比较文学与世界文学

第四期

主编　陈跃红　张　辉

北京大学出版社
PEKING UNIVERSITY PRESS

图书在版编目(CIP)数据

比较文学与世界文学. 第四期/陈跃红，张辉主编. —北京：北京大学出版社，2013.12
ISBN 978-7-301-23648-2

Ⅰ. ①比… Ⅱ. ①陈…②张… Ⅲ. ①比较文学—文学研究—中国②世界文学—文学研究 Ⅳ. ①I206②I106

中国版本图书馆 CIP 数据核字(2013)第 315468 号

书　　　名：比较文学与世界文学(第四期)
著作责任者：陈跃红　张　辉　主编
责 任 编 辑：黄瑞明
标 准 书 号：ISBN 978-7-301-23648-2/I・2696
出 版 发 行：北京大学出版社
地　　　址：北京市海淀区成府路 205 号　100871
网　　　址：http://www.pup.cn　　新浪官方微博：@北京大学出版社
电 子 信 箱：zbing@pup.pku.edu.cn
电　　　话：邮购部 62752015　发行部 62750672　编辑部 62754382　出版部 62754962
印　刷　者：北京大学印刷厂
经　销　者：新华书店
787 毫米×1092 毫米　16 开本　12.25 印张　280 千字
2013 年 12 月第 1 版　2013 年 12 月第 1 次印刷
定　　　价：32.00 元

目　录

学术动态

新书快递

稿约

Contents

编者的话

陈跃红　张　辉

本期“学术焦点”发表了来自英国、日本、韩国和中国台湾四位学者的文章，这些文章都是提交给2013年8月由复旦大学举办的“乔伊斯与东方”国际学术会议的论文。饶有意味的是，主持人戴从容教授告诉我们，三位非英语国家的作者更愿意选择乔伊斯的母语——英文发表他们的高见，而与之相对照，来自英国的福德姆则选择要将自己的英文文章翻译为中文发表。

这或许不仅仅是一个有趣的巧合。推而广之，跨文化的交流和沟通，需要的不就是这种难能可贵的“换位思考”吗？也许只有当我们学会使用对方的语言去表达各自的思想，学会站在对方的文化位置上来反观彼此的传统，我们才能更好地达成互相理解，而不是貌似面对他者却始终在自说自话。

正是在这个意义上，真正的比较研究有助于克服约定俗成的诸多“常识”，也事实上有利于我们打破现代哲学解释学对所谓“主体”和“前见”的片面肯定。因为，从根本上说，理解并不是要简单重复“主体”已有的知识、情感和思想，更不是要让被解释对象就范于某个人为设定的范式与窠臼，而是要在对他者的理解中获得新的、拓展的视域，解除似是而非的成见。本期“批评空间”中的几篇文章，都在不同程度上涉及对古今经典作家和经典作品的理解和解释。林国华的《沃格林的〈柏拉图〉》一文，其问题意识来自于对柏拉图文本的再解读，这是他破解沃格林“前理解”的方便法门；而王柯平对柏拉图《法礼篇》的讨论，则显然试图摆脱现代学科对“法”的“前把握”，使人们将之与哲学乃至诗联系起来；与上述两篇文章遥相呼应，金永兵的《经典的美学特征》，使我们更进一步认识到作为解释结果的文学经典的生成性与其恒久美学价值之间的解释学张力；而孙柏的文章以斯特林堡《鬼魂奏鸣曲》从剧本到电影的演进，给出了一个跨文类的解释个案；韩加明的《新世纪的几部西方文学史研究述评》，则提供了一个长时段的文学解释的历史参照系。

本期的译文，一则是“西马”老将杰姆逊的访谈；一则是中生代学人伦敦大学讲座教授提哈诺夫(G. Tihanov)关于巴赫金小说观的长文。据悉，提哈诺夫2014年将首次访问中国。杰姆逊的访谈，开篇就涉及“知识体系”的来源，或许这又是在提示我们关注整个现代思想的“前理解”；而提哈诺夫文章的副标题是“巴赫金小说论的知识背景和独创性研究”，无疑与杰姆逊有可以对观之处。注意知识和理解的背景和源起，或许本来是学术研究的题中应有之义，但是，是简单认同前理解的合理性甚至将之视为主体性的体现，还是对这种前理解加以细致辨析、反思乃至质疑，则似乎不仅仅是知识旨趣上的分野。

本期还有几点值得一提。“学术动态”的篇幅明显增加;“青年园地”也由通常的两篇增加到三篇;此外,编委名单中还增加了几位来自海外的学人。这样做,目的无他,只是期望有更多的同仁加入到我们这个对话、交流、沟通和理解的共同事业中来,“群贤毕至,少长咸集”。

学术焦点

主持人语

戴从容

爱尔兰作家詹姆斯·乔伊斯从来没有来过中国。一开始在乔伊斯的笔下,他也像20世纪初期众多没有到过中国,只靠着《中国纪行》这类哗众取宠的"游记"来理解中国的西方人一样,把中国简单地想象为皇帝统治下的异教徒社会,一心只想着鸦片,觉得白人身上有一股尸体的味道。在《尤利西斯》中,乔伊斯曾借一位水手之口,把中国描写成人人会变戏法,会炖老鼠汤喝的怪异民族。事实上那时的中国对乔伊斯来说只是一个符号,代表着一切与自己不同的"他者"。

但是这个印象随着乔伊斯对其他民族的关心而发生了改变。这个变化不是乔伊斯早年相信的顿悟(epiphany)式的,而是在与周围的中国人的交往中,在对真正的东方著作而不是二手文献的阅读中逐渐获得的。在《芬尼根的守灵夜》中,乔伊斯对东方的描述依然说不上深刻,但已完全不同于以往的怪诞滑稽。这表明两个文化的相互理解不是不可能的。这种理解永远不可能达到完美,但是却可以通过不断深化而建立起彼此之间的宽容和善意。

英国学者芬·福德姆和日本学者伊东荣志郎都注意到《芬尼根的守灵夜》中闪和肖两兄弟形象中包含的中国与日本的冲突,以及这一对立呼应着爱尔兰人与英国人之间的冲突。不过非常有趣的是,作为欧洲人(虽然是爱尔兰人)的福德姆倒更关注《芬尼根的守灵夜》中被戏仿的历史上的"东方主义",即欧洲人将中国人视为蛮族,因为担心"黄祸"而梦想着汉人的消亡;而作为亚洲人(虽然是日本人)的伊东荣志郎则更看重乔伊斯试图通过孙中山的"天下为公"思想,来提供一种中日可以在其中和平共存的"人类世界史"。欧洲研究者的反躬自省和亚洲研究者的执着蓝图,正是文化交流必不可少的两个阶段,没有自省无以走出自身的局限,没有信心无以走向相互理解。

理解异国文化是一个永远不会穷尽的过程,在这个方面,译介和研究是比较文学为文化交流所筑轨道的两条钢轨。《芬尼根的守灵夜》的翻译与芬·福德姆和伊东荣志郎对书中中国意象的研究一样,都是希望为不同的乃至对立的文化之间的相互理解搭建渠道。台湾大学的曾丽玲教授指出《芬尼根的守灵夜》中译本与德里达的《丧钟》之间的相似之处,更印证了不同文化在思想上的暗合。《芬尼根的守灵夜》在英语世界也以艰涩著称,但这不妨碍它成为影响当代文学的经典作品;同样,《芬尼根的守灵夜》被译介到中国也许会有暂时的水土不服,但是正像乔伊斯在《芬尼根的守灵夜》中坚信的不同文化之间有着相通之处,《芬尼根的守灵夜》与中国的译入语文化在相互作用中也必然都会有所改变。

《芬尼根的守灵夜》描写了一条河，它自己也是一条河，一条充满着无限生命力量的河。正如韩国学者申恩景教授注意到的，乔伊斯在书中赋予了这条河巨大的变化力和可塑性。从这一点说，乔伊斯早就用这部融合了六十余种语言的作品预言了文化交流必将带来的改变，这个改变已经像河流般流淌在我们的生活之中，并且也将像河流般奔流不息。

“直到汉与匈的消亡”

——乔伊斯，中国和种族化的世界史

芬·福德姆

陈莹 译

【内容提要】 在一战后全球对整体叙述的要求这一语境下，乔伊斯在《芬尼根的守灵夜》中不但呈现了世界历史的纷争，而且呈现了种族化的世界历史如何把中国脸谱化。本文分析了乔伊斯如何通过使人物和叙述类型增殖，而不是消解它们，来揭示出世界历史结构的缺陷。要颠覆性地揭露世界史的局限，关键是扩展性的叙述，而非排除性的叙述。

【关键词】 詹姆斯·乔伊斯 《芬尼根的守灵夜》 世界史 中国

“Until Hanandhunigan's Extermination”: Joyce, China and Racialised World Histories

【Abstract】 Influenced by the new global imaginary which required new global narratives after the First World War, Joyce not only staged a world historical conflict in Finnegans Wake, but also showed how the stereotypical roles given to China in racialised world histories found their way into Finnegans Wake. The central point of this paper is that Joyce engages critically with and against the structures of world histories not through a dissolution of character and narrative types, but through their proliferations. The proliferation of narration rather than its expulsion is key in the subversive revelations of the limitations of world histories.

【Key Words】 James Joyce *Finnegans Wake* world history China

1922 年末，詹姆斯·乔伊斯那部被禁的“两个种族(以色列—爱尔兰)的史诗”搅乱了欧美文化知识界，他自己却获得了充分的信心，或者说野心，将叙述转向了一个更大的主题：人类种族。[①] 乔伊斯对他的赞助人哈里特·肖·韦佛宣布，他要写一部“普遍的历史”[②]。我认为，乔伊斯是在创造大历史的趋势下突然转向于此，这种倾向也同样影响了众多出版人和作家，比如 D. H. 劳伦斯、埃兹拉·庞德、约翰·巴奇、奥斯瓦尔德·斯宾格勒，还有受到更大影响的 H. G. 威尔斯。第一次全世界范围内的战争——一战显然已经结束，国际联盟也建立了起来，多个国家签订了凡尔赛和塞夫尔条约，这些大事件导向了一种要求整体叙述的全

① 詹姆斯·乔伊斯：《詹姆斯·乔伊斯书信集》，斯图亚特·吉尔伯特编，伦敦：Faber and Faber 出版公司，1957 年，第 146 页。

② 帕特里夏·哈金斯：《詹姆斯·乔伊斯的世界》，伦敦：Methuen 出版社，1957 年，第 140 页。

球构想。在似乎是达到高潮的1924年,指向世界史的文章标题层出不穷。[①] 正如1905年到1907年任爱尔兰事务总管(Chief Secretary of Ireland)的布莱斯子爵在1919年的发言中所说的(这也可能是乔伊斯所想的):

> 这是地球上有史以来第一次我们的居民变为了一个整体,这个整体的每个部分都被其他部分的命运所影响……因此,第一次在真正意义上可以书写世界史了。[②]

与创伤和恢复这类问题有关的话语为意识形态的产生提供了机会。世界史在被暴力释放和煽动的话语中被大写,尤其当暴力发生在资本主义的中心的时候,在那里资本可以传播这些话语。类似的事件在世界贸易中心遇袭之后也发生了,于是萨缪尔·亨廷顿关于"文明的冲突"的世界历史理论又重新被提及和讨论。[③] 一战期间和战后对于阐释性叙述的需要产生了意识形态间的竞争:保守派的、自由党的、费边主义者的、社会主义的,还有女性主义的世界史出现了。一些(但绝不是全部)战后的文章标题是为学校教学准备的,但是,我们没有理由将出版人对说教课本的要求和知识分子对微妙且复杂的描述的需要视作来源于不同的领域。他们的解释也许是相互矛盾的,比如斯宾格勒的悲观主义与学校教科书的乐观主义格格不入,教科书认为学生应该获得"一些社会发展的概念,并意识到自石器时代以来人类是向前发展的"[④]。尽管如此,他们却拥有共同的出发点:正是那些构成主要纷争的东西——一战和战争爆发的条件,推赶着"现代主义"不断前进。因此,乔伊斯的世界历史计划是世界史话语的有机组合的一部分。这套话语的理论也可以在维柯和黑格尔的论著中找到,乔伊斯也认同这些理论依据。本文考察了这样的世界历史被种族化的方式,正是在这一语境下乔伊斯在《芬尼根的守灵夜》的早期构思中呈现了世界历史的纷争,在这里他转向远东以扩大全球视野。作为乔伊斯东方转向的更进一步的背景材料,我将在种族化的世界史和维柯及黑格尔的作品中考察中国是如何被关注的。把乔伊斯放入世界史话语的语境中,强调了差异和文本间多元的可能性。我把中国历史作为一个案例(并关注中国自身的权益),展现出在种族化的世界历史中中国被赋予的模式化脸谱如何在《芬尼根的守灵夜》中得以表现。这一章的核心是乔伊斯对世界历史结构的批判性参与和反对,他通过使人物和叙述类型增殖,而不是消解它们,来揭示出世界历史结构的缺陷。

---

① 这些叙述可以在以下著作中找到:(按时间顺序排列)M. W. 基廷,N. L. 弗雷泽:《世界历史介绍》,伦敦:A and C, Black,1916年;J. B. 博茨福德:《世界简史》,伦敦:Macmillan出版社,1917年;奥斯瓦尔德·斯宾格勒:《西方的没落》,第一卷:《格式塔和现实》,慕尼黑:C. H. Beck出版公司,1918年;布莱斯子爵:《世界历史》,伦敦:牛津大学出版社:1919年;厄内斯特·施尔特:《世界历史介绍》,伦敦:Waverley书局,1920年;E. M. 威尔莫特·布克斯顿:《世界简史》,伦敦:Methuen出版社,1921年;莱斯利·西西尔·史密斯:《世界历史主流》,伦敦:Revingtons出版社,1922年;赫顿·韦伯斯特:《世界历史》,伦敦:Health出版社,1922年;阿尔弗拉德·巴尔顿:《给劳工的世界史:一个从时间伊始时被剥削者立场出发的人的行为的故事》,伦敦:Labour出版公司,1922年;约翰·巴乔编:《当今的国家:新世界历史》,伦敦:Hodder and Stoughton出版社,1923年;玛格丽特·科尔:《世界史介绍》,伦敦:Labour研究系出版,1923年;H. G. 威尔士:《世界简史》,伦敦:Cassell出版社,1922年;吉尔伯特·T. 赛德勒:《简而言之的世界史》,伦敦:C. W. Daniel出版社,1924年;F. J. C. 赫恩肖:《第一部世界历史》,伦敦:Macmillan出版社,1924年。

② 布莱斯子爵:《世界历史》,第4页。

③ 萨缪尔·P. 亨廷顿:《文明的冲突和世界秩序的评论》,伦敦:Simon & Schuster出版公司,1996年。

④ 韦伯斯特:《世界历史》,第三章。

世界历史中的种族

种族化和对人类多样性的种族意识被诊断为社会达尔文主义的一种特征。19世纪前对世界史的叙述同样促进了这种意识的形成。种族主义和种族差异论在世界史上独霸的原因很明显:首先,叙述者通常认定种族主义可以成为一个群体被历史选中——或值得被选中的合理化解释。比如,在宇宙论和神学的框架下,《旧约》对犹太人(或者犹太“族”、犹太“国”)历史的讲述。在《创世记》中,我们可以看到对毁灭性惩罚的叙述策略是如何被用来解释世界上明显不同的种族的存在的,比如大洪水和唯一幸存的父亲诺亚。诺亚之子,闪、含和雅弗继承了他的世界里的不同部分,这将被当作一个神话来架构和解释三个主要的“种族”:黑种人、白种人和黄种人,以及他们是如何被世界历史区别对待的。[①] 诺亚之子也可以用来解释白种人中的三个类型。赖因·普拉特正是从“诺亚”历史叙述传统审视了《芬尼根的守灵夜》中乔伊斯对这一问题的处理。[②] 这样的历史叙述希望解释人类社会的不平等。布莱斯的《世界历史》(1919)就是此意识的典型论调:“我们欧洲的血统享受着许多继承来的好处,在现在的赛跑中与其他人拉开了距离。但这将会是一次漫长的比赛,他们中的一些也许会赶上我们。”[③]布莱斯无力的双关语在乔伊斯的故事标题“赛车之后”中得到了充分的说明——在欧洲人的赌局中赛车的失败是作为“欧洲最落后的种族”的标志。[④]

其次,世界史的形式产生了精减的必要,创造粗线条的事件而不是描述例外和复杂的细节。因此,在既有原则基础之上对元素进行选择很有必要,这样一来,一些特定的纪念物、文件和事件就被边缘化了,因为他们不足以对说明历史“主流”做贡献:比如,爱尔兰就是个典型的国家,在世界历史中,它过于边缘化而未被关注。J. M. 罗伯特的《世界历史》(1976)(I. R. 摩尔称为不可超越之作)中写道:“迷人尤卡坦半岛……津巴布韦的毁灭……复活节岛的神秘雕塑,始终待在世界历史的周围。”[⑤]罗伯特表示,文明必然会在一定程度上证明这一点是合理的。这样,带着对特定现象的叙述,比如彻底拒绝的、排除的、乐观的、建设性的,羞耻的和恬不知耻的叙述就可以被创造出来。在1924年,甚至有理由将中国排除在“当下将创造出‘欧洲文明’(我们研究的主要目标)的主流努力之外”。[⑥] 相比之下,D. H. 劳伦斯的历史——虽然仅仅关注欧洲——却记录了中国人对于欧洲历史基本层面的原初影响。比如,中国人成功抵御了3世纪蒙古人的侵略,“匈奴转向了西方”,继而导致了古罗马的灭亡。[⑦] 排除在外并不是一个解决实际问题的好方法。它反映出一个有缺陷的观念:世界史基本上等同于欧洲史,这种观念广泛流

---

① 种族三分的理念绝不是普遍的:通俗科学的作者和达尔文主义者路易斯·菲吉耶在1872年的著作中将人类种族划分为“白种人种、黄种人种、棕色人种、红色人种和黑色人种”。对此也可参见桑德勒的相关章节。

② 赖因·普拉特:《乔伊斯、种族和〈芬尼根的守灵夜〉》,剑桥:剑桥大学出版社,2007年,第29—30页。

③ 布莱斯子爵:《世界历史》,第20页。

④ 埃尔斯沃兹·梅森、理查德·艾尔曼:《詹姆斯·乔伊斯评论集》,纽约:维京出版社,1964年,第70页。

⑤ J. M. 罗伯特:《世界历史》,纽约:Knopf出版社,1976年,第八卷,参见I. R. 摩尔:《世界历史》,见M. 本特利编:《历史编纂学读本》,伦敦:Routledge,1997年,第952页。

⑥ 施尔特:《世界历史介绍》,第13页。

⑦ D. H. 劳伦斯:《欧洲历史的发展》,牛津:牛津大学出版社,1921年,第66页。

传，并催生出更多对种族优越性的叙述。当能从丰富的史料中选择如何叙述时，世界历史也同样要填补史料不足的空白——尤其是那些较早的记录中的裂缝。

这些裂缝不一定导致种族主义，但这些空白却能促进一些理论，阐释其中可能发生了的事情，19、20 世纪的种族主义的意识形态塑造了填补这些空白的理论。由于尊敬种族主义，世界历史获得了一个坏名声。I. R. 摩尔于 1997 年将种族主义描述为“狂热分子，假木偶和鼓吹家手中多变的工具 ”。他呼吁长期处于边缘地位的世界历史重新崛起，并指出这种边缘化来自一种对“宏大和邪恶视角的结构的恐惧，历史学家将这种结构与斯宾格勒和汤因比的名字联系在一起”①。但是这种结构之所以过时同样也与历史上不能避免的欧洲中心的种族化和种族主义相关。种族和它们的“旁支”和“宗族”常常好像戏剧演员，具有固定特点，甚至既定的命运，在一种展开的叙述中扮演他们的角色。在世界史的种族戏剧层面，黑格尔具有重要的地位：“历史进程中的每一步都有固定的原则，在历史上，这些原则是精神的特质——罕见的民族天才……那种或这种特质构成了一个人的特殊才能，这是我们要询问的，也是必须……被历史证明的。”②布莱斯的思考也与此相应：“在文明的源初，一个平静却显著的变化成为了一个稳定且被明确界定的族群的结构，每个族群都有显著的情感和精神的特点，它们形成了我们所谓的民族特点……这些族群……如何进化却是一个模糊却引人注目的问题。”③威尔莫特·巴斯顿在她教科书的开篇展现出一个使人联想到乔伊斯的“纪念馆/缪斯屋”④的意象：

> 设想有一段足够长的饰带来环绕地球，在上面我们也许会注意到男人和女人的形象……带有典型的种族和时代特征的男人女人。有时他们促进种族向共同的目标前进，有时他们成为阻碍……但整体上总是向一个目标前进，那个目标就是人类的幸福。⑤

为了书写世界历史，乔伊斯面临着被归入某个种族话语类型的风险，“人物”（种族偏见）和“叙述”（殖民，帝国的种族主义和民族主义的历史编纂学的重复）的问题将会加重这种风险。但是，乔伊斯并不拒绝“人物”和“叙述”中的任何一个。他与这些类型和偏见合作，通过它们迅速地构思，然后将让它们在碎片化叙述的重复海洋中漂浮。这其中的风险并不因消解了“人物”和“叙述”的负面意义而减轻，而是恰恰相反：通过与它们的深入接触而缓解。要颠覆性地揭露世界史的局限，关键是扩展性的叙述，而非排除性的叙述。

乔伊斯对世界史纷争的表现

乔伊斯将爱尔兰作为他的六七张底稿的背景，开始了他对世界历史的书写。在第四张

① 摩尔：《世界历史》，第 942—943 页。

② G. W. F. 黑格尔：《历史哲学讲演录》，J. 希伯列译，伦敦：George Bell and Sons 出版社，1888 年，第 66 页。此后引为“LPH”。

③ 布莱斯子爵：《世界历史》，第 17 页。

④ 詹姆斯·乔伊斯：《芬尼根的守灵夜》，伦敦：Faber and Faber 出版公司，1964 年，8.9，此后引为“FW”。

⑤ 威尔莫特·布克斯顿：《世界简史》，第 1—2 页。

底稿中的伯克利——帕特里克辩论是一个特例,因为这是乔伊斯第一次将远方世界中地理的、政治的和语言学上的回音编织进来。由此,乔伊斯触及了全球想象的边缘,将他的视野设定为"世界文学"的在场①,这个经典的文学术语自歌德提出以来就引来不断的讨论。乔伊斯在其中一张底稿中将"普遍历史"视为"描述了爱尔兰使圣帕特里克皈依"②。它讲述了一个具有预言能力的异教牧师和一个务实的基督教传教士之间荒谬的相遇。乔伊斯根据公元 432 年爱尔兰大德鲁伊主教鲁赫鲁(他的理想主义因与伯克利相关而被强调)与英国出生的圣帕特里克的历史性相遇来给这些人物类型分级。这次相遇围绕一个关于视野与颜色的哲学论辩展开,它植根于一种混杂的、部分来自于中文的美拉尼西亚语。乔伊斯将一份副本寄给了韦弗:③

> 宾伯在神的洋泾浜人鲁赫鲁·伯克利上面,爱尔兰亲亲神的大德鲁伊,穿着他的七重消色七重色彩的……披风,他给客人帕特里克展示了……太多造物主的多彩的泛显灵世界的幻象,从矿物到植物再到动物所组成珊瑚的装饰,似乎在一起也没有满足堕落的人,而是在阳光下几个爱尔兰等级的照片反射的下面……展示它自己……不能吸收。

帕特里克不懂伯克利的意思,于是伯克利解释说,所有不同色彩的物体事实上都是绿色的影子。比如说:

> 因战争获得的紫色的创伤的至高无上的大独裁者全身整齐地涂染了很多如同你看到的番泻树的神的颜色。④

"如果读我的东西有任何困难",乔伊斯曾说,"那是因为我使用的材料……我的思想通常是简单的。"⑤透过术语和洋泾浜的面纱,我们可以看见"joss pidgin fella"(神的商人),伯克利主教指出"堕落的人"面前出现的世界的幻象,它们被一组差异明显的色彩区分出来,然而在现实中,一切物质都具有一种因内在本质色彩造成的整体性。伯克利提出,各种色彩构成的混杂是一种普遍存在的绿色——我们要考虑到辩论恰巧发生在爱尔兰,在三叶草绿的天主教爱尔兰开始之时。与帕特里克肤浅的认知不同,伯克利主教认为宇宙是一个整体,一个"一"。正如文森特·程所说,伯克利的"相对多元论"产生了一种色盲,它看不到导致了种族的人类群体之间的差别。⑥ 乔伊斯的世界历史将展示出这几种认知之间的冲突,它们如同军事力量之间的冲突一样。

韦弗一定感到非常困惑,于是表达了她对此构思的失望,所以,乔伊斯在接下来的回信中说:"我很遗憾帕特里克和伯克利没有成功地表达他们自己。我想,这个答案将是派迪·

① 见大卫·达姆罗施:《世界文学是什么》,普林斯顿:普林斯顿大学出版社,2003 年。

② 麦克·格勒顿等:《詹姆斯·乔伊斯全集》,纽约:Garland 出版社,1977 年,第 63 卷,146e。

③ 乔伊斯有些洋泾浜词取自奥托·耶斯佩森的《语言:本质,发展和起源》,纽约:Henry Holt 出版公司,1922 年。包括"joss","chinchin"和"chowchow"——意义为"神"、"问候"和"混合保存"或"食物"。"joss"和"pidgin"被认为是中文"deos"的翻译和英语中的"商业"一词。见此书的第 222 页。

④ 格勒顿:《詹姆斯·乔伊斯全集》,第 63 卷,146e。

⑤ 弗兰克·巴金:《詹姆斯·乔伊斯和〈尤利西斯〉的产生》,伦敦:Granson & Grayson 出版社,1934 年,第 291 页。

⑥ 文森特·程:《乔伊斯,种族和帝国》,剑桥:剑桥大学出版社,1995 年,第 273 页。

迪格纳穆的幽灵:轮回。或者(在黑格尔和维柯之后)四位杰出的编年史家建立的历史理论也许能部分表达我的意思。"[①]无论这些理论是什么,就像我前面写的,乔伊斯将之归于"那些乏味的、重复的、怀旧的、消极的、说教的四个老人",他们醉酒后以一种模拟历史形态的相似物来重复自己(无论这是不是那类黑格尔的辩证法或者维柯的时代循环),他们的重复贯穿了整个世界史的叙述。[②] 乔伊斯非常关注相关的讨论,将这些讨论描述为"对于此书本身的辩护和证词"。[③] 当乔伊斯修改了后三十章的片段后,我们更能明显地辨认出帕特里克的日本人身份,这样乔伊斯就可以把19世纪90年代和20世纪30年代的中日的冲突编织进来。[④] 他思考着:

> 让两个男人,一个中国人和一个日本人在都柏林的凤凰公园的一个酒吧里彼此交谈难道不是一件矛盾的事吗?但是,它却又是表达强烈冲突和不能化解的对立的一种理性和客观的方式。[⑤](原文为法语)

胜利的殖民者和溃败的被殖民者之间的相遇成为世界史叙述的主要内容。我们如何把这一段与中国在一个种族化了的世界史中的角色联系起来呢?我准备通过四个层面来回答这个问题:其对殖民的和民族的历史编纂学的倒置;对文学方言的使用;把东方和西方当做代表着两种对立观念的辩证性;最后还有对超历史学的分层和重复的运用。最后一个层面也将导向简要讨论《芬尼根的守灵夜》中的世界史模式,在"预先重复"的时候为什么总被理想化。

首先,圣帕特里克是被爱尔兰改变了信仰,而非改变了爱尔兰的信仰。乔伊斯对圣帕特里克改变信仰的重新解释颠覆了典型的殖民编年史学,因为在典型编年史学中,殖民传教士使野蛮的当地人改变信仰,或者说交易人造就商人,权力全部导向一方,而被殖民者被剥夺了任何力量。海拉·辛格联系印度的历史,表达了对这种编年史学的一种具有代表性的批判:

> 不仅是欧洲的政治经济改变了印度的封建制度,印度的封建制度也同样改变了欧洲的政治经济……殖民渗透不是单向的,殖民地对于大都会的反渗透是事情的另一面。[⑥]

殖民焦虑的、清教徒式的反面便是游牧民族推翻一个堕落的社会,正如威尔莫特·巴斯顿1921年所说:"一个毫无活力却有太多文明和奢华的生活方式的种族在一个过着简单生活的游牧民族面前的崩溃是历史时常重复出现的桥段之一。"[⑦]

---

① 乔伊斯:《詹姆斯·乔伊斯书信集》,吉尔伯特编,第204页。

② 费恩·福特汉姆:《〈芬尼根的守灵夜〉的普及和真实的H.C.E.》,见安德鲁·吉布森和赖因·普拉特编:《乔伊斯,爱尔兰和英国》,盖恩斯维尔:佛罗里达大学出版社,2006年,第198—211(202)页。

③ 乔伊斯:《詹姆斯·乔伊斯书信集》,吉尔伯特编,第206页。

④ 见伊藤英四郎:《"亚洲合众国":詹姆斯·乔伊斯和日本》,载于理查德·布朗编:《詹姆斯·乔伊斯读本》,牛津:Blackwell出版公司,2008年,第203页。

⑤ "让两个男人,一个中国人和一个日本人在都柏林的凤凰公园的一个酒吧里与彼此交谈难道不是一件矛盾的事嘛?但是它又是一种表达一种强烈的冲突和不能化解的对立的理性和客观的方式。"(本文作者的翻译)雅克·默坎顿:《詹姆斯·乔伊斯的时间》,巴黎:L'Age D'Homme出版社,1967年,第23页。

⑥ 希拉·辛格:《高贵地表述,乡野地抵抗,建立国家》,社会运动研究,2/2,2003年10月,第223页。

⑦ 威尔莫特·布克斯顿:《世界简史》,第9—10页。

其次，乔伊斯对语言变化和混杂的语言类型很有兴趣，这一类型的语言有时在国际贸易的交汇中产生，它的增多很明显标志了一种全球化的未来。洋泾浜语言为乔伊斯的巴别塔式的相遇提供了一种模式，这种相遇既内在于也来源于他的“全球想象”。《芬尼根的守灵夜》推进了对文学方言戏拟可能性的探索，混杂语言的使用颠覆了发现这种语言时其中包含的种族标记。第485页上的（“我不是盎格鲁的后代，我说黄人的语言”）和第89页（“确确实实”）都是典型的乔伊斯对中国的文学方言的展示。[①] 舞台上的中国人与爱尔兰人相近，他们如同戏剧家布希考特的主角，即使是带有偏见的，也成功地迷惑了英国讯问者的理性企图，为了捍卫真理，在傻瓜面前装傻。《芬尼根的守灵夜》中这种总是转瞬即逝的腹语策略性地指出这一时刻的舞台表演性，以及文学语言的人工构造性。但这并不意味着乔伊斯想要这些种族印记彻底消失：文学方言中非标准形式的程式化有效地制造了被选择的各类话语之间的坡度和距离，这些话语被强制性地彼此亲近。在这些不同的话语之间移动，喜剧和颠覆可以流动和跳跃，文学方言对于《芬尼根的守灵夜》的喜剧和颠覆主题至关重要。

第三，书中的场景表现了有关世界观的现象学之间的辩证关系——表面不同、内在同一，这些现象学于是可以被绘入种族和文化差异的地图，或者实际上，同一的地图中。根据黑格尔的东方学传统，宇宙是一个整体的概念构成了中国哲学的基础（LPH 69）。在黑格尔的时代，有一种说法声称正因为如此，中国哲学的系统与斯宾诺莎的系统相似，这种说法困扰了黑格尔。乔伊斯重复了这些说法，显示他的道家“先知”的视野与伯克利的“无物质主义”之间的联系。东西方之间的冲突和统一被认为是哲学和意识形态上有关中心和边缘、帝王和平民、实践和理论、矛盾双方辩证冲突的象征。

第四，与此相关，乔伊斯对比较性超历史分层的使用因“轮回”方法而合理化，在这里古代的冲突思想（清教徒对基督徒）可以重新出现在更近代的冲突（中国人对日本人）中。正如乔伊斯所说，作为一种“巨大的冲突，一种前所未有的对抗，都柏林酒吧里关于观念的争论代表了文明的碰撞（东方和西方）、民族的碰撞（中国和日本，或者爱尔兰和英国）、种族的碰撞（凯尔特和不列颠，“中华名族”和“大和民族”）、文化的碰撞（神秘的和实际的）或者意识形态的碰撞（孤立主义和帝国主义）。正如格蕾丝·埃克利注意到的：“这些邻近的国家处于哲学和政治、大陆和岛屿的战争中，也为英国和爱尔兰提供了一个东方对等物。”[②]带着对文学方言的矛盾性使用，这可能颠覆了，但也同样支持了乔伊斯在维柯和黑格尔的作品中发现的文化差异和历史形态的神话。乔伊斯将会多次进行这种表演，重复日本人和中国人之间的冲突，比如，将这种冲突并入拿破仑与惠林顿的冲突中：

> 这个涉及面更广的事件预先重复了它自己。这一对（不论是拿破仑与惠林顿交战或者德·里兹克企图侦查巴克利夫将军，人们也许会说），明显地挣扎了很长时间。
>
> （FW，81.32—81.36）

拿破仑变成了“一个日本人”，一个英雄（如同战士肖恩），惠林顿吸收了“道”的概念，一

① 见赖因·普莱特在《“展示种族”：乔伊斯，种族和〈芬尼根的守灵夜〉》，第121—145页。

② 格蕾丝·艾克利：《对光明日的期待：第四本，第一章》，见麦克·H. 孟加拉和弗里茨·塞恩编：《〈芬尼根的守灵夜〉导读》，大学公园：宾西法尼亚大学出版社，1974年，第224页。

种当代的自我流放的形式(与闪相似)。对这些相遇的预期结果被系统地颠覆了,乔伊斯所说的“客观表述”也同样颠覆了这些预期结果的代表性地位。“预先重复”听起来像“再重复”,一种再做一遍之前修正做过的事情的企图,它本身就是对先前表演过的原创事件的一种重复。但是因为它是“预先重复”的,它对已经发生事件的重复,应该发生在这个原创事件之前。这概念也许与“répétition”(法语中“排练”)更相近,事件在它的最终形式出现之前不停重复,展示那些还没有发生的事,上演一出还未被写好的戏,意味着一种与真实和一些从未实现的表演的理想之间的延迟关系。实际的相遇于是永远是理想的,仅仅在它的陈述中“预先重复”过,从来不存在一次最终的表演,因此,实际上也没有首次或者连续重复过。《芬尼根的守灵夜》中的种族或其他的冲突仅仅是对历史叙述认为的确定事件的排练,然而这些事件却永远无法精确地确定形态。

世界历史里的中国

乔伊斯在他的老朋友庞德和叶芝身上也发现了类似的对于远东文化的思考。不过,这种思考也反映出中国在世界史中是一个分裂的存在。17 世纪耶稣会士的报告发现了中国文化的博大精深,这为重写世界史提供了动力,因为在这之前的世界历史主要关注近东,认为近东是文明的发源地——正如博须埃 1681 年开创性的著作《宇宙历史》所言。中国在世界史中常与以下三方面相关(或归类于以下三方面):中国文明的早熟和持续性,中国与世界其他国家的隔绝和她相对停滞的发展。中国人的种族被认为是“蒙古人”或黄种人的一部分,但他们在 1922 年也同样代表了这一分类中的一个特例:“黄种人”也许处于一种“野蛮或原始的文化阶段”,而“中国人、印度支那人和日本人多少是非常重要的例外”。[①]

维柯和中国象形文字

维柯也许不是现代主义的世界史学家,但与黑格尔一样,他是在现代主义时期讨论世界历史类型的关键人物。因为他们与乔伊斯的特殊关联,我将把他们作为现代主义的重要部分来关注。

维柯是将有关中国的新内容整合进普遍历史的理论的先驱者之一。他认识到自己是在“中国人带着一种贸易优势的眼光,最近向我们欧洲人打开国门”[②]的时刻来写作的。他广泛阅读了耶稣会士的笔记和关于中国的含义的二手资料,他的《新科学》能为上文提及的三种联系提供坚实的根据。关于中国的内容甚至也许促进了维柯的理论的产生,因为他的理论主要在解释已知中国的一切,来描绘虽然处于不同时代,却有着相似历史阶段的历史进程中的异族的来临。他论证说,中国的发展停滞在埃及的阶段,理由是中国人对象形文字的使

① 韦伯斯特:《世界历史》,第 21 页。

② 詹巴蒂斯塔·维柯:《新科学》,第三版,T. G. 伯金、M. H. 菲斯克译,纽约伊萨卡:康奈尔大学,1948 年,第 303 页,此后引为“NS”。

用。书写系统被看作民族个性和能力的标志:不同的种族在不同的时代发展出相异的书写实践。1922年,阿尔弗雷德·巴尔顿以社会主义的视角写了一部世界史,小心翼翼地展示了他对书写实践与文化发展之间关系的想法:

> 中国在8世纪所达到的文明就已经类似于18世纪的西方文明的水平,在这以后却没有明显的进步,其中的原因很难解释,H.G.威尔斯认为,主要是中国繁复的语言使得阅读和书写的习得变得非常困难,以至于学习了古代经典的知识阶层已经没有精力去创新或创造,工商阶层更没有时间或机会去学习。①

了解了这个观点,有人会问那么纸、印刷术、火药和指南针是如何能被“非字母化”且有着“繁复语言”的人发明出来,甚至早于那些使用了一千多年“更为先进”的字母系统的人?

维柯关于中国汉字与古埃及文字相似的误解导致将中国人的世界观奇异化,认为中国人的世界观更接近于他提出的“诗性智慧”。这种异化的观念在厄内斯特·费诺罗萨建立的中国汉字诗学中延续,也同样影响了庞德,后来被乔伊斯批判性地利用。

> 自然中不存在真正的名词和孤立的事物。事物仅仅是终端,或者是运动的接口,动作的十字截断面,简单的印象。同样,也不存在纯粹的动词和抽象的运动,眼睛将名词与动词视为同一:运动是事物的运动,事物是运动中的事物,所以,中国的概念倾向于表现。②

在《意象主义宣言》中,庞德认为通过阅读和使用中国汉字,他可以更接近“事物本身”。在一篇有关中国诗歌的论文中,庞德补充说:“中国诗歌‘非常凯尔特式’”,“我发现叶芝先生提出过一个关于安瑞岛人的相似故事”,于是,中国书写系统决定了另外一种中国人的世界观,这是另一种异域的、民间的凯尔特(和他们的薄暮)。但是,正如钱兆明的观察:“费诺罗萨对于中国书写语言图画性的赞赏是荒谬且误导的。”③乔伊斯在《芬尼根的守灵夜》中也指出了庞德-费诺罗萨的诗学的缺点:“如果我们‘口头地’看待它,也许在生动的自然中不存在真正的名词,万事万物都变成了混沌的眼球。”(FW,523,10—12)按伯克利的理解,中国再次与一种空想的认知方式联系起来。乔伊斯用“口头地看”来嘲笑费诺罗萨的逻辑,显示出费诺罗萨“通过文字”而不是“通过眼睛”来观看世界的局限。中国用“馄饨”,一种被认为是分开的“眼球”的汤饺暗示了发音相似的“混沌”。每个人都在变化,转变为眼睛。乔伊斯借用费诺罗萨的“自然”,在斯宾诺莎“自然的自然”的基础上,创造出“动态自然”,创造出自然的统一的神。自然中“每个生物都在转变”,如果我们将这些活动理解为“名词”的对应,“事物”则不能严格存在。并且当每种存在都呈现出对自身的吸引力,在它自己的眼中,“转变”为自身,名词—事物也不能存在。在它们眼中,自己总在发展,永远在“转变”,没有停顿。这种关于动态自然的视角并不是在论述语言的缺陷,而是为了反映出一个没有休息与静止的世界。

① 巴尔顿:《给劳工的世界史》,第97页。

② 引自埃兹拉·庞德:《早期作品》,伊拉·纳德尔编,纽约:Penguin出版社,2005年,第290页。

③ 钱兆明:《东方主义和现代主义:庞德和威廉姆斯作品中的中国传说》,北卡罗来纳州德勒姆:杜克大学出版社,1995年,第105页。

维柯甚至从中国绘画中推断出埃及绘画的样子："我们可以推断出埃及人与现在的中国人一样缺乏技术。"(NS,46)正如中国被隔绝了一样，埃及也一定如此。维柯用这种与真实的隔绝来解释神话传说里中国人傲慢地相信他们自己伟大遗产的原因，这种信念即使与希伯来真理接触后也同样没有改变。(NS,32)因此，通过对中国和埃及的比较，维柯提出了国家进步需要特殊力量的阶段论。这种比较与乔伊斯对当代中国与古代爱尔兰的的超历史的分层类似。

黑格尔与凤凰

维柯将中国发展的停滞不前归罪于儒家的著作，认为它们"如同埃及人的僧侣书一样，对物质自然的提及是原始和笨拙的……几乎全部转向庸俗的道德准则，也就是说，道德如同自然法则一样约束着人们" (NS,50)。黑格尔重申了这一点："对中国人而言，他们的道德法则如同自然法则——外在地、积极地控制他们——中国人声称道德法则是在暴力、强制责任和对彼此的尊敬的基础上建立的。"(LPH,74)道家也成了黑格尔的批判对象，这是维柯没有考虑的，因为直到 1788 年，维柯死后的 45 年，《道德经》才被翻译成拉丁文。对道家的发现和解释标志了西方对中国建构的重要进展。在黑格尔的时代，关于道家的一个典型的(误导的)观念是"它对世界上的事情漠不关心"①。于是，道家的服从本能和对知识理性的弱化也许与中国的文化停滞和历史循环思想相一致。对黑格尔而言，"自然的"道德法则证明了中国如同印度一样"完全缺乏对自由观念的本质理解"(LPH,74)。自由的缺失表明这两个国家无法回应"追求完善的冲动"，或者无法依据任何"转变辩证"的关联来建立一个不断进步的、最终成为同一的整体。(LPH, 56,59)于是，黑格尔将中国划分在以种族为界的"亚细亚"范围内，这也将保留在西方的思想和精神中。

黑格尔使用了乔伊斯熟悉的意象来说明这种差异，这种修辞也可以在《尤利西斯》和《芬尼根的守灵夜》中找到：

> 在轮回的观念中，我们发现(再循环的观念)在它与个体存在的联系中发展。但是，一个更广为人知的传言表明，凤凰是一种自然的生命类型；它永远为自己准备火堆，然后飞入火中燃烧自己，但却从它躯体的灰烬中产生出新的、再生的新鲜生命。但是，凤凰这个意象不仅是亚洲的，它不仅是东方的而且也是西方的。精神……不仅仅……从它先前形体的灰烬中焕然新生；它也来自于一种光荣的、纯粹的、升华了的精神。它显然与自我对抗——消耗自我的存在；但是在毁灭中又产生出一种新的存在形式，每一个连续的阶段转变为一种具体的实在，努力将自己升华到一个新的级别。(LPH 76)

中国历史给黑格尔的系统造成了一个难题：在它早熟的文明中，中国肯定曾经已经"将自我提升到了新阶段"，但是从未有过一种"精神"将它带领到那里。中国的先进是技术上的，但绝不是道德和精神上的。只有在西方才有精神的进步，而且仅仅是通过暴力来实现

① 亨瑞·艾利斯：《晚期驻中国大使的进展》，伦敦：John Murray 出版社，1818 年，第二卷，第 293 页。

的:在东方仅有自然的循环(转世,生命的轮和凤凰般的重生)。于是,中国是弱小的,不能对抗自身,相反,一个西化了的东方(以日本的形式为例)却可以与自我为敌。

变黄与黄祸

关于中国弱小的意识与西方变为世界历史中的本土有关,正如它的对立面,对中国文化重生的恐惧也随即产生。正如一本学校教科书所言:“中国文明在其宗教和智性方面曾经是(现在也是)弱小的。”[①]斯宾格勒认为,在技术层面上东方与西方都曾开拓了世界,但是却以截然不同的方式:“中国文化将几乎所有欧洲的发现也列入其中——包括指南针、望远镜、印刷术、火药、造纸术、瓷器——但是中国人没有从自然中夺取,而是骗取了这些东西。[②] 种族化的世界史在区分白种人、黑种人和黄种人的策略中暗示了一系列相对的力量的联盟:

> 白种人……逐渐吞食了这些落后的种族,有时灭绝他们,或者产生出一个混杂的种族,比如现代的印度人,他们中的最高种姓代表了更纯粹的雅利安血统,但在世界上其他地区,白种人只将自己作为黑人或混杂人群的统治者……在中国……蒙古人种似乎是这片领地的第一位统治者,因此无需消灭黑人或与他们混杂就发展了起来。[③]

乔伊斯将一个中国牧师与一个日本传教士的相遇设定为一个土著的中国/爱尔兰哲学对日本/英国的侵略哲学的转变,颠覆了中国与爱尔兰因过分与世隔绝或缺乏足够的侵略性而不能成为世界历史的一部分的叙述。

然而,乔伊斯也愿意把中国与弱小和谦卑联系起来,正如他在接下来对习俗化了的羞耻文化和中国妥协的反叛的明确提及中说:1900 年爆发了义和团运动,孙逸仙在 1924 年于汉口成立了短暂的中华民国——“但是为什么是手绢? 孙逸仙从哪里来的第二种声调? 他有磕头。”(FM,89.36—90.2)为什么你有一块手帕? 为什么你用(第二声)悲叹,我的孩子? 因为有些霸道的人(牛)踢了、击打和剥去了他的脸? 屁股(“buxars”是荷兰语中的裤子):贬低他,使他失去脸面(“脸面”在中国文化中是个很重要的成分,根据《牛津英语大词典》记载,19 世纪 90 年代第一次被西方分析),变为一个身份低微的人(磕头)。乔伊斯似乎将耻辱融入一系列的历史的提醒:从 1850 年到 1940 年的中国历史可以被阐释为一系列首先是西方,然后是日本的帝国主义的压迫下的耻辱。

强大的西方与弱小的东方的种族化的二元对立在 19 世纪被广泛地接受了,对它的设想的批判与对东方文化的授予的暗示,可以看做一种进步式的思想和现代主义希望结束前代神话的标志。斯宾格勒又一次为乔伊斯与这些建构的关键联系提供了一种有用的语境,因为目前为止他们是建构。对斯宾格勒而言,

---

① 赫恩肖:《第一本世界史书》,第 37 页。

② 斯宾格勒:《西方的没落》脚注,第 389 页。

③ 史密斯:《世界历史的主流》,第 10 页。

“现代”一词，在西方的土地上……提供了一幅历史不断进步的画面。而东方的画面则是静止的。它呈现出一种自我约束的对立，与其结果和一种神圣行为一样，它的转折点也具有一种平衡。但是，一旦被一种全新类型的人类采用，就马上转变……成为一种线性发展的观念。[①]

斯宾格勒根据它们如何服务于相关文化的活动，将两者都视为可以转化的结构、画面或理念。乔伊斯在利奥波德·布鲁姆的他者观的杂交式变体中将西方视角与东方视角戏剧化，转而与西方社会进步的梦想和无目标的循环空想联系起来。布鲁姆的理念被认为有一个亚洲的成分，它与1904年在都柏林人中热议的外来的轮回思想联系起来，这种轮回的思想侵扰了他们政治和文化进步的主张，强调了他们炼狱般的停滞。在《芬尼根的守灵夜》中，黑格尔的“亚洲”的凤凰神话作为一种“自然生命的类型”，也是一种叙述次序循环的象征。它占据了“火鸟化为灰烬”的凤凰公园，好像在这本书中，在它的循环结构如同内部再生了一样。(FW，24.11)但是在《芬尼根的守灵夜》中，东西方的两面性被戏剧可能性淹没了，与此同时，它比《尤利西斯》更明确地被乔伊斯颠覆。东方的他者性目前仅仅被视为一种威胁，因为它包含了对东西方二元对立的戏拟，或者，如同在他们的时代被描绘的那样，在自然和精神之间藏着一种“无法化约的敌对主义”，一种由在对立中对自我“预先重复”的对立结构带来的辩证。

黑格尔关于中国历史停滞的观念为丁尼生的著名对句诗《洛克斯里大厅》提供了语境。诗中动态的叙述成功地在两行自信的扬抑格八韵步诗中简化了黑格尔复杂的公式：

在世界的影子里我们度过了年轻的岁月：
欧洲的五十年好过神州大地的整个循环。

无论乔伊斯是否了解黑格尔东方主义理论的细节，他戏拟了丁尼生诗中的东方主义：“我们已经从中国周年那里听到，这只母鸡如何不仅仅是第二个12分之8的第一个4分之5后的一两声嘀嗒——香江香港三十二——而是一年年地20去9的另一个和第30。”(FM，119.22—6)丁尼生的“中国周年”现在与在“咖啡圈”中听到的八卦的循环联系起来，八卦的内容扭曲为一种模糊的数字符码(包括勃拉瓦茨基恶毒的凯瑟琳车轮的象限的历史循环，也许还有黄道日历)。因为他们都是高度编码的符号，这种符码将中国和它假定循环的历史简化为一种循环密码和极简形式，外交官和传教士的传言建立起一种来自世界历史的建构。《芬尼根的守灵夜》存在一些这样的符码，因此，一个符码化了的中国成为了另一象征：《守灵夜》自身是被神秘的八卦和传言建构的，它可读性很低的杂乱草稿被乔伊斯说意大利语的女儿形容为“中国的”，这令他很高兴。[②]

在现代主义时期影响世界历史的还有中国在他们的当下叙述中达成的共识：中国不再是与它的神秘的过去一样拥有无限未来的国家。拿破仑在逃亡圣海伦娜的一次演讲中说：

① 斯宾格勒：《西方的没落》，第39页。

② 乔伊斯：《詹姆斯·乔伊斯书信集》，第三卷，理查德·吉尔伯特编，纽约：维京出版社，1966年，第134页。

“中国是一个生病了的沉睡的巨人。但是当她醒来，世界将会颤抖。”[1]拿破仑是较早的反对“黄祸”观念的人，这个观念在19世纪90年代美国移民中产生，在接下来的一系列世界历史事件中重新上演：“过去发生的事情也许可能会再发生。当今的世界了解‘黄祸’的威胁。”[2]这种恐惧在世界史和他们种族化的叙述中加深，表现为对世界史前的叙述的投射：

> 原始居民以他们的耐心勤奋著称，他们的财富和人口急剧增长，直到他们宁静的生活招来了中亚草原凶猛的游牧民族的嫉妒和轻视。这些掠夺的游牧部落一次又一次骑着战马穿越戈壁沙漠，扫荡了他们的财产，摧毁他们的村庄，抢夺了他们的供给，带走并囚禁了他们的孩子。[3]

在《芬尼根的守灵夜》中，这种威胁被嘲弄般地放入一种变形了的吉尼斯广告中：“吉尼斯对你很好”变成了“Genhis is ghoon for you.”（FW，593.17—18）在东方出现的暴君将颁布一系列命令：“飞……烧……是！无规则动词。”（FW，594.1—3）中国人虽然与游牧民族远远不同，但是作为部分的“黄种人”，他们也常是被这种“游牧恐惧”的对象。这种恐惧产生了根绝其来源的渴望：这种恐惧只有在没有差异的时候才能消失，正如在爱尔兰主教的空想夜晚对于根本统一的设想，或者通过一种“实际的办法”，消除这些造成威胁的差异，如同“直到汉与匈的消失”一句所写，（FW，6.20—1）它指向未来某个时候，当人类不停（又一次）重复自己，汉（中国人）和匈（游牧民族）被消灭，如同“直到犹太人的皈依”一句所说，一个完全不可能的目的论错觉。但是，它揭示了在基督教主导的西方，种族主义者和帝国主义者对于“灭亡蛮族”的幻想和渴望，而令他们终止的谣言始终只是一种夸张的假定。世界历史被视为一个拥有不同人种和特点的种族化戏剧，它对“终结”的正式渴求中产生了这种幻想。乔伊斯这种模拟的世界历史将这些幻想戏剧化，如同给予这些幻想以简单的生命。戏剧在一种含混的语言中结束，这种语言通过它特有的艺术建构和多样的种族化话语，尽可能清晰地组成了这些类型的结构。

作者简介：芬·福德姆，伦敦大学教授，《都柏林乔伊斯学刊》编辑，主要研究领域为当代英国文学。

---

① 这种归因逐渐被接受但却是我能找到的最接近的资源：“我听说巴拿马曾说东方渴望一个人：一个真正的人，或者一种精神，被等待了很久来挽救自然的美好，于是，我们种族中的大部分来自于独裁无知和迷信的压制。”（埃利斯：《后期驻中国大使纪要》，第二卷，第252页。）无论拿破仑是否说过，这句话被认为在1909年广泛流传：“我们常常听说中国被比作一个既没有梦想着它安静的力量也没有意识到如何使用这种力量的沉睡的巨人。”莱曼·哥顿少尉，引自威廉姆·萨菲尔：《萨菲尔的政治词典》，牛津：牛津大学出版社，2008年，第666页。

② 施尔特：《世界历史介绍》，第14页。

③ 赫恩肖：《第一本世界历史书》，第35页。

Asia Was, Laozi Is, Plurabelle to Be: China and Japan through Joyce's "Cracked Looking Glass"[①]

伊东荣志郎

【Abstract】 This paper aims to explore how James Joyce described East Asia, especially China and Japan: Joyce's "cracked looking glass" reflects the two countries like an inseverable pair. Throughout *Finnegans Wake*, the pair of China and Japan is often seen probably because of "geographical vicinity, similarity of exotic flavor, and like appearance of the script" as George C. Sandulescu suggests in *The Language of the Devil* (66).

It was probably in his Jesuit school days that Joyce began to be conscious of China and Japan. In the retreat scene honoring St. Francis Xavier of *A Portrait of the Artist as a Young Man*, the rector tells about the missionary life of the saint who "wished then to go to China to win still more souls for God but he died of fever on the island of Sancian" (*P* 111).

After the Russo-Japanese War, Joyce wrote to his brother Stanislaus that "Japan, the first naval power in the world" (November 6, 1906; *Letters II*, 188). In *Ulysses*, Leopold Bloom remembers Simon Dedalus imitating Larry O'Rourke saying, "The Russian, they'd only be an eight o'clock breakfast for the Japanese" (*U* 4. 116—17). However, Joyce seems to have noticed that numerous Asians came to hate Japanese imperialism. Sheldon Brivic argues in *Joyce through Lacan and Žižek* that "England and Japan have much in common as aggressive islands invading the mainland" (208).

In the morning of *Ulysses*, Leopold Bloom walks "in the track of the sun"(*U* 4. 99—100). Bloom shows his interest in the Orient including China and Japan especially in "Calypso" and "Lotus Eaters." Later in "Ithaca," readers recognize that it is also the title of the book he owns: F. D. Thompson's *In the Track of the Sun* (1893).

One of the highlights of *Finnegans Wake* is the dialogue between the Chinese Archdruid and the Japanese St. Patrick in Book IV (*FW* 611—613). Joyce parallelled the relationship between China and Japan with that between the Celts and Christianity or George Berkeley and the English evangelists to Ireland. This scene reflects the tensions between China and Japan around 1938. Joyce finalized and published the novel in 1939 and died in January 1941.

【Key Words】 James Joyce China Japan Orientalism (Post-)Colonialism

Introduction

This paper aims to explore how James Joyce described East Asia, especially China and

---

① This paper is a revised version of the paper presented at the 2013 Shanghai James Joyce Symposium held at Fudan University, Shanghai, China between 14—15 August 2013.

This research is supported by a Grant-in-Aid for Scientific Research (C) (No. 21520266) by the Japan Society for the Promotion of Science under the title of "James Joyce and the Genealogy of Oriental Studies."

Japan: Joyce's "cracked looking glass" (*U* 1.146, etc.) reflects the two countries like an inseverable pair. Throughout *Finnegans Wake*, the pair of China and Japan is often seen.

It was probably in his Jesuit school days that Joyce began to be conscious of China and Japan. In the retreat scene honoring St. Francis Xavier of *A Portrait of the Artist as a Young Man*, the rector tells about the missionary life of the saint who "went from country to country in the east, from Africa to India, from India to Japan, baptizing the people. He wished then to go to China to win still more souls for God but he died of fever on the island of Sancian" (*P* 111).

In the morningscene of *Ulysses*, Leopold Bloom walks "in the track of the sun" (*U* 4.99—100). Bloom shows his interest in the Orient including China and Japan especially in "Calypso" and "Lotus Eaters." Later in "Ithaca," readers recognize that it is also the title of the book he owns: F. D. Thompson's *In the Track of the Sun* (1893), a record of the author's world trip via Japan and China, taking over seven months.

Finnegans Wake includes numerous non-European elements including Chinese and Japanese compound words. Many Chinese place names are alluded to in the text: Peking [北京; Beijing; cf. VI.B.24.293; *JJA* 34: 480]: "the Pekin packet" (*FW* 507.28) and "spekin" (*FW* 533.6), Huang/Zijin Cheng [紫禁城; The Forbidden City; cf. VI.B.24.293; *JJA* 34: 480]: "Hwang Chang evelytime" (*FW* 130.35) and "hwen ching hwan chang" (*FW* 322.6), Shanghai [上海]: "he praze savohole shanghai" (*FW* 398.27—28) and "How big was his boost friend and be shanghaied to him?" (*FW* 485.23—24) The Anna Livia Chapter (Book I, Chapter 8) contains approximately 963 river names including presumably 194 rivers of Asia and Oceania, and a washerwoman refers to the Yellow River, or Huang He (黄河), known as China's Sorrow: "Hoangho, my sorrow, I've lost it!" (*FW* 213.6—7; cf. 47474—164; *JJA* 48: 95) It clearly indicates that Joyce knew that the river was called so because it frequently caused devastating floods sweeping away many people and their houses, villages, etc. on its banks.

I. China and Japan through Jesuit Missionaries

The Society of Jesus (*Societas Iesu*), widely known as the Jesuits, is famous for their global missionary activities. They came to Japan between 1549 and 1644, and to China between 1579 and 1724 according to the historical record. The Jesuits introduced Western science, astronomy and arts to Asian countries, while they were very active in conveying Asian knowledge and philosophy to Europe. However, as the result of a series of political and economic conflicts, the suppression of the Jesuits became serious in Europe in 1750 and continued until the 1814 restoration when they started to establish Jesuit colleges and universities around the world.

Joyce went to two Jesuit secondary schools, Clongowes Wood College, and Belvedere College which is also known as St. Francis Xavier's College.

Naturally the Jesuit education had a significant influence during Joyce's formative years.

A brief summary of the life of St. Francis Xavier was told by the rector[Fr. William Henry, S. J.] on the three-day retreat at Belvedere College in Chapter III of *A Portrait of the Artist as a Young Man*:

> The rector went on gravely:
>
> — You are all familiar with the story of the life of saint Francis Xavier, I suppose, the patron of your college. He came of an old and illustrious Spanish family and you remember that he was one of the first followers of saint Ignatius. They met in Paris where Francis Xavier was professor of philosophy at the university. This young and brilliant nobleman and man of letters entered heart and soul into the ideas of our glorious founder and you know that he, at his own desire, was sent by saint Ignatius to preach to the Indians. He is called, as you know, the apostle of the Indies. He went from country to country in the east, from Africa to India, from India to Japan, baptizing the people. He is said to have baptized as many as ten thousand idolaters in one month. It is said that his right arm had grown powerless from having been raised so often over the heads of those whom he baptized. He wished then to go to China to win still more souls for God but he died of fever on the island of Sancian. A great saint, saint Francis Xavier! A great soldier of God! (*P* 111)

The rector preached that Xavier is said to have baptized as many as ten thousand idolaters in one month. The truth is that while staying in Japan for two years and three months Xavier baptized roughly 100 in Kagoshima, 100 in Hirado and 500 in Yamaguchi: the total number is about 700 (*Hibiki*, 34, 5). However, taking the great language and culture barrier into account, 700 is a good number for the initial mission. The significance of Xavier's achievements in Japan is not baptism but making the guidelines and facilitating missionary work for the followers.

Portugal and the Society of Jesus asked the Pope the permission for missionaries for the Portuguese East Indies under the Padroado agreement between the Holy Sea and the kingdoms of Spain and Portugal. In 1540 King Joao III of Portugal nominated Xavier as Apostolic Nuncio or the first papal diplomatic representative to the new world. ① In October 1545 Xavier went to Portuguese Malacca where he met a Japanese *samurai* named Anjiro [or Yajiro] from Kagoshima in December 1547: It was the first time for Xavier to hear about Japan. Anjiro had fled from Japan, having been charged with murder in Kagoshima. Anjiro enthusiastically told Xavier about Japanese culture and customs, which tempted him to go to Japan. Preceded by Anjiro, Xavier, boarding on a Chinese flatboat, finally reached Kagoshima, Japan on August 15, 1549 with three other Jesuits.

① Cf. Henry Venn, *The Missionary Life and Labours of St. Francis Xavier Taken from His Own Correspondence*, p. 18.

Monument to the Arrival of St. Francis Xavier, Kagoshima (made by Louis Francen in 1978)

They were welcomed by Lord Takahisa Shimazu (1514—1571) who allowed them to be engaged in missionary activities in his dominions, expecting trade benefits from Portugal. Japanese people were not easily converted because most of them believed in Buddhism and *Shinto* (*FW* 539. 11: benefits though shintoed), the indigenous spirituality of Japan. However, the Western pictures of the Virgin Mother and child and the representation of the cross attracted Nipponese people. In order to explain Christianity Xavier asked Anjiro to translate Christian terms into Japanese: For God he chose *Dainichi* [*Skt.* Vairocana; *Ch.* 大日如来], and for heaven or paradise the word was *jodo* [Pure Land; *Ch.* 净土], which means the celestial realm or pure abode of a Buddha or Bodhisattva.① However, Anjiro, who was a converted *samurai* from *Shingon* [*Skt.* Mantra: *Ch.* 真言] Esoteric Buddhism (*U* 9. 68—70), did not know that both words indicate typical Buddhist terms. Then the Jesuits were welcomed not only by the common people but also by the Buddhist monks.② Xavier and his companions were engaged in missionary work in several places in Western Japan such as Kagoshima, Hirado and Yamaguchi.

In January 1551 with the support from the powerful merchant Ryokei Hibiya of Sakai they finally arrived in the capital Kyoto (*FW* 534. 02 & 550. 28) to greet the emperor and other highbred people to obtain the permission to preach Christianity all over Japan, but those noblemen in Kyoto refused to meet the Jesuits. This did not matter since they did not have any influential power because it was still in the Warring States Period (1467—1573). Xavier gradually came to think that they should have preached in China, so that it would have enabled them to proselytize in Japan much easier. Thus in November 1551 he decided to go back to Goa to start missionary works in China. However, he died of fever on December, 3, 1552 on Shangchuan Island (上川岛), China, before he could realize his ambition. The Society of Jesus distinguished itself from other Catholic societies by Francis Xavier's mission to Asia in the age of the Counter-Reformation. Xavier and Loyola were canonized by Gregory XV (1554—1623; p. 1621—1623) on March, 12, 1622.

---

① Ross, Andrew C., *A Vision Betrayed*, p. 29.

② Cf. Ross, p. 29: "Xavier was furious when, after using it for some time in public preaching, he discovered that Dainichi was a particular manifestation of the wisdom which illuminates the universe worshipped by Shingon Buddhists."

As Andrew C. Ross notes, Xavier's life and vision links the Jesuit mission in Japan and China, and it was a Neapolitan Jesuit Alessandro Valignano (1539—1606) who shaped the mission in the two countries (Ross 32). He made the first visit to Japan from 1579 to 1582 and formed a basic strategy for conversion of the heathens to Catholicism in Japan, which was later called "adaptationism." He wrote *Il Cerimoniale per i Missionari del Giappone* (*The Ceremonial for Missionaries in Japan*) for the Jesuit missionaries in 1581, although their luxurious lives like the high-ranked Japanese Buddhist monks then were severely criticized not only by the late-coming Franciscans and Dominicans (cf. P. 157—158) but even by some Jesuits. Valignano thought that the key to reform the mission was to produce Japanese priests. He and other Jesuits transformed a recently emptied Buddhist monastery into a nascent *seminario* [seminary] in 1580 in Arima Province [now Minami-Shimabara City, Nagasaki] and built a *noviciado* [Jesuit convent] in Usuki, Bungo Province [now Oita]. At the *seminario* twenty-two young Japanese converts began to receive Christian education both in Japanese and Latin [cf. "japlatin" (*FW* 476. 14)]. Next year they founded another *seminario* in Azuchi, the castle town of Nobunaga Oda (1534—1582), and a *collegio* [college] in Funai, Bungo Province with the support of the powerful Christian lord Sorin Otomo (1530—1587). In 1582 Valignano planned for his famous Japanese Embassy to Europe known as "Tensho-Ken-o-Shonen-Shisetsu" (The Boys' Embassy to Europe of the Tensho Period). He took with him to Europe four young Japanese Christian boys of aristocratic stock (Mancio Ito, Miguel Chijiwa, Julião Nakaura and Martinão Hara) as "ambassadors" to lay before the Pope and the Catholic monarchs and princes of Europe the needs of the Japanese Church (Ross 67). The ambassador party left Nagasaki (cf. *FW* 315. 22 & 535. 19; also the setting of Puccini's *Madama Butterfly*) on 20 February 1582 for Lisbon via Macau, Malacca and Goa. They went to Madrid to meet Felipe II (1527—1598; *r.* 1554—1598), then to Florence to join a ball hosted by the Medici family. Finally they visited Rome to greet the popes Gregorius XIII (1502—1585; *p.* 1572—1585) and Sixtus V (1520—1590; p. 1585—1590) and these four Japanese boys were subsequently granted citizenship of Rome. The party came back to Nagasaki in 1590, three years after the invalid deportation order called "Bateren [<*Pg.* padre]-tsuiho-rei" (the Purge Directive Order to the Christian Missionaries) by Imperial Regent Hideyoshi Toyotomi (1537—1598) who was the most powerful man at that time.① However, Hideyoshi began to assume a firm attitude towards them after the San Felipe Incident in July 1596.② Thus all the Christians over Japan were gradually subjected to the suppression:

① During the 1577 battles of Kyushu, a Portuguese Jesuit Gaspar Coelho (converted Jew; 1530—1590), the first chief of the Japanese Branch of the Society of Jesus (the Jesuits), proudly showed Hideyoshi his battleships of the newest European type. By that time, Hideyoshi had already noticed that the Jesuits, with the Spanish Invincible Armada's overwhelming naval power, planned to bring Japan and China into subjugation by colonialism. Cf. Eishiro Ito, "Unveiling Histories of the Tohoku District: Juan Goto and Crypto-Christians."

② In July 1596 the Spanish ship San Felipe was wrecked off the coast of Tosa Province [now Kochi] and Hideyoshi learned from the pilot that the Spanish Franciscans were in the vanguard of an Iberian invasion of Japan. In response, Hideyoshi ordered the crucifixions of twenty-six Catholics in Nagasaki on February, 5 of that year (the Twenty-Six Martyrs of Japan).

The total number of the Jesuit martyrs in Japan from 1549 to 1644 is 111. ① The next government Tokugawa *Shogunate* (1603—1867) was also fascinated by the profits from trading with Western countries at the start, but they gradually came to fear that like some Asian countries Japan might have been colonized by Spain and Portugal if Japan continued to trade with them and allowed their Christian missions to Japanese people. The *Shogunate* also feared that their favored order of Neo-Confucianism (the teachings of Zhū Xī [朱熹 1130—1200]) might have been destroyed by Christianity. So in 1639, the government closed its door to foreign countries (except China, Korea and the Netherlands) until 1854: no foreigners (except licensed Dutch merchants, etc.) were officially admitted into Japan, and no Japanese could go abroad. It was only through the medium of the Dutch at Nagasaki that the exclusive Japan learned about the Western World.

Three decades later after Francis Xavier's death, in 1582, some Jesuits including the two Italians Michele Ruggieri (罗明坚 1543—1607) and Matteo Ricci (利玛窦 1552—1610) restarted the mission in China and introduced Western science, mathematics, astronomy and visual arts to the Imperial Court: Such contacts between China and Europe can date back to the thirteenth century contingence between the Papacy and the Mongol Empire in the days of Marco Polo. ② The Jesuits also carried on a significant inter-cultural dialogue with Chinese scholars such as Confucians or "confusianist"(s) as Joyce spelled (*FW* 131. 33—34). According to the research by David. E. Mungello, a total of 920 Jesuits participated in the China mission from 1552 (the death of Xavier) to 1800: of whom 314 were Portuguese, and another 130 were French. ③

In 1557, the Portuguese established a permanent settlement in Macau, about 100 km closer to the Pearl River Delta (珠江三角洲) than Shangchuan Island. Alessandro Valignano founded Colégio de São Paulo, Macau (St. Paul's College of Macau) in 1594 to train the Jesuits for mission work in China. Ricci, Ruggieri and their followers studied Chinese language and culture enthusiastically and adapted some Chinese religious qualities including Buddhist, Taoist and Confucian elements to create a Sino-Christian civilization. Their strategy went very well in the beginning: Even Emperor Chongzhen (崇祯帝 1611—1644; *r.* 1627—1644) was nearly converted to Christianity. However, the fall of the Ming Dynasty (cf. *FW* 57. 5) in 1644 and the conquest of China by the Manchu Qing regime conduced to some hardships to the Jesuits. During the subsequent years of war between the Qing and the remnants of the Ming some Jesuits stood on the different sides of the front line.

While the Jesuits were intent on building churches and demonstrating Western

① Cf. Kiefer, James E., "Jesuit Missions in Non-Christian Countries."

② The earliest Chinese document of Christianity entering China was in the seventh century, which is known from the Nestorian Stele erected in AD 781 in the age of the Tang Dynasty China and discovered buried (probably during religious suppression) near Chongren Temple (崇仁寺) in the suburb of Xī'ān in 1625. The heading on the stone is "Memorial of the Propagation in China of the Luminous Religion [Nestorian Christianity] from Daqin" (大秦景教流行中国碑). The Jesuit Alvaro Semedo was the first European to visit the stele (some time between 1623 and 1625).

③ Mungello, David E., *The Great Encounter of China and the West*, p. 37. The total number of 920 does not include Chinese members of the Society of Jesus.

architectural styles, they were also very ardent in conveying Chinese knowledge to Europe. For instance, Ricci introduced the philosophy of Confucius (cf. *U* 12.191) in *De Christiana expeditione apud Sinas* (*Concerning Christian Expeditions to China*, 1615).[①] In 1662 Father Prospero Intorcetta (殷铎泽 1626—1696) published *Sapientia Sinica* (*The Wisdom of China*) related to the study of the Four Books (四书; *Sìshū*: *FW* 587.19).[②] Intorcetta also published *Sinarum scientia politico-moralis* (*Politico-moral Science of the Chinese*) in 1667, and *Confucius Sinarum philosophus* (*Confucius, Chinese Philosopher*) together with Philippe Couplet (柏应理 1623—1693) in 1687. In fact, the Jesuit writings greatly contributed to Chinoiserie in Europe. Some Chinese Christians were also taken by the Jesuits to Europe: one of the earliest Chinese travelers to Europe was Cheng Antelo (郑安德勒; also known as Andreas Zheng or Wade-Giles), who was sent to Rome by Emperor Yongli (永历帝 1623—1662; *r.* 1646—1662) of the Southern Ming Dynasty along with the Polish Jesuit Michal Boym (卜弥格 1612—1659) and stayed in Rome and Venice from 1652 to 1655.[③] The Jesuits' reports on the *Ba gua* (八卦: the Eight Trigrams of Taoist cosmology; cf. *FW* 476.36) and the Yin/Yang principles (阴/阳; cf. *FW* 8.21, 109.6, 246.31 & 578.21) attracted many European thinkers such as Gottfried Leibniz in the late seventeenth century.

However, the situation gradually changed in the Qing Dynasty as the number of Christian missionaries dramatically increased with the arrival of the Franciscans and Dominicans from the Spanish colonies such as Formosa and the Philippines from 1632.[④] The newcomers began to criticize the Jesuit strategy of "adaptationism" carried out all over the world and informed Rome of the Jesuit missionary method, which greatly offended the Catholic Church. The controversy over the Chinese practices of ancestor worship and Confucianism badly affected all the Christian missions. Emperor Kangxi (康熙帝 1654—1722; *r.* 1661—1722) tried to ban Catholicism but he was not successful. Finally in 1724 Christianity was banned by Emperor Yongzheng (雍正帝 1678—1735; *r.* 1722—1735). The Italian Jesuit Lorenzo Ricci (1703—1775) was elected the 18th Superior General of the Society of Jesus in 1758: He was the last before the Suppression beginning in 1773 (cf. *P* 57). Pope Clement XIV (1705—1774; *p.* 1769—1774) dismissed the Society of Jesus in July 1773. The withdrawal of this great missionary force exposed Christian churches in China to successive waves of persecution.

Instead of the Jesuits, Protestant Christianity began entering and taking root in the Qing Dynasty China in the early nineteenth century. Taking a neutral position on religion, Bloom shows some sympathy with the Protestant missionaries here. Around the time of the two Opium Wars (鸦片战争 1839—1842/1856—1860), the role of the Jesuits in China

---

① Ricchi primarily wrote the manuscript in Italian on his "journals" during his twenty-seven-year life in China. In 1612, two years after his death, it was expanded, edited and translated into Latin by Nicolas Trigault (金尼阁, 1577—1628) to be published in 1615.

② Brockey, Liam Mattew, *Journey to the East: The Jesuit Mission to China*, 1579—1724, p. 278.

③ See Brockey, p. 112.

④ Cf. Ross, pp. 178—200.

was largely taken over by *La Société des Missions Étrangères de Paris* (shortly MEP; The Paris Foreign Missions Society).

II. *In the Track of the Sun* in *Ulysses*

In the sunny morning scene of "Calypso" Leopold Bloom goes out from his apartment at 7 Eccles Street toward St. George's Church in the south (Hardwicke Place) "in the track of the sun" (*U* 4.99—100). Bloom's longing for the East intimately associates with F. D. Thompson's *In the Track of the Sun* (New York/London 1893), which is included in Bloom's library, although it is reported that the title page is missing (*U* 17.1395). The book is Thompson's itinerary of the seven-month-and-four-day globe trotting starting on October 14, 1891—from New York to the East—Japan, China (Hong Kong and Canton), Ceylon [now Sri Lanka], India, Egypt and Palestine: Thompson's itinerary roughly covers the range of Bloom's association with the East in "Calypso" and "Lotus Eaters." Thompson sailed back to New York via Europe. The book is full of attractive illustrations and photos. The title page (recto) of *In the Track of the Sun* has a photo of a Japanese girl playing the *samisen* as Bloom remembers: "A girl playing one of those instruments what do you call them: dulcimers" (*U* 4.97—98). [1]

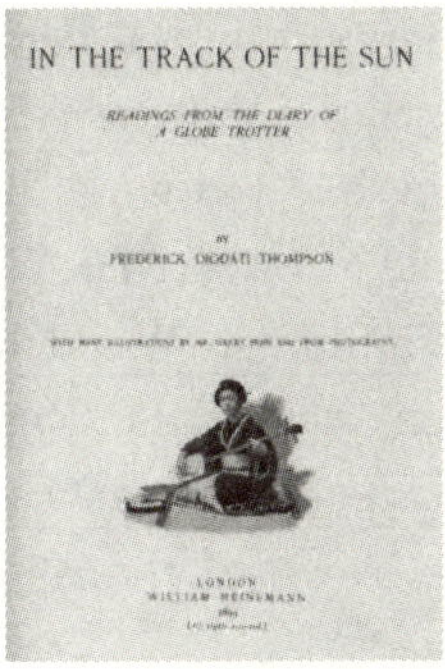

The title page of *In the Track of the Sun*

---

[1] In "KIOTO AND ITS TEMPLES" of Chapter IV. "FAREWELL TO JAPAN," the same photo appears again and the writer comments: "After dinner I visited a Japanese theatre, and saw some curious dancing. The dancers, wearing very rich and handsome dresses, kept time, in slow and graceful movements, to the music of flutes, guitars, and small drums, played by twelve Japanese girls" (55). The verso of the title page is the "stately and plump" "Statue of Daibutsu, or Great Buddha" which is probably the Great Buddha of Kamakura, Kanagawa, Japan:

Bloom later associates the title with women's wear: "Fashion part of their charm. Just changes when you're on the track of the secret. Except the east" (*U* 13. 804—5).

In the opening passage of "Lotus-Eaters" Bloom imagines the East on a sunny, warm morning. In Westland Row he halts before the window of the Belfast and Oriental Tea Company and reads a tea poster "choice blend, made of the finest Ceylon brands" (*U* 5. 18—19): he soon associates it with "The far east. Lovely spot it must be: the garden of the world, big lazy leaves to float about on, cactuses, flowery meads, snaky lianas they call them..." (*U* 5. 29—31). Ceylon is famous for tea products since a tea plant was brought to Ceylon by the British from China in 1824 and Sir Thomas Lipton, son of poor Irish immigrants, started a tea business in 1890. It is also the place where Henry S. Olcott's *Buddhist Catechism* Joyce once owned in Dublin was first compiled in 1881 as the author noted at the end of the booklet. Next Bloom imagines the people's idle lives there like the Lotus-Eaters in the *Odyssey*" (*U* 5. 33—36) which seems to be based on what Edward Said calls "Orientalism."

For a time Bloom forgets the East while he walks westward to check his post-box at Westland Row Post Office, encounters C. P. M'Coy talking about Paddy Dignam's death, etc. and reads Martha Clifford's letter in the lee of Westland Row Station wall. After finishing it, he resumes his walk and reaches the open backdoor of All Hallows [St. Andrew's Roman Catholic Church]. He steps onto the porch and doffs his hat:

> Same notice on the door. Sermon by the very reverend John Conmee S. J. on saint Peter Claver S. J. and the African Mission. Prayers for the conversion of Gladstone they had too when he was almost unconscious. The protestants are the same. Convert Dr William J. Walsh D. D. to the true religion. Save China's millions. Wonder how they explain it to the heathen Chinee. Prefer an ounce of opium. Celestials. Rank heresy for them. Buddha their god lying on his side in the museum. Taking it easy with hand under his cheek. Josssticks burning. Not like Ecce Homo. Crown of thorns and cross. Clever idea Saint Patrick the shamrock. Chopsticks?
>
> (*U* 5. 322—30) (Underlining mine.)

In the Roman Catholic church, Bloom remembers and mocks the Jesuit missionaries in China showing his sympathy for the "heathen" Chinese people. He associates Fr. John Conmee with the Jesuit mission to Africa, and with China after the two Opium Wars between Britain and the Ching Dynasty China. However, as Don Gifford notes, despite the strong Chinese xenophobia the Jesuits maintained missions in several cities in China in the nineteenth century: One crisis in the resistance to the missionaries was the death of five Jesuit priests in Nanking during the Boxer Rebellion (义和团运动, 1898—1901) in 1900 (Gifford 92). In Bloom's imagination the Chinese people prefer opium to Christianity, and Buddha is the Chinese god as he and Molly saw the reclining statue in the National Museum, Kildare Street, but Molly knows that it is "that Indian god" (*U* 18. 1201—2). ①

① Cf. Ito, Eishiro, "Orienting Orientalism in Ulysses," pp. 61—64.

Then he remembers the reclining Buddha statue he saw in the National Museum of Ireland in Kildare Street. The Buddha statue, actually from Burma, is very beautiful, well-proportioned and, sensual, when compared with "stately and plump" Buddha statues in East Asia. The Buddha statue was presented in 1891 by Colonel Sir Charles Fitzgerald as "a trophy of Britain's newest colony exhibited to the people of her oldest" according to John Smurthwaite (3).

Bloom mistakenly associates the Buddha's reclining pose with idleness, "taking it easy with his hand under his cheek" (*U* 5. 328—29). In fact, the reclining Buddha statue was made to express how the Buddha attained the Nirvana after he had eaten a pork dish offered by Cunda, the smith, which made his stomach totally in curable: "he had bedding spread with the head towards the north according to the ancient custom. He lay upon it, and with his mind perfectly clear, gave his final instructions to his disciples and bade them farewell" according to Olcott (22). So Bloom's association can be read as a parody because his sleeping pose is later described to look like the reclining Buddha by Molly (*U* 18. 1199—202).

Li Hongzhang①

In *Ulysses* there is only one example of the China-Japan pair in a catalogue of "Cyclops": "Hokopoko Harakiri, Hi Hung Chang" (*U* 12. 564). This is a possible allusion to the First Sino-Japanese War (1894—1895). "Hokopoko" might be a Japanese mimetic word "pokopoko" (a rumbling noise of borborygmus) or "bokoboko" (burble), and "Harakiri" means "cutting bowels" or "ritual suicide by disembowelment formerly practiced by Japanese *samurai.*" "Hi Hung Chang" indicates Li Hongzhang (Li Hung Chang; 李鸿章, 1823—1901), a Chinese politician, general and diplomat who signed the

① Cf. "Liaotung Convention."

Treaty of Shimonoseki ending the First Sino-Japanese War on April, 17, 1895. As Fritz Senn notes, Joyce's spelling also implies the popular voice of resistance in China (*JJQ* 13. 1, 245).

After the Russo-Japanese War (1904—5), Joyce wrote to his brother Stanislaus about "Japan, the first naval power in the world" (November 6, 1906; *Letters II*, 188). In *Ulysses*, Leopold Bloom remembers Simon Dedalus imitating Larry O'Rourke saying, "The Russian, they'd only be an eight o'clock breakfast for the Japanese" (*U* 4. 116—17). However, Joyce seems to have noticed that numerous Asians came to hate Japanese imperialism when he was working for *Finnegans Wake* in 1930s after the foundation of Manchukuo (满洲国). Sheldon Brivic argues in *Joyce through Lacan and Žižek* that "England and Japan have much in common as aggressive islands invading the mainland" (208).

III. China and Japan on the Noh Stage of *Finnegans Wake*

It has been often argued that *Ulysses* is a book of the day while *Finnegans Wake* is a book of the night. To conclude the night novel, even showing the Viconian cycle of *recorso*, to describe the sun-rising seems to be most appropriate. As Sheldon Brivic implies, the last chapter of *Finnegans Wake* can be called an Asian chapter full of Oriental elements from the Near East to the Far East (197). The word "Orient" was derived from the Latin word "*oriens*, *orient-em* rising sun, east" (*OED* 2). "Japan" literally means the origin of the sun, so the design of the national flag suggests the rising sun while "China" literally means the most flourishing country in the center of the world as the nation is actually now. So Joyce chose to transfer a highlight scene of the dialogue between St. Patrick and the Archdruid to that between a Japanese Buddhist monk and a Chinese philosopher/sage, reflecting the military tension between China and Japan especially after 1937.

Joyce was interested in China, especially Confucius or "Kung fu-Tze" as Joyce often spelled after Ezra Pound's spelling according to James S. Atherton's *The Books at the Wake*: "folk who may not have had many momentums to master Kung's doctrine of the meang" (*FW* 108. 11—12) (Atherton 227). Joyce often amusingly spelled his name purposely mixing it up with the English word "confusion" in *Finnegans Wake*: "confusium" (*FW* 15. 12), "confucion" (*FW* 417. 15), "Hell's Confucium and the Elements!" (*FW* 485. 35), etc. Joyce was presumably interested in Taoism, too, through the entry under "Lao-Tsze" (Laozi: 老子) of the 11th edition of the *Encyclopædia Britannica* (1910—1911): "laotsey taotsey" (*FW* 242. 25—26). The article was written by James Legge, translator of Lao Tzu's *The Tao Te Ching in The Text of Taoism* (Oxford: OUP, 1891).

Joyce sometimes confused several Chinese words with Japanese ones, or he tended to combine some Chinese words with Japanese on purpose, as Joyce's language list shows. The sounds he tried to represent with the alphabet are not often correct, or very frequently sound like Pidgin Japanese. George C. Sandulescu argues concerning Joyce's language list in *The Language of the Devil* that the order of the languages is very significant: "... Next on the list, two languages —Chinese and Japanese— are placed together for reasons of geographical vicinity, similarity of exotic flavor, and like appearance of the script" (sic) (66). This is the list of China/Japan contrasts in *FW*:

CHINA/JAPAN CONTRASTS IN *FW*		INSERTION DATE *	MS NO. (*JJA*)
81. 33—34	Nippoluono/Wei-Ling-Taou	May 1938	47476a—189v (*JJA* 49: 400)
343. 15	yup/ scoopchina's	1937	47480—26 (*JJA* 55: 49)
435. 27	chine/ jupan	c. 1936	47486b—386 (*JJA* 61: 407)
485. 36—486. 1	chinchin/ nipponnippers	c. 1936	47486b—456 (*JJA* 61: 443)
486. 11—12	a chink / a jape	April-May 1937	47487—56 (*JJA* 62:109)
583. 18	china's/ japets	? 1925	47482a—42 (*JJA* 60: 81)
611. 4—5	tappany/ chin chinjoss	Mid 1938	47488—169v (*JJA* 63: 169)

* Each date indicates the time when the insertions of both elements were completed.

As Louis O. Mink indicates in "*Finnegans Wake*" *Gazetteer*, *FW* regularly pairs China with Japan. It is noted that most references to the China/Japan pair were inserted after 1936. It reminds us of the fact that the Chinese passage (*U* 5. 323—30) of "Lotus Eaters" was also inserted into the 1922 text of *Ulysses* after the *Little Review* version. As Jacques Mercanton tells in "The Hours of James Joyce," he was asked by Joyce, "Isn't it contradictory to make two men speak Chinese and Japanese in a pub in Phoenix Park, Dublin?" (213) It suggests the dialogue between Archdruid Berkeley, speaking Pidgin English and St. Patrick speaking "Nippon English" (*FW* 611—613) where the Japanese St. Patrick argues "colors" with the Chinese Archdruid/Bishop Berkeley. The first draft of the episode was sent to Harriet Shaw Weaver on August 2, 1923 and it was considered to be the first piece to be written in the Wakean language that Weaver worries about the opaque nature of its linguistic experiment and that Joyce replied that he was "sorry that Patrick and Berkeley are unsuccessful in explaining themselves" (October 9, 1923; *Letters* I, 204) as Dirk Van Hulle explains (C&S 442—443). It is uncertain that Joyce could really differentiate between Japan and China. However, it was not until 1938 when St. Patrick clearly turns into a Japanese monk and Berkeley a Chinese philosopher. Like Gilbert & Sullivan's *The Mikado*, the pidgin Japanese/Chinese conversation continues like a quarrel. Joyce added some Japan/China elements later to express the strife between Shem and Shaun, the Archdruid and St. Patrick.

As Thornton Wilder points out, St. Patrick first appears as a Japanese, "Patriki San Saki" (*FW* 317. 2). ① The Japanized monk reappears in the final chapter of the novel, to discuss religious problems with the Chinese Archdruid (*FW* 611—613). It seems that their

① Cf. Graham, p. 6.

conversation occurs on the Noh stage. It is well-known that two influential figures to Joyce, W. B. Yeats and Ezra Pound, were very interested in the Noh play [*Jp.* 能] and enthusiastically introduced it to the West.

Yeats became interested in the Noh through his two Japanese friends, Yonejiro Noguchi (野口 米次郎, 1875—1947) and Michio Ito (伊藤 道郎, 1892—1961) who stayed in London in the mid-1910s. Yonejiro Noguchi was a famous writer of poetry, fiction and literary criticism in both English and Japanese. Michio Ito, born in Tokyo in 1892, was a dancer and choreographer. Pound wanted Ito to help him with the editing of Ernest Fenollosa's manuscripts on Noh. However, Ito's answer was, "Noh is the damnedest thing in this world."① Pound managed to persuade Ito to help him. Fortunately Ito studied *Kabuki*, which is based on Noh with plots, music and dance but performed in vulgarized form. Later, wearing a partial *Kabuki*-style mask, he could perform the hawk-like Guardian for Yeats' play *At the Hawk's Well*. In fact, his costume and moves seemed ancient Egyptian rather than Noh-style, although his exotic performance impressed Yeats and the audience very much. Ito had never trained as a Noh actor/dancer, but he played the role of the Hawk woman (the Guardian of the Well) at the premiere of Yeats' symbolic masque *At the Hawk's Well* (1916), which is full of the Noh elements.② In the play, the Hawk woman corresponds with "shite" (primary actor) and the Old Man waiting for fifty years for the water of immortality to flow and the Young Man (Cuchulain) can be considered as "waki" (subordinate actors/primary spectators). The effect of the play largely depends on the skill of the dancer, different from traditional Irish dramas. Both Pound and Yeats had never seen a real Noh play, but they struggled to learn something new to them from the traditional Japanese play to apply it to their Modernist works. Yeats learned to insert the dance into his plays to get the mystic mood of unreality to realize the Celtic legend.

In April 1916 when brave Irish men took up arms for independence from the British Empire, W. B. Yeats wrote an introduction of *Certain Noble Plays of Japan* by Fenollosa and Pound. It was printed in 350 copies and published near Dublin by William's sister Elizabeth Corbet Yeats as the Cuala Press edition in the year of the Easter Rebellion. For Yeats, the Noh play was an *Eastern* rising. Ezra Pound worked as a secretary of Yeats between 1913—1914 when he began to contact Joyce. Joyce was very interested in the theatre when he was young. When Joyce frequently corresponded with Pound and Yeats, he struggled to write his only play *Exiles*, which was deeply influenced by Henrik Ibsen's *A Doll's House*. In his letters to Joyce between 1914—1916, Pound often mentioned his joint work with Fenollosa to introduce the Noh play to the West, although Joyce did not

① Cf. Caldwell, Hellen & Ito Michio: *The Dancer and His Dances*, p. 44: "Twenty-four years later Pound extolled the Noh singing in no uncertain terms, but when he first heard it he was 'not interested in it.' Ito said, 'I told you so!'"

② Later Yeats published Four Plays for Dancers (1921), all of which are based on certain Noh plays: *At the Hawk's Well* is based on *Yoro* (「养老」), *The Only Jealousy of Emer* on *Awoi no Uye* (「葵上」), *The Dreaming of the Bones* on *Nishikigi* (「锦木」) and *Calvary* on some religious Noh plays (source unidentifiable).

seem to show particular interests in their work at that time. ① Richard Ellmann and Michael Patrick Gillespie reported, however, that Joyce owned a copy of *'Noh' or Accomplishment: A Study of the Classical Stage of Japan* (New York: Knopf, 1917) inscribed to Joyce by John Quinn, June 29, 1917, when Joyce was still looking for a publisher for *Exiles*. ② It is not surprising that Joyce was gradually concerned about the Noh play.

In general, the Noh play has something in common with *Finnegans Wake*. According to Maruoka and Yoshikoshi, the Noh play is a lyric masque accompanied with dances, which pursues the beauty of dances and music (24). The plot is not so important in the Noh play. Rather, more significant for the Noh play is to describe only one concept or one sentiment like the compassion between father and son, love, jealousy, revenge, the *samurai* spirit, etc. The plot of *Finnegans Wake* is very complex. Very few skilled readers can follow the plot. In other words, to enjoy *Finnegans Wake* for ordinary readers is to give up following the plot and enjoy wandering about the multiple meanings of one word, one sentence and one page. Also, main characters, Shem and Shaun often transform into other pairs of Butt and Tuff, Mutt and Jute, Muta and Juva, etc. like wearing and changing different masks one after another in the theatre. Shem and Shaun exchange each other's role to play the main actor and the narrator in turn, just like "shite" and "waki" in the Noh play. "Shite" can be used as an English vulgar word "shit." Also, "waki" is in cluded in "waking," a very important English word for the night novel *Finnegans Wake*. Needless to say, there are numerous allusions to dances and music throughout *Finnegans Wake*.

The first Noh theatre setting is adapted from *FW* 244. 13 to 245. 3. As Louis Armand notes, there is a possible reference to the Noh adaptation of Noah's Ark in the pantomime or in the Noh theatre: "O! Amune! Ark!? Noh?!" (*FW* 244. 26). ③ In this scene the plot is based on the Bible story of Noah's Ark setting in the Noh theatre: "And of every living thing of all flesh, two of every *sort* shalt thou bring into the ark, to keep *them* alive with thee; they shall be male and female" (Genesis 6:19, *KJV*). Several Japanese words are in cluded: "Haha" (*FW* 244. 19) meaning mother and "Tcheetchee" (*FW* 244. 20) meaning father suggests the pair (male and female) of every kind of animals. "Kikikuki" [*Jp.* kiki (危機): crisis; *Jp.* kiku (菊) chrysanthemum; kiku (聞く): to hear; *Jp.* kuki (茎): stalk, stem] (*FW* 245. 2) implies Noah and his family's circumstance in the Ark during the 40 days and nights of raining. The Noah's Ark/Noh theatre setting is employed again in the dialogue between St. Patrick and the Archdruid: "saving to Balenoarch (he kneeleths), to Great Balenoarch (he kneeleths down) to Greatest Great Balenoarch (he kneeleths down quite-somely)" where the Chinese Archdruid seems to kneel down to

---

① See Pound/Joyce, pp. 17, 33, 53, 56, 73, 83 and 85: "MacMillan are doing a Japanese play book, a good deal bigger than the small one at Cuala" (p. 83: Pound's letter to Joyce dated 1 and 2 September 1916 from 5, Holland Place Chambers, Kensington. W.).

② Cf. Ellmann, *The Consciousness of Joyce*, p. 124 and Gillespie, p. 95.

③ Louis Armand, "The Art of the War: Declaration of the Other."

Noah's Great Ark (*FW* 612.26—29).

In the section one of Book II, Chapter 3 where the hunchbacked Norwegian captain (HCE under the name Pukkelsen) ordered a suit from a Dublin tailor J. H. Kersse (punning "curse") but the suit did not fit the hunchback, the Japanese Buddhist monk "Patriki San Saki" (Shem) first appeared at *FW* 317.2. The spelling "Patriki" echoes the typical Japanese pronunciation of the word, and "San" meaning Mr./Mrs. etc. and "Saki" meaning above or ahead is Joyce's unique Japanese translation of the English word "Saint" while "sake" also conveys any alcoholic beverage in Japan. The scene is adjusted to the Noh theatre of black and white (cf. "you pore shiroskuro blackinwhitepaddynger," *FW* 612.18): "— Nohow [*Jp.* Noh play] did he kersse or hoot alike the suit and solder skins," ... "before him, from Sheeroskouro [*Jp.* shiro to kuro: white & black], under its zembliance [Zen + alliance/resemblance/ compliance, etc.] of mardal mansk [man/mask]" (*FW* 317.22—34).

The typical pattern of the beginning of the *Mugen Noh* (梦幻能; dream/ phantasmal Noh plays) that Yeats and Pound loved, a travelling Buddhist monk appears and encounters a ghost telling his/her tragic past. In Book IV, the Japanese avatar of St. Patrick appears again with the Chinese in carnation of the Archdruid Berkeley (Shaun) in the Noh theatre (*FW* 611—613). Joyce paralleled the relationship between Japan and China with that between the Celts and Christianity or Irish Bishop Berkeley and the English evangelist to Ireland. In the Yeats' Noh play ["yeh not" (*FW* 611.11)], the Japanese bonze St. Patrick, with the Buddhist monk Fenollosa ["monkafellas" (*FW* 611.10) practically propagates Buddhism/Christianity to the Chinese philosopher Archdruid ["joss pidgin fella Balkelly, archdruid of islish chin chinjoss" (*FW* 611.4—5), who seems to preach Confucianism and Taoism, especially "tauttung" [*Ch.* tao-tung; 道德] and takes, according to *Ulysses*, the "veil of space with coloured emblems hatched on its field" (*U* 3.417—8).

Joyce mentioned this conversation in a letter to Frank Budgen on August 20, 1939: "Much more intended in the colloquy between Berkeley the arch druid and his pidgin speech and Patrick the arch priest and his Nippon English. It is also the defence and indictment of the book itself, Berkeley's theory of colours and Patrick's practical solution of the problem" (*L* I, 406). The Japanese "Patriki San Saki" (*FW* 317.2) reappears as the "Same Patholic," (*FW* 611.10)/ "Rumnant Patholic" (*FW* 611.24) to discuss color/ colorism/ colonialism with the George Berkeley who wears a mask of Chinese Archdruid, reflecting the two Sino-Japanese Wars (*FW* 611—613).① Using two Japanese words related to colors, "shiroskuro" [white & black (*FW* 612.18); cf. "Sheeroskouro" (*FW* 317.33)] and "Iro" [color (*FW* 612.20)], "Same Patholic" (*FW* 611.10), an aggressor "quoniam [*L.* since], speeching, yeh not [W. B. Yeats] speeching noh man" in the Noh theatrical performance (*FW* 611.10—11), finds the practical answer for "pidgin fella

① Cf. Ito, Eishiro, *"United State of Asia"*: *James Joyce and Japan*, p. 202.

Balkelly," (*FW* 611. 5)'s argument on colors. [1] Their conversation seems to suggest the Chinese resistance against the Japanese army in the late 1930s.

In the process of the dialogue, the relationship between the Japanese and the Chinese are as close as that between "shite" (principal actor) and "waki" (subordinate actor). In this section the Chinese Archdruid appears first and introduces the Japanese St. Patrick as the principal actor/dancer. The whole setting is on the Noh stage in Phoenix Park, Dublin. The word "Iro" means "color" in Japanese. It also presumably implies the surname of Michio "Ito", the principal dancer/actor for the first performance of W. B. Yeats' Noh-like play *At the Hawk's Well* in 1916. "Rumnant Patholic" (*FW* 611. 24), "principalest of" (*FW* 612. 20) Michio Ito, did "kirikirikiring" (*FW* 612. 11 [*Jp.* "kirikirimai": to put the screw on; screw dance [in the fog] as the "shite" of the Noh play. Ito acts a kind of "Shite" or the Hawk-like Guardian of the Well as Pound wrote to Joyce dated 23 October 1915 (*Pound/Joyce* 58). The Japanese St. Patrick performs the Young Man (Cuchulain) who wants the miraculous water of immortality or the Yellow River drainage basin when alarm bells are ringing ["hunghoranghoangoly" (*FW* 611. 30; cf. *FW* 213. 6—7)] and the Chinese Archdruid (the Old Man) chooses fight sending the Chinese swordsmen ["tsinglontseng" (*FW* 611. 30)]: Here comes the flood. [2]"Iro" [*Jp.* color]'s "Irismans ruinboon" [Irishman's rainbow] dazzles the relationship of St. Patrick and the Archidruid, or the world of white (*Jp.* shiro) and black (*Jp.* kuro), so that none of them can get the miraculous water forever. Finally the oracle of death is told: "Onmen" (Amen＋omen) (*FW* 612. 30). In the typical Noh context "Onmen" or the Japanese word "on-nen" (怨念) means a grudge, which inevitably makes the ghost (the Chinese Archdruid) encounter the Japanese monk St. Patrick. "Onmen" was begotten even to the putty-faced Chinese Berkeley ["uptoputty Bilkilly-Belkelly-Balkally" (*FW* 612. 32)]. Somebody was shouting, sweating and thumping. An earthquake ["Jeeshees" : *Jp.* earthquake (*FW* 612. 34)] happened and something fell down in the climax scene (*FW* 612. 32—36). This is definitely alluding to the two Sino-Japanese Wars, although it was written around 1938 when Japan still dominated over China with its military power. Joyce never knew what happened to East Asia during and after World War II because he died on January 13, 1941.

However, this esoteric dialogue between the Japanese St. Patrick (possibly modeled after the Zen Buddhist author, Daisetsu Suzuki [铃木大拙; "szszuszchee" (*FW* 333. 5)] from whose writings Yeats learned Zen Buddhism), and the Chinese Archdruid (presumably modeled after the founding father of the Republic of China, Sun Yat-sen (孙文) is very significant, and even predictive. Dr. Sun's famous saying, "Tiān xià wèi gong" [天下为公; literally, "everything under Heaven belongs to everyone"] is originally from Chapter 9. "Liyun" (礼运) of *The Book of Rites* (礼记; *Liji*). In the letter-style chapter of Book I, Chapter 5, the unidentified narrator tells about Early Christian Ireland

---

① Cf. Ito, Eishiro, *"United State of Asia": James Joyce and Japan*, p. 202.

② It seems to suggest the 1938 Yellow River flood (花园口决堤事件). Here the Chinese Archdruid overlaps Chiang Kai-shek (蒋介石) who studied at the Tokyo Shinbu Gakko (东京振武学校), an Imperial Japanese Army Academy Preparatory School for Chinese students in 1907.

using Sun Yat-sen's idea: "We who live under heaven, we of the clovery kingdom, we middlesins people have often watched the sky overreaching the land. We suddenly have. Our isle is Sainge" (*FW* 110. 4—6). Later, the Japanese St. Patrick expresses himself implying Dr. Sun's idea that he is just an inhabitant of this earth: "I know not, O cashla [*Jp.* okashira: boss > O God], I am sure offed habitand this undered heaven" (*FW* 483. 26—27). Joyce seems to have known that Sun Yat-sen is a key person who can connect China and Japan.

Conclusion

As we have seen, St. Francis Xavier's and his Jesuit followers' missions to East Asia influenced Joyce in his formative years. Their missionary strategy of "adaptationism" was not a new method in Ireland where the diverse elements of the Celts and the Classical Roman Church merged as we can observe in the Celtic arts such as the High Crosses with the ringed Celtic cross and *The Book of Kells*. The early Jesuit adaptationism must have been easy to be accepted by Irish Catholics especially in the Jesuit schools. What Joyce was excellent in is that he applied the old Jesuit method to his novels, particularly to *Ulysses* and *Finnegans Wake* in which he merged various elements from numerous languages with English and other European languages to create his revolutionary fictions.

Bloom's ambivalence about the Orient is rooted in his ambiguous "Asian" background. Bloom thinks of the Orient as an Orientalist who escapes from the reality and fantasizes of being in some Oriental place. However, he also notices: "Probably not a bit like it really. Kind of stuff you read: in the track of the sun" (*U* 4. 99—100).

The whole book of *Finnegans Wake* is a giant riddle consisting of numerous small riddles and various dialogues. If the reader tries to interpret it from a perspective of the Noh play and Zen Buddhism, it can be sometimes much easier because the essence of Noh and Zen is simplicity and profundity. One is reminded of the Noh and Zen elements of Charles Kay Ogden's "Basic English" translation of the Anna Livia chapter. Through the Joyce's "cracked looking glass," especially Book IV of *Finnegans Wake*, we could see what we have not seen very well. The reflected images of his lookingglass, even half-broken, seem very neutral through many phases.

The former president of Germany, Richard von Weizsäcker, once said, "Wer aber vor der Vergangenheit die Augen verschließt, wird blind für die Gegenwart" ("But whoever closes his eyes to the past becomes blind to the present," Rede am 8. Mai 1985 vor dem deutschen Bundestag). Weizsäcker indicates the Holocaust, the notorious Nazi persecution of the Jews. Generally speaking, at Japanese schools, teachers do not enthusiastically teach the details of Japanese Imperialism/colonialism to their students while in China and in Korea, teachers are very keen to tell the details of modern East-Asian history to their students, featuring Japanese Imperialism. It is time for Japanese people to open their eyes to the past, to gaze the present and to make a better future with the neighboring countries, and other parts of the world. *Asia was*, *China is*, *Prosperity to be*.

Works Cited

Armand, Louis. "The Art of the War: Declaration of the Other": <http://web. ff. cuni. cz/~lazarus/jjht_declarations. html>. Accessed: 6 September 2013.

Atherton, James S. *Books at the Wake: A Study of Literary Allusions in James Joyce's "Finnegans Wake."* Carbondale and Edwardsville, IL: Southern Illinois University Press, 1959.

Bowman, John and Ronan O'Donoghue, eds. *Portraits: Belvedere College* 1832—1982 [*PBC*]. Dublin: Gill and Macmillan, 1982.

Bradley S. J., Bruce. *James Joyce's Schooldays*. New York: St. Martin's Press, 1982.

Brivic, Sheldon. *Joyce through Lacan and Žižek: Explorations*. (New Directions in Irish and Irish American Literature) New York: Palgrave Macmillan, 2008.

Brockey, Liam Matthew. *Journey to the East: The Jesuit Mission to China*, 1579—1724.

Cambridge, MA and London: The Belknap Press of Harvard University Press, 2007.

Caldwell, Helen. *Michio Ito: The Dancer and His Dances*. Berkeley: University of California Press, 1977.

Crispi, Luca and Sam Slote, eds [C&S]. *How Joyce Wrote "Finnegans Wake": A Chapter-by-chapter Genetic Guide*. Madison, WI and London: The University of Wisconsin Press, 2007.

Dai, Congrong. "A Chinese Translation of *Finnegans Wake*: The Work in Progress." *James Joyce Quarterly*, 47. 4 (Summer 2010), 579—88.

Ellmann, Richard. *The Consciousness of Joyce*. Toronto and New York: Oxford University Press, 1977.

—. *James Joyce*. New and revised ed. Oxford: Oxford University Press, 1983.

Gifford, Don. *Joyce Annotated: Notes for "Dubliners" and "A Portrait of the Artist as a Young Man."* 2nd ed. Berkeley, Los Angeles and London: University of California Press, 1982.

Gifford, Don and Robert J. Seidman. *"Ulysses" Annotated: Notes for James Joyce's "Ulysses."* 2nd ed. Berkeley, Los Angeles and London: University of California Press, 1988.

Gillespie, Michael Patrick with the assistance of Erik Bradford Stocker. *James Joyce's Trieste Library: A Catalogue of Materials at the Harry Ransom Humanities Research Center, The University of Texas at Austin*. Austin: The University of Texas Press, 1986.

Graham, Phili p. "Addenda (No. 5): Japanese." *A "Wake" Newslitter*, 9 (1963), 6—7.

Ito, Eishiro. "The Japanese Elements of *Finnegans Wake*: 'Jishin, Kaminari, Kaji, Oyaji.'" *Joycean Japan*, No. 15. The James Joyce Society of Japan, June 2004, 36—50.

—. "Journey to the Far East: Reading Joyce in the Jesuit Context Featuring St. Francis Xavier." *James Joyce Journal*, vol. 16, no. 2. The James Joyce Society of Korea, Winter 2010, 53—78.

—. "Mediterranean Joyce Meditates on Buddha." *Language and Culture*, No. 5. Center for Language and Culture Education and Research, Iwate Prefectural University, January 2003, 53—64.

—. "Orienting Orientalism in *Ulysses*," *James Joyce Journal*, vol. 14, no. 2. The James Joyce Society of Korea, Winter 2008, 51—70.

—. "United States of Asia: James Joyce and Japan." Ed. Richard Brown. *A Companion to James Joyce. Blackwell Companions to Literature and Culture*. Oxford: Blackwell Publishing, 2008.

—. "Unveiling Histories of the Tohoku District: Juan Goto and Crypto-Christians": <http://p-www. iwate-pu. ac. jp/~acro-ito/Japan_pics/Japan_MZS/Juan_Goto. html>. Accessed: 6 September 2013.

Joyce, James. *The Critical Writings of James Joyce*. Eds. Ellsworth Mason & Richard Ellmann. Ithaca, NY: Cornell University Press, 1989 (1st ed. 1959).

—. *Finnegans Wake*. New York: The Viking Press, 1987.

—. *The James Joyce Archive* [*JJA*]. 63 vols. General ed. Michael Groden. New York & London: Gerland Publishing Inc., 1978.

—. *Letters of James Joyce*, I. Ed. Stuart Gilbert. New York: The Viking Press, 1966.

—. *Letters of James Joyce*, II. Ed. Richard Ellmann. New York: The Viking Press, 1966.

—. *A Portrait of the Artist as a Young Man* [*P*]. The Definitive Text corrected from the Dublin Holograph by Chester G. Anderson and edited by Richard Ellmann. London: Jonathan Cape, 1968.

—. *Stephen Hero* [*SH*]. Ed. John J. Slocum and Herbert Cahoon. New York: New Directions, 1963.

—. *Ulysses*. Ed. Hans Walter Gabler. London: The Bodley Head, 1986.

Referred to as*U* x. y (x= the episode number, y = the line number in each episode).

Kiefer, James E. "Jesuit Missions in Non-Christian Countries": <http://justus. anglican. org/resources/bio/42. html>. Accessed: 6 September 2013.

Lennon, Joseph. *Irish Orientalism: A Literary and Intellectual History*. New York: Syracuse University Press, 2004.

Li, Baldwin. "The Tao of James Joyce." (private essay) December 2003.

—. "The Tao of James Joyce." (IJJF conference paper) June 2004. "Liaotung Convention": < http://www. taiwandocuments. org/liaotung. htm>. Accessed: 6 September 2013.

Maruoka, Daiji and Tatsuo Yoshikoshi. *Noh: Kansho no tameni* [*Noh for Appreciation*]. Color Books no. 104. Tokyo: Hoiku-sha, 1966. (in Japanese)

McHugh, Roland. *Annotations to "Finnegans Wake."* Third Edition. Baltimore: The Johns Hopkins University Press, 2006.

Mungello, David. E. *The Great Encounter of China and the West, 1500—1800*. Lanham, MD: Rowman & Littlefield, 2005.

Olcott, Henry S. *The Buddhist Catechism*. London: Theosophical Society, 1903.

Potts, Willard, ed. *Portraits of the Artist in Exile: Recollections of James Joyce in Europeans*. San Diego, New York and London: Harcourt Brace Jovanovich, Publishers, 1986.

Pound, Ezra. *Certain Noble Plays of Japan*, 1916; repr. Whitefish, MT: Kessinger Publishing LLC, 2010.

—. Ed. with commentary by Forrest Read. *Pound/Joyce: The Letters of Ezra Pound to James Joyce with Pound's Critical Essays and Articles about Joyce*. New York: A New Directions Book, 1967/pap. 1970.

Ross, Andrew C. *A Vision Betrayed: The Jesuits in Japan and China*, 1542—1742. Edinburgh: Edinburgh University Press, 1994.

Said, Edward W. *Orientalism*. New York: Vintage Books, 1979.

Senn, Fritz. "Notes." *James Joyce Quarterly*, 13. 2 (Winter 1976), 244—45.

Skrabanek, Petr. "St. Patrick's Nightmare Confession." *A "Finnegans Wake" Circular*, vol. I, no. 1, Autumn 1985, 5—20.

Smurthwaite, John. "That Indian God." *James Joyce Broadsheet*, 61 (Feb. 2002), 3.

Staples, Hugh. "More Trivia Ulysseana." *James Joyce Quarterly*, 15. 1 (Fall 1977), 93—94.

Sullivan, Kevin. *Joyce among the Jesuits*. New York: Columbia University Press, 1958; Westport, CT: Greenwood Press, Publishers, 1985.

Thompson, Frederick Diodati. *In the Track of the Sun: Reading from the Diary of a Globe Trotter*. London: William Heinemann. 1893.

Venn, Henry. *The Missionary Life and Labours of St. Francis Xavier Taken from His Own Correspondence*. London: Longman, Green, Longman, Roberts, & Green, 1862.

Wilson, Robert Anton. "Joyce and Tao." *The James Joyce Review*, 3, 1—2, 8—16.

Yee, Cordell D. K. *The Word according to James Joyce: Reconstructing Representation*. Cranbury, NJ: Associated University Press, 1997.

作者简介：伊东荣志郎，日本岩手大学英文系助理教授，主要研究领域为詹姆斯·乔伊斯、叶芝及谢默斯·希尼等。

Anna Livia Plurabelle's "River-Speech" and *Finnegans Wake*: A Life Force and A Textual Force

田恩卿

【Abstract】 The text of *Finnegans Wake*, like a living being, moves perpetually in flux. In its flux the drive of the text denies both a limit and closure. As an emblem of a mysterious and vital dimension of the life force, Anna Livia, a female character of the text, is continuously wandering, circulating, and producing: she is the river Liffey flowing across Ireland. Her perpetual movement, her ceaseless turning, goes beyond daylight reason and reflects the desire of the *Finnegans Wake* text, which produces irreducible content. In the complicating and dense texture of the work, everything is interlocked through the flow of the life force of Anna Livia. The proliferating quality in the textuality resists any fixed form of the reality of life. The essential function of the "force" is to make things move, and it both separates the united and holds together the dispersed. The vital flux produces without reason or logic because it has impulse instead of aim.

Anna Livia Plurabelle and her flux of the life force are the products of the unique rhetoric of the two chattering washerwomen on the banks of the river Liffey. The sound of their discourse is the sound of the river's flowing water, or its fluidity. The playful polyphony of their talk and the incessant and delicate variation of the meaning in their words are liberating because they are never stabilized. The rhetorical form of gossip becomes the channel through which repressed voices are released. Concerned with the subject of Anna Livia's constant fluidity and proliferating energy, the unique qualities of the gossips' conversation are especially effective. Their fragmentary and ceaslessly shifting flow of talk becomes the carnivalisque writing of *Finnegans Wake*.

The dynamic, mobile, and intense energy of their narrative forces the text of *Finnegans Wake* into perpetual movement like a living flux. The text generates meanings infinitely, though there is no direct connection between its generated meanings. Taking the form of flux, the fragmentary text of *Finnegans Wake* does not have an immediate goal, but aimlessly flows, always ready for connecting and distorting to produce new meanings. In the dense and complicated texture of the work, the only constant is the deep flow of life's unpredictable possibilities.

【Keywords】 textuality narrative representation life force desire seim anew

I

James Joyce's *Finnegans Wake* is apparently a disparate text both in its subjects and language. Various subjects are woven together in a disorderly form, and every word and sentence in the text constantly creates new meanings. Its disruptive and deregulated plot is never coherent, and characters transform themselves at any moment as stories are evolving. The work creates an ostensibly chaotic world by threatening conventional linguistic systems and by destabilizing conventional views of reality. However, this does not mean that the work is in complete disorder. There is a peculiar mechanism in the text. Though the text generates meanings infinitely and gaps between the meanings are never filled, everything is in some way interlocked and connected to everything else. In the carnivalesque writing of *Finnegans Wake*, there seems to be some "potential link" which works as a "binding force" of the fragmentary and ceaselessly shifting talk, though it is not a hierarchical organization. In the dense and complicated texture of the work, the only constant is the deep flow of life's unpredictable possibilities. The vibration of meanings from the work's sustaining force, that is, the implication of life's unpredictable possibilities, is palpable though not easily defined.

The peculiar textuality of *Finnegans Wake* is made discernible most effectively in the discourse of the washerwomen in the chapter "Anna Livia Plurabelle" (Book 1, Chap. 8). As Anna Livia's movement and her nature is dynamic, so the narrative device of this chapter is most alive and animated. Though Anna Livia does not speak within the chapter, the chapter is primarily about her, and the proliferating quality of Anna Livia is produced not only by the river, the symbol of her, but also by the unique rhetoric of the gossipy narrative of the washerwomen doing their laundry on the bank of the river. Their narrative takes the form of flowering "river-speech."

II

As the figure of a mysterious and vital dimension of the life force, Anna Livia is continuously wandering, circulating, and producing. She is the river Liffey flowing all over Ireland. Anna Livia, in the washerwomen's conversation as well as in her own nature, is indeed the "Bringer of Plurabilities" (104. 2): she has 1001 children in Dublin. Her name "Anna Livia Plurabelle" itself is deeply associated with the vitality of the life force and with the quality of proliferating. From the Celtic tradition, "Ana" is the name of one of the oldest goddesses of life. "Livia" is derived from the river Life, or Liffey. It is also similar to the word "to live" (Boldereff, 124). "Plurabelle" implies life's plurality, productivity and variety.

As both a character (person) and water (nature) at the same time, Anna Livia first appears in *Finnegans Wake* as a flowing stream that meanders past mountains and fields and becomes the river Liffey. The washerwomen assume her origin (or the source of water) to be Wicklow, which flows down toward Dublin Bay. When Anna Livia is in her girlhood, the stream flows liberally and even wantonly. The men with whom she is sexually related are associated with the stream; she is faithless and adulterous as vigorously flowing water. The washerwomen say mockingly of her free and gay attitude: "She must have been a gadabount in her day ... Casting her perils before our swains from Fonte-in-Monte to Tidingtown and from Tidingtown tilhavet. Linking one and knocking the next, tapting a flank and tipting a jutty and palling in and pietaring out and clyding by on her eastway." (202. 4—12) The word "til havet" means "to the sea" in Danish (McHugh, 202). The voyeuristic washerwomen suggest that Anna Livia might have been raped several times when she was young in the county Wicklow: "Waiwhou was the first thurever burst? Someone he was, whuebra they were, in a tactic attack or in single combat. Tinker, tilar, souldrer, salor, Pieman Peace or Polistaman." (202. 12—14) Perhaps her first amorous experience was initiated by a hermit, Michael Arklow, who bathed his hands in the river and drank her water, though there is a rumor that two Picts waded through her before that (203. 17—204. 9). So cool and sweet is Anna Livia that even the local hermit Michael Arklow could not contain his passion. In their imaginativeness, the washerwomen's narrative is inflamed with passion:

> Well, there once dwelt a local heremite, Michael Arklow was his riverend name, ... and one venersderg in junojuly, oso sweet and so cool and so limber she looked, ... the kindling curves you simply can't stop feeling, he plunged both of his newly anointed hands, the core of his cushlas, in her singimari saffron strumans of hair, parting them and soothing her and mingling it, that was deep-dark and ample like this red bog at sundown.
>
> (203. 18—26)

When Michael Arklow is strongly attracted to Anna Livia, the social ethics embodied in the hermit collapse before Nature, embodied in Anna Livia. Before the strong power of the life force (or desire), metaphysical reasoning is helplessly destroyed: "He cuddle not help himself, thurso that hot on him, he had to forget the monk in the man so, rubbing her up and smoothing her down, he baised his lippes in smiling mood, kiss akiss after kisokushk (as he warned her niver to, niver to, nevar) on Anna-na-Poghue's of the freckled forehead." (203. 32—204. 1)

It is not by accident that the man who is drawn to Anna Livia is associated with religion. The world religious men represent is a holy one. "Holy-ness" implies wholeness, completion; the security of completion will bring entropy, death. The confrontation between Anna Livia and the hermit is that of fertility and sterility, dynamics and stasis, or vitality and regularity. For the religious man, Anna Livia is a threatening figure who enthralls him with her natural charms.

However, when she becomes a mother, the stream sounds more affectionate in its motherly flowing. When she comes to her son, Shem, he describes her movement in rhythmical and flowing speech:

> with a beck, with a spring, all her rillringlets shaking, rocks drops in her tachie, tramtokens in her hair, all waived to a point and then all inuendation, little oldfashioned mummy, little wonderful mummy, ducking under bridges, bellhopping the weirs, dodging by a bit of bog, rapidshooting round the bends, by Tallaght's green hills and the pools of the phooka and an place they call it Blessington and slipping sly by Sallynoggin, as happy as the day is wet, babbling, bubbling, chattering to herself, deloothering the fields on their elbows leaning with the sloothering slide of her, giddgaddy, grannyma, gossipaceous Anna Livia.
>
> (194. 33—195. 4)

The river, all-pervading, becomes the source of all living things, and of life itself.

Anna Livia as the embodiment of the life force is symbolized by the river, and the river flows from the beginning to the end of *Finnegans Wake*. In Book I, Chapter 7 of *Finnegans Wake* Anna Livia comes to her sons while they are quarreling and saves her remorseful, distressed, and guilt-ridden son, consoling him in the caring and motherly murmurs of a brook: "O me lonely son, ye are forgetting me!, that our turfbrown mummy is acoming, alpilla, beltilla, ciltilla, deltilla, running with her tidings." (194. 21—23) To her husband, HCE, who is sleeping and awaits the mobilizing Psyche, Anna Livia calls, "Rise up, man of the hooths, you hooths, you have slept so long!" (619. 25—26)

Life-giving Anna Livia, however, is not always redeemed. Since the drive of the life force is aimless and ego-less, its embodiment, Anna Livia, cannot be limited to either one of the two contradictory roles of the redeemer or the temptress. Therefore, she is a figure of Eros and motherhood at the same time. As other characters in *Finnegans Wake* are the embodiments of various types of vital forces, Anna Livia, rather than being just an individual, becomes the pure and formless energy of feminine qualities that can take any form. Anna Livia in her youth was herself a temptress but has grown to be a mother as the seductive young Issy will also grow towards motherhood. Deprived of their individuality, the two are transformed into figures, but still retain their basic roles. This explains the archetypal characters of *Finnegans Wake* who are deprived of any particularity. An allegorical representation, they are assembled repetitively with variations according to their roles or functions in different situations. There is no integrity to these characters—only their roles are consistent. They act as pure and formless energies which are in a constant state of assemblage and flux, conglomeration and dispersion, condensation and spread. The essential function of the "force" is to make things move, and the "force" both separates the united and holds together the dispersed. Release of the force (drive or energy) produces various representations.

III

The fluidity of Anna Livia as water closely corresponds to the gossipy narrative of the two chattering washerwomen on the banks of the river Liffey. The river's flow is rambling and winding, straying away from any presupposed fixed direction. Similarly, the gossip of the two washerwomen, unwritten and unfixed, disperses in the wind and mixes with the sounds of the flowing water. The babbling of Anna Liffey's flow is discursive, but it is consistent and free. The washerwomen's chattering, which is interwoven with the names of numerous rivers, is like the river's fluidity, or the flow of its water: their continuous words are never stabilized.

The rhetorical device of women's gossip helps to activate the narrative. The gossip becomes a channel through which repressed voices of women are released. Although the connotation of gossip is negative and gossip is considered unreliable, unconvincing, and casual, its messiness is used in *Finnegans Wake* most efficiently. The very qualities which make the gossiping dialogue unconvincing become a series of displacements that dissolve any controlling principle.

Two unique qualities of the gossip are especially effective: one is the washerwomen's digressions that follow interruptions, and the other is the washerwomen's repetitive return to the point of origin. One interruption is made by the sound of Nature: "Can't hear with the waters of. The chittering waters of. Flittering bats, fieldmice bawk talk" (215. 31—2); another constant interruption comes from the form of the dialogue, as one speaker both stops and encourages the other with the refrain of "tell me."

The refrain of "tell me" brings another subject. One of the washerwomen tells the story of Anna Livia and her husband again and again in different ways. Directed only by a desire for more proliferation, the washerwomen's conversation has no coherence, nor is its content filtered. It is significant that the washerwomen's narrative is moved by questions rather than by facts. Though the subjects of their conversation are mainly Anna Livia's past and the scandal of her husband, Earwicker, the washerwomen do not seem to care about facts. Their conversation clarifies neither who Anna Livia is nor what really has happened to her husband. The washerwomen seem to enjoy just a feast of words. As they wash Earwicker's dirty clothes, they wonder what he would have done: "Whatever it was they threed to make out he thried to two in the Fiendish park." (196. 9—11) And looking at the stains of his underwear they imagine some obscene acts he might have done: "Look at the shirt of him! Look at the dirt of it! He has all my water black on me.... I know by heart the places he likes to saale, duddurty devil!" (196. 11—15)

Like the shallow and precarious waves in the river, in the washerwomen's talk are ceaseless replacements and shifts of subject through the interruptions and through each speaker's own creation of the story. Consequently both of the subjects of Anna Livia's activities and the scandal of Earwicker become more and more mysterious and unfathomable as the conversation continues. Their digressions are often mistakes: addition, subtraction, substitution produce only unfixed truth. Naturally, they need to go back to the origin again and again. A device of connecting the digressions is the frequent return to the same subject, each time with the women reinterpreting it. Every return brings about another digression, adding further different stories interwoven with experiences, prejudices, or faulty memories. This rhetorical device also becomes a fundamental aspect of the textuality of *Finnegans Wake*: many stories within the text are one story with many variations. In the text, there is no progress in the story, and the same subject is returned to again and again. Thus the principle of the process of the text is "the seim anew," so the cyclical structure in *Finnegans Wake* is to "return." In fact, the ending of the novel is connected with the beginning of it.

The many stories of *Finnegans Wake* are "the seim anew," or one story. Always the same, they are so many versions of a story, as one narrator in Chapter 5, Book I, says: "Yet is it but an old story, the tale of a Treestone with one Ysold, of a Mons held by tentpegs and his pal whatholoosed on the run, what Cadman could but Badman wouldn't, any Genoaman against any Venis, and why Kate takes charge of the waxworks."(113. 1822)

Anna Livia's fluid language, arising from the unconsciousness that belongs to Nature, brings forth the continual dissolution of narrative. Likewise, in *Finnegans Wake* the primal mobility is some desire or force through which the various characters and stories are created, or improvised in psychoanalytic free associations, as trauma is. There are, therefore, no coherent stories in the work; instead, disconnected events and unrelated characters ceaselessly combine into different versions of the same subject. There is no true or original version in the variant accounts of the major themes in the work: the only certainty is that of unresolved and indissoluble conflicts of human desire. Therefore, the consequential building of theme is impossible in *Finnegans Wake* as blind desire prevents any representations. The proliferating quality in the textuality of *Finnegans Wake* resists any fixed view of the reality of life. From the peculiar language and textuality of *Finnegans Wake*, Anna Livia, an ever-elusive reality, is created.

IV

Anna Livia's life force, like water, flows in all directions. As the river Liffey meanders, so Anna Livia's movements do not seem to have any sense of direction. Thus, she flows "not knowing which medway or weser to strike it" (209. 22). The vital force produces without particular reason or logic since it has impulse instead of aim. The fundamental nature of the human force is unstable and inorganic, though, paradoxically, the human mind always tends to have nostalgia for eternal truth. In this sense, Anna Livia, as a river, as Nature, transcends the human level.

The life force of Anna Livia works by some unknowable and even inhuman force, like Deleuze and Guattari's ineluctable and ceaselessly energizing force of the "producing machine," and this force provides the fundamental mechanism in the textuality of *Finnegans Wake*. The sound of her voice is lyrical and poetic, but it is, above all, the liberating language of desire released from any repression, any fixed interpretation. Anna Livia's dynamic and mobile river-speech produces the perpetual movement in the text of *Finnegans Wake*.

Finnegans Wake, like a living being, moves perpetually in flux. Reading of the text is always a state of process, and it is the record of the deep flowing of life in its vital and kinetic energy. Moving beyond daylight reason, the vibration of the life force in the text produces irreducible content, blurring the boundary between center and digression, or depth and surface. In the complicating and dense texture of the work, everything is interlocked through the flow of the life force. As life forces, neither the text of *Finnegans Wake* nor Anna Livia is ever stable: by continuously moving, colliding, displacing, and shifting, both of them become the matrix for permanent renewal and rearticulation. The Wakean language is treated as a "process," rather than a "function": it gives meaning, and it takes it away at the same time. Through the continuous displacement of meaning, through its capacity to shape and re-shape forms, the language of the text has a self-generating order. The flux of the force has an ineluctable power. The movement that comes from the force, which is implicit in the Wakean stories and characterizations, makes the text of *Finnegans Wake* an on-going process.

Works Cited

Boldereff, Frances Motz. *Reading "Finnegans Wake": A Study of James Joyce's Masterpiece*. Barnes & Noble, 1959.

Deleuze, Gilles and Felix Guattari. *Anti-Oedipus: Capitalism and Schizophrenia*. Minneapolis: University of Minnesota Press, 1983.

Joyce, James. *Finnegans Wake*. London: Paladin. HarperCollins Publishers. 1992.

McHugh, Roland. *Annotations to "Finnegans Wake."* Baltimore: Johns Hopkins UP; London: Routledge, 1980.

作者简介:田恩卿,韩国崇实大学英语语言与文学系教授,主要研究方向为詹姆斯·乔伊斯及其他当代英国作家。

《芬尼根的守灵夜》的准对应中文文本

曾丽玲

【内容提要】 戴从容译的《芬尼根的守灵夜》采用了数个独特的翻译策略——比如将每一多义的原字词的数个诠释一一列出，只以短竖符号与主意义相隔；此数个意义之间再以不同字号（小四号标示主意义；小五号标示其他可能含意）做区隔；登录乔伊斯小说里的自创字词的拉丁字母原文于译文上；以上种种出现在书左页的排版设计加上书右页动辄上百则的注释使得《芬尼根的守灵夜》的中译本呈现出的文本效果趋近西方解构大师德里达一举解构哲学与文学书写的反骨著作《丧钟》，可说成功地重现了《芬尼根的守灵夜》里意义驱散的原始精神。以上呈现在书左页的种种文本设计其实复制《芬尼根的守灵夜》意义不定或具有多重意义的文本特质，即便是连对西方解构传统不娴熟的中文读者，也因为戴译的独特安排，不由自主地参与到文本诠释的再创造，戴译本身就重现如乔伊斯原文如出一辙的“具有书写能力的”的文本特性。

若将戴译与德里达的《丧钟》做一比较，则会发现戴译成功地传递了乔伊斯的文字革命，虽然此译作目前只及第一卷，戴译为中文读者开天眼、通天声的重责已功德圆满，而且戴译本身所成就的文本特质足以匹配乔伊斯的原小说，成为与乔伊斯小说自成一格的准对应文本。

【关键词】《芬尼根的守灵夜》 德里达 《丧钟》 具有书写能力的文本

The Chinese Paratextual Counterpart to *Finnegans Wake*

【Abstract】 The unique strategy of juxtaposing several possible meanings in the rendering of each multivalent word—separated by a vertical bar and marked by disparate font sizes—together with trimmed-down numbers of footnotes, plus Joyce's original neologisms printed above the word rendered—all of the foregoing on the verso page—combined with all the necessary and numerous explanatory notes listed on the recto page, successfully yields Dai's Chinese translation into a paratext akin to Derrida's *Glas* (in English translation, in particular)—approximating the right effect re-creating Joyce's original meaning-diffusing event as chiefly witnessed in *Finnegans Wake* (refered to as *FW* afterwards). The move to print Joyce's original words above the words rendered into Chinese signals an act soliciting the local readers' own participation in deciphering Joyce's original meanings. This replicates *FW*'s decisive gesture of rendering a "writerly," instead of a "readerly," text by exploiting the utmost polysemy of almost each word and thus decentralizing the authorial control of interpretation. Thus, Chinese readers, albeit even given little exposure to the English language, are encouraged—precisely by their translator—to form their own opinion concerning the translation, thus gaining access to experiencing a uniquely writerly text.

Though risking arousal of discontent from some critics with regard to the lack of the translator's authoritative decision made on choosing the one definitive meaning for each multivalent word, Dai's rendition which sticks to Joyce's hallmark indecision on interpretation creates a literal/textual counterpart to a deconstructive text to which *FW* rightfully pertains. The innovative topographical design of the Chinese *FW* forcibly acts out deconstruction of the logocentric meaning and, instead, prompts proliferation (and hence *differance*) of meanings and interpretations.

A comparison of Derrida's *Glas* in its English-translated form and Dai's Chinese *FW* will show that Dai has felicitously recreated Joyce's revolution of the word. Though only Part I is completed, Dai's translation has hit off on a propitious track and set Joyce's text on the right tune and topography for Chinese readers' ears and eyes.

【Keywords】 Joyce *Finnegans Wake* Derrida *Glas* the writerly text

Almost twenty years on since the Chinese *Ulysses* came into print[①], Chinese readers are now ready to welcome and even digest Dai Congrong's translation of *FW*, the epitome of Joyce's difficult art. Granted, Dai's translation makes things no less difficult. Instead of opting for the more traditional and expected way of rendering a straightforward translation of the text, in which case abundant explanatory footnotes are predictably called upon to solve the translator's problems, Dai reproduces Joyce's hallmark multivalence literally on top of the page, studiously compiling hundreds of footnotes. For the main text, she insists on itemizing several more prominent options for each of Joyce's multivalent word, with a further decision on listing the most likely meaning first in sequence and separating it from the rest by means of variations of type and a bar mark. Being pluralist, such an unfamiliar and reader-unfriendly rendition is yet to be diversified by her decision to keep Joyce's original word above his coinage. As a result, the Chinese readers are for the first time utterly defamilarized by this translational strategy, hampered by the seeming lack of decision made on the pluralist conundrum. Admittedly, Dai's translation yields heavy materiality with such pluralist display of chosen texts, be they Chinese or of Joyce's own language. Dai's experimental and obscure translation easily evokes an equally experimental and obscure predecessor, equally inspired by Joyce's *FW*—that is, Derrida's *Glas*. Dai's text can be properly mentioned in the same tone as the English-translated *Glas* for their effects on evoking and activating the deconstruction scenario.

Glas defies the generic distinction of philosophy and literature by commenting in juxtaposition on Hegel and Genet's dramatic text. Derrida constructs his exploration of these two writers "by postioning separate and discrete textual columns next to each other so that it is necessary to read intertextually and follow the ways in which the textual play operates across and between the margins or borders of the page(s) and space(s) separating the columns" (Roughly 45). As a result, the two diverse texts of *Glas* are readily criticized as defying genre, yielding a practical question as to how to read the book. As John Sturrock puts it, the question arises as to "how to read the two main columns of print"—consecutively or alternatively from section to section—and Derrida's "futuristic... text"

① *Ulysses* was first translated into Chinese in 1994 by Jin Di.

blatantly demands "too much of one's patience and intelligence" and risks being "unread" as its ill fortune (1987). Though risking engendering no less a conundrum of how to read her text and perhaps incurring a speculation on the fate of being unread in the long run after all the hype concerning the first ever Chinese translation of *FW* is gone, Dai's pluralist text positively replicates the uniquely writerly experience which Joyce's original is set out to produce, first and foremost.

Joyce's Wakese language is notoriously polyglot. It is often made up of composite words from some sixty to seventy world languages, with the purpose of generating numerous puns, words and phrases meant to convey pluralist levels and layers of meanings at once. Both Roland Barthes' model of "listening" and Stephen Heath's "optical listen" should be recommended to Joyce's readers in the face of his abstruse text. It is vital to receptively listen or even "optical listen" to Joyce's polyglot in order to access "all forms of polysemy, of overdetermination, of superimposition" as contained in Joyce's numerous puns and composite words (Barthes, *Empire* 258). However, "what is listened to here and now... is not the advent of a signified... but the very dispersion, the *shimmering* of signifiers" (Barthes, *Empire* 259). Both the speech form and the written or printed form of all the puns should be paid attention to, as Heath prescribes in his method of "optical listen." The signifying, rather than signification, power, thus, can be fully initiated (Barthes, *Empire* 259). This active mechanism involved ties in with Barthes' idea of a writerly text. For such a text, the reader is "no longer a consumer but a producer of the text" (*S/Z* 4). Writerly texts and ways of reading constitute, in short, an active rather than passive way of interacting with a culture and its texts. Reading for Barthes is "not a parasitical act, the reactive complement of a writing," but rather a "form of work" (*S/Z* 10).

With Dai's essentially pluralist translation strategy put in place, the Chinese readers must practically work themselves hard in being forced to "optically listen" to Joyce's original now being rendered into multiple forms and plural options, as it were, of meanings. As a result, readers must make decisions all the time concerning how to string the words together—a practically DIY process contributing to the Barthesean process of signifiying and hence unwittingly turning themselves into a collaborative, or interactive, writer of a kind worthy of Joyce's original. The innovative topographical design of the Chinese *FW* forcibly acts out deconstruction of the logocentric meaning presumably having existed in any original text and, instead, prompts proliferation and hence difference of meanings and interpretations.

A similarly disconcerting precedent has existed with Derrida's unconventional philosophical text of *Glas*, a text supposed to illuminate both Hegel and Genet's writings, the way any translation should contribute to the illumination of the original text. However, an unconventional typology is chosen for the book: there are multiple texts on the same or across the page. The book is written on two columns in different type-faces. The left column is a discourse on Hegel, and the right on Genet. Each column is then interspersed with all kinds of notes and quotations which Sturrock calls "side notes" designating "marginalia, supplementary comments, lengthy quotations, and dictionary definitions" (Todd 67). Chances are these side notes may last several pages, floating freely (Sturrock) and cutting the two major columns sometimes in the middle of their textual flows. Derrida's readers thus experience a very discontinuous reading experience, having to "break us of our nasty linear habits" (Sturrock), for it is literally "bifurcated writing" (Roughly 54) with "metempsychosis of One and Other" as taking place in all letters, words, and writings, hence creating "a set of doubles, doubled" as Derrida sees them (Benstock 1984, 173). The novelty and then disorientation of such a doubling reading experience will be exactly what's in store for the readers of the Chinese *FW*. Dai's strategy of doubling or folding up interpretations creates a disconcerting effect of meaning diffusion, the one the readers of *Glas* encounter head on. Taking into account negative reception of Derrida's *Glas*—being commented variously as evincing "playfulness" but proving a "disadvantage" to ordinary readers (Hartman 1981) or "dizzying" (Dickstein 2007)—Dai's readers may be put into a disadvantage, too, due to their limited exposure to classics of experimental writings, the epitome of which is Joyce's *FW*.

Derrida acknowledges Joyce's influence in conceiving *Glas* in the way it is. He describes *Glas* "as a sort of a wake," clearly in reference to *FW*. Alan Roughley explicates, "It is clear that his reading of Joyce's text haunts the way in which Derrida has constructed his exploration of Hegel and Genet..." (45) With Derrida's own confession as a clue, one certainly can see precedents of such textual patchwork and the anti-linear mode of reading thus created in the "lessons section" of *FW*. Chapter II of Part II of *FW* (260—308) is a long section titled "Nightlessons." This is the most graphically oriented chapter of the entire book. The margins of the main text are suffused with many mini textual columns spread across, including a big number of footnotes. Alan Rougley specifies "the arrangement of the text on the pages of *Glas* is similar to the *Wake*'s lessons section and provokes a similar double and chiasmic reading of the text" (53). Shari Benstock has analyzed how the columns of the lessons section "operate deconstructively" (in Roughley 55) and finds the footnotes of the lessons section "produce a subversion of... authorial prerogative" (Benstock 1983, 211). Rather than the conventional footnotes found in scholarly texts, they are more like discrete texts in a deconstructive "grouped textual field" as explicated in Derrida's *Positions* to be "the only site... in which a deconstructive overturning of classical philosophical hierarchies can 'be marked'" (Roughley 54). Compare the effect of Joyce's unconventional footnotes with interpolations into the two main columns of Derrida's *Glas*. According to Sturrock, at the side of the columns are Derrida's interpolations; they are "like footnotes insofar as they relate to matters raised on the page in question, but they are unlike footnotes in that they do not relate to any particular word or reference," as a result of which "Derrida's side notes float free and can be read at whatever point you fancy" (Sept. 13, 1987).

Even though Dai has finished only Part I of *FW*, and this legendary "Nightlessons" section is yet to appear in Dai's future ongoing translation project, the Chinese readers are intriguingly at a vantage point of already being exposed to the novel's doubling, chiasmic, and in brief, deconstructive textual field via Dai's experimental translational strategy. Dai's rendition—which sticks to Joyce's hallmark indecision on interpretation by exploiting the full force of textual doubling—creates a literal/textual counterpart to the deconstructive novel, making her text a unique text deserving attention and yielding weight among the genre of Chinese-translated Western classics. Dai has carried out Joyce's own imperative that reading be a kind of "raiding" (*FW* 482.32) to its fullest potential in her rendition. She raids Joyce's original to make it splinter into multiple interpretations as many as which are faithfully kept and recorded all on the same page where the main column/text is rendered. While the Chinese language medium seems to render Joyce's difficult text ideally comprehensible for the first time, Dai's unique brand of translation renders Joyce's text less than immediately accessible at the same time—a double bind, yet meritoriously escaping Alan Roughley's skepticism in questioning the fundamental translatability of Joyce's original in the spirit of the Derridean deconstruction: "Once the reader has translated [Joyce's] question ['Dyoublong'] into a more readily comprehensible form, then he is no longer reading Joyce's text but the results of an operation that has performed upon it." (109) For a word like "Dyoublong," the way to bypass reduction of Joyce's original into one definite interpretation as other more conventional translator would opt for can be found right with Dai's rendition (48), juxtaposing the more obvious, or primary reference to the city of Dublin by way of the normal type and the just as obvious overtone of "Do you belong" by way of a smaller type, then topped with Joyce's original word above the primary meaning. Such multiple renditions of this one word (literally into three meanings) avoid the illusion of pigeonholing Joyce's original meaning and furthermore facilitate proliferation of meanings to the full and plain view of the readers. In other words, Dai has most felicitously recreated Joyce's revolution of the word. Though only Part I is completed at this stage, Dai's Chinese *FW* has hit off on a felicitous track and set Joyce's text on the right tune and typography for Chinese readers' ears and eyes.

Works Cited

Barthes, Roland. *Empire of Signs*. New York: Hill and Wang, 1983.

—. *S/Z*. New York: Hill and Wang, 1975.

Benstock, Shari. "At the Margin of Discourse: Footnotes in the Fictional Text." *PMLA* 98.2 (1983): 204—25.

—. "The Letter of the Law: *La Carte Postale* in *Finnegans Wake*." *Philosophical Quarterly* 63 Spring (1984): 163—5.

Derrida, Jacques. *Glas*. Trs. John P Leavey, Jr. and Richard Rand. Lincoln: U of Nebraska P, 1986.

Dickstein, Morris. "Praising Not the Hedgehog but the Fox." *The New York Sun*. 26 December 2007. http://www.nysun.com/arts/praising-not-the-hedgehog-but-the-fox/68566/. Retrieved 16 July 2013.

Hartman, Geoffrey H. "How Creative Should Literary Criticism Be?". *The New York Times*. 5 April 1981.

http://www.nytimes.com/1981/04/05/books/how-creative-should-literary-criticim-be.html?pagewanted=all. Retrieved 16 July 2013.

Heath, Stephen. "Ambiviolences: Notes for Reading Joyce." *Post-structuralist Joyce: Essays from the French*. Eds. Derek Attridge and Daniel Ferrer. Cambridge UP, 1984. 31—68.

Joyce, James. *Finnegans Wake*. Penguin, 2000.

—. *Finnegans Wake*. Tr. Congrong Dai. Vol. 1. Shanghai: Renmin, 2012.

Roughley, Alan. *Reading Derrida Reading Joyce*. Gainesville: UP of Florida, 1999.

Sturrock, John. "The Book is Dead; Long Live the Book!". *The New York Times*. 13 September 1987.

http://www.nytimes.com/1987/09/13/books/the-book-is-dead-long-live-the-book.html. Retrieved 16 July 2013.

Todd, Jane Marie. "Autobiography and the Case of the Signature: Reading Derrida's *Glas.*" *Jacques Derrida: Critical Thought*. Ian Maclachlan, ed. London: Ashgate, 2004. pp. 67—86.

作者简介：曾丽玲，台湾大学外国语文学系暨研究所教授，研究领域为乔伊斯研究、贝克特研究、20世纪英国小说。

批评空间

沃格林的《柏拉图》

林国华

【内容提要】 本文以沃格林对《理想国》中的三处细节的解读为例，尝试分析其得与失。沃格林把《理想国》的第一个字"*kateben*"（往下走）与古希腊的"下地狱"的神话联系起来，虽然富有"想象"与"才情"，却不过是"新柏拉图主义"的陈词滥调在现代的翻版；他对克法洛斯的解释别具一格，却不够完整、公正；他对"腓尼基人的传说"的阐释极富洞见。

【关键词】 新柏拉图主义　克法洛斯　腓尼基人的传说

Voegelin's *Plato*

【Abstract】 This paper intends to analyze the merits and demerits of Voegelin's interpretation on Plato' Republic with three specifical cases. According to Voegelin, the first word of *the Republic*, i. e., "kateben"(going down) is associated with the Greek mythology of "going to the underworld," though rich in "imagination" and "talent," this idea is yet nothing more than a repetition of the Neo-Platoic cliché. In addition, his explanation on Cephalus is insuficient and therefore appears short of justice. Nonetheless, despite of all these defects, Voegelin's interpretation of the "Phoenician tale" is indeed very insightful.

【Key Words】 Neo-Platonism　Cephalus　Phoenician tale

（一）

2006年坊间出版的《理想国》研究文献《〈王制〉要义》（华夏出版社），收录了三篇解释，其中最后一篇是沃格林（Eric Voegelin）的。第一篇具有哲学思辨气质，甚至还带点20世纪"解释学"文艺理论的味道；第二篇偏重古典学套路。与两者不同，沃格林是一个政治哲学家和政治思想史家，但他的研究风格可用四个字概括："想象"与"才情"。

沃格林的这种风格在开篇就一览无遗：他效仿古老的新柏拉图主义解释传统，从《理想国》的第一个字"*kateben*"（往下走）窥探到了远望深渊和地狱的神秘象征，并继而和古希腊的"下地狱"的神话传统勾连起来——在沃格林看来，苏格拉底"下到"比莱乌斯港就是哲人下到地狱。《理想国》的谈话是在比莱乌斯港进行的，这无异于说，哲学是一种来自地狱的教导，或者说，哲学必须从地狱开始。难道真是这样吗？沃格林奔放但不失精致的想象力似乎在《理想国》结尾可以得到明确的认可:《理想国》正是以一个被柏拉图改写的“下地狱”的神话结束的。

几年前我在和朋友的通信中讨论但丁《神曲》,涉及到维吉尔《埃涅阿斯记》第六卷的埃涅阿斯下地狱的神话,那个神话的中心内容是安奇塞斯的亡魂对自己的儿子、未来罗马国父埃涅阿斯的政治教导。笔者以那次讨论为基础,写了一篇随笔,其中有这段文字:

> “我相信,在《苏格拉底的申辩》末尾一段极其重要的有关死亡的文字中(41a—c),柏拉图暗示了哲学是一种来自冥间的思考和探究。《尤塞弗罗篇》、《苏格拉底的申辩》、《克力同篇》和《斐多篇》四部对话被认为是柏拉图的早年作品,在柏拉图的作品整体结构中也多被古代注疏家排列在最前面。从这个意义上讲,这四部对话实际上可以被当作是哲学的序言。同时,四部对话的主题是苏格拉底之死,这样的次序安排可能意味着,只有在苏格拉底进入冥间之后,哲学才真正开始。——这意味着,在时间序列的意义上讲,《斐多篇》之后的所有柏拉图作品都是被假定成一个亡魂的谈话,这个亡魂被神从冥间遣入人世,正如苏格拉底的自白:‘雅典公民们,我这样一个人是神灵赐给城邦的,你们如果听我的劝告,就留下我吧!’(《苏格拉底的申辩》31a—b)”。

写这段文字的时候,自觉想象有余,说理不足,朋友也不置可否,那篇随笔也就慢慢淡忘了。今天看到沃格林竟然也有类似的想象,自然念及旧文旧事。

这几年,读书问学逐渐偏离古代的故纸堆,但是“下地狱”的问题倒也不曾彻底忘掉,甚至还研读了这个问题史的重点文献——西塞罗《国家篇》第六卷“西比阿之梦”(*Somnium Scipionis*)以及古代晚期密教学者马克罗比乌斯(Ambrosius Macrobius)和文艺复兴时期西班牙大文豪维弗斯(Vives)的传奇解释。可是,才情不够,斩获甚少。

很难确定为什么希腊人在崇尚生命的同时,又对“地狱”这类死后的事情怀着隐秘的感情。那究竟是一种什么样子的感受,我们也不易把握。但不论如何,正如希罗多德的作品充满童真的素朴与世俗的欢乐,修西底德的作品交织着现世的冷峻和智者的教导,古希腊人的生活与心境大抵就是这样。死后的事情在他们的生活中似乎从来没有占据过重要地位,正如“下地狱”在《理想国》里仅仅是最后的修辞,它的多余被一些中古阿拉伯哲人看得很清楚。——阿维罗伊的《理想国》讲疏到第九卷就毫无征兆地终止了,给人感觉似乎《理想国》本来就没有第十卷似的。

古代晚期,希腊人以及那些被希腊文化教化过的罗马人的文明日渐衰败,文人对现世不再抱有先辈们曾经有过的热爱,生命变得平静、内敛,终至消极、枯萎,这种生命态度的思想结晶就是斯多亚道德哲学,在它的教诲下,灵魂的美德不再是往昔那种具有向外展开的、具有侵略性的政治德性,而是自利的、冥思苦想式的理论生活,它不再追求名声,而转而低声谈论沉思的幸福和哲学人生,它尤其称道平静地面对死亡,因此,苏格拉底之死——这颗柏拉图早早埋藏在雅典政治的黄金时代中的斯多亚种子——开花结果了,“下地狱”的问题顺理成章地进入文人视野,它自然地表达了古代道统的“遗老遗少”们对现世的愤懑和对来世的想象,并且作为一种学问的形态被发扬光大——这就是“新柏拉图主义”。新柏拉图主义不仅是一种学问方式,而且是一种生活方式,它酷似“毕达哥拉斯主义”,而且两者也的确一度

联手，共度古代晚期的艰难岁月。这一点，没有人比奥古斯丁体察得更细致入微了。（参《上帝之城》第8—9卷）

“新柏拉图主义”学人由于自身所属的旧体制的衰落，对“现实主义”思想风格没有兴趣，转而执迷于神秘的“象征”和“符号”，期待来自另一个世界的隐秘指令。在他们眼中，朴素自然的世界和事物已经发生了严重的变形，阿普列乌斯的《变形记》的出现绝对不是偶然，柏拉图对话也未能幸免。以波菲利（Porphyrios）、普罗克鲁斯（Proclus）、杨布利柯（Iamblichus）等人为代表，柏拉图对话被大规模地给以象征和寓意化的解释，哲学的、政治的对话成了玄妙难解的神话学，这种状况一直持续到文艺复兴的费奇诺（Marsilio Ficino）。在马基雅维里时代，新柏拉图主义传统在费奇诺的手里已经是强弩之末，他撰写的鸿篇巨制《柏拉图神学》是这个传统的最后堡垒。马基雅维里和费奇诺共存于同一个时代、同一座城市，这是我每每想起来就感到惊讶的事情：前者殚精竭虑地致力于重建被查士丁尼大帝取缔的柏拉图学园的同时，后者孜孜以求的却是统治新世界的新君主。马基雅维里之后，新柏拉图主义传统终于被霍布斯流放到“黑暗王国”中去了，那是它最后一次给人印象深刻的出场。尽管如此，在启蒙后的现代，这种浸透着玄奥智慧的学问偶尔还会吸引个别富有“才情”和“想象”的头脑，比如沃格林。——沃格林的《理想国》研究只不过是“新柏拉图主义”的陈词滥调，这不仅体现在他对“*kateben*”的解释中，也体现在他对《理想国》第十卷“厄尔神话”的解释中，更体现在他对“洞喻”这个新柏拉图主义者最能施展身手的论题的解释中。

究其精神气质而言，“下地狱”的神话也许源起于古老的东方，比如古埃及、古推罗、古腓尼基、或甚古犹太之类的以迷信立国的祭司民族，不过这不重要，重要的是要看到被古希腊人淘洗过了的“下地狱”又是一副什么光景。这个神话从荷马开始，就被一代又一代的希腊文人改写，有俄尔甫斯样式的，有奥德修斯样式的，也有柏拉图样式的，甚至到了罗马时代，做过共和国的掌门人但心仪希腊文化的西塞罗也不忘记改写一篇让世人惊奇不已的“西比阿之梦”。然而，所有的这些努力，所有的这些文献，在古代晚期的“新柏拉图主义”学统中都发生严重变形。和以往的变形不一样，这是一次本质性的变形，一次足以重新塑造生活方向（*periagoge*）的变形，它支配了从古代晚期到中古晚期的漫长而精巧的神学解释路径以及以此为灵感的粗鄙难耐的民间宗教性的“梦幻文学”传统。最后，所有这一切在但丁的《神曲》中得到了最夸张的展示以及最彻底的变形。

撰写一部“地狱神话”在新柏拉图主义传统中的“变形记”未尝不可，那如梦如幻的玄奥情调足以令人忘掉现世。不过，此刻，有一件也许是更为重要的事情需要我们知道，那就是：《神曲》之后，也正是梦醒时分。

（二）

《理想国》无疑属于年轻人，正如完成整个对话的人都是年轻人一样。对话持续了一个晚上，这需要充沛的体力。当然，苏格拉底除外，此人是神灵赐给雅典的神物，另当别论（《苏格拉底的申辩》31a—b）。然而，在这个热烈的言辞国度的边缘，柏拉图塑造了一个几乎是无声无息的老者——虔敬正义的克法洛斯。

克法洛斯出现在这部哲学戏剧的开端。老练的读者都知道，开端的地方往往是应该引起注意的地方。老克法洛斯引起了很多读者的注意。布鲁姆(Allan Bloom)在其《理想国》英译本导言中表述了颇有见地的观察：老克法洛斯在这部戏剧中的沉默寡言乃至最后缺席象征着法律的不容讨论、不容置疑的性质。这个观察富于教益。沃格林是一位极有才情和想象力的政治思想家。他阐释过八部柏拉图对话，其中对《理想国》用功最多。在这项研究中，沃格林对老克法洛斯的解释别具一格，可谓点睛之笔。

苏格拉底在他的对话中必须面对一些有着"无可指责"但是却又"令人同情"的性格的人。沃格林说，老克法洛斯就是这种性格的范例。这位老人对年轻人的生存疑惑、政治沙龙和哲学讨论都没有兴趣，但他虔敬守法，过着合理正义的生活。在这一点，他无可指责。但是，沃格林认为，正是这一点恰恰令人同情。老克法洛斯代表了危机时代中的"老一代人"，类似于我们的"老革命家"。他来自于一个德行纯良的美好年代，并获得了在那个年代养成的正义虔敬的品行。现在，那个年代逝去了，但是，光荣的革命传统仍然使他保持古老的美德。在这个问题上，一切都无可置疑，他不需要任何灵魂的拷问和艰深的思考就可以做一个有德行的、正义的人。——他的德行和正义来自他因循多年的传统，与理论思考无关。用沃格林的话说，"他不是由于'爱智慧'而正义"，而是由于习传的品行而正义。换言之，他的正义似乎没有经过哲学的检审，似乎也没检审的必要。对于这种理所当然的正义，老人从未质疑。甚至他的整个生活都不曾遭受过"置疑"(*aperion*)的侵扰。前苏格拉底时代的自然哲学家阿纳克西曼德所谓的那种万物得以产生的"没有固定形态和性质的物质"(*aperion*)对于老克法洛斯来说是全然陌生的，他老实地赚钱，并且真心诚意地供奉神祇。——沃格林认为，老克法洛斯的生活平静安逸，灵魂没有动荡，这不是"爱智"的生活，他的正义与德行没有经受过哲学的问责，恐怕也经受不起哲学的问责。因此，当一个危机四伏的年代，一个传统的习俗与德行饱受质疑、濒临崩溃的年代到来之际，克法洛斯代表的"老一代人"既没有能力反思老传统的缺失，也没有能力辨析新时代的弊病，结果，他们也就没有能力向嗷嗷待哺的年轻人提供什么有用的教导了。

老一代人在年轻人的教育问题上所体现出来的无能被沃格林很不耐烦地指斥为老年人特有的"衰弱"，这很容易让人想起卢梭在《爱弥儿》中所强调的，老年人不适合承担教导幼童的任务。不管怎么说，老克法洛斯的情况起初令人"同情"，继而引人"鄙视"，因为在传统断裂的危机时期导致突如其来的精神空虚的，正是这一代人，他们生活在光荣传统的庇护之下，却从来不曾过问那个老旧传统的可持续性发展空间有多大。接下来，"一切似乎都是瞬间发生的：老一代人忽视了在年轻人心中树立正确而具体的秩序观念，而冷淡与迷惑在几年之内就转变成可怕的社会灾难"。波勒马霍斯不是开始天真地把正义理解为商人的诚实了吗？——这就是沃格林笔下的老克法洛斯，他确实令人同情，也招人鄙视。

然而，事实也许是，在柏拉图笔下，老克法洛斯固然令人同情，但未必招人鄙视。当苏格拉底把一群轻浮暴躁、嗷嗷待哺的年轻人聚拢在一起并且将要开始一场喧闹的"自由教育"的时候，老人安静地离开了，并走向自己供奉一生的神殿。这其中，悄然离开无疑体现了老人的节制，一种基于自知的节制；而走向自己供奉一生而今却门可罗雀的神殿，这体现的未必不是古老律法的孤傲！也许最终证明布鲁姆是正确的：克法洛斯孤守古旧的律法正义，拒绝与人交谈，因为律法不是爱智者的清谈，而是立法者的独白。值得一提的是，在柏拉图所营造的以苏格拉底为中心的世界中，神殿似乎从来没有一个显赫的位置，在这个意义上，这位古代哲人比《新大西岛》的作者、现代哲人培根似乎更缺乏虔敬。

一代人有一代人的事情去做，一代人有一代人的命运去接受。就像荷马笔下的草木，岁岁枯荣，周而复始——太阳底下真的没有什么新鲜的事情。这或许就是希腊人留给世人的最高智慧。克法洛斯的时代结束了，新时代是祸还是福与他再没有关系，他只和他的神在一起。在这一点，他酷似《苏格拉底申辩》中的苏格拉底最后的样子："公民们，你们活着，我却该死了，哪条路更好，唯有神知道。"

不管克法洛斯如何平庸，苏格拉底如何高妙，有一点他们是一样的：他们都老了，正是这一点把他们和年轻一代断然分开。这是命运女神赐给凡人的不可更改的事实，这是大自然不可违抗的命令。克法洛斯顺应了这个事实，心怀敬畏，选择离开。苏格拉底却留了下来，试图更改命运女神早已为凡人谋划好的棋局。在这一点上，也只有在这一点上，苏格拉底尤其显出其渎神的性格，而这也正是这个老哲人的伟大和疯狂的地方。他的失败也正是在这里。雅典城在他身后的政治乱相说明了一切。

苏格拉底貌似哲人，貌似敬畏恒定不变的自然，其实骨子里对"自然"深怀警惕，并且妄图凭借自己的技艺（教育）改变自然的进程和秩序，在这一点上，他和近代的卢梭没有太大区别，二者都相信自然的"可完善性"。所以，我们不无理由地说，在 19 世纪大遭鞭挞的"进步"理念并非始于卢梭，而可能早在苏格拉底那里就埋下了伏笔。苏格拉底的渎神，克法洛斯的虔敬，只有从这个角度去思考才能得到完整、公正的理解。

（三）

赫拉克利特支离破碎的文字凝聚着足以穿透灵魂的神秘："对于醒着的人来说，只有一个单一而普遍的世界，而在睡眠中，每个人都转向他自己的私人世界。"（《残篇》89）

《理想国》第三卷结尾，柏拉图辗转讲述了一个同样神秘的"腓尼基人的传说"。政治哲学家沃格林（Eric Voegelin）看到，这个倍受争议的传说渗透着赫拉克利特"残篇 89"对平等精神的暗示。在立法者为其"样板城邦"确立了森严的等级（劳动者、辅助者、护卫者）之后，全体公民被要求聆听一个"腓尼基人的传说"。传说告诉公民们，他们接受的不同教育、他们的身份连同城邦的等级，都只不过是他们的想象，"如梦如幻"。自然的真实情况是：他们曾经居住在大地深处，在他们被孕育养成后，被大地母亲打发到世界中来。因此，土地是他们的母亲，而他们彼此又皆为兄弟。可是，这个传说忽然话锋陡转：虽然所有人皆为血缘兄弟，但是神在铸造他们的时候，在有的人身上加入了金，使他们成为统治者，在有的人身上加入了银，使他们成了辅助者，在有的人身上加入了铜和铁，他们就是低微的农人和工匠。

可以看到，"腓尼基人的传说"由两部分内容组成。其一：所有人由大地生育（*physis*），皆为兄弟；其二，所有人皆为神所创造（*techne*），并被区分为金质人、银质人、铜质人和铁质人。前者说的是自然的平等,后者说的是技艺所导致的不平等。这两部分内容的意义显然截然相反,但却共处于一个神话中,简直匪夷所思。

在形态上,柏拉图笔下的"腓尼基人的传说"是对赫西俄德"五世神话"的改写,但是却别有意蕴。后人对这个传说的解释似乎大都专注于金质人、银质人、铜质人和铁质人的技艺性的划分,换言之,传说的第二部分内容倍受瞩目。在现代,这部分内容几乎成为那些平等主义者籍以控告柏拉图的最大罪状。相应的,柏拉图的辩护者也应运而生,他们大都以所谓"高贵谎言"为柏拉图开脱罪责。究其本质,控告者也好,辩护者也罢,两者似乎都瞩目于"腓尼基人的传说"的第二部分内容,换言之,两者都承认,柏拉图凭借这个传说,确实是在传授万恶的不平等政治教义。

对于上述这两种貌离神合的解释路线,沃格林(Eric Voegelin)不以为然。他试图从"腓尼基人的传说"的第一部分发现更加根本的真相。从传说所在的上下文里,沃格林也看到,它是立法者出于城邦福祉的考虑而讲述的一个善意的"神话",亦即"谎言"(389b—c,414b)。这个谎言是什么呢?沃格林说,"它只是一个简单的真理,即人人都是兄弟"。遗憾的是,这个曾经一度口口相传的真理已经很少人相信了,所以,当它再度出现的时候,只好披上神话的外衣,甚至甘愿被人视为谎言。心思敏感的沃格林对此感到难过,他在《理想国》的字里行间发现(414d),在苏格拉底看来,人间的差异和不平等仅仅是一场梦幻(*oneirata*),兄弟间的平等才是被掩盖的真相(*aletheia*)。——

> "把这最高真理当作不可信的谎言来述说,这是《理想国》这部作品中最痛苦的一页,饱含着【苏格拉底】对雅典痛心疾首的鄙视。"

以神话的方式引入平等,这不仅表明了使"平等"成为可能的、在城邦时代还无法言说的对"共同人性"的感知体验,也暗示了城邦之内派系林立和邦国之间征战杀伐、毫无兄弟骨肉之情可言的城邦时代所特有的苦况(参《理想国》卷五对希腊世界内讧的论述,比较格劳秀斯《论战争法权与和平法权》开篇对基督教世界内讧的论述)。

"腓尼基人的传说"出现在"样板城邦"森然的等级制确立之后,在这种等级制中,统治阶层高高在上,并接受为了巩固它们的地位而被精心设计的教育和训练。这样的布局,在沃格林看来,只不过为了一个目的,那就是让所有公民(尤其是统治者)意识到那个使世人被区分、被离异的政治等级以及那个等级赖以存在的所有教育、训练等技艺都是梦幻般的东西(*oneirata*),真相是:人皆来自大地,四海皆为兄弟。梦幻与真实的区别,被苏格拉底用来反对"邪恶的傲慢",这种傲慢正在支配着权贵们。沃格林深刻地洞见到,这种傲慢正浓浓地弥漫在城邦之中,吞噬着所有脆弱的东西。没有什么能够阻止这种邪恶的激情,即使是四海皆兄弟的古老真理也于事无补。因此,构成"腓尼基人的传说"的第二部分应运而生:既然连骨肉兄弟的平等神话都无力抑制权贵的傲慢,那么索性把权贵之所以成为权贵的一切教育、训练和等级秩序全都归结为一场梦幻般的神话。——"腓尼基人的传说"的第二部分没有把人间的不平等归因于教育等一系列属人的技艺,而是归因于造物神在不同人群中掺入的不同金属。这样,由于把孕育了权贵和傲慢激情的不平等提升到神话领域,不平等的政治制度的整体结构就获得了一种"梦幻"的特征,一种人力所不能左右的、近乎命运的神秘作弄般的特征。

沃格林对“腓尼基人的传说”的总结富于理性精神，也具有卢梭式的鼓荡人心的民主修辞品质：

> 在这场梦幻与真理的戏剧之后，又一次清楚明白地显映出赫拉克利特的影子。我们想起那些梦游者，他们放弃了那些拥有清醒理智的人所拥有的共同世界，只活在他们的私人世界中。如果人们为当下的地位和天赋感到骄傲，并想方设法为不肖子孙维持权势，而不视这种思想为真理的堕落，那么，好城邦中的社会差异极有可能引发私人世界的战争。当统治者提拔他的子弟们进入统治层，哪怕他们并不具有其父辈的金质，而低阶层的子弟即使拥有金质也决不被擢升之际，国家就要完蛋了。因为它不再是智慧统治的、清醒的生活世界，而是变成了混乱的私人世界，在这个世界中，人们沉迷各自的梦幻激情。如果人们忘了，它们的存在所具有的真实性只不过是为了表现神的梦幻戏剧，那么，好城邦也会变为一场噩梦。

“腓尼基人的传说”所传达的无疑是一个伟大的政治讯息：人人平等，皆为兄弟。这个讯息首先来自柏拉图，柏拉图委之于苏格拉底，苏格拉底委之于一个“立法者”，那个“立法者”又委之于“腓尼基人”，“腓尼基人”则为之裹上一袭如梦如幻、屡遭误解的神话花衣。一个如此判然自明的真理，其来历竟然如此辗转曲折、费尽心机，这实在令人难以置信。时光荏苒，到了18世纪的时候，卢梭重述了这个真理，但是剥掉了腓尼基人缝制的神话外衣：人生而平等，但由于技艺的作弄，却无往不在枷锁之中。——如此简单、如此有力，同样令人难以置信。

作者简介：林国华，供职于西南政法大学法学研究所、华东师范大学政治学系、华东师范大学世界政治研究中心。

《法礼篇》中的喻说与哲思

王柯平

【内容提要】 古希腊语"喻说"或"比喻"是一种常见的修辞技艺，其主要作用在于言此而喻彼，或以比喻方式来表达与解释。柏拉图对话文本中所用的多种喻说，既是其书写方式的组成部分，也是其进行哲思的有效手法，这有助于展现其言说的魅力和丰富其哲学的话语。本文以《法礼篇》中的"医生喻说"、"渡河喻说"与"玩偶喻说"为例，尝试揭示"喻说"与"哲思"之间的内在有机联系。

【关键词】 《法礼篇》　喻说　医生喻说　过河喻说　玩偶喻说

Plato's Philosophizing through Allegories in *The Laws*

【Abstract】 The Greek word *allēgoria* denotes one of the rhetorical techniques. It literally means "speaking other" or "speaking otherwise than one seems to speak". Its key service involves two corresponding procedures: a way of composing a work and a way of interpreting it. Often found in Plato's dialogues are allegories of different kinds, which are used not merely as part of the Platonic approach to writing, but also as an effective strategy to engage in philosophizing. Consequently, it helps manifest the appeal of the speech and enrich the discourse of philosophy in Plato. This paper attempts to expose the internal and organic link between Plato's allegorizing and philosophizing through the analysis of the doctors' allegory, the river-crossing allegory and the puppet allegory taken from *The Laws*.

【Key Words】 *The Laws*　allegory　the doctors' allegory　the river-crossing allegory　the puppet allegory

诗学与哲学的互动关系，在柏拉图的书写方式中表现得尤为突出。这种书写方式包括诸多要素，其中柏拉图式的喻说(Platonic allegories)占据显著位置。通常，柏拉图采用的喻说方式，具有比喻、寓言和象征等作用，也具有启迪、解释和澄明其哲学思想等功能。

在古希腊，"喻说"有着悠久的传统。从词源与语义上看，表示"喻说"的希腊名词是allēgoria，其动词是 *allēgoreō*，原本由副词 *allos* 与动词 *agoreuō* 组成；通常，allos 表示"去往另一处"或"用另一方式"，*agoreuō* 表示"言说"或"发布"，*allēgoreō* 则表示"言此而喻彼"或"以比喻方式来表达与解释"。这便使"喻说"(allegory)一词"包含两种彼此相关的意思：其一是以比喻的方式写作，其二是以比喻的方式解文。前者是用比喻方式创构一件作品，以其外显用意来表示'别的'用意；后者是用比喻方式来解释一件作品，旨在以此表示此作品包含

'别的'用意"。①

值得注意的是，在早期解释荷马时代神话的过程中，由比喻方式所形成的具有奥妙玄幻特性的神话学(*mythologyia*)，与童年时期强调爱智求真要旨的哲学(*philosophia*)密不可分，导致这一现象的原因之一就在于喻说的效用和神话的魅力。有的西方学者因此断言："喻说"不仅与神话有关，而且与哲学的起源有关。柏拉图以前的哲学研究，有时被神话的喻说方法所遮盖。而喻说作为一种解释模式(interpretative mode)，对研究早期希腊哲学的生成具有重要意义。但是，古代哲学史家在论及希腊哲学发展时很少提及这一点。②现有的研究表明，"自哲学以降，哲学与喻说不仅关联密切，而且喻说使哲学与诗歌之间古来有之的争论变得活跃和复杂起来"。③有鉴于此，本文特意从《法礼篇》里列举出下述三则喻说，即"医生喻说"、"渡河喻说"与"玩偶喻说"，藉此证明和彰显柏拉图在其书写方式中，是如何借助"喻说"来表达和传布其"哲思"的。

一、"医生喻说"中的法理原则

在柏拉图所构想的"次好城邦"里，虽然依法治邦(the rule of law)为主、以哲治邦(the rule of philosophy)为辅已成国策，但是，如何立法的问题，对于柏拉图来讲，既是法学问题，也是哲学问题，不仅事关城邦建制与发展的前景，而且事关法治与管理的成效。因为，柏拉图明白，立法的目的是为了管教城邦居民，但其有效性取决于居民的服从与遵守，而服从与遵守又取决于所定法规是否符合居民的实际需要。在古希腊，城邦居民通常分为自由民与奴隶两大类。鉴于他们不同的社会地位与政治权利，立法家务必考虑如何区别对待的立法原则。为此，柏拉图这样写道：

> 我们委任的立法家，在他制订出的法典前面就没有令人满意的序述吗？难道他只是简单地宣布该做什么或不该做什么，再加上一些惩戒违背行为的措施，然后就转入下一条法律了吗？难道就不附加上一句鼓励与说服大家的话了吗？这就好比给人看病各用一套方法的医生(*iatros*)。我们要像儿童恳求医生采用最温和体贴的方法给他们看病一样，提醒立法家注意这两种方法的差异……其中一类医生是奴隶出身(*oi douloi*)，他们是在师父的指导下学医，凭借观察和实习行医；另一类医生是自由民出身(*oi eleuthroi*)，他们是通过研究自然来学医，老师将系统的知识传授给学生……一般说来，城邦里的病人既有奴隶，也有自由民。奴隶出身的医生通常给奴隶看病，决不在意病人的抱怨，也不询问病人的病情，他就像一位鲁莽的抄写员，蛮不在乎地根据自己的经验，

① Gerard Naddaf, "Allegory and the Origins of Philosophy," in William Wians (ed.), *Logos and Muthos: Philosophical Essays in Greek Literature*, Albany: Suny Press, 2009, p. 111, also see Jon Whitman, "Allegory," in Alex Preminger and T. V. F. Brogan (eds.), *The New Princeton Encyclopaedia of Poetry and Poetics*, Princeton: Princeton University Press, 1993, pp. 31—35.

② Gerard Naddaf, "Allegory and the Origins of Philosophy," in William Wians (ed.), *Logos and Muthos: Philosophical Essays in Greek Literature*, pp. 99—100.

③ *Ibid.*, p. 119.

> 好像看一眼便能确诊似的，随即就给病人开出处方，然后匆匆忙忙地去看下一个病人，全然一副独断独行的派头（*kathaper tyrannos*）。自由民出身的医生则不然，大多都能以科学的方式给自由民看病，像对待朋友那样与病人亲切交谈，认真了解发病的过程，尽力向患者说明情况，排忧解难，在未得到患者的同意之前，不会给其开出处方；他会耐心劝导患者，使其平心静气，继续合作，然后对症下药，直到患者康复。上述两种治疗疾病的方法，哪一种是医术比较高明的医生或健康教练员所使用的方法呢？这两种方法中哪一种应当考虑运用于立法呢？①

在此喻说中，至少有四点值得我们关注，即：医生的诊治态度，患者的社会地位，医生的职业培训与立法的基本原则。

首先，从医生的诊治态度来看，这两类医生对待这两种患者的态度截然相反，一是直接诊断就立刻开方，二是详问病情后对症下药；前者冷漠专断，不由分说，简单鲁莽，犹如给士兵下达命令一般；后者耐心友善，注重交流，说明病理，凸显人文情怀与科学精神。这两种不同的医治方式，使人不由想起荷马史诗里描述政治决策过程中的两种不同做法。在《伊利亚特》第二卷里，希腊联军统帅阿伽门农据梦神所托之梦，扬言要放弃攻城，准备领军回国，以此试探军心。但为了避免误解和骚乱，他先请心高志大的长老会议事，彬彬有礼地重述神梦，仔细说明原委，赢得大家赞同。随后，他让传令官召集军队，自己手握权杖，对将士大声宣布：你们要按照我的吩咐服从命令，让我们坐船逃回亲爱祖国的土地，因为我们攻不下街道宽阔的特洛伊城池。未料想军中有一士兵特尔西特斯十分倔强，不但不听招呼，反而大声叫嚷，责骂阿伽门农贪图女色，私下藏娇，虽然身为统帅，却是懦夫恶徒，不该让阿开奥斯人遭受灾难。在场的长老会成员之一奥德修斯闻言，即刻来到这位士兵身边，用权杖将其打得肩膀淌血，满面流泪，吓得再也不敢吱声。经过此番波折，最后的结果是军心振奋，饱餐战饭，继续攻城。②从中可见，阿伽门农深谙权变之术，做法因人而异：对待长老，他重在说服；对于士兵，他下达命令；这与医生对待自由民和奴隶的不同态度颇为相似。

其次，从患者的社会地位来看，有一方是奴隶出身，另一方是自由民出身。在当时，不同的出身是前定的或与生俱来的，这便决定了他们各自不同的社会地位。相应地，不同的社会地位也决定了他们各自在城邦里的工作范围、生活方式乃至医疗条件。换言之，在医疗方面，奴隶出身的患者理应就诊于奴隶出身的医生，自由民出身的患者通常就诊于自由民出身的医生。这样一来，医生采取何种诊治态度与患者接受何种医疗方法，都是因循城邦既定制度的结果。于是，我们可以由此推知古希腊自由民与奴隶在城邦生活中的不同境遇。在普遍实行奴隶制的古代社会，奴隶通常被当作从事苦役的工具与财产的组成部分，其教育、权利、尊严、福利乃至生老病死几乎可以忽略不计。自由民则不同，他们享受着城邦公民所赋予的诸多权利，包括参政议政、立法诉讼、宗教祭祀、节日庆典、管理义务与社会福利等等。柏拉图本人所关注的对象，是作为城邦公民的自由民而非奴隶，因为奴隶或奴隶制对他来

① Plato, *Laws*, trans. R. G. Bury, Cambridge and London: Harvard University Press, 1994, 720.

② 荷马：《伊利亚特》，罗念生、王焕生译，北京：人民文学出版社，2003年，第二卷——阿伽门农召开全营大会试探军心。25—390行，第26—40页。

说，只不过是历史遗留下来的习俗惯例而已。在其对话作品《欧绪弗洛篇》(*Euthythro*)里，柏拉图曾描写过一桩奴隶被主人虐待致死的案件，但并非是为了替这位死去的奴隶伸张正义，而是为了论辩“何为虔敬?”这一带有宗教色彩的德行问题，其潜在用意则是为了澄清“虔诚”观念的模糊性乃至危害性，因为当时掌权的雅典政客正是借用“不虔诚”的“不实之罪”，特意挑动民众将他们的严厉批评者或“政治牛虻”苏格拉底判处死刑。总之，在这篇对话里，柏拉图是言此而及彼，旨在为师辩护，至于他对待奴隶与奴隶制的态度，显然是因循旧制、听之任之，这也是他屡遭后世诟病的要点之一。现追究这个问题，已超出本文范围，我们还是回到“医生喻说”的讨论上来。

这里要说的是第三点，也就是医生的职业培训问题。在当时，医生这一职业的培训方式也取决于医生本人的出身。据上所述，奴隶出身(*oi douloi*)的医生，是在师父的指导下学医，其传授医道的过程虽然也包括临床观察与实习，但其主要方法通常是“灌输式的”，师父一般要求徒弟切记“应该如此”的医疗手段，而不鼓励他们进行“为何如此”的科学探讨；相比之下，自由民出身(*oi eleuthroi*)的医生是通过研究自然来学医的，老师会将系统的知识传授给他们，要求他们视野广阔，刨根问底，求真说理。通常，老师采用的教学方法是“启发式的”，会鼓励学生探讨“为何如此”的科学道理，而不会要求他们死记硬背，以免堕入只知“应该如此”而不知“为何如此”的陷阱。自不待言，不同的职业培训方式必然养成不同的行医方式或诊病态度。因此，当奴隶出身的医生以简单鲁莽的态度对待奴隶出身的患者，而自由民出身的医生以耐心温和的态度对待自由民出身的患者，也就是一种司空见惯的“医疗习俗”了。当然，柏拉图在此贬低的是前者，推崇的是后者。他之所以如此，并不只是出于自身惯例性的政治立场，而是出于如何建构一套“实实在在的法礼”的目的性追求。

最后，需要特别关注的便是立法的基本原则问题。从“医生喻说”的内在要旨来看，柏拉图是以医生与患者的关系为例，来宣示立法者及其立法程序的原则要求。这一要求所标举的是劝导或说服，所贬斥的是独断或专制。因为，若从医道的角度看，医生诊断病情，不仅要知其然，而且要知其所以然，这样才有可能对症下药，治病救人。若从康复的角度看，如果患者也能通过医生的说明，对自己的病情不仅知其然，而且知其所以然，那就有助于自己配合医生的治疗方案，使自己早日康复。如果将这种医治方式运用于立法牧民或治国理政，那就有助于立法者与民众、治人者与治于人者相互理解，彼此配合，达到法立民遵、政通人和的预期目标。否则，仅靠自上而下、自以为是的单边式强权专制，就有可能导致法规受阻、政令不畅或民怨沸腾的负面后果。或者说，虽有多种立法，却无有效司法，亦无自觉守法。由此可见，柏拉图借用这种喻说，就是要人们从日常的就医求诊中，从生命攸关的感受中，从关乎切身利益与推己及人的心态中，去反思立法的有效方式及其科学的法治教育过程。

实际上，在随后的讨论中，柏拉图借用那位雅典人之口，以婚姻法为例，向同行的斯巴达人和克里特人阐明了强制与劝说并用的立法原则，认为只靠强制性的威慑不够，单凭劝说性的告诫也不成，这两种方式务必综合利用，交替行使，才会收到更好的效果。如果只限于其中一种，必然会顾此失彼，陷入片面。[①]因为，法治的对象不同，有的因威慑而生畏，故不敢非

① Plato, *Laws*, 721—723.

为;有的因劝说而臣服,故不越雷池。再者,从实际效果上看,法无强制性威慑之力则不立,法无劝说性告诫之能则难行。为此,柏拉图特别建议,要在每部立法条款之前,加上简明扼要、言之成理的"绪论"(*prooimia*)部分,其目的就在于说服教育民众,知晓立法的用途,轨导自身的行为,养成遵纪守法的意识或德行。

显然,柏拉图所采用的这种喻说方式,既是一种化远为近的说理策略,也是一种化抽象为具体的比喻说辞。在其对话中,柏拉图经常采用不同的喻说(其中包括自己创构的神话或故事),意在表达更为深刻的哲理或立法的艺术。实际上,这也正是其对话作品富有戏剧性、文学性,并能给人留下深刻印象的重要原因之一。可以肯定地说,举凡读过《理想国》的人们,都会记得那个著名的"洞穴喻说"(the Allegory of the Cave);举凡读过《法礼篇》的人们,也不会忘记这个有趣的"医生喻说"(the Allegory of the Doctors)。不消说,对于熟悉这则喻说及其用意的读者,面对柏拉图所提出的这两个问题——"上述两种治疗疾病的方法,哪一种是医术比较高明的医生或健康教练员所使用的方法呢?这两种方法中哪一种应当考虑运用于立法呢?",我相信他们想必都会做出合理的选择。

颇为有趣的是,柏拉图在《法礼篇》里还使用了其他喻说和神话,这一方面体现了"由艾索克拉底引入阿提卡散文里的文体优雅之美"(the graces of style introduced into Attic prose by Isocrates),[①]另一方面延续了柏拉图充满诗性智慧的写作与论说艺术。这两个方面实际上也是柏拉图诗学与哲学交融嬗变的重要特征。为了进一步体认这一特征,我们不妨再看看另外两例。

二、"渡河喻说"引发的哲思

论及宗教信仰等神学问题,灵魂或心灵的作用举足轻重。为了帮助同行的克里特人和斯巴达人明白这一复杂的论证,那位见多识广的雅典人出于解释的目的,便以"渡河喻说"(the allegory of crossing a river)为契机,来表明自己所扮演的角色与所提出的论证。如其所述:

> [有关灵魂的]这一论证极其吊诡。我们老年人务必审慎,不要受其新鲜感或新奇性的迷惑,否则我们就会上当,使自己看上去就像是荒唐的傻瓜一样,其雄心勃勃的思想竟然在微不足道的小事情上遭遇败绩。要仔细斟酌。想想看,我们三人要渡过一条突然涨水的河流,我相对年轻一些,且有不少渡河经验。假定我说:"我应当自己先去试试,让你们两位待在安全地带,我去探明这条河流是否也适合你们两位老者去渡,如果发现不适合,那也要弄清情况到底糟糕到什么程度。如果我发现此河适合你们去渡,我就会招呼你们过来,将我的经验告诉给你们,以便帮助你们渡河。如果发现此河不适合像你们这样的老者去渡,那么只好让我一人来冒此风险了。"你们觉得这样是否合理呢?我们所遇到的情况是一样的:后面的论证过于深奥,像你们这样体弱的老人或许难以理

① A. E. Taylor, *Plato: The Man and His Work*, New York: Meridian Books, 1956, p. 19.

解。我想，为了不让你们这些初学者被一连串问题搞得晕头转向，因为那样会使你们感到没有面子和非常不爽，我想最好还是这样：我先向自己发问，你们只听不答。随后我再逐一回答这些问题，我将用此方式完成这一论证，直到对灵魂做出深究，对灵魂先于物质做出证明。①

乍一看来，这好像是一个自告奋勇的年轻人，在遇到河水暴涨时努力帮助两位老翁的友善之举。其实，这位自称“较为年轻”的雅典人也是一位老者，只不过与同行的另外两位老翁相比，他自己略小几岁罢了。他用这种婉转客气的语调和甘冒风险的喻说方式，试图在安慰和说服同伴之时，也显示出自己尊老的品质和为人着想的素养。当然，其真实用意并非像看上去那么简单，这里仅从如下四个方面予以分析：

1. 经验意义

在《法礼篇》行将讨论如何立法之始，也就是在第一卷 634c－635 a 处，分别来自雅典、克里特和斯巴达的三位老者达成协议，认定只有老人才有资格私下讨论法礼的长短，但决不允许在年轻人面前公开议论法礼，同时也不允许年轻人探询法礼的好坏，这不只是因为年轻人缺乏经验与判断能力，而且是因为法礼是神明参与制定的产物，是所有人应当遵守的规约。很显然，这一协议偏向于极力维护老人统治(gerontocracy)的观念，为此断然杜绝或限制了任何想要自由探讨立法的权利。雅典人是见证过民主制度的优劣并享用过言论自由的公民权利的，但克里特人克莱尼亚斯和斯巴达人麦吉卢斯则没有这类经历，他们的视野仅限于自己知道的城邦制度及其相关事务。于是，为了让他们两位便于理解将要谈论的问题，雅典人利用渡河的比喻，强调和凸显了经验的意义。这种意义不仅在于表明渡河的经验有助于人们渡过危险的河流，而且还意味着相关的经验有助于人们认识相关的对象或克服相关的难题，等等。雅典人有意自称“年轻”，但却富有“经验”，由此成为另外两位“老翁”的向导。这似乎告诫他们，年龄不是问题，经验才是关键。这便给为雅典人随后的长篇大论打开了方便之门，当然也有意保全了克里特人和斯巴达人“自尊的颜面”。

2. 象征意义

雅典人宣称下面的论证过于“吊诡”和“深奥”，认为同行的这两位“体弱的老人”或许难以理解，于是慨然提议自问自答，仅让后者听而不答，免得他们昏头转向，不知所云，感觉不爽。所谓“体弱的老人”，看似一种富有同情心的表述，实则暗含一种善意的讥讽；看似意指他们的体能或生理状况，实则是指他们智力或理解能力的欠缺。相比至下，雅典人知识渊博，受过良好的哲学教育，而克里特人与斯巴达人见识有限，没有受过哲学训练。而接下来所要讨论的灵魂问题，既涉及宗教信仰，也关乎宇宙秩序，显然是一个哲学话题。这便表明雅典人属于“哲学家”(the philosopher)，克里特人与斯巴达人属于“非哲学家”(non-philosophers)。双方的区别在于：“哲学家”所熟悉的深奥论证，是“非哲学家”难以理解或难以想象的。由此推想，“渡河”是由此岸走向彼岸。如果此岸象征无知、彼岸象征有知的话，那么，哲学家就是帮助人们“渡河”的向导，即协助人们从无知的此岸到达有知的彼岸的导

① Plato, *Laws*, 892d—893a. Also see the Penguin version of *The Laws* translated by Trevor J. Saunders.

师。随后的“讨论”表明，雅典人的哲学思想与论证方法，让洗耳恭听的克里特人和斯巴达人深感折服、不断点头称道。

3. 现实意义

我们很难想象，在一个崇尚法治的城邦里，知识贫乏或不懂哲学的立法者会制定出优良的法律，治理好公共的事务，教育好广大的公民，维护好社会的秩序。《法礼篇》里的三位老者，都是立法者与护法者。在他们中间，雅典人是“哲学家”，而克里特人和斯巴达人是“非哲学家”。这一差别不仅关系到立法的完善与城邦的治理，而且关系到公民的教育与社会的秩序。故此，雅典人借用“渡河喻说”，试图劝导他们接受哲学训练，帮助他们提高理智水平，期待他们成为合格的立法者与护法者。因为，他们应当“像哲学家一样，要能够言之成理地向听众说明事物的真相”①。而要说明相关“真相”，譬如宗教根基、信仰缘由、灵魂作用、万物生成与宇宙秩序等等，他们就必须接受相关的教育或训练，尤其是哲学的教育或训练。如此一来，雅典人便昭示出高等教育的必要性和重要性，并且在随后的论述中，提出了建立“夜间议事会”这一立法和护法机构的设想，要求他们不仅要德高望重、经验丰富，而且要学识渊博、公正无私，除了担负“护法”与“监督”的职责之外，还担负着深入研究法律、哲学和完善法律建设等职责。②这实际上是从现实需要出发，为“次好城邦”的哲学教育奠定了合法的基础。这里所说的“哲学教育”，理应涵盖其他高等学科领域。

我们知道，在柏拉图的政治哲学中，有三部对话文本最具代表性：其一是《理想国》，其二是《治邦者篇》，其三是《法礼篇》。比较说来，在《理想国》里，城邦主要是靠“哲人王”执政，所倚重的是以哲治邦，所借助的是认识和道德法则；在《治邦者篇》里，城邦主要是靠贤能理政，所强调的是领导科学，所认同的是法治系统；而在《法礼篇》里，城邦主要是靠“夜间议事会”监管，所依据的是法治律令，所兼顾的是哲学研究。如果联系起来看，这三篇对话构成了一个从人治到法治的演进与转化过程。但无论其怎么演进与转化，哲学始终占有不可替代的重要位置。

至于法律的作用，虽然三者都未忽略，但各有侧重。譬如，在《理想国》里，“哲人王”以哲治邦，以德化民，遵守“美好城邦”的法则，这些法则通常以道德为本位，主要包括作为城邦道德与政治立法基础的理念学说，作为规定诗乐教育及其适宜内容的审查条例，作为管理农商和司法程序的具体法规等等。在《治邦者篇》里，明智的执政者深知立法的重要，认为此法包括成文法与不为文法，前者为具体的实在法律，后者为祖传的习俗惯例，均用于范导或规约民众的言行，使其符合城邦管理的要求。但是，真正的治邦者当属贤能之士，应知城邦和民众的根本利益所在。他不仅具有科学知识，而且掌握领导艺术（譬如修辞、兵法与管理等），能够英明决策，统领全局，指派各类专家处理不同事务。这样便使科学知识优先于法律本身。在《法礼篇》里，作为个体的“哲人王”或“治邦者”均被“夜间议事会”这一领导群体所取代，依法治邦成为城邦管理的核心方略。但是，法礼的作用已经扩展，一方面用于维系城邦的秩序和稳定，另一方面用于培养民众的德行与责任，因为城邦的最终目的关乎公民的道德

① Plato, *Laws*, 857.

② Ibid., 961—968.

与福祉。①但从立法、执法到释法的整个过程来看，显然都离不开“哲学护国者”(philosophy-guardians)，也就是那些经验丰富、德高望重和精通哲学的“夜间议事会”成员。在这里，依法治邦与以哲治邦非但没有彼此对立、互相掣肘，反倒相得益彰，协作无间。这无疑是柏拉图孜孜以求的理想管理模式。

4. 理论意义

雅典人随后所阐述的理论，涉及宇宙创化与万物生成的本源与过程。尽管他用铁饼的旋转与半径不同的圆周来解释运动与变化的现象，但其复杂性和理论性显然超过了克里特人和斯巴达人的知解能力。不过，他用巧妙的询问方式让这两位同伴积极参与进来，诱使他们在随声附和中聆听他的独白并认同他的学说。

总其要旨，雅典人的理论是从物体运动的类别谈起，继而论及宇宙创生的起因与万物化成的过程，最终追溯到灵魂的运动特征及其与神相若的绝对本质。他认为物物相因，彼此互动，生生灭灭，增增减减。若一运动物体碰撞一静止物体，就会导致分解；若一运动物体相遇运动方向相反的其他物体，就会产生结合。只要其存在状态未受损害，分解就会减少物体总量，结合则会增加物体总量。如果分解与结合导致存在状态废止，相关的物体就会毁灭。

这一切是如何引发的呢？其根本起因或始基到底何在呢？雅典人就此提出三阶段论：首先是冲动阶段，其次是运动阶段，再者是变化阶段。万物正是在变化过程中诞生的。究其根本，这都是两种运动所为：一种是永远能够推动他物但不能推动自身的运动形式，该运动形式只能将运动赋予他物，但其自身的变化则取决于另一运动形式。而另一种运动形式凭借结合与分离、增加与减少、产生与毁灭等作用，既能推动自身，也能推动他物，是所有存在物中变化与运动的始基或起因。无论从祖谱还是从能量上讲，只有这种既能自生运动又能推动他物的运动形式，才是万物运动、变化和生成的原因，也就是引发一切运动和变化的第一原则或原初动力。

这一原则或动力不是别的，正是与神相若的灵魂。这灵魂先于物质，如同精神秩序先于物质秩序一样。这灵魂是万物生成的第一起因，不仅内在于而且主导着运动中的一切，其中包括地上的万物，海里的众生与天上的星体。这灵魂依据理性，用一种规则的、一致的、围绕固定中心并借此推动他物的运动形式，主宰着宇宙万物。其掌控太阳的方式，就像驾车一样驱而动之，从而使人享受到阳光，使人将灵魂视若神明。此外，灵魂还伴随着热与冷、轻与重、白与黑、苦与甜、光滑与粗糙等特性，利用由其自身引发的相关运动，主导物质的次级运动和刺激万物或增或减、或分或合。再者，灵魂自身就是神明，能够利用种种手段，抑或持守神圣的理性，引导万物善始善终；抑或联合非理性，产生完全相反的结果。因为，灵魂有多种，但主要分两类，其一是“最美的灵魂”(tēn aristēn psychēn)，是以平衡而有序的方式成就美、善、正义的原因；其二是“恶的灵魂”(tēn kakēn psychēn)，是以失衡而混乱的方式产生丑、恶、不义的原因。②在随后的讨论中，柏拉图关注更多的是“最美的灵魂”，并从积极参照的立场出发，肯定和推崇这种灵魂在引导和监管宇宙万物时所呈现的道德功能。对于“恶的灵

① Robert W. Hall, *Plato*, London: George Allen & Unwin, 1981, pp. 81—89.

② Plato, *Laws*, 893b—899b.

魂”,柏拉图只是点到为止,存而不论。因此,我们只能这样推断:凡是丑、恶与不义之类现象以及不敬神明的异端妄为,均发端于“恶的灵魂”,但它们在终极意义上都无法与“最美的灵魂”抗衡。这一先验设定,既是柏拉图的神学原则,也是其道德原则,两者均在“厄洛斯神话”(the myth of Er)与“劝诫神话”(the myth of exhortation)中得到确证。①

上述有关灵魂、运动、变化与万物生灭这一系列过程的理论意义,主要可从以下几点予以审视:第一,灵魂如同神明。灵魂的自生运动和推动他物的双重运动特征,俨然成为宇宙创化与万物生成的本源或第一推动力,与其他存在物相比享有绝对的优先性。这样一来,灵魂便与神明等同了起来,因为其主宰万物的合理方式就像“真神”(oion orthōs theos)一样,②同时也取代了原先被视为形上实体的“善自体理念”,因为其推动、创化和主宰的能力已然超过了后者。

第二,灵魂依据理性。在这个灵魂生运动、运动生变化、变化生万物的三阶段逻辑程式中,作为第一推动力的灵魂,能够借助各种手段,掌控天体的运动,引导万物的变化,成为宇宙或世界的主宰。这一切之所以可能,是因为灵魂持守神圣的理性,因循“理性运动的本质”(dē nou kinēsis echei),围绕某一中心和相同的物体协调一致地运转。③如此看来,理性乃是灵魂万能的内因。但这“灵魂”并非一般灵魂,而是“宇宙灵魂”;这“理性”也并非普通理性,而是“宇宙理性”。此两者似乎形成某种一而二、二而一的内在关系。

第三,灵魂无法直观。灵魂与理性一样,都是不能直观的实体。人们如果认为自己能用肉眼直接看到和充分理解灵魂与理性,那就如同在昊昊阳午时分用肉眼直接观看太阳一样,必然会两眼昏花,失去视力,所看到的只能是夜幕一般的黑暗。为了免于这种无效之劳,最好还是先看看作为其外在表象的运动形式,也就是那种在空间里围绕一个中心与相同事物周而复始的规律性运动。灵魂推动这一切,理性轨导这一切,两者浑然一体、隐而不显。这就如同太阳的形体,每人都能看见;而太阳的灵魂,无人可以直观。亦如其他生物形体,无论死活与否,均用肉眼可见,但其灵魂全然不同。④灵魂如同周围的空气一样,包裹着肉体和感官,但就是视而不见,惟有用理性方能认识其存在与作用。有趣的是,柏拉图在此又使用了“观日喻说”,但与先前在《理想国》里所用的“日喻”相比,⑤这里显然更为简要,估计是出于提醒读者回忆前说而无需赘述的考虑。这也正是若想理解柏拉图的一篇对话就需要熟悉其全部对话的原因之一。

---

① 王柯平:《厄洛斯神话的哲学启示》,见《哲学研究》2011年第1期;《柏拉图的劝诫神话解析》,见《哲学动态》2012年第6期。

② Ibid., 897b.

③ Ibid., 897d.

④ Ibid., 897d—898e.

⑤ Plato, *Republic*, 516b ff. 在从教育角度来论述人性问题时,柏拉图借助“洞喻”予以说明。在描写那位爬出洞穴的人时,柏拉图认为这里需要一个逐步适应或学习的过程,并由此引出这则“观日喻说”。如其所言:“要让此人看到高处的物体,就需要一种逐步习惯的过程。起先,他最容易看到的是物体的影子,随后是人或物在水中的倒影,再后来是物体本身,再往后他便可以凝视天体的表象或天宇本身,夜间借助星光与月光观看较易,白天借助太阳与阳光观看较难。直到最后,在不借助其水中倒影或其他背景中的幻象情况下,他才能直观太阳本身,看清太阳的真实本性。此时此地,他通过推理得知:正是太阳提供了一年一度的四季变化,主宰着可视领域里的万事万物,因此才是所有可见事物的起因。”

第四，灵魂分有善恶。世上的事物是相对而出的，有美必有丑，有善必有恶，有正义必有不义，人类及其社会更是如此。所有这一切，均取决于两种灵魂及其运作方式：其一是"美的灵魂"与平衡有序的方式，其二是"恶的灵魂"与失衡混乱的方式。这种二分法，实为道德判断，由此引出的因果律，便成为宇宙道德原则。在随后讨论宗教信仰与"劝诫神话"的过程中，这一宇宙道德原则被用于末世论中的最后审判，由此演化为业报轮回法则，在统摄过去、现在与未来的时间向度中，始终监管和安排着人类各式各样的灵魂与命运。与此同时，那位雅典人，作为柏拉图的代言人，正是根据这项宇宙道德原则，逐一批驳了不敬神明的三大疑问——诸神不存在；诸神虽然存在，但对人类漠不关心；诸神会受到祭祀和祭品的影响，容易被人收买。[①]

第五，灵魂数目未定。人若没有灵魂，就成为行尸走肉；物若没有灵魂，就必然走向消亡。无论是对于具有生命的人或物还是天上活动的日月星辰，灵魂必居于其中，推动其运行，虽自身无形，但却有潜能，主导人体、物体与天体运动。但灵魂如何推动他物运动呢？柏拉图说是从外部发力推动。就天体运行而言，会不会是"通过天体外部的物理接触或通过其他方式"呢？[②]柏拉图语焉不详，说不清导致天体运行或主宰宇宙万物的"灵魂是一个还是多个"(psychē men ē psychai)，也说不清神明的确切数字以及神明与天体之间的关系。但有两点可以肯定：一是这灵魂无论多少都是"善的和有德的"(agathai de pasan aretēn)，因为它们能力超常且手段多样，堪称主宰一切的"神明"；二是灵魂如同"神明无处不在"(theōn einai plērē panta)，内在于宇宙万物之中。[③]"神明无处不在"是泰勒斯(Thales)的格言。柏拉图此处引用，不只是要佐证灵魂无处不在的观点，而且是要借此为不信神明者设定"限度或规则"(nomizonti)。[④]

顺带说一句，举凡仔细阅读过《法礼篇》的人们知道，此书开头第一字是古希腊语"神"(Theos)，接下来则把克里特城邦的法律尊为"神"的作品。在《法礼篇》第十卷里，无论是万物生成，还是宇宙秩序，其根源均被归于"世界灵魂"，实际上也就是归于"神"这位万能的造物主。这等于确立了宗教信仰的绝对基础，也等于将立法程序和城邦政治纳入了宗教神学和宇宙神学的领域。在柏拉图看来，采用这一宗教或神学策略，不仅将业已制定的法礼神圣化了，而且也把正在建构的"次好城邦"神圣化了。不过，可惜的是，他这种试图拯救古希腊"城邦理想"的不懈努力，终究经不起更为强势的现实政治力量和历史变革动力(譬如马其顿王国和希腊化时期)的冲击，最后无法超越城邦衰落与消亡的必然宿命。

三、"玩偶喻说"里的人性问题

晚年的柏拉图，思想更为成熟，观察更为深邃，对人性的认识更为透彻。在《法礼篇》里，

---

① Plato, *Laws*, 885b.

② R. F. Stalley, *An Introduction to Plato's* Laws, Oxford: Basil Blackwell, 1983, p. 173.

③ Plato, *Laws*, 899a—b.

④ Ibid., 899c.

他将《理想国》里的灵魂三分说简化为灵魂两分说，在关注理智与情感两个部分的同时，也关注这两者之间形成的内在张力或紧张关系。这种关系一方面凸显出理智的非凡优越性，另一方面展示出诸多情感驱力的混合多样性。对此优越性，柏拉图持积极态度，试图通过“正确教育”加以涵养培育，促其走向神性，以便确保明智之士管好人类事务；对此多样性，柏拉图持消极态度，认为人类受情感的制约，难以克服自身弱点，因此管不好自身事务，缺乏自立自足的能力。不过，柏拉图终究是人不是神，他虽然鄙视人性的固有缺憾，但也怜惜人类的存在状况。为此，他将人比作“神的玩偶”，其言如下：

> 我们不妨这样想，我们每个活着的人都是神的玩偶(pauma theon)。我们是否与生俱来就是神的玩物(paignion)呢，或者与生俱来就是为了某种严肃的理由呢，这是超出我们认识范围之外的事情。但是，我们的确知道这一点：我们自身具有这些情感，它们如同四下拉扯我们的绳线一样。它们东拉西扯，彼此对立，结果使我们采取了与其相应的行动，也就是彼此抵牾的行动；我们反反复复，经常跨越善恶交接的界限。依据我们的论证，在这些牵动力量中，有一种要求我们永久臣服，从而成为我们不得不依赖或听任其摆布的一种牵动力量；我们务必抵制其他绳线的拉拽。但有一根绳线是金线或神线，所传布的是“估算”的力量，它是城邦的公法(tēn poleōs kainon nomon)。这条金线是柔韧的，而其他绳线则是僵硬的，是由多种其他物质力量组成的。公法行使的力量是有德的或卓越的，每个人总应同这股力量合作，因为，“估算”是高尚之事，其性能柔和而不暴戾，但其作为则需要协助，这样一来，我们身上的含金部分就会胜过其他物质力量。假如我们给予自助的话，那么，在我们显现为玩偶的这则寓言中，其道德寓意就会贯通始终，得到巧妙而真实的表示；“自优部分”与“自劣部分”之类说法的含义就会变得更为清晰，城邦与个体的责任就会得到更多赞赏。个体务必知悉有关拉拽他的那些牵动力量的真相，务必在其一生的行为中遵从这一真相；城邦务必从我们言及的某一神明或某一人杰那里了解这一真相的好处，务必将其吸纳进法礼的形式之中，借此管理好城邦内部的事务和处理好本城邦与其他城邦的关系。倘若再进一步，那就要更为明确地厘清德行与恶行之别；对这一问题的昭示继而会有助于澄明教育(paideia)的主旨和各种其他实践活动……①

对于这则喻说的用意，我们不妨从以下四个方面予以解析：

1. 情感与理智

显而易见，“玩偶喻说”隐含着复杂的人性。在柏拉图那里，人类自身的“这些情感”，与人类自身的多种欲望是彼此关联的，所谓七情六欲与衣食住行，几乎尽列其中。这一切是人类的天性使然，本来无可厚非，但若过度迁就或贪求，又将成为人类的弱点所在。相比之下，柏拉图认为人类易犯三种过失，即：对快乐的追求与喜爱，对欲望的屈就与遵从，对痛感的回避与恐惧。此三者通常与人的内在情感纠结一起，形成种种内在驱力，促动或左右着人的心态、念头乃至行为。

---

① Plato, *Laws*, 644d—645c.

在上述中，柏拉图将人的“这些情感”或欲望，比作拴在人这具“玩偶”身上的绳线。这些绳线相互纠结，彼此拉拽，形成杂乱的反向运动，由此引发出心理世界里的自我内斗，进而转化成外在行为上的矛盾冲突。结果，出于情感的需要和欲望的满足，人人为己，盲目竞争，“每个人在公共领域都是其他人的敌人，每个人都在进行一场抗击自我的战争”①。对于这些由情感或欲望扭成的绳线，有的学者将其喻为“僵硬而死板”的“铁线”(the iron strings)。它们所代表的牵动力量，其自身是客观存在的，其本质是非理性的；一旦放纵或过度，就会对人的心理产生消极影响，对人的德行产生妨碍作用。

相对于这些“铁线”，人身上还幸存一根“柔和而灵活”的“金线”(the gold string)。这根“金线”作为一种牵动力量，是基于理智的“估算”能力或“实践智慧”(phronēsis)，不仅能使人权衡利弊、考虑因果，而且能使人辨别善恶、趋利避害。鉴于人的理智是由神所赐，这根“金线”也被喻为“神线”。此线所象征的牵动力量，实际上就是金贵和神圣的“城邦公法”(tēn poleōs kainon nomon)。②所谓“城邦公法”，就是城邦公民务必遵从的规矩与衡量其行为的准则，不仅可以用来抵制源于情感或欲望的牵动力量，而且可以用来引导人们步入遵纪守法的正途。通常，人只要诉诸理智，遵循公法，就能认清内在的牵动力量，克服自身的弱点，分辨行为的善恶，做出合理的决定，成为合格的公民。不过，在柏拉图心目中，这种“城邦公法”并非纯属人为，而是在人神的传授或启示下得以建立。由此可见，人无论作为“神的玩偶”，还是作为神启的对象，都终究处在神的掌控中或影子里，或者说，人终究生活在神的佑护下，这可以说是柏拉图神学思想的基点所在。

值得指出的是，柏拉图的心灵学说，在《理想国》里采用的是“理性、激情与欲求”三分法，在《法礼篇》里却采用了“情感与理智”或“非理性与理性”两分法。这后一种做法，在柏拉图学园的早期阶段曾流行一时。③在其最后这篇对话中，柏拉图化繁为简，合三为二，这样不仅便于表述，而且适合一般人的理解能力，尤其是适合那两位非哲学家(克里特人和斯巴达人)的理解能力。但这并非是说，“激情”(thumos)因素在《法礼篇》中已被柏拉图完全摒弃了。其实不然，《法礼篇》里每谈及“喜爱胜利”(philonikia)与“喜爱荣誉”(philotimia)时，“激情”作为一种潜在要素总是处处在场。当然，在柏拉图心目中，“激情”既是一个积极因素，也是一个消极因素，前者表现在城邦卫士对胜利和荣誉的追求中，后者则反映在诸如傲慢与爱欲等情感之中。这类情感“如同其他情感一样，也属于铁线范围，总与金线相左，将人这具玩偶向不同的方向拉扯”④。

另外，从情感与理智的内在心理冲突来看，被视为“玩偶”的个人，在这里全然是被动的

---

① Plato, *Laws*, 626d.

② Ibid., 644d—645c.

③ D. A. Rees, “Bipartition of the Soul in the Early Academy,” Journal of Hellenic Studies, 77 (1957), 112—18. 桑德斯并不赞同这种观点，他认为柏拉图不会轻易放弃“心灵三分”的生动想法，其后期的“心灵两分”说也不会排除“心灵三分”说。为此，他特意通过细读《法礼篇》里的心灵学说，竭力表明“激情”(thumos)要素在柏拉图探讨心理驱力中所发挥的重要作用。Cf. T. J. Saunders, “The Structure of the Soul and the State in Plato's Laws” [‘Structure’], Eranos, 60 (1962), 37—55.

④ Maria Michela Sassi, “The Self, the Soul, and the Individual in the City of the *Laws*,” in *Oxford Studies in Ancient Philosophy*, 35 (2008), p. 135.

存在，任由情感或欲望的绳线东拉西扯，亦如波布尼奇(C. Bobnich)所言，“此人似乎就是一个被动的容体，所盛的是彼此牵扯的情感，或者就是一个被动的看客，所见的是相互纠结的牵动力量”。孰不知人不仅有情感，而且有理智，因此可以主动地参与到这一感受过程之中，若用波布尼奇的话说，那就是“我们能够牵动自己的绳线”。[①]

再者，所谓“城邦公法”，是理性的至高原则，既促使“理性的规定”(tēn tou nou dianomēn)，[②]也代表“城邦的共识”(dogma poleōs koinon)，[③]其最终目的在于将健康的节制或自律之德灌输到心灵之中，使人的欲望不会过度泛滥，不会危及城邦的管理秩序与共同福祉。[④]至于遵守“城邦公法”，从来不是一个简单的问题。这既涉及自由意志，也关乎实践智慧，此两者互为表里，在很大程度上取决于道德修为与法礼习俗。一般而言，道德修为是由中出，法礼习俗则由外作，彼此相辅相成，二者缺一不可。

2. 人与神

人与神的关系，一直是柏拉图神学与伦理学所关注的焦点。但就“玩偶喻说”来看，柏拉图在《法礼篇》第一卷与第七卷里先后重复这一类比，其遣词虽显轻佻而含讥讽，但其态度认真且用意严肃。他在颂扬神明和贬低人类的同时，有意将人与神联系起来，并要求人务必认同自身的“玩偶”处境，务必参照这一品性度过一生，务必利用这一“最佳部分”，积极参与“最高贵的消遣游戏”，借此养成与其现存状况截然不同的心智。[⑤]

在古希腊语里，所谓“最佳部分”(to beltiston)，也就是“最善、最好或最美部分”。根据柏拉图言说的语境，我认为该部分既是“人”与“神”产生关联的契机，也是“人”完善自身和成就德行的基础。因为，“人”正是作为“神的玩物”或“玩偶”，才使“人”攀上了“神”，从而结成三种关系，即：操控关系，游戏关系与教育关系。

首先，就操控关系而言，“人”不如“神”，无论在理智、德行与能力上，“人”都逊色于“神”；因此，“人”被“神”摆弄，受“神”操控，就像“克洛诺斯神话”所描述的那样，人的事务只能由远胜于人的神来安排和管理。而人只能打点和照料比自身略逊一筹的牛群与羊群。[⑥]

其次，就游戏关系而论，“神”以“人”为伴，将“人”作为自己玩耍、消遣或解闷的对象；相应地，“人”也借此以“神”为伴，成为“神”从事娱乐活动的组成部分。这便构成一种彼此依赖、互为对象、各取所需的游戏关系。通过这种游戏关系，“神”关爱和怜惜“人”，将理性或理智当作礼物赋予人，从而使“人”具有了“像神一样”的质素；与此同时，人凭借这种游戏关系，既可接近神，亦可摹仿神，从而使自己成为“像神一样”(esesthai theion)[⑦]的存在。于是，“人”便由此“向神生成”(becoming divine of the human)，成为不断完善自我和追求超越的生灵。

最后，就教育关系来看，它一方面源自上述“游戏关系”，另一方面源自“参与最高贵的消

① C. Bobonich, *Plato's Utopia Recast: His Later Ethics and Politics*, Oxford: Oxford University Press, 2002, p. 266, pp. 247—292.

② Plato, *Laws*, 714a.

③ Ibid., 644d; cf. 636d, 663b—c.

④ Ibid., 835e—836a.

⑤ Plato, *Laws*, 803b.

⑥ Ibid., 713a—714b. Also see Plato, *Statesman*, 271c—273d.

⑦ Ibid., 792d.

遣活动”(kallistas paidias)。在柏拉图那里，“游戏”(paidia)经常被用来预示“教育”(paideia)，适宜的“游戏”被视为“正确教育”(orthōs paideia)的不二法门，尤其是在“儿童”(paida)阶段。譬如，木匠与士兵，都是在游戏过程中学会并掌握各自技艺的。故此，“正确的教育”要充分利用游戏活动(paizonta)，借此将儿童的趣味和欲求导向他们最终的目标，养成他们敬业的习惯，塑造他们良好的灵智，使他们通过寓教于乐的游戏，喜爱上他们所应学会的本领，一旦他们长大成人后，就必然能够精熟地掌握和运用这些东西。①至于“参与最高贵的消遣活动”，实指“参与最美好的游戏活动”，这涉及神赐予人的另一类礼物——诗乐歌舞。柏拉图认为，由神所赐的诗乐歌舞，不仅是为了犒赏人们，使他们在辛勤劳作之余放松自己的心情并满足自己的审美需要，也是为了教育人们，使他们借此“养成与现在截然不同的心智”。②故此，教育的起源可以说是“发端于日神阿波罗与诗神缪斯”。③不过，若要实现以上目的，务须遵从下述规定：每一个人，无论男女，都应参照人即“神的玩物”“这一品格特性度过一生”。④这一设定，不仅成为上列三种“人”“神”关系的联结枢纽，而且正是柏拉图先前所言的那种“严肃目的”(spoudē tini zunestēkos)。⑤如此一来，通过“人”“神”之间的三重关系，人的事务增添了神性的维度，再也不同于往前了。换言之，人的事务已转化为“严肃的事情”，已成为“务必认真对待”的对象，从而看似具有与“悲剧”相若的“严肃性”了。

3. 德行与恶行

在“玩偶喻说”里，人受情感或欲望的干扰与拉扯，会贸然采取相互抵牾的行动，在反反复复的混乱之际“跨越善恶交接的界限”。这一界限，可以说是由功效对立的“铁线”与“金线”形成。代表情感与欲望的“铁线”所产生的牵动力量，一旦趋于过度或泛滥，就会把人拽向恶的一端，由此导致恶行；相反地，象征理智或“估算”的“金线”所产生的牵动力量，如若能够统摄情感与欲望，就会将人推向善的一端，由此成就德行。

在这里，柏拉图特意强调，人应当接受神明的启示或人杰的教诲，要设法认清那些拉拽自己的牵动力量的真相及其好处，并将其吸纳进法礼的形式之中，借此管理好城邦内部的事务和处理好本城邦与其他城邦的关系，进而判明德行与恶行之间的差别，一生中要勤而行之，最终要确立自己的德行，消除自己的恶行。为此，柏拉图提醒人们，一方面要明确“自优部分”与“自劣部分”之类说法的含义，承担城邦与个体的责任，另一方面要发挥理智的作用，在遵纪守法的前提下，积极主动地参与“自助”活动。所谓“自优部分”，也就是自我优良的品性，主要涉及爱好和平和重视友爱的精神，这不仅有助于加强城邦公民之间的团结或消除人与人之间的战争，同时也有助于保持自身心态的平和与避免内心世界的冲突。至于“自劣部分”，一般是指自我低劣的品性，主要关乎自私自利或巧取豪夺的恶行，这不仅会导致城邦内部的战争，而且会激发内心世界的冲突。⑥

---

① Plato, *Laws*, 643c—d.

② Ibid., 803c.

③ Ibid., 653d.

④ Ibid., 803c.

⑤ Ibid., 644d—e.

⑥ Ibid., 627—628.

说到底，柏拉图试想告诫人们，每个人至少有两个自我，一方比较善好，一方比较恶劣，彼此相互争斗，总想压倒对方。而情感与欲望这些心理驱力，通常助纣为虐，使人处在内心纠结、冲突与焦虑的状态之中。要想解除这一困境，就需要借助理智的力量，克服自己的弱点；遵守城邦的法礼，培养自己的德行。古人云："人心惟危，圣心惟微。"从柏拉图的角度来看，我们似乎可以这样归纳：在普通人那里，人心惟情而危；在爱智者那里，人心惟理而安。前者反映人性的弱点，如若情感不通过理性的过滤，就会趋向危险的恶行；后者表示人性的优点，经理性估算而获实践智慧，从而引致安和的德行。

4. 悲观与乐观

柏拉图曾郑重宣布：严肃的事务需要认真对待，不严肃的事务无需认真对待。在他所认定的严肃事务之中，神与神的事务居于首位；而在其以为不严肃的事物之中，人的事务位列其上。如他所言，人的事务没有任何值得严肃对待的东西，严肃对待人的事务实属不得已而为之。[①]因为，柏拉图深知人性的复杂与弱点，谙悉人情与人欲对人生构成的多种困扰。虽然人亦有理智这一神赐的礼物，但是，一旦情胜于理或情理不合(diaphōnia)，就会引发最为糟糕的"无知"(amathia)，而"无知"则是一种"蠢行"(anoia)，是导致"恶行"的重要原因之一。[②]在此意义上，柏拉图对人、人性与人的事务的态度，显然是相当消极或悲观的。

不过，柏拉图也认为，没有人会自愿作恶事或履恶行。人屈就快感、惧怕痛苦或发狂发怒，是因为缺乏有关善恶的知识。[③]为此，柏拉图强调"教育"(paideia)的主旨与作用，赋予"教育"一种特有的积极功能。当然，柏拉图所推崇的"教育"，是"正确的教育"，是关乎"公民德行"和"城邦福祉"的"教育"。这种"教育"，包括诗乐和体操教育，数学与科学教育，法治与道德教育，神学与哲学教育等等。

概而言之，诗乐教育以善心为本，旨在培养年轻人的良好的趣味，从而使其爱其所应爱，恶其所应恶。体操教育以强身为用，旨在培养年轻人勇武善战的体魄与能力，造就其美善兼备的身材与素质。数学与科学教育以理智为上，旨在培养人们推理、分析、抽象与归纳的认知能力。法治与道德教育以公正与德行为鹄，旨在规范人们日常的合法行为，培养人们善于节制的自律意识，鼓励人们追求自我完善的品格修养。神学教育以神为善因，强调人以神为范型，确立神为量万物的尺度，以此培养人的自我超越精神和传布人向神生成的必要性与重要性。哲学教育以智慧和真知为认识对象，意在引导人们爱智求真，充分发挥理智的积极作用，塑造自己完善的人格与发展自己非凡的洞察力，最终使自己成为"像神一样的存在"(god-like being)。在此意义上，柏拉图的态度不仅是严肃认真的，而且是积极乐观的。为此，他一生竭尽绵薄，试图改革雅典的教育传统，努力推行自己的教育理念，建议人们务必"掌握实践智慧"和"服从神性法礼"，最终设法使人们"养成与其现存状况截然不同的心智"。[④]

---

① Plato, *Laws*, 803b; *Republic*, 604b.

② Ibid., 653a—c; 659d—660a; 689a—d; 696c.

③ Ibid., 860d; 863b—c; 864b—c.

④ Ibid., 942a—c; 739b—d; 803b.

由此可见，柏拉图在《法礼篇》里所建构的理想，既指向理想的城邦，也指向理想的心灵。而这两种理想范式，都与柏拉图的教育思想密不可分。究其本质，理想的城邦亦如理想的心灵，均能与各自内在的冲突和平相处。在这里，法礼的作用举足轻重，“其如一剂灵丹妙药，旨在克服情操与情感所引发的不稳定影响。这剂灵丹妙药的权威主义性相或许会让当代读者感到担心，但柏拉图力挺这种救治方式，假定此乃消解人性极端弱点的关键所在。特别值得一提的是，法礼对理性的规定作用是强制性的，并假定每个人只要是一个神性动物，他就潜在地拥有这种理性规定能力，但是，只有‘少数人’才能够运用这种能力。简言之，柏拉图要求我们为了政治秩序而付出的代价，就是要压抑我们‘比较糟糕的’但却是更为人性的自我”①。

综上所述，柏拉图在喻说中所表达的哲思，隐含着诗性的智慧与念兹在兹的道德和政治目的，他力图通过诗乐、体操、科学、法治、道德、神学与哲学等多种教育形式，以期实现自己所设定的理想追求。此外，无论是从柏拉图的上述书写方式来看，还是从哲学与神话这种“剪不断”的关系来看，我们都会发现哲学从其发轫之初，就处于一种双重性的模糊地位。诚如韦尔南(Jean-Pierre Vernant)所言，哲学的灵感及其发展在一开始就与神秘仪式和集市论争有关，这便导致哲学摇摆在宗教团体特有的玄秘感觉与城邦政治特有的公开论辩之间。前者以毕达哥拉斯教派(the Pythagorean sect)为代表，偏好秘密结社与传播秘传学说；后者以智者运动(the Sophistic movement)为代表，强调城邦公共生活与推行有偿传授。相应地，哲学家也游离于两种相互冲突的态度或诱惑之间。他有时自命不凡，俨然摆出一副主神的派头，借用知识的名义为城邦管理出谋划策；有时则沉浸于思索纯粹私密的智慧之中，故而超然出世，索居离群，带上几名弟子，在城邦里组成小城邦，试图通过学习与思索来探寻救世之道。②柏拉图的特殊情况似乎很能佐证这一论断。我们知道，柏氏在毕达哥拉斯学派与希腊文化传统的影响下，试图通过神话的言说传统，将哲学思考与玄秘的宗教意识连接起来，以期使其在城邦民众中得到更为有效的传播或接受；与此同时，他继承了智者学派喜好争论的传统，采用了神话、喻说和逻各斯混合交汇的论辩策略，试图借助笔下的苏格拉底或雅典客人之口，将他的哲学思想应用于城邦政治或城邦管理。同样有趣的是，柏拉图作为哲学家，自身态度也表现出双重性或矛盾性，既有入世的内在驱力，又有出世的心理倾向。换言之，他一方面参与政治实践，标举“以哲治邦”的理念，不断探索建构理想城邦的可能途径，甚至冒着生命危险三访舒拉古，试图造就他心目中的“哲人王”；另一方面，当他的政治抱负遭受失败之后，便退而办学，隐居于市，在雅典城邦内建立“雅典学园”，在那里倾力探讨治邦理政之道，培养经世济民之士。我以为，从这两方面来理解柏拉图哲学的目的论追求，将有助于“还原”其真实思想的历史风貌。

作者简介：王柯平，博士，北京第二外国语学院跨文化研究院教授，中国社会科学院哲学研究所研究员。

---

① Maria Michela Sassi, “The Self, the Soul, and the Individual in the City of the *Laws*,” p. 147.

② Jean-Pierre Vernant, *The Origins of Greek Thought*, London: Methuen, 1982, pp. 59—60.

经典的美学特征[①]

——哈罗德·布鲁姆“文学经典”理论再解析

金永兵

【内容提要】 本文深入布鲁姆思想的整体内容，通过探寻其思想的内在根源，揭示出他关于文学经典的美学特征的思考，即经典的审美性、主体性、原创性和终极性等相互关联的层面。对文学经典的美学特征的把握，既是深入理解布鲁姆相关思想的重要途径，同时也是在我们时代语境中探寻和发挥文学经典的文化价值建构作用的一个基本的理论前提。

【关键词】 哈罗德·布鲁姆　经典　审美自主性　主体性　原创性　终极性

On Aesthetic Characteristics of the Canon

——Reinterpretation of Harold Bloom's Canon Theory

【Abstract】 The paper reveals the realistic significance of Harold Bloom's antithetical criticism in the cultural studies era, by discussing his opinions on literary canon's aesthetic characteristics, namely aesthetic autonomy, subjectivity, originality and ultimacy, and exploring the intrinsic root of his thought.

【Keywords】 Harold Bloom　canon　aesthetic autonomy　subjectivity　originality　ultimacy

“读书必有取舍”，究竟什么样的文学作品堪称经典，值得阅读，同时，我们又该怎样阅读经典，经典于读者、社会文化有何意义？正如美国学者哈罗德·布鲁姆(Harold Bloom)的一部著作的名字所提出的问题那样：“怎样阅读，为什么？”关于经典，任何试图给出一个清晰定义的尝试似乎都显得非常艰难，并且永远可以被找到漏洞或含混之处。然而矛盾的是，这一试图给出标准的努力又是必须的，因为毕竟还是存在一些被普遍认可的价值。即使没有明确的标准我们也会秉持一些习以为常的见解或者惯例。什么样的作品是经典，这并非文学本身所能全部统摄，它还必然牵涉到审美传统、教育体制、文化价值观、话语权力等复杂而强大的因素，可供切入的角度非常多。本文将深入布鲁姆思想的整体内容，通过探寻其思想的内在根源，揭示出他关于文学经典的美学特征的思考，即经典的审美性、主体性、原创性和终极性等相互关联的层面。对文学经典的美学特征的把握，既是深入理解布鲁姆相关思想的

① 本文是作者所主持国家社科基金项目：“‘中国问题’与‘中国经验’——新时期文艺理论研究”(项目号12BZW001)的阶段性成果。

重要途径，同时也是在我们时代语境中探寻和发挥文学经典的文化价值建构作用的一个基本的理论前提。

一、审美性：具有“美学尊严”

布鲁姆承袭了康德等人的审美学说，认为艺术本身就是其目的，审美判断是非功利的且主要是关乎主观的心理力量等。布鲁姆认为，“审美价值”不只是像人们所认为的那样只是康德的一个观念，而是“一种现实存在”。他说：“只有审美的力量才能透入经典，而这力量又主要是一种混合力：娴熟的形象语言、原创性、认知能力、知识以及丰富的词汇。”[①]他十分推崇伍尔芙在《奥兰多》中写下的一段关于阅读的见解：“谁读书又是为了达到什么目的呢，不管这目的多么可取？我们的某些追求难道不是因为它们本身的美妙和乐趣吗？阅读不就是这样一种追求吗？”[②]我们从诗中获得的认知和反思能力、那种艰辛的愉悦本身就是一种奖赏。布鲁姆称自己从童年时读到这段话开始，便一直将开头的三句奉为信条并身体力行。事实上，这也是布鲁姆全部经典理论与批评实践的支点。他认为，经典必须具备崇高的审美特征，这是经典作家和经典作品的根本特征，是一个清晰的、无法借鉴的标志，类似波德莱尔所说的“美学尊严”。就像波德莱尔最著名的诗作《恶之花》的诗题本身表明的那样，诗最伟大、最高贵的目的是“美”，是要表现“纯粹的愿望、动人的忧郁和高贵的绝望”[③]，诗要把“善”同“美”区分开来，“恶”中也可以发掘出美，而“真”同样不是诗的目的，诗表现的是更为真实的东西，是另一个世界的真实，要深入地狱天堂、到未知世界的底层去发现。

这不仅仅是对文学本质观或者一种批评策略的表述，我们更应该把它读作一种世界观。在论及伍尔芙的经典性时，布鲁姆指出她与尼采持有一个同样的观念，即认为“人类的存在与世界最终只有作为审美现象才是合理的”，其实，布鲁姆同他们一样，“最适宜被描述为天启式的审美家”[④]。这里，布鲁姆的理论不同于通常意义上的审美本质论强调文学的审美价值的核心地位或者审美批判的终极维度，而不否认文学的其他价值和批评维度，布鲁姆却是把文学的唯一的目的和价值确定为审美，他要“维护审美自主性”。他的困难并不在于阐释经典的审美价值或者以波德莱尔、佩特、王尔德等人为例讨论文学的审美价值，而在于他要以纯粹审美视角来筛查西方文学以构建经典谱系，他必须面对的事实是“自品达以降，力争经典地位的作家会为某一阶级而战，正如品达为贵族而战那样”，但丁也好，弥尔顿也好，“都为了自己所坚信的某种精神上丰富而正义的政治事业而牺牲甚大”，如何将他们解读为“天启式的审美家”，如何论证那些“伟大的文学即使面对最有意义的事业也会坚守其自足性：不论是女性主义、非裔文化主义，还是当前各种政治正确的事业”，社会与文学之间是“不可干预”的关系？[⑤]

---

① [美]哈罗德·布鲁姆：《西方正典——伟大作家和不朽作品》，江宁康译，南京：译林出版社，2005年，第20页。

② 同上，第349页。

③ [法]波德莱尔：《波德莱尔美学论文选》译本序，郭宏安译，北京：人民文学出版社，1987年，第3页。

④ [美]哈罗德·布鲁姆：《西方正典》，第343页。

⑤ 同上，第19—20页。

这正是他与“憎恨学派”(“School of Resentment”)的分歧。所谓“憎恨学派”，是布鲁姆对新马克思主义、女权主义、心理分析等文学“外部”研究不满的称呼，他认为这一派别的人内心都充满愤怒，完全失去了对美学的尊重。在布鲁姆看来，这些术语背后代表的是一种社会能量和权力意识，这些研究者将莎士比亚等伟大作家都缩减为社会能量的表征，然而在他看来“权力”并不比个人情感更加重要，文学研究应该采用自己的术语，它不是哲学、社会学或者心理学的附庸。尽管布鲁姆自己深受弗洛伊德心理学的影响，但是他非常反对对文学作品进行社会学或心理学的研究，反对称莎士比亚有“俄狄浦斯情结”，而是宁愿认为弗洛伊德有“哈姆雷特情结”，主张对弗洛伊德作莎士比亚式解读，而不是对莎士比亚作弗洛伊德式解读。这不是一个简单的反转，而是一种文学批评立场的转变。他认为莎士比亚是审美自由与原创性的完美典范，弗洛伊德虽然以心理分析蜚声各种文化圈，但他真正的意义在于其著作描述了人类复杂的本性，这“远比日薄西山的弗氏疗法更具生命力”①。他所认定的文学经典只是在诗本身意义上而言的。另一方面，布鲁姆对于某些文学“内部”研究同样是质疑的，他对浪漫主义文学的价值重估，其实并非只是反对意识形态式的文学批评，而是抵抗形式主义，比如艾略特等人对于诗歌“非个人情感”的表述以及弗莱的“原型批评”。形式主义虽然是着眼于“内部”，然而并未在其中找到合理的立足点，原型批评借用荣格等人的“集体无意识”来分析诗作背后的普遍原始心理，不断标榜一种放之四海而皆准的阅读方法，声称据此能够阅读任何时代任何诗人的作品，然而实际上这种愿望只能是空中楼阁，最终很可能简化化为一种见物不见人的技术操作；布鲁姆希望实现的是更加具有人文色彩、关注诗人主体的诗歌批评。

正是基于这种文学审美观，无论他对西方经典作家谱系的构建，还是对其中作家的生活及其作品经典性的解读，都是围绕“审美自主性”这一维度甚至是唯一维度来展开的。譬如，面对浪漫主义诗人拜伦、雪莱等人对革命政治活动的积极介入，布鲁姆有自己的“审美自主性”意义上的解释。他将浪漫主义诗歌分为两大阶段：普罗米修斯阶段和“想象和真人”阶段。布鲁姆以普罗米修斯来代表浪漫主义诗人如雪莱、布莱克等人对于社会革命的热情与介入，他们一度以诗歌为武器致力于对腐朽的社会体制、刻板的宗教观念进行嘲讽和攻击，而当他们感到变革的无望之后，便转入“想象和真人”阶段，这一阶段的特征是诗人们相对远离论战和讽刺，精力更多地集中于“自我”本身。布鲁姆认为，第一阶段诗人的抗争可以理解为类似于利比多对压抑的反抗，雪莱等诗人卷入革命政治活动的行为实际上是在释放受压抑的冲动和力量，为进入第二阶段自在自为的自我心灵状态提供准备。这样一来，浪漫主义诗人的社会介入便也被归入到美学意义上的选择，而并非出于政治考量。② 面对有研究者认为一些诗作反映了社会斗争，布鲁姆指责研究者在“寻求自己的自私的目的”，“看不到冲突性就是高雅艺术的内在特性”，③从而实现对诗歌审美自足性的维护。

---

① [美]哈罗德·布鲁姆：《西方正典》，第295页。

② 关于布鲁姆对浪漫主义诗歌的分期，参见张跃军、古克平：《布鲁姆早期浪漫主义诗歌理论初探》，济南：《山东外语教学》2004年第3期。

③ [美]哈罗德·布鲁姆：《西方正典》，第20页。

尽管伍尔芙被后来的女权主义批评追溯为先驱，布鲁姆却认为这并非她真正的价值所在，她的重要意义在于敏锐的感知能力，而这来自于家学渊源和长久的阅读，即便伍尔芙在一定程度上为后来的学者提供了女性主义资源，也绝不能把她压缩为激进的政治理论家。布鲁姆反复强调伍尔芙本人"将她的女性主义政治学建立在佩特式的唯美主义之上"[①]，"不论伍尔芙可能在某一时刻会压抑什么，她都绝不会压抑自己的审美感受力"。在此，布鲁姆还进一步清楚地表明了自己的审美立场："我们的文化注定仍将是一种文学文化，而那些仍未名誉扫地的意识形态最终会被排除出去。"[②]

至于普鲁斯特小说主人公之所以基本上都不是同性恋、并未带有一半犹太人血统，不是因为犹太人的历史境遇或1922年同性恋仍被视为耻辱，而只是因为这样的安排会使小说成为一部更好的小说，一位伟大艺术家所拥有的审美尊严鞭策我们"为那些本质上的审美决定寻找审美动机"。[③] 即便是被认为书页中散发着道德芬芳的乔治·艾略特，她之所以具有经典性也在于把握住了"道德和审美共鸣的那一块中间地带"[④]，如果小说家不能将公开的道德说教转化成一种审美的美德，就会陷入一场文学的灾难。在布鲁姆看来，真正出类拔萃的艺术家的强大个性是无法被某个时代的社会机制禁锢的，真正的思考与社会政治无关，因此，经典的意义必须在审美角度上来认知，他很赞同黑兹利特所说的艺术并不是以进步为鹄的。

二、原创性："使美感增加陌生性"

如果说布鲁姆只是康德等人美学思想的重要继承者和实践者，可能会在很大程度上忽视掉其自身的价值。布鲁姆在坚守经典的审美自主性过程中进一步提出经典特质的另一层面，即独创性问题。布鲁姆强调文学作品成为经典的原因在于"陌生性(strangeness)"，即"一种无法同化的原创性，或是一种我们完全认同而不再视为异端的原创性"。并且，他认为沃尔特·佩特关于浪漫主义的定义，即"使美感增加陌生性"，"适用于所有的经典作品"，"从《神曲》到《终局》的成就实际上就是从陌生性到陌生性的循环"。[⑤] 因此，"在陌生性意义上而言的原创性超越其他一切品质，是能够使一部作品成为经典的品质"[⑥]。布鲁姆最为推崇英国批评家塞缪尔·约翰逊的话"原创是对天才的最高赞誉"[⑦]。在布鲁姆后来的著作*Genius: A Mosaic of One Hundred Exemplary Creative Minds*中，每每谈及这些文学巨擘的独特天才时，也往往围绕着这一点。他讨论莎士比亚的经典意义时指出，"不管你是谁和身处何处，他总是在观念上和意象上超过你。他使你显得不合时宜，因为他包含你，而你却无法包括他"，"弗洛伊德的心灵地图是莎士比亚的，前者似乎只是对后者的肤浅解说"。正因为如

① [美]哈罗德·布鲁姆：《西方正典》，第342页。
② 同上，第347页。
③ 同上，第317页。
④ 同上，第253页。
⑤ 同上，第2页。
⑥ 同上，第262页。
⑦ 转引自[美]哈罗德·布鲁姆：《西方正典》，第151页。

此，只能从审美角度来解读经典，而不能从“外部”例如社会、心理的角度来透视，因为那是多余而可笑的[①]。

布鲁姆的“原创性”或者说“陌生性”并不是单指形式，他认为，后辈诗人为了克服“影响的焦虑”，不断地发掘新的思考角度（认知的原创性）与新的表现形式（表现的原创性），正是这种努力成就了一部文学史。就认知的原创性而言，譬如但丁对《神曲》的描绘，他对宗教世界的想象带有一种狂野的陌生性，而普鲁斯特对性嫉妒的描写则超越了莎士比亚与弗洛伊德，洞悉到情欲困扰的深处。狄金森更是以超凡的认知原创性著名，她很难被解读，因为她永远在质疑，在力求将确定转变成空白，抛开一切我们熟知的看法与定见。就表现的原创性而言，则可以是塑造人物的具体技巧、词汇的丰富程度、语言的风格、修辞的新颖和结构篇章的布局方式等。布鲁姆以乔伊斯关于时间的表现为例解释了这种原创性：普鲁斯特和贝克特等人根据他们的生活经历写作，而乔伊斯则不同，“他艺术地使自己超出时间之外，以便解脱时序和因果关系对发展的影响……（他的作品中）事件的发展是间歇式的，人物和主题虽然服从某种近乎疯狂的内在必然性，在表现和发展它们时显示出陀思妥耶夫斯基式的对事件平庸串联的轻蔑。”[②]这种特殊的时间呈现方式无疑会加强小说的独特性，使得读者惯常的思维被打破，获得一种新鲜的体验。

这里，我们感受到俄国形式主义理论家什克洛夫斯基关于“陌生化”的思想：“正是为了恢复对生活的体验，感觉到事物的存在，为了使石头成其为石头，才存在所谓的艺术。艺术的目的是为了把事物提供为一种可观可见之物。艺术的手法是将事物‘奇异化’（陌生化）的手法，是把形式艰深化，从而增加感受的难度时间的手法，因为在艺术中感受过程本身就是目的，应该使之延长。”[③]文学，可以使我们在重复性的日常生活中退化了或者说“自动化”了的感受力得到恢复，使我们看到习以为常的生活中一些新的可能。

在俄国形式主义那里，显得陌生的既是被程式化惯例性表现方式所提供的那一“现实”本身，也包括惯例性表现方式本身。布鲁姆无疑是接受这一看法并在批评中加以实践的，他始终以审美感受和语言特征（如语言形象、修辞手法等）作为批评的主要关注对象，但他不局限于艺术技巧层面的陌生化，更进一步，他还依据他早期浪漫主义诗歌研究和尼采以及弗洛伊德心理分析，提出关于“陌生性意义上而言的原创性”得以产生的创造性心理根源：艺术想象和“创造性误读”（creatively misreading）。

“想象”被他视为浪漫主义诗歌理论的全部中心，是一种对于反叛与创造的膜拜。“我们的生命毕竟就是……一场‘持久的苦难和孤独’。只有一种力量，即想象能够拯救生命。”[④]浪漫主义有着不屈的创造的意志，带有狄德罗所说的罪犯式的艺术气质：蔑视规则，热爱权利、崇高和辉煌，不愿也不屑被正常的生活所约束，因此超拔的想象是其突出的精神标志。在对浪漫主义文学的研究中，布鲁姆非常重视那些具有超凡想象力的诗人。他认为莎士比亚最

---

① 参见[美]哈罗德·布鲁姆：《西方正典》，第17页。
② [美]哈罗德·布鲁姆：《西方正典》，第393页。
③ [苏]维·什克洛夫斯基：《散文理论》，刘宗次译，南昌：百花洲文艺出版社，1994年，第10页。
④ [美]哈罗德·布鲁姆：《批评、正典结构与预言》，吴琼译，北京：中国社会科学出版社，2000年，第233页。

高超的技艺便是卓越的想象，惠特曼则具有一种神话般清新的创新性，每一位强者诗人都有着杰出的想象能力。在描述很多诗人的经典性时，布鲁姆其实就是对其启示性想象的描述，譬如在论述伍尔芙时，布鲁姆描绘了伍尔芙这样一种物我合一、以内在本性去融合和亲近外物来体察世界本质的方式："每一次新鲜的领悟与感知都会引起现实在她面前摇曳不定，而思想只是出现在她那受恩时刻边缘的暗影。"①

"创造性误读"针对的是强力作家面对强大的文学传统和前辈作家及其文本所产生的"影响的焦虑"时的一种创造策略。在他看来，诗歌文本不是自足自律的封闭体系，诗歌中存在着"内在互文性"，一部诗歌的话语总是与先驱诗人的经典文本话语之间发生着互文性联系，彼此交涉对照，诗人们相互阅读并相互影响，可以说，"诗的历史是无法和诗的影响截然分开的"。由此，在前辈巨大影响笼罩下的后辈诗人便有了一种俄狄浦斯式的对"父亲"的憎恨，并具有强烈的否定父权的欲望，渴望通过对前辈诗人的象征性弑父行为，开辟出属于自己的诗歌领地。因此，诗人必须具有一种勇于与前辈大师们"竞争"的精神，布鲁姆所心仪的"诗人中的强者"，就是那些"以坚忍不拔的毅力向威名显赫的前代巨擘进行至死不休的挑战的诗坛主将们"，他们以创造性的误读来摆脱影响的焦虑而获得审美原创性。他说，"一部诗的历史就是诗人中的强者为了廓清自己的想象空间而相互'误读'对方的诗的历史"②，每一首诗都可以看做是诗人——作为诗人——对另一首前驱诗或对诗歌整体做出有意的误释。"伟大的作品不是重写即为修正"，从而"获得一种必然与历史传承和影响的焦虑相结合的原创性"。③

三、个人主体性："增进内在自我的成长"

关于文学的审美价值，各种文学理论几乎都给予强调，但在布鲁姆看来，作为其对立面的"憎恨学派"在这个问题上的基本原则是"所谓的审美价值也出自阶级斗争"，把审美与阶级、阶层、族群等建立联系。布鲁姆虽然无法全然否定人的社会性存在，但是他反复强调，"个体的自我是理解审美价值的惟一方法和全部标准"④，"审美只是个人的而非社会的关切"⑤，因而"审美批评使我们回到文学想象的自主性上去，回到孤独的心灵中去，于是读者不再是社会的一员，而是作为深层的自我，作为我们终极的内在性"⑥。

有研究者将布鲁姆的美学立场定义为"唯我主义"⑦，是有道理的，这在很大程度上正是源自他所继承的浪漫主义的大写的"我"。浪漫主义代表着一种高度内向化、自我化的诗学，它最大的特征便是热情地张扬自我肯定自我崇拜自我和自由无羁的意志，抗拒一切外在于

---

① [美]哈罗德·布鲁姆：《西方正典》，第 344 页。
② [美]哈罗德·布鲁姆：《影响的焦虑》，徐文博译，北京：三联书店，1989 年，第 3 页。
③ [美]哈罗德·布鲁姆：《西方正典》，第 8 页。
④ 同上，第 16 页。
⑤ 同上，第 12 页。
⑥ 同上，第 8 页。
⑦ 阎景娟：《文学经典论争在美国》，北京：社会科学文献出版社，2010 年，第 67 页。

自己的规则，这种主体自我曾被黑格尔说成是可以创造一切也可以毁灭一切。从早期关于浪漫主义诗歌分析开始，布鲁姆就非常重视作家关于自我、存在等问题的思索，欣赏内化的带有孤独感的诗歌氛围，鄙薄所谓社会意义，在其后对于经典特质的研究中这种观念表现得更加充分，他不断强调经典背后“君王”般自我的存在。在对华兹华斯诗歌及其影响的分析中，布鲁姆概括了一个“浪漫主义的自我神话学”。他说：“在《徒步远足》中，孤独者的形象是浪漫主义最基本的原型的一个典型代表，这种人与他人不相往来，整天沉浸在自己的过分的自我意识中……（这是）对浪漫主义的自我神话学作的最充分的陈述。”[①]在他眼中，海明威和托尔斯泰等作家也都在文字间注入了深刻的自我崇拜，把他们的自我融入事物的本性之中。经典作品中也许不一定会流露出强烈的自我意识，但是一定会标有作家的明显个人印记。布鲁姆认为有些作家在写作中会故意隐匿自我，以尽量客观冷静的姿态来描述对象，有些则毫不掩饰地热情颂扬，但这都是指作为叙述者的自我，实际上，在其背后的作家自我则无一例外都是非常强大而有力的。任何伟大的诗人都在永久地敏锐地倾听自我，这是其全部创造活动的源泉，代表着旺盛的生命力。同时从文学阅读的角度说，布鲁姆认为，经典是面对每个人自身的，是内省的，“获得审美力量能让我们知道如何对自己说话和怎样承受自己。莎士比亚或塞万提斯，荷马或但丁，乔叟或拉伯雷，阅读他们的作品的真正作用是增进内在自我的成长。深入研读经典不会使人变好或变坏，也不会使公民变得更有用或更有害。心灵的自我对话本质上不是一种社会现实”[②]。

实际上，这里布鲁姆不是简单地重复康德、尼采意义上审美与个人主观心理的内在关系，也不只是在浪漫主义意义上肯定这种对主体自我的崇拜，他还是在寻找、维护美国精英文化传统，在建构一种美国文化精神的意义上寻找这种审美主体“自我”。布鲁姆将自己定位为一个爱默生主义者——“没有历史，只有传记（no history, only biography）”[③]。爱默生是对美国文化精神的形成具有重要意义的诗人，他告诫人们要信任自身、依赖自身，其学说被认为是美国的世俗宗教。他曾经这样宣示美国精神的新纪元：“我们依靠别人的日子、我们漫长的学习其他大陆的日子，渐进结束了。”[④]爱默生关于“自我”的肯定为美国精神的建立提供了充分的可能性，他认为人们需要相信自己是创造世界的力量，那种认为自己是自然世界的迟来者、世界在很久以前便已经完成了的观念是有害的，他还以极其高涨的热情宣称“我”就是上帝，只要“我”将自己从肉体、欲望和个人意志中那些脆弱与不洁的部分中解救出来，就可以达到自我的这种神性。对于先哲与他们曾经创造的历史，爱默生提醒后人不必过分谦逊和膜拜，“人应当学会发现和感受他自身心灵内部瞬息划过的微弱的光芒，这要胜过流连于诗人和先哲天空的光辉。不注意自我的思想——只因这思想是人自己的——会使人自我消解。在每一部伟大的著作中我们都可以辨识出我们自己的忽视掉的思想：它们以一

---

① ［美］哈罗德·布鲁姆：《批评、正典结构与预言》，第 206 页。

② ［美］哈罗德·布鲁姆：《西方正典》，第 21 页。

③ Harold Bloom, *Genius: A Mosaic of One Hundred Exemplary Creative Minds*, New York: Warner Books, 2002, p. 359.

④ Harold Bloom, *Genius: A Mosaic of One Hundred Exemplary Creative Minds*, p. 180.

种带有陌生感的尊严重新回归到我们这里。”[①]布鲁姆认为爱默生最重要的天才即在于，他认为我们在文学中感受到的光辉本就是我们自身的，阅读就是找回本来就属于自己的东西。

惠特曼是布鲁姆文学经典序列中所确认的美国诗歌源头，是他极为推崇的“美国风土的诗人”（“the poem of our climate”），布鲁姆盛赞他成功而永久地改变了美国的声音和形象，改变了美国人的自我和美国宗教。而布鲁姆对于惠特曼诗歌的赞赏很大程度上也在于惠特曼对“自我”的歌唱，他将惠特曼理解为一个真正的忠实于自我的浪漫主义诗人，反对从社会政治层面理解惠特曼，认为“对惠特曼的解读必须要超越于‘民主诗人’，虽然惠特曼坚称这是他自己的身份，但他实际上是一个与外界隔绝的、犹疑的和个人化的诗人，远比他自己公开标明的情形要复杂”。[②]他借用斯蒂文斯的看法，认为惠特曼“不是神灵，但他与日出日落共进退，吟唱着分裂的自我和那不可知的灵魂，点燃了比自然之火还明亮的火焰”[③]。这里他将经典的陌生性、审美性和个人自我的主体性统一了起来。

四、终极性：“使人善用自己的孤独”

在布鲁姆看来，好的文学必然包含着对于终极问题的探求，这些是无法用政治立场来衡量的；而文学研究的最终目的就是探寻能够超越一时之社会需求及特定成见的某种价值观，这是文学及批评得以存在的根本，经典的特质与意义就在于此：“西方经典的全部意义在于使人善用自己的孤独，这一孤独的最终形式是一个人和自己死亡的相遇。”[④]

强调文学经典的终极关怀与布鲁姆的宗教研究密切相关。他一直表示自己是古代和现代诺斯替主义（Gnosticism）的虔诚信徒，他还曾经深入地研究过美国的“摩门教”。这深刻地影响了他的经典理论。在布鲁姆看来，“经典是具有宗教起源的词汇”[⑤]，因此，他用来界定“经典”的“canon”一词不同于“classic”，在后者的等级感之外是带有浓厚宗教意味的。美国学者曾评论布鲁姆的经典阅读理论：“这种指导就是一度归于宗教的职责范围的，从根本上来讲布鲁姆是在世俗的写作中寻找宗教体验：‘因为我本人偏好在莎士比亚或爱默生和弗洛伊德的文本中寻找上帝的声音，根据我的需要，我对但丁戏剧的神性可以毫不费力地注意到’”。[⑥]

布鲁姆认为，没有经典，我们会停止思考，经典赋予了我们认知的能力，它们往往渗透着一种面对孤独、死亡的自我拷问和强烈的内省意识。他比较认同安格斯·弗莱彻在论崇高时对雪莱的新阐释：“崇高会让我们放弃轻松愉快而去追求更难得和痛苦的快乐。”[⑦]在布鲁姆看来，写作是一种让灵魂战栗或安宁的力量。布鲁姆批评畅销书作者斯蒂芬·金的一个

---

① Harold Bloom, *Genius: A Mosaic of One Hundred Exemplary Creative Minds*, p. 180.

② Ibid., p. 303.

③ [美]哈罗德·布鲁姆：《西方正典》，第215页。

④ 同上，第21页。

⑤ 同上，第14页。

⑥ Paul, Gray. *Hurrah for dead white males*!, New York: Time, Oct 10, 1994, Vol. 144, Iss. 15, p. 62.

⑦ [美]哈罗德·布鲁姆：《西方正典》，第230页。

重要理由即认为他完全不懂得人生的认识论终极价值，只是迎合大众部分浅薄的需要。他引用过蒙田作品中的这样一个句子："不过，你不会因病而死，你因活着而死。死亡无需借助疾病即可利索地杀掉你，疾病却拖延了某些人的死亡，这些人因为老想着自己迈向死亡而活得更久些。"[①]"因活着而死"勾勒出一种浑浑噩噩的生命状态。在布鲁姆看来，蒙田在不断地指点着人们寻找和拷问着自我。

布鲁姆在《西方正典》一书中多次提及对"死亡"的表现，譬如认为布朗宁和狄更斯"共同的幻想方式里有一种死亡的梦魇在主宰着"[②]，"（托尔斯泰）与其说是为对垂死或死亡的一般恐惧所动，不如说是为自己异常的活力和活力主义所动，因而不愿苟同任何消亡无存的感受"[③]，死亡也是《等待戈多》里明显的沉重主题，贝克特对死亡的认知在于认为爱会很快消逝。

布鲁姆集中探讨了托尔斯泰笔下哈吉·穆拉特的死亡所呈现的美学尊严，认为这是托尔斯泰最杰出的虚构。在战斗中被子弹击中，死亡阴影袭来的时刻，哈吉的脑海中迅速掠过一连串战友、敌人、亲人的片断，不过此时他昏昏沉沉地已不再感到怜悯、愤怒抑或任何欲望了，他聚起全身力气开了最后一枪，随后沉重地爬出壕沟，手执匕首步履蹒跚地径直走向敌人，随着几声枪响，他又一次倒下了，几个民兵随即高呼胜利地奔过来。托尔斯泰以这样一种表述展现给我们他对于死亡的理解——即便肉体行将终结却依旧保持着顽强的意志力，这就是英雄主义的死亡美学。从终极与死亡的角度，布鲁姆又一次回到对强大自我主体的呼唤。

描绘了时代的阴郁、病态和迷惘感受的贝克特的《终局》则被布鲁姆认为反映了一种无法摆脱的焦虑感："当你等待戈多时，你就处在渺渺之中；《终局》的前景就是《等待戈多》，我们回到渺渺之中，一场干涸的大洪水，空旷浩渺的虚空。"[④]在戏剧人物汉姆和克罗夫的对话中，"昨天"被描绘为很久以前的糟糕透顶的一天，今天则依旧是一个倒霉日子，碌碌庸众眼中的世界是广阔田地间茁壮生长的玉米和成群结队捕鱼的帆船，似乎"一切都那么可爱"，然而被所有人认为是疯子的艺术家却在这世界的欣欣向荣面前感到惊惶失措，在他眼中末日已经来临、"一切都是灰烬"，于是他独身一人蜷缩在自己的角落中。布鲁姆认为"疯子"指的是威廉·布莱克，他通过自然看到了诺斯替创造即堕落的预言，因而在他眼中一切都是灰烬，世间繁华忙碌的表象不过是一场虚幻，人则始终无法摆脱危机的状态。[⑤] 这种孤独的焦虑与前面所谈到的无法被打败的强大个体精神共同构成了布鲁姆眼中个体生命的辩证法。

在布鲁姆那里，文学经典的诸种美学特征密切结合、协调统一为一个整体，这也就是他所坚守的"审美自主性"。但是，文学经典只是从这样的立场和角度去认识，是不是会丢失掉太多丰富而有价值的东西？正如文化研究者从批判的意义上所归纳的那样，经典被认为"代表了人文学科及其批评的特定的文化的衡量标准"，它们构成了"文化材料宝库"，"代表了文

① [美]哈罗德·布鲁姆：《西方正典》，第117页。

② 同上，第248页。

③ 同上，第259页。

④ 同上，第404页。

⑤ 同上，第405页。

化的本质”，也就是说，经典“正是建立在对于什么是学生们应当了解的和熟悉的知识中最为重要和最有价值的假设上”，那么这一套标准和规则里面必然存在着大量的等级制的经济基础、话语权力以及意识形态力量等复杂的问题。[①] 从布鲁姆对“憎恨学派”的批评中可以看出，他是清楚这一点的，但是他认为那不重要，因为他的理论有自己的时代问题，他并不是无的放矢，而是有着非常深刻的现实背景或者他所不喜欢讨论的意识形态指向，他要以一种“对抗性批评”挑战的是“回避或者压抑审美在所谓的高等教育机构中是普遍风气”[②]的时代，是“文化研究”席卷一切的时代，是美国个人主义审美传统逐渐丧失的时代。因此，他这里“美学立场本身就是一种意识形态”。我们当然可以对布鲁姆关于经典的美学特征和标准的看法有很多的批评，诸如他呈现出来的精英主义倾向、西方中心主义倾向、审美乌托邦、以及各种具体见解的牵强，等等。但是，任何理论都只有放在其所身处的时代语境才能彰显其独特价值，面对西方价值平面化的“后学”时代和“文化研究”的势不可挡，布鲁姆以矫枉过正的理论态势守护着审美文化传统，他是在通过寻找文学传统，匡正文化生态，难能可贵，这不仅仅是一个文学问题，而是在通过文学经典的阐释，建构美国的时代文化精神[③]。其实，不是谈论政治的学术研究就一定是关心社会的，谈论审美问题的就一定是脱离社会的，在一个泛政治化的时代，布鲁姆用他的方式“介入”到一个时代的文化价值建构和对民族历史文化传统根基的再阐释再创造。在中国当代文化价值建构中，我们有怎么样的民族文化根基，我们如何确定经典、激活传统，这又是怎样的历史谱系呢，应该怎样去阅读这些经典并发挥经典的当代文化价值建构功能呢？我想，这是值得深入思考的。

作者简介：金永兵，文学博士，北京大学中文系副教授。

① 参见亨利·吉罗等：《文化研究的必要性：抵抗的知识分子和对立的公共领域》，罗钢、刘象愚主编《文化研究读本》，中国社会科学出版社，2000年，第83—84页。

② 同上，第16页。

③ 参见金永兵、陈曦：《文学经典的阐释与美国精神的建构——哈罗德·布鲁姆“文学经典”理论解析》，《北京大学学报》2011年第4期。

叠印:斯特林堡式场面调度(从戏剧到电影)

孙　柏

【内容提要】 在“后地狱时期”的梦幻剧创作中,特别以《鬼魂奏鸣曲》为范例,斯特林堡创造性地使用了一种可借自电影术语来命名的场面调度手法,即叠印。它实际上是现代性的危机在再现领域中的一个反映。随着全球化也是全球分裂进程的展开,世界的完整连续性被打破,时空的结构也失去了它在经典现实主义时期的那种整一性。斯特林堡的形式革命在于他将消失在中心透视之外的外部世界叠加在舞台再现的时空之上,从而创造了一种幽灵化的观看,使过去和现在同时进行、幻想与现实一并展开。从世界—历史的角度来看,斯特林堡所提供的现实及其重影,源自于西方现代文明自身的幻灭,即根源于它所创造的辉煌的现在正不断地被它充满剥削、掠夺的不光彩的过去所袭扰。那幽灵不只是不断地回返,他始终就在那里,在谋杀者身边,在同一块舞台上面。
【关键词】 叠印　场面调度　《鬼魂奏鸣曲》　幽灵化的观看　现代性危机

Lap-dissolve: Strindbergian Mise-en-scène (from Theater to Film)

【Abstract】 In the “dream plays” written in his post-Inferno era, especially in *The Ghost Sonata*, Strindberg created a kind of mise-en-scène which could be named as “lap-dissolve” as borrowed from film terminology. Eventually it is a reflection on the crisis of modernity in the theatrical representation. With the proceedings of the globalization as well as the global rift, the temporal and spacial continuum of the world has been broken. In his formal creation, Strindberg made the outer world excluded from the perspective picture of Weltanschauung over-lapped on the scenic representation on stage, producing a spectro-scopic effect, in which the past and the present, the illusionary and the real, go side by side in the one and same vision. The reality and its double, as Strindberg drew on his imaginary canvas, resulted in the World-History collapse occurred in the imperialist period. For the westerns, the splendid present was enduring the unbearable disturbance made by its own past full of blood and dirties. The spectre, the murdered, not only came back again and again in order to declaim, but was still there on the same stage, just beside the murderer, as he never left.
【Keywords】 Lap-dissolve　Mise-en-scéne　*The Ghost Sonata*　Spectro-scopic　Crisis of Modernity

一

在应对现代性的危机的过程中,易卜生创造了一个形式主题:“幽灵式的回返”,即总是有一个来自过去的被放逐者,背负着家族或地方性社会的隐秘历史,突如其来地闯入舞台呈现的现实空间，宣示本应属于他、却被剥夺了的权利，作为一个再度归来的幽灵重新占领这个地方也即再现的空间。“Gengangere”的原意就是“不断回返者”，不过这一形式主题并非始于《群鬼》，而是从《社会支柱》就已确立的：约翰·汤尼森出人意料地突然归来，不仅带回了博尼克不光彩的发迹史和丑闻，而且喻示着老欧洲的沉沦和新大陆的兴替在整个现代殖民主义史上的复杂纠葛。

相比较于易卜生，斯特林堡似乎并没有更多地专注于舞台上下的分别，并没有通过这种(精神分析学所说的)“屏忆(screen memory)”的调度来唤起被压抑者的回返。他所采取的形式策略要更为激进：他将外部世界直接叠加在舞台的再现空间之上，使过去的幻影融入到剧情展开的现在进行时中去，让消逝的画面与现实的场景交迭在一起，并产生一种剧场性的或演述性的互动。——总之，这里最好借用一个电影术语来予以概括，斯特林堡创造的是戏剧舞台上的叠印。

作为一个电影术语，“叠印(lap-dissolve)”指的是两个画面相融重叠在一起，经常是在淡入淡出、渐隐渐显中用于表示场景转换中的时间流逝，或为引入闪回而促成从现实到回忆的过渡；在被用做一种影像特技时，它最显著的效果就是视像的重叠，仿佛现实世界被鬼魂所缠绕。叠印是最早体现电影化精神的技法之一，它的技术起点一般可以追溯到乔治·梅里爱偶然发现的停机再拍。然而，如果说，梅里爱只是出于机缘巧合而发现了停机再拍的幽灵效果，那么，斯特林堡则是在视觉的形而上学的意义上“发明”了叠印这一电影化技巧的。就是说，他以一种真正的电影精神创造了对于世界的全新的观看(Weltanschauung)，这种观看是在后来属于电影的世纪中愈形明显起来的。世界的破碎、时空的断裂使得再现的整一性失去了内在逻辑和自身依据；对于戏剧来说，特别是对于直到十九世纪中叶才发展成形的现实主义客体剧，既失去了与舞台之下的外部世界的连续性，又失去了自身得以确立的稳固性，它的存在本身逐渐成为戏剧再现必须要解决的难题，就象是一块浮冰一样漫散地漂移在人类之孤寂的海面上。易卜生之伟大是在于他第一个揭示了舞台上下、内部外部之世界的深刻断裂；而斯特林堡之伟大则在于他用一种时空的对折来予以解决，当过去和现在同时进行，幻像与现实一并展开，包围着人类生活的那片黑暗就被带到了舞台脚灯前面。这就是叠印最终可能达成的效果，它并没有拓展人们的视野以穿越舞台再现的界线，但它至少还保有这块舞台本身，至少还维系了这种再现的时空存在感，尽管那种总是表现为不可知之命运的黑暗仍然紧紧地包围着。

诚然，斯特林堡在个别作品中，也曾使用过易卜生式的场面调度手法，最典型的一例出现在1901年的《复活节》①中。从舞台置景的技术角度来说，海斯特一家的窗子也就是博尼克家能够望见花园的那扇窗子。人物可以通过它来观望外面的世界，却没有勇气也没有能力去真正越过那条界线走出去，他们宁愿蜷居在这个闭锁的家居内室的空间里，将自己囚困在各自以及整个家庭不名誉的过去。《复活节》里最重要的戏剧动作就是林德奎斯特的登门造访。斯特林堡以极其娴熟的舞台技巧来推延他这一戏剧动作的完成：因为他作为这户人家的债权人，随时可以要求支配这房间里的一切所有，而海斯特一家似乎也一直在等待这一

① August Strindberg: *Easter and Other Plays*, translated by E. Classen, Frome: Butler & Tanner Ltd, 1929.

时刻的最终到来;他的身影一次比一次巨大地投映在拉上帘子的门窗上,仿佛马上就要破门而入。这个悬念直到剧终时才以一种喜剧的方式得到圆满解决,林德奎斯特放弃了他的债权,但要求男主人公埃利斯直面他自己良心上的亏欠。

综观当时欧洲的戏剧舞台,通过视窗的分隔来表现现实与幻境的交织,绝非罕见。例如在《铃声》(列奥波德·刘易斯编剧、亨利·欧文主演)[①]这部已成为现代演剧史上一段传奇的经典之作中,已贵为阿尔萨斯市长的马蒂阿斯总是在铃声的幻听里,不断看到自己当年为财起意、谋杀波兰犹太商人的画面;终日受这梦魇困扰的马蒂阿斯,最后不堪内心的折磨,在供述了曾犯下的罪行之后,心脏病发作而死。不过,严格说来,这部通俗剧中制造幻像的并不是舞台后部的窗子,因为窗户仍需用来维系内景空间和外部世界的连续性(所有登场人物都会先走过窗外短暂露面),演出使用的舞台技法是使绘有旅馆内墙的纱幕升起或变得透明,看上去就象是那堵墙壁溶解掉了一样,于是便显现出后面的幻觉场景来。更为重要的是,这部剧中的现实与幻境仍然是相互区分开来的,两者并未真正混合在一起;即便在第三幕的高潮段落,梦游般的马蒂阿斯也是从一个暗室进入到另一个表演区,仿佛回到几十年前的案发现场,来到一个他幻想中的法庭接受审判。说到底,负罪的过去对现时的侵扰尽管得到了表现,但仍然不能逾越时空划分的界线。

二

经历了"地狱"时期之后的斯特林堡,在如《通往大马士革之路》三部曲这样的重要剧作中,已经创造和使用了叠印的手法。[②] 但最淋漓尽致地发挥了这种场面调度效果的,仍然是1907年问世的《鬼魂奏鸣曲》,这种剧场效果的重点是,现实主义表演的外部特征在最初的观演契约中完全抹除了活人和死人、现在与过去之间的区别。这一现实的魅影最终指向的,是世界—历史构造的无法匡正的脱节。[③]

《鬼魂奏鸣曲》使幽灵与活着的人站在同一块舞台上,那个送牛奶的姑娘已死去多年,现在她借助大学生的灵媒式的中介回来,向老人(何梅尔经理)索还命债。——不过在这明显的叠印手法之外,斯特林堡为整部剧作设定的观看结构要更为复杂。实际上,这部"室内剧"并非从室内开始,它所划分的三个场次可以被看做是同一戏剧动作的分解和演进,它们有层次、有节奏地展开,最后推向一个绝境般的死地,即那个被壁纸所掩饰、用屏风来遮挡的密室,在那里,所有人物都将沦为"壁橱里的枯骨"。老人试图闯入他想要侵占的房子,用他的仆人约翰松的话说,就是:"他想占有一切……他看到房子,就推倒它们,开辟街道,建筑广

① 见 David Mayer 编:*Henry Irving and* The Bells:*Irving's Personal Script of the Play*,London:Butler & Tanner Ltd,1980. 另可参考 David Mayer:"*The Bells*: a Case Study—A 'Bare-ribbed Skeleton in a Chest'",收入 Joseph Donohue 编:*The Cambridge History of British Theatre*,*Volume 2:1660 to 1895*,第 401 页,Cambridge University Press,2004.

② 如第二部第三幕第一场的"宴会厅"场景,或第三部第一幕陌生人与女儿的会面。见 August Strindberg:*The Road to Damascus*:*A Trilogy*,English version by Graham Rawson,London:Jonathan Cape Ltd,1939.

③ "The time is out of joint. O cursed spite, / That ever I was born to set it right."Shakespeare:*Hamlet*,Act I,Scene V,第 215—216 行。

场；但是也闯入民宅，从窗子爬进去，左右人的命运，打死自己的敌人，从不饶恕。”[①]老人的这一阴险企图为全剧的戏剧动作提供了初动力。如果对照《复活节》标准的现实主义客体剧的结构来看，《鬼魂奏鸣曲》是预设了那个闯入者（林德奎斯特/老人[②]）的视点来进行统摄性的观看的，让他站在即将被摧毁的房子外面进行谋划并做出评估。因此，剧中的第一个场景就已经是将传统剧场的成规惯例中舞台下面的空间调度到了舞台上面，就此而言，老人在看到他的未婚妻关窗子时所说的话就格外耐人寻味：“……在反光镜里她看不见自己，只是外部世界，但是世界可以看见她。”[③]——长久地待在一所腐朽的房子里面，人们除了相互折磨就无事可做（毫无疑问这正是斯特林堡在他的婚姻生活中所经受的地狱般的折磨），其结果就是导致人的木乃伊化。主观视界与外部世界完全断绝了联系，除了将这个封闭的空间彻底夷平之外、除了通过这种荡涤一切的毁灭将那条划定了内外之分的界线彻底抹除之外，实际上不存在任何救赎的可能。老人也是自陷于此，而成为另一具木乃伊的。

因此，叠印首先意味着一种幽灵式的观看（spectro-scopic，这个词曾经在《父亲》里出现过，当时上尉在向医生解释自己用“分光镜”对陨石进行光谱分析；詹姆斯·麦克法兰正确地指出“spectrum”的原意为“幽灵或魅影或鬼魂”，所以他建议《鬼魂奏鸣曲》应译为 *The Spectral Sonata*，《幽灵奏鸣曲》[④]，也就是双重视点的设定，以制造某种分光镜效果的视像。尽管老人阴谋的目光笼罩着整个场景，但是送牛奶的姑娘却是由大学生的视点引入的，只有这个礼拜天出生的孩子可以看到她，看到她的幻影。然而，关键并不在于大学生所具有的灵异功能，如何成就了一个鬼影幢幢的舞台，而是在于这来自于他的主观视界；或者说，只有对于大学生而言，主观视界与外部世界之间的连续性依然得以保存，尽管那个被放逐者、被排除者不是从他或她（送牛奶的姑娘或者出现在即将倒塌的建筑物墙角的孩子）的悲惨的过去回来的，而是作为一种并置的现实获得舞台的显影。再现的逻辑和规则本身由此被打破了：世界可以看见某些人，也可以对某些人视而不见；但幽灵式的观看却制造了现实的重影，把戏剧舞台铺演为一张错版的因而有着更宽光谱的世界地图。

空间的套层构成了这部剧中最后一层意义上的叠印手法。出于并不仅仅只是自私的目的，老人想方设法要让大学生参加在上校的圆形客厅举行的鬼魂宴，从而真正进入到那个内部空间。老人这一角色的复杂性堪比易卜生的约翰·盖勃吕尔·博克曼，甚至是歌德的浮士德（他一心要铲除这所长满毒草的房子、以便为年轻人开辟新的生活）。因为在他的积极的、肯定性的方面，他仍然代表着资产阶级的进取心和开拓精神，这是他自信地以为“世界在握”的根本原因，斯特林堡的诗作《林荫大道》完全可以被读做是对何梅尔经理的宏伟规划的

---

① 斯特林堡：《鬼魂奏鸣曲》，收入李之义编、译：《斯特林堡文集》第5卷，第87页，北京：人民文学出版社，2005年。

② “老人”和上校之间的关系不也就正是林德奎斯特和海斯特一家的关系吗？甚至他们可能带给他们拟想中的猎物的致命威胁都如出一辙：“因为这里能看到的东西都属于我——家具、窗帘、餐具、柜橱……一切东西！能看到的一切东西都属于我，都是我的！”——见斯特林堡：《鬼魂奏鸣曲》，收入李之义编、译：《斯特林堡文集》第5卷，第98页。

③ 斯特林堡：《鬼魂奏鸣曲》，收入李之义编、译：《斯特林堡文集》第5卷，第85页。

④ 斯特林堡：《父亲》，收入李之义编、译：《斯特林堡文集》第3卷，第170页。James McFarlane：“Strindberg's Vision：Microscopic or Spectroscopic?”，收入 Göran Stockenström 编：*Strindberg's Dramaturgy*，第140页，Minneapolis：University of Minnesota Press，1988.

充分肯定:“拆掉这里的旧房子,获得更多的空气和阳光;/这个理由还不正当?”[①]然而就象他的双重身份显示的那样,他所背负的肮脏的过去、血污斑斑的发迹史,仍然化身做复仇女神追逐着他。在戏剧文本中,老人的形象凝结的双重时间性直接通过台词和动作表达出来,现代性规划的钟摆被木乃伊制止,这并不代表任何的善胜恶败,而只表明何梅尔经理不过也是另一具木乃伊而已;鬼魂宴以老人走进柜橱而告终,它显示出,整个由现代性规划所造就的世界本身就是一个僵局。圆形客体、糊了墙纸的柜橱以至最后一幕的风信子花房,都可视为同一的封闭空间,包括作为一个再现之视界/世界的剧场、舞台也是如此——叠印只是这种僵局、绝境和死地的叠加:“睡吧,不要做梦,当你醒来的时候,一个不燃烧的太阳会迎接你,在没有灰尘的房间里迎接你……”[②]在这一幕里,斯特林堡又一次呼应了易卜生的主题:温室或花房,在其中生养、成长的孩子总是因为隔绝于外部世界的现实,而孱弱不堪、难经风雨,最终总不免夭折或被毁灭;“玩偶之家”实际上正是这一空间意象最著名的一个变奏,因为它本来就是指给孩子玩的迷你家居,除此之外,如《群鬼》中的温室或《野鸭》里的阁楼,都起到同样的象征作用。[③]《鬼魂奏鸣曲》里的小姐(上校的、其实是老人的女儿)也是这群资产者之子中的一员,某种先天不足导致她不可能真正成长,是父辈的罪孽窒息了她、使她最终夭折,但是屏风的遮挡使她永远成为这座坟墓一样的房间中的一件家什、这块舞台上的一件道具,和她的母亲一样,成为木乃伊、成为雕像。《鬼魂奏鸣曲》是以一种全然电影化的方式结束的,落幕时刻已成为斯特林堡戏剧最具标志性的画面,它同样是一次叠印、一次淡入/淡出:“房子消失;勃克林的画《死亡之岛》变成了后幕。”[④]

三

叠印既是一种场面调度手法,又提示着对这个世界的一种幽灵式的观看。较之于戏剧舞台,电影作为二十世纪的艺术似乎更为突出地继承了斯特林堡赠与后人的这份遗产。

如前所述,电影中的叠印的技术起点一般可以追溯到乔治·梅里爱偶然发现的停机再拍。梅里爱在1897年拍摄于巴黎歌剧院广场的一段影片里,因为机器一时卡壳,稍隔了一段时间才又正常运转起来,于是画面上一辆行驶中的公共马车忽然变成了运灵柩的马车。[⑤]类似的特技摄影和魔术照相很快发展成为叠印、合成照相、二次或多次暴光等技巧,并被广泛地应用于电影拍摄一直到今天。(附带说一句,深深迷恋于摄影艺术的斯特林堡也留有一祯题为《三度暴光》的照片,那同样是一种从影像直观上即可辨认出来的叠印。[⑥])电影史上最

---

① 斯特林堡:《林荫大道》,收入李之义编、译:《斯特林堡文集》第5卷,第179—181页。

② 斯特林堡:《鬼魂奏鸣曲》,收入李之义编、译:《斯特林堡文集》第5卷,第116页。

③ 参考 Asbjørn Aarseth:“The Glass Cabinet—a Key Concept for the Approach to Ibsen's Modern Prose Plays”,收入 *North-West Passage:Yearly Review of the Centre for Northern Performing Arts Studies*,第27—40页,University of Turin,2004.

④ 斯特林堡:《鬼魂奏鸣曲》,收入李之义编、译:《斯特林堡文集》第5卷,第117页。

⑤ 乔治·萨杜尔:《世界电影史》,徐昭、胡承伟译,北京:中国电影出版社,1995年,第24页,。

⑥ August Strindberg:“Triple Exposure”(1907—1908),收入 *Strindberg:Painter and Photographer*,第92页,New Haven and London:Yale University Press,2004.

充分运用这一影像魔术的影片即出自瑞典,维克多·斯约斯特罗姆根据塞尔玛·拉格洛芙小说改编的《幽灵马车》[1]讲述的是一个浪子回头的故事:男主人公大卫·霍尔姆直等到死后变成鬼魂,才感悟到救世军女孩对他改过自新、良知复萌的深切期盼,于是回到被他离弃、陷入绝境的妻儿身边。这部影片自始至终大量使用叠印,特别是幽灵马车出现将要带走死者灵魂的场面,极为震撼。只有当那个浪子重新皈依上帝、被特赦回到人间,现实世界与属灵的世界才被再度区分开来,死亡的阴影才停止对阳光下人们美好生活的缠绵。

放在1920年代欧洲电影的整体环境中,斯约斯特罗姆的这部《幽灵马车》并不会显得特立独行,因为在默片时代的哥特式电影、特别是早期的恐怖片当中,叠印都得到了极为广泛地应用,其原因自然是它所具有的那种幽灵化的观视效果(最具代表性的影片可举茂瑙的《诺斯费拉图》和德莱叶的《吸血鬼》为例)。

不过,真正将斯特林堡式的场面调度直接用到电影里的,还要等到阿尔夫·斯约堡执导的《朱莉小姐》[2],这不仅是一部斯特林堡戏剧改编作品,而且是一部体现了斯特林堡艺术风格与精神的影片。导演理解了斯特林堡后期戏剧的电影特征,并用它来重新演绎了斯特林堡的早期作品。其中有两个重要的回忆段落,导演都避免使用淡入/淡出溶入闪回的传统手法,而直接采用斯特林堡式的场面调度,因为淡入/淡出根本上说还是属于剪辑(往往通过后期的洗印工序来实现),而更理想的方式则是用同一个镜头将过去和现在、回忆和现实括入在一起。例如,有一场重头戏是朱莉小姐向男仆让讲述她悲戚的童年生活,当说到父亲发现母亲的阴谋的时候,镜头横移括入站在母亲画像前深感痛苦的父亲;镜头剪切,回到朱莉小姐的童年,她亲眼目睹父亲就是在母亲的画像前自杀未遂的;接着是这个被吓坏了的小女孩的特写画面,然后一身黑色外出服装的母亲入画,抱起了年幼的朱莉;当画面再次回到现在时,当年的母女竟从沉思着的朱莉小姐身后走过,不仅如此,她们还经过听得入神的让的身边。类似的段落分析我们还可以进一步展开,但重点已很清晰:尽管《朱莉小姐》是斯特林堡早期的自然主义剧作,但是斯约堡却运用他后期剧作的剧场性重新诠释了这部作品,他不仅突出了银幕影像缠绕在现实与梦幻之间的媒介特征,而且将叠印从剪辑的技术单元回复到场面调度的艺术运思——也就是说,他一方面用电影重新创作了斯特林堡的剧作,另一方面是用斯特林堡重新创造了电影本身。

斯约堡对斯特林堡精神的深刻领会,恰如彼得·沃特金用电影对蒙克绘画进行的再创造。论及斯特林堡与视觉艺术之间的关系,有一个他的同时代人无法绕过的人,这就是爱德华·蒙克。两位北欧艺术巨匠在柏林和巴黎的交往可称过从甚密,更重要的是两人还分享着诸多创作主题,如摩西、吸血鬼、嫉妒,等等。蒙克成长经历中的一个巨大伤痛,来自他妹妹索菲的早夭,后来这成为在他画布上反复呈现的场景。蒙克于1893年创作了《病室中的死神》,死神居于作品的中心却是看不见的,家人包括蒙克自己除了默默祈祷再没有任何办法,只能眼睁睁地看着死神将索菲带走。重要的是这幅画描绘的是十六年前(索菲1877年死于肺结核)的家中惨事,而蒙克所画的家人——凯伦姑妈、父亲、兄弟姐妹安德烈斯、英格

---

① *Körkalen*, Victor Sjöström 编剧、导演并担任主演,瑞典1921年出品。

② *Fröken Julie*, Alf Sjöberg 导演, Anita Björk, Ulm Palme 主演,瑞典1951年出品。

和劳拉——却都处在1893年时的年纪和容貌,因为索菲之死直到此时仍在发生着,不仅是在蒙克的心里,而且是在命运与共的整个家庭生活中(蒙克本人以及他的兄弟都曾患有肺结核病)。[①] 当彼得·沃特金拍摄他著名的传记片[②]时,蒙克生活与创作之间的这层关系也成为影片的主要线索,并且他使用蒙太奇将蒙克的叠印手法转现到银幕之上。影片中反复出现这样的段落,现时中蒙克做画的情景、他年少轻狂时热烈追求图拉·拉尔森的画面、索菲之死的撕心裂肺的悲惨记忆以及他为摆脱孤独而欢场买醉的场景,以很简短的镜头快速地交替剪接在一起。

当然,不必赘言,无论在剧场还是在银幕上,斯特林堡遗产的最重要的继承人无疑是英格玛·伯格曼。他在封镜之后拍摄的电视电影《排演之后》[③]对他剧场生涯的一个片断进行了不无自省的重现。剧情中声名卓著的舞台剧导演亨利克·沃格勒正为排演斯特林堡《一出梦的戏剧》而焦虑不安,但就在此时,他与母女两代御用演员在舞台上下的情感纠葛却又面临着更大的危机。因年老、酗酒已遭弃用的母亲拉克尔回来向亨利克要求重新登台的机会,也是在要重新得到他的爱;而女儿安娜则倾述着自己因来自母亲、来自亨利克、来自舞台生活的情感讹诈混淆了现实与虚构、真情与谎言的痛苦。影片中,在母亲登场之后,现在与过去的接线开始模糊起来,当亨利克和拉克尔的对话似乎回到二十年前,镜头摇过,原来坐在一旁沙发椅上的安娜已变回了从前的那个小女孩。在母亲离开之后,这一场面调度手法再次重复,亨利克回到女孩安娜身边、吻她的额头,继而在沙发的另一边坐下;特写镜头中,他握住了她的手,随之镜头上移,又重现为成年的女演员安娜。与斯约堡的《朱莉小姐》一样,伯格曼这里采用的技巧明显在于景框的设定,可以认为,景框内外的划分其实就等同于舞台上下边界的限定;镜头移动将过去与现在括入同一影像界面,这一动作可以被看做是对斯特林堡时空对折的叠印手法的重复和再创造。

在伯格曼的后辈中,欧洲艺术电影的新一代大师也频频在各自的作品中用到这种舞台剧化的叠印手法。例如塔尔科夫斯基在他自传性的影片《镜子》的结尾处,使剧情世界中的母亲与导演自己的母亲出现在同一影像段落中(几年后他在瑞典拍摄的最后一部作品《牺牲》不仅使用伯格曼的御用演员和摄影师,而且影片本身就是对斯特林堡式室内剧传统的一次再传承)。而在安哲罗普洛斯的杰作《尤利西斯的凝视》中,主人公是一位东欧裔的美国导演,他回到已然面目全非、实际不复存在的"祖国"寻找一截历史胶片、一段光影记忆(值得注意的是,这部影片中,同样有伯格曼的御用演员厄兰·约瑟夫森的出镜,他扮演的恰好是一位电影博物馆馆长)。在他的探询中,巴尔干半岛的苦难历史与支离破碎的现实相互交织,影像的光尘和血脉根源的记忆交迭在一起,特别是一个很长的镜头段落中,历史象是一场家庭舞会一样在他的回忆中展开,时间跨越了战后的数十年,而固定机位拍摄的影像既没有移动也没有剪切,只有字幕提示着逝水流年。

---

① 参考 Arnold L. Weinstein:*Northern Arts:the Breakthrough of Scandinavian Literature and Art, from Ibsen to Bergman*,第317—322页,Princeton University Press,2008.

② *Edvard Munch*,Peter Watkins 编、导,Geir Westby 主演,挪威、瑞典1974年出品。

③ *Efter Repetitionen*,Ingmar Bergman 编、导,Erland Josephson, Ingrid Thulin, Lena Olin 主演,瑞典1984年出品。

不必更多地举例，我们已经看到，斯特林堡所创造的这样一种场面调度，以及由这一舞台表现手法所构成的对于再现结构及其可能性的探询，是怎样深入地渗透在了 20 世纪的电影艺术中。叠印动摇了稳定的现实存在感，它提供了一种审视世界的全新的视点，一种幽灵化的观看，使我们有能力（无论通过戏剧还是电影）去扣问现代性危机的历史根源。从世界—历史的角度来看，斯特林堡式场面调度所提供的现实及其重影，源自于西方现代文明自身的幻灭，即根源于它所创造的辉煌的现在正不断地被它充满剥削、掠夺的不光彩的过去所袭扰。那幽灵不只是不断地回返，他始终就在那里，在谋杀者身边，在同一块舞台上面。

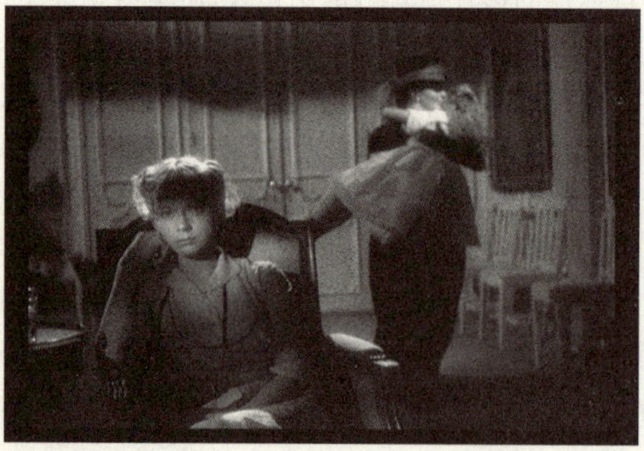

作者简介：孙柏，北京大学文学博士，人民大学文学院副教授。

新世纪的几部西方文学史研究述评

韩加明

由李赋宁先生任总主编的新编《欧洲文学史》是全国哲学社会科学八五规划重点项目，从20世纪90年代初开始启动，到2001年第三卷出齐，历时十多年。“编者说明”指出：“我们孜孜以求的目标，是写出一部能比较全面、客观、科学地反映欧洲文明诞生以来文学嬗变的全过程，又有强烈时代感的新的《欧洲文学史》。为此，我们在坚持以历史唯物论为指导，以坚实丰富的材料为基础的同时，努力把握国内外关于欧洲文学研究的最新进展和成果，吸收新的材料和观点，在实事求是、尊重历史的原则下，融会贯通地运用当代的一些文学理论和文学研究方法。”（第1—2页）原版《欧洲文学史》叙述到20世纪初为止，新编《欧洲文学史》增加第三卷介绍20世纪欧洲文学。虽然前两卷与原版《欧洲文学史》的时间划分基本相同，但是篇幅大大增加，原来上卷约22万字，下卷约30万字；新编《欧洲文学史》第一卷就53万字，相当于原版全书；第二卷60多万字；新增的20世纪卷分上下两册，篇幅几乎相当于前两卷。

从目录就可以看出新编《欧洲文学史》内容有较大补充，对欧洲文学发展的介绍更加全面。原版第一章古代文学，包括古希腊和罗马文学，新版分为古希腊文学和古罗马文学两章，各有七节和十节，按照文体文类介绍当时的各类文学。原版第二章中世纪文学只有四节，介绍英雄史诗和骑士文学、城市文学、从中古到文艺复兴的过渡和意大利诗人但丁。新编《欧洲文学史》第三章中世纪文学有九节，分别介绍宗教文学、英雄史诗、骑士文学、城市文学、但丁和意大利诗歌、俄罗斯文学、东欧文学、北欧文学。从这些标题可以看出宗教文学是新增的，因为以前的外国文学研究对宗教文学往往采取简单的否定态度，而现在的态度则比较客观，恰当地评价中世纪宗教文学的贡献。后面新增的三节则对欧洲其他地区中世纪文学有了一定的介绍。从文艺复兴时期开始，各章分节介绍欧洲主要国家的文学，与原版《欧洲文学史》最大的区别是各节标题只提某国文学，不再提作家的名字。这样做的好处是避免人为地把主要作家与其他作家区分开来，而是把重点放到对国别文学的总体介绍和评价上，体现了较强的理论把握。如对18世纪法国文学的介绍，原版只有两页介绍法国当时的社会背景与总体文学状况，紧接着就转入具体作家的介绍。新版则以较大的篇幅介绍法国的启蒙运动发展和“古今之争”，并论述了曾经被完全否定的洛可可艺术的产生和影响（第379—86页）。书中写道：“毫无疑问，洛可可艺术直接参与了现代美学的创立，它以表现人生、满足人的感官、精神需求为特色，为新生的美学提供理论和实践两方面的依据。当人们谴责它使色情在法国文化中泛滥时，也不应该忘记它的历史功绩。”（第388页）在对具体作家的评述中，新版纠正了原版只重视内容，忽视艺术的偏差，对于作家的艺术特点给予更多的关注。如对狄德罗的名著《拉摩的侄儿》新编《欧洲文学史》对其叙事艺术就有这样的评述：“作品从整体上可分为对话段落与叙事段落两条主要脉络,它们各司其职,交错进行:对话段落推动情节发展,叙事段落则起到承上启下的'铰接'作用,从而把对话引向不同的主题。此外,当话题无法深入之时,'我'就会出面进行干预,以评论的形式对文本情境作一小结。"(第 396 页)

比较原版《欧洲文学史》下卷和新编《欧洲文学史》第二卷即 19 世纪卷,最大的区别就是淡化政治或阶级划分,取消消极与积极浪漫主义的区别,重点从文学创作方面客观描述不同作家的贡献。从目录中可以看出,原版刻意强调的宪章运动和巴黎公社等政治事件,以及浪漫主义和批判现实主义等流派划分都取消了,各节标题只表明不同的国别文学。这样的修正是完全必要的。宪章运动和巴黎公社是重要的政治事件,但对于欧洲文学史的影响则是有限的;浪漫主义和批判现实主义在各国文学中的表现各有不同,贴上同样的标签无益。对具体作家的介绍也有很多修正。如在第一章第三节介绍 19 世纪早期英国文学时,与原版主要突出拜伦和雪莱不同,新编《欧洲文学史》对五个主要浪漫主义诗人都有比较全面的介绍和评价,并对现在被西方学界归为浪漫主义文学的彭斯和布莱克的创作进行了实事求是的介绍。在原版《欧洲文学史》被忽视的华兹华斯在新版得到重视,但是编者对于其诗歌的矛盾有清醒的认识:"华兹华斯诗歌中自然与自我两概念并非总能协调一致,他的诗似未能清楚解答一个人如何在忠实于自然的同时也忠实于自我。"(第 62 页)原版《欧洲文学史》对德国浪漫主义运动基本持否定态度,如"早期浪漫主义运动并没有持续多久,但是他们的言论和作品反映了德国资产阶级向封建势力的投降,在德国文艺界起了很大的消极反动作用"(第 36 页);又如"浪漫主义文学除了极少数的例外,几乎都是消极的,为反动的封建制度服务的"(第 40 页)。新编《欧洲文学史》在对 19 世纪早期德国文学史的介绍中摈弃了过去片面强调歌德席勒为代表的古典主义,贬低德国浪漫主义文学的做法,中肯地介绍了德国浪漫主义文学的发展和贡献。书中写道:"与只有歌德和席勒为代表的古典文学相比,德国的浪漫主义则拥有大量的作家……耶拿派从事的主要是浪漫派理论的探讨和确立,涉及的主要是抽象的哲理思考,尤其是施莱格尔兄弟,而诺瓦利斯及蒂克则是实践者。海德堡派的作家则大力从事创作,突出地体现了德国浪漫派在童话、民间故事、神话传说、民歌等领域里的挖掘、整理及传播所作的贡献。"(第 13 页)像第一卷一样,新编《欧洲文学史》第二卷也对以往重视不够的东欧文学和北欧文学给予了较多的关注。

与原版《欧洲文学史》统一规划,统一定稿不同,新编《欧洲文学史》尊重撰稿人的意见,不强求文体的统一。"编者说明"写道:"许多撰稿人是国内有影响的专家,他们的稿子包含多年研究的心得,按预定的字数硬性删节,不免削足适履。为使专家们的特点不致湮没,尤其为使那些启人心智的宏论能够完整地保留下来以飨读者,对字数的限制便在不知不觉之中放宽了。"(第 2 页)这样做虽然出现了不同作家之间在篇幅上不均衡的问题或缺陷,却给了撰稿人自由发挥的空间,使一些重点作家的评介几乎就像学术论文。如果说以原版《欧洲文学史》为参照修订的新编《欧洲文学史》第一、二两卷在有些作家的叙述上表现出某些失衡,新撰写的《欧洲文学史》第三卷则更突出了不同撰稿人的特点。如第三卷上册对现代派诗人 T. S. 艾略特的介绍就长达 17 页,对其重要诗歌作品和文学批评甚至社会批评著作都有精到的分析,对其复杂性给予了充分关注。书中写道:"艾略特试图用基督教来改造已经世俗化的西方社会,徒劳无功,但他对英美工业文明的批判至今读来仍未过时";"他希望确保全世界文化的多样性,因而不以'进步'和'落后'等观念来为不同的文化定性。艾略特的文化观与后殖民批评家的'杂交'和'越界'理论格格不入。他担心彻底的混杂将抹煞各种文化之间的差异性从而导致文化的死亡"。"现代派往往被理解为精英文化的倡导者,其实艾略特要维护的并不仅仅是欧洲古典文学的高情逸兴。他非但不拒绝通俗文化,甚至还写过下流小调。"(第72—74页)这样的介绍和评论使读者对艾略特能有比较鲜活的印象。又比如对意识流小说家普鲁斯特的介绍,既指出"《追忆似水年华》这部长达240余万字的鸿篇巨制,以主人公马塞尔怀念和追忆逝去的青春年华为主线,向我们展现了一幅19世纪末20世纪初法国上层社会的图景",又点明它也是"对心灵'深层矿脉'的开掘,是主人公潜在意识的记录"。既关注"时间是贯穿小说始终的一个主题",也不忘"爱情是这部小说的另一个重要的主题"(第187—9页)。关于小说的结构,则强调"普鲁斯特把这部长篇小说当作一座大教堂来设计,一开始就精心安排了对称的结构,即代表资产阶级的斯万家那边,和代表贵族的盖尔芒特家那边。看似相互独立的部分逐步展开,那么多细部在两翼遥相呼应,那么多石块在开工伊始就砌置整齐,渐渐形成一个有机的整体,到全书最后呈现出一座宏伟教堂的全貌"(第190页)。这对于读者把握普鲁斯特的巨著很有帮助。

从总体来看,在具体写作规范上新编《欧洲文学史》编写体例继承原版,把学术观点揉入叙述中,很少直接引文注释。特别是由于原版的直接引文注释主要为马列经典作家的话,新版对此大多删除,因此新版的直接引文注释很少。但在对现代派作家乔伊斯和艾略特的介绍中,撰稿人发挥自己特长,写出了很有分量的学术论著,其引证之频繁与学术论文无异。这种写法的长短还是值得探讨的。原版侧重欧洲文学史整体叙述,对各国重要作家也特别关注其在欧洲文学整体发展的意义,而新编《欧洲文学史》(特别是新增的20世纪卷)则更像是各国别文学史的汇编,因为到了20世纪,欧洲版图已经大变,总体意义上的欧洲文学已经难见了。新编《欧洲文学史》三卷四册,约200万字,篇幅几乎四倍于原版《欧洲文学史》。这样的好处是容量大为增加,可以对丰富的欧洲文学史内容做比较充分的阐述介绍。但是也自然带来相应的缺陷,那就是篇幅太大,不适宜用作教材。正因为如此,郑克鲁在谈到此书时说"有必要再组织一批教师和专家重新编写一个《欧洲(美)文学史》,供外语系使用"。[①] 但我们也可以从另一方面来看待这个问题。不论是在原版《欧洲文学史》上卷出版的1964年,还是在上卷修订再版下卷首版的1979年,《欧洲文学史》都具有教科书、研究性著作和普及性读物的三重功能,因为那时它是唯一的。对于大学生它是指定教科书,对于研究者它是前辈学者的研究著作,而对于广大社会读者它又是唯一的欧洲文学史。但是,在新编《欧洲文学史》问世的2000年前后,虽然它仍然是唯一用《欧洲文学史》为书名的著作,类似的著作却已经大量涌现,那就是各种各样的外国文学史教材。因此,新编《欧洲文学史》的教材功能大大降低,更像是一套研究专著。它的读者对象主要不是大学生,而是对欧洲文学史有兴趣并希望进行相关学术探索的学者。《欧洲文学史》1979年版印数9万册,新编《欧洲文学史》第

① 郑克鲁:《谈谈对外国文学史的编写》,中国外国文学学会编(何辉斌执行主编)《外国文学研究60年》,浙江大学出版社2010年,第254页。

一卷印数3千册似乎证明了这一点。

陈惇主编的《西方文学史》(四川人民出版社2003出版的)是我国第一部以《西方文学史》为书名的著作，此前出版的同类著作多用“欧美文学史”为书名。全书共十章，与《外国文学史(欧美卷)》分章相同，但是90万字的篇幅则是扩大了约二分之一。第一卷(古代—18世纪文学)，陈惇、刘洪涛著，共分五章。第二卷19世纪文学，共三章。第三卷20世纪文学分为两章。本书的重要特点是目录不仅各章内容清晰，而且在每一节内还列出不同的要点，显得一目了然。如第十章第五节“德语文学”：战后的德国——民主德国文学——联邦德国文学——具体诗——左翼作家西格斯——“我们的世纪”的作家格拉斯——悲喜剧作家迪伦马特——“谩骂关注”的汉特克。这四个作家中西格斯为民主德国作协主席；格拉斯为联邦德国作家；迪伦马特为瑞士作家，而汉特克是奥地利作家，这可以说很好地照顾到了不同地区或国家的德语文学。第十章第六节“英国文学”：福利国家与货币主义——“人性恶”的揭露者戈尔丁——实验小说家福尔斯——“反戏剧”作家贝克特——“恐吓”喜剧作家品特，这些标签让读者对重要作家的特点有清晰的认识。

看各卷目录可知，“德国文学”只用于第五章第四节，介绍德国古典文学黄金时代和第六章第二节介绍“古典的”与“浪漫的”并存的时代；19世纪中期和后期文学都没有专节介绍德国文学，而20世纪两章都是用“德语文学”的标题。与德国文学史发展不平衡形成对照的是从文艺复兴开始，每章都有专节介绍英、法文学；从19世纪初开始每章都有专节介绍俄罗斯文学。美国文学则比较特殊，第一次介绍包括从独立战争到南北战争，因此在19世纪中期文学一章没有专节介绍美国文学，但在其他各章都有专节介绍。同时，从这个目录还可以看出，所谓西方文学基本上就是几个大国的文学，特别是英、法、俄、美；德国或德语文学在20世纪前发展不平衡，而在19世纪中后期东欧和北欧文学发展成就突出。曾经在历史上取得辉煌成就的希腊、意大利和西班牙在近现代文学成就却不太突出。20世纪关于“苏维埃时期的俄罗斯文学”的两节形成鲜明对比：20世纪上半一节内容介绍提到十个重要作家，而20世纪下半一节则没有提一个人名：卫国战争与军事题材文学——“解冻”与“解冻文学”——“奥维奇金派”与农村题材小说——反官僚主义的小说——封闭、开放与回归——80年代以后的俄罗斯文学。美国文学则在20世纪上下半期都有代表作家领衔：第九章第六节：美国文学的两度繁荣——现实主义小说家德莱塞——意象派诗歌与庞德——“南方文学”的代表福克纳——“迷惘的一代”与海明威——美国戏剧史上的丰碑：奥尼尔。第十章第四节：美国文学：“冷战时期”与世界政治经济中心——垮掉派与金斯堡——黑色幽默——元小说——“枯竭的文学派”作家巴思——“在路上”的凯鲁亚克——“黑色幽默作家”海勒——阿尔比。这样细致的标题就像内容梗概，对于学生读者很有帮助。

第一卷开头的“绪论”虽然不长，但有一定理论性。第一节先解释了“西方”概念，其中提到“‘西方国家’就成了资本主义列强的同义词”(第1页)。接着指出在研究世界文学时用“东方”和“西方”的概念主要“是从文化体系的意义上来划分的”。西方文学有统一的文化传统，东方文学或文化则没有这种统一性，而是分成“相对独立的中国文化、印度文化、波斯阿拉伯伊斯兰文化和黑非洲文化”(第2页)。第二节谈文学史编纂方法，指出各种类型都有其局限，“所以，正确的科学的文学史研究应该全面认识文学发展的动力，把审美的分析和历史的社会的分析这两个方面结合起来，才能避免片面性，使文学史走上科学的道路”(第4页)。第三节强调东西方文学的互相影响，特别是远古亚非文学对古希腊文学的影响，阿拉伯文学对西方文艺复兴的影响等，因此本书在每章的文学史概述中增加了一些有关东西方文学交流的内容。第四节强调本书的教材性质，篇幅不能太大，既要保证学生必须掌握基本知识，又要做到材料充足，观点明确，重点突出。他提出了大学生学习西方文学史的三个要点，掌握基本知识，了解重点作家作品，提高分析鉴赏能力。“这就是说，我们在设计教材的体系上，必须兼顾西方文学的全面知识、文学史的发展线索和代表性作家作品三个方面，全面地、适当地处理好面、线、点三者的关系。这也许是教材与学术专著在写法上的不同之处。”(第7页)

《西方文学史》内封有这样的介绍：这是一本有新意的外国文学史著作，它把西方文学放在世界文学的总体格局和东西方文化交流的背景中，从一个新的角度审视其成就，注意吸收最新的研究成果，内容涉及从古代到20世纪的西方文学的近三千年的历史，重点介绍了大约200个作家。全书史料翔实，论述具体，分析深刻，而且图文并茂，配有100幅作家图像。全书最后一节(第十章第七节)为拉丁美洲文学：一片神奇的土地——“先锋派文学”——“文学爆炸”——魔幻现实主义——加西亚·马尔克斯——“作家的作家”博尔赫斯——“拉美的乔伊斯”科塔萨尔——诗坛新星帕斯。著者认为拉丁美洲文学的发展大体经历了五个阶段：史前时期，殖民地时期，独立革命时期，民族文学繁荣时期和当代文学时期：“20世纪五六十年代，拉丁美洲文学在世界文坛异军突起，在西方，乃至整个世界形成了一股‘拉丁美洲文学热’，或称‘文学爆炸’。一时间，作家辈出，群星灿烂，流派纷呈，争奇斗艳……而就现实主义而言，在拉丁美洲文坛就活跃着十几种流派，诸如心理现实主义、动物心理现实主义、社会现实主义、结构现实主义、魔幻现实主义等不同风格和流派的文学(第354页)。”关于当代拉丁美洲文学大繁荣的原因，著者列举了地理因素、文化因素、社会因素和外部因素等四个方面，外部因素主要是超现实主义以及西方现代主义文学的影响和启迪。总起来看，陈惇等长期从事西方文学史教学研究的学者合作编著的这套三卷本《西方文学史》既给读者勾画出了西方文学发展的大体脉络，又提供了对一些重点作家作品的分析解读，是西方文学史研究方面的突出成果。

匡兴主编的《外国文学史(西方卷)》2010年由北京师范大学出版社出版，53万字。全书11章，章节安排与南开大学版《外国文学史(欧美卷)》大同小异，而且篇幅也差不多，只是把20世纪俄罗斯文学单独列为第十一章。从撰稿人的情况来看，陈惇撰写前五章，基本上与他主编的《西方文学史》第一卷内容差不多；匡兴撰写第六到第十章的大部或全部，还有刘象愚、黄晋凯等十几位学者参与撰稿。从所收的作家来看，18世纪末之前的作家只比《外国文学史(欧美卷)》少拉伯雷、伏尔泰和席勒，19世纪作家增加了华兹华斯和勃朗特姐妹，但是删除了雪莱、海涅、密茨凯维奇和惠特曼，20世纪作家则有大调整，删除了普鲁斯特、马雅可夫斯基、帕斯基尔纳克和贝克特，增加了艾略特、奥尼尔、尤内斯库、贝娄、莱辛、格拉斯、莫里森等，还有苏联作家普拉东诺夫、布尔加科夫和特里丰诺夫等。从这个名单变化来看，18世纪以前的作家基本稳定，19世纪略有增删，而20世纪作家则见仁见智，很难有比较统一的名单。本书20世纪作家名单的特点是增加了三位女作家，纠正了以往外国文学史教材对女性作家重视不够的偏差。《外国文学史(西方卷)》新增的三位苏联作家中有两位是在斯大林时代创作但没有发表机会的作家:普拉东诺夫“那过于玄奥、冥远的思想探索和奇异的艺术思维与那狂热而残酷的年代显得格格不入而被冷落、排斥”(第475—6页),而布尔加科夫“从1928年直到病故,毅然熬忍着事业的坎坷、生活的窘迫、精神的苦闷,呕心沥血,惨淡经营,批阅十二三载,修改八次之多,一直修改到逝世前不久,为后人留下的一部奇书《大师和玛格丽特》”1973年在苏联全文发表后,“引起持续性、全球性轰动,被誉为俄罗斯文学的高峰”(第485页)。而本书介绍的最后一位苏联作家特里丰诺夫1950年刚25岁就以长篇小说《大学生》一举成名,后来却因“致力于暴露和批判社会的阴暗和腐败”引起非议,“但在他逝世以后,评论界对他的社会心理小说的评价却越来越高”(第491页)。这种对苏联时期受到否定的非主流作家的重视有重写文学史的味道。

除了多种通史之外,断代史方面最为引人注目的是杨慧林、黄晋凯著《欧洲中世纪文学史》(译林出版社2001)。“前言 中世纪欧洲文学的研究方法及其针对性问题”是一篇颇有分量的理论文章,从中世纪欧洲文学研究的跨文化、跨学科性质,中世纪欧洲文学从“非国族化”到“本土化”的特征,中世纪欧洲文学与中世纪的美学和文学观念,中世纪欧洲文学研究的资料依据与未来延伸四个方面作了系统论述。本书共分四编23章。第一编“中世纪欧洲文化概说”有四章,分别介绍中世纪的欧洲文化品格、基督教宇宙观的文化意味、基督教释经学的深层影响和基督教早期至中世纪的神学发展。第二编“语言形成时期”也有四章,介绍中世纪欧洲民族俗语的形成、早期英雄史诗(如《贝奥武甫》)、早期基督教文学和基督教文学批评的兴起。第三编“族群独立时期”共七章,介绍欧洲文学的本土化、北欧的埃达与萨迦、英雄史诗与骑士叙事诗(如《罗兰之歌》、《熙德之歌》、《尼伯龙根之歌》和《伊戈尔出征记》等)、平民诗谣(如列那狐故事、《玫瑰传奇》、《罗宾汉传奇》等)、吟咏诗人与抒情诗和游记。本编第七章综合介绍基督教文学理念的成熟,包括从加洛林王朝到经院主义时期和托马斯·阿奎那对经院时代的总结。第四编“文学成熟与文化转型时期”有八章,前三章分别介绍欧洲文学的文人化、教会戏剧的发展和城市化的世俗文学,此后的四章介绍中世纪到文艺复兴过渡时期的五位重要作家:但丁、彼特拉克与薄迦丘、乔叟、维庸。第八章是全书最后一章,综述基督教神秘主义的流变及其对文学观念的影响,涉及四个方面:一、伪狄奥尼修斯与基督教神秘主义的缘起,二、西都教团,三、圣维克多学派,四、变革中的基督教晚期神秘主义。附录“中世纪欧洲文学研究文献述要”包括较有影响的英语研究文献118项,并注明以上文献述要的主要依据为克罗斯比等编著的《中世纪研究文献编目》和比利时鲁汶大学神学院图书馆藏书。附记介绍本书的缘起:“数年前,在一个关于人文社科发展规划的座谈会上,黄晋凯建议外国文学界应组织力量撰写一批有分量的断代文学史,以在现有的基础上进一步深化外国文学的研究(第379页)。”此后译林出版社编辑约稿,除两位作者外徐京安和杨恒达撰写了部分重要章节,作者当年的研究生做了大量资料准备工作。

本书的第一个突出特点是理论性强。传统观点认为中世纪是所谓“黑暗时代”,是古希腊罗马与文艺复兴两大高峰之间的低谷,文学上除了但丁之外乏善可陈。本书的前言对中世纪文学研究的跨文化、跨学科、跨国别等特点有精湛的阐述,让人读来耳目一新。其次,基于对中世纪文学特点的清醒认识,本书不是专注于文学作品研究,而是从中世纪欧洲文化发展、民族俗语的形成、族群演变过程和文学成熟与文化转型等四个方面来论述中世纪欧洲文学，从而勾画出中世纪欧洲文学与文化相辅相成，交融发展的过程。第三，在整个论述过程中充分重视基督教的作用。以往我们对基督教的认识比较片面，主要强调其对世俗生活、人文情感的压抑，忽视了基督教之所以产生发展的内在原因，更没有清醒认识其对欧洲后来文化发展的深刻影响。本书紧紧抓住基督教产生发展这个中心问题，客观公正地评价了基督教对中世纪文学和文化发展的复杂影响。

本书借鉴西方中世纪研究的大量最新成果，对于一些常识性问题给出了新颖的解释。比如，希伯来和希腊两大文化传统的融合一向被认为是欧洲文学和文化的基本特点，但是对于两者为什么能够融合，是怎样融合的这些根本问题却少有探讨。本书第一章第二节"古希腊传统与基督教"对此问题有精到阐释。著者首先指出以注重人的地位和尊严为特点的"希腊精神""似乎始终存在着两个难以解决的致命问题"，一是希腊晚期的怀疑主义、斯多葛主义等包含着对于人类的悲观认识，为希伯来的"原罪"观念的侵入留下了缺口；二是希腊神话中"神"的"人化"暗含着危险，因为"人类找不到绝对的坐标"（第 12 页），而希伯来传统的上帝则提供了答案。著者还指出希腊历史学之父赫西俄德所述人类历史从黄金到白银再到青铜和黑铁时代的不断堕落"这种一代不如一代的趋势，刚好同希伯来人从原罪到救赎，从'失乐园'到'复乐园'的 U 字形描述构成了反差；其中可以会通之处，必然是 U 字形的谷底"（第 13 页）。此外，"古希腊文化还体现着一种对于道德和'至善'的普遍关心，这是苏格拉底哲学所奠定的传统，也是'二希'文化之所以能通过基督教相融的基础"（第 13—14 页）。这就清楚地解释了为什么二希文化可以成为欧洲文化传统的共同源头这一关键问题。除了对二希文化融合的强调，本书还特别指出日耳曼、凯尔特等北欧蛮族的南侵对中世纪文化发展的影响，从而勾勒出南方的二希传统与北方的蛮族南侵相互影响，最终形成中世纪文化复杂特点的三方合一图景。著者强调："在中世纪的'蛮族'文化中，影响最大的是日耳曼人。日耳曼人的入侵曾经打断希伯来文化与希腊文化的融合，并使中世纪的欧洲动荡不堪。直至他们逐渐接受了基督教文化之后，中世纪的欧洲才开始复苏，而他们自身的文化也已经蕴入其中"（第 15 页）。关于日耳曼人的特征，著者参考塔西陀的《日耳曼尼亚志》，指出"在塔西陀的笔下，日耳曼人特点是好动的，懒散是这个民族极端厌恶的品质"（第 15 页）。在 21 世纪，特别是在不少南欧国家深陷债务危机，被戏称为懒散的"笨猪"国家时，我们似乎还能看到塔西陀描述的准确性。《欧洲中世纪文学史》指出："罗马帝国的崩溃所留下的政治真空，也许只有在北方'蛮族'融入基督教的精神之后，才真正得以填补。从这一意义上讲，公元 496 年克洛维皈依罗马教会，标志着一个新欧洲的出现。"（第 18 页）

杨周翰先生多年以前曾经提醒说不了解中世纪就不能充分理解现代欧洲。[①] 今天，我们可以告慰前辈说杨慧林和黄晋凯合著的《中世纪欧洲文学史》为更加客观全面地了解中世纪文学文化打开了方便之门。本书撰写十分严谨，书后附录"中世纪欧洲文学研究文献述要"给人深刻印象："我们关于西方的一切讨论，当然都无法离开中国自身的背景和经验，但是这必须以了解对方为前提。否则，除去强调基督教对于西方文学之重要、除去批判以往的偏见或忽视，就

① 杨周翰：《攻玉集》，北京大学出版社 1983 年，第 8 页。

很难再有所推进。相对而言,外国文学研究在基督教神学和中世纪文学方面的准备似还比较薄弱。谨整理出西方较有影响的英语研究文献,凡118项,并注明其所及内容,供有关学人参考。"(第364页)这个书目对研究者很有帮助,只是书目内容的排列方式若做解释则更好。第一章第四节"罗马—拜占庭传统与基督教"提到拜占庭时有这样的解释"(即今天土耳其的君士坦丁堡)"(第20页)。这可能会让读者产生误解,以为这是拜占庭今天的名字,而实际上1930年君士坦丁堡就已经改名为"伊斯坦布尔"了。还有如"凯尔特"在个别地方又称为"克尔特","典雅爱情"又译为"优雅爱情"和"文雅爱情"。希望再版时能够改正这些疏漏。

人民出版社2010年出版的崔莉著《欧洲文艺复兴史 文学卷》可以说是一部欧洲文学断代史。本书是刘明翰主编的"欧洲文艺复兴史"系列丛书的一卷,丛书包括总论、政治、经济、法学、文学、历史、哲学、宗教、艺术、教育、科学技术、城市与社会生活等共有12卷。正文前的丛书主编"总序"指出:"现在呈献给读者们的多卷本《欧洲文艺复兴史》,是国家社会科学规划的一个研究项目。它是我国首次系统地梳理和全方位地阐析欧洲文艺复兴思想精华的一次尝试,也是多层面地探究文艺复兴成果和历史经验的纵深耕耘。"(第1页)著者撰写的"导论"首先综合介绍文艺复兴时期文学的辉煌成就,然后提出"文艺复兴时期文学的新探索",在这个方面主要关注两点:一是"本书提出欧洲各国王权对于文艺复兴运动的支持和扶佑,是文艺复兴盛世出现的客观因素之一"(第5页),二是强调"文艺复兴时期女性作家和作品的社会进步意义。作为一种尝试,本书将文艺复兴时期的女性作家和作品独立成章"(第7页)。正文共八章,第一章介绍文艺复兴文学兴起的历史背景,涉及中世纪基督教文学、世俗文学、古希腊罗马文学的影响和各国开明君主的支持和庇护等。从第二章开始依次介绍主要欧洲国家文学,首先是意大利文学,因为但丁的出现预示着文艺复兴的开始,彼得拉克和薄伽丘是早期文艺复兴巨匠;第三章介绍法国文学,主要是维庸、拉伯雷和蒙田。第四和第五两章介绍英国文学,其中第四章从英国诗歌之父乔叟写起,然后介绍莫尔的《乌托邦》、斯宾塞的《仙后》和培根的散文随笔。第五章专门介绍莎士比亚戏剧。第六章介绍西班牙与葡萄牙文学,第七章介绍德国、俄罗斯和欧洲其他国家文学,因为这些国家当时还没有形成强大的民族国家,文学成就较小。第八章介绍文艺复兴时期的女性作家,涉及意大利、法国、英国、瑞典等国女性。单独介绍女性作家的确是本书的一个特色,这可能与作者是女性和近三十年女性批评迅速发展有关。最后一章综合介绍欧洲文艺复兴文学风格、美学意义及其他,带有某种总结评断的特点。

综上所述,新世纪西方文学史研究出现各种著作争奇斗艳繁荣局面。如果说《欧洲文学史》出版时我们关注的还主要是20世纪以前的西方文学,那么今天得到最广泛重视的却是20世纪西方文学。50年前我们提供给读者的还只是关于欧洲文学的一般性介绍,今天则在戏剧史研究、小说史研究、中世纪研究、文艺复兴时期文学研究等不同领域出现了有相当深度的可喜成果。这些成果的出现不仅满足了教学的需要,而且为研究者和大众读者提供了满足不同需要的著作。与过去相比成绩可喜,但是从更高的要求,从在西方文学史研究中提出有影响力的中国学者的观点来看,我们还有很多工作要做,可以说是任重而道远。

作者简介:韩加明,北京大学外国语学院教授。

异邦新声

充满活力的杰姆逊

——弗雷德里克·杰姆逊访谈录

史岩林 译

访谈人:伊恩·布坎南(英国卡迪夫大学批评与文化理论教授,杰姆逊研究专家,主编和发表过多部杰姆逊研究著作)

伊恩·布坎南(以下简称布):我们先谈一下你的"知识体系"是如何形成的吧。

弗雷德里克·杰姆逊(以下简称杰):我的知识体系形成于20世纪50年代,而不是20世纪60年代(尽管我的知识体系建构是以欧洲为中心的,但当我说"我的"或"我们的"时候,当然指的是与欧洲相对的美国)。虽然我主要与法国和德国联系紧密,但我必须说明我很早就开始接触第三世界国家,尤其是20世纪50年代的墨西哥,还有从北非直到印度尼西亚这一大片伊斯兰世界。我到北非各地考察过,当然北非也可以纳入法国情势的框架下来考察。事实上,我在阿尔及利亚度过了[在北非的]最初几周——我想那应该是阿尔及利亚革命前的一两个月——当时它仍是法国的一个省,是法属殖民地。这些经历是我背景的重要组成部分,后来在20世纪60年代逐渐发挥了作用。在20世纪50年代,对于像我这样的白人大学生,最令人激愤和极端的政治事件莫过于麦卡锡主义和军队/麦卡锡听证会。直到我去欧洲,没有比这更令我激进化的事情了。

无论是当时还是现在,像我们后来称之为西方马克思主义的那类东西的完全缺失都是美国知识界面临的主要问题;我自己的贡献是(如在《马克思主义与形式》等书中)让世人了解这些传统。我不想作任何特殊的自我表扬,但我认为自己可能是[在美国]第一个撰写有关阿多诺、布洛赫、甚至本雅明和萨特评论的人。我现在仍旧为自己所做的这些工作感到骄傲。至于那时马克思主义的实际任务,你要知道那是所谓文化研究之前的事情,其重点是文学批评,因此我构思了第一本书,将其作为设计新型文学批评的一种方法:不局限于介绍一些一般或广义地称为马克思主义文学批评、文学社会学的东西。我们始终想把这种新"方法"与旧的文学和文化社会学严格区分开来,因为后者与马克思主义的做法完全不同,但是我也提倡对传统的马克思主义批评进行一种具体的改革和创新。我们在这一新领域工作的人,几乎没有人在知识体系上与旧的苏联传统建立密切联系。我想我们和其他所有人一样,都把后者理解为将作品按意识形态简单分类,并判断他们是进步还是保守。

我认为,我和其他人开始重新思考这项任务所用的方法,不是简单地找出这个或那个作家在意识形态上的相似之处，而是要重点搞清保守或反动作家的作品如何会具有一些可以认为是进步的特征。因此，这就演变成了一种与过去的马克思主义方法不同的文学文本分析方法。后来，理论（即法国理论，结构主义，后结构主义等）开始盛行，这种方法得到进一步扩展，因为我们不仅需要考虑马克思主义理论的发展，还需要看看其他的理论是与马克思主义理论关系不大，还是完全无关——他们在何种意义上适合新的马克思主义理论化。因此，在这种情况之下，我认为问题不在于简单地使用某种政治分类系统或进行阶级属性分析，而是要在非政治、反政治的文献和其他哲学传统中寻找可用的元素。

布：你曾在很多采访中说过，至少有三位老师对你有过重要影响，他们是巴尔特、本雅明和萨特。接着前一个有关知识体系形成的问题，你能否描述一下这三个人物是如何与你产生联系，又是如何影响你的知识体系形成的呢？

杰：我认为阿多诺对我的影响远超过本雅明，因为我们对本雅明的了解仅仅来源于各种零散的片段，而非完整的著作，当然有些东西还在陆续出现，作为一种统一整体仍会产生新问题。但最初带给我震撼体验的是萨特的作品，那是在大学时代，甚至更早。萨特作品中的那种可能性（那一代很多人[包括法国的]可以感受到）使你突然间获得一种理论化的、哲学化的分析模式，这种分析模式能将一切——从日常生活和存在经验到政治和历史——真正地哲学化。弗洛伊德对我也一直很重要：他的理论是个重要发现，它强化了日常生命本身的哲学感，使人们可以从内在把握它。所以，对我来说，我的早期著作的确受到萨特的启发，因为巴尔特对我的影响主要是《写作的零度》和《神话学》这些早期作品，在我看来，它们在本质上仍旧是萨特式问题的延续。

阿多诺则不同，我想可能不只我一个人通过托马斯·曼的《浮士德博士》间接接触了阿多诺，我们隐约感觉到《浮士德博士》是以阿多诺一些未发表的论音乐的手稿为基础写成的，而这些手稿就是《现代音乐的哲学》。

我在德国学习的时候，开始接触阿多诺已出版的书稿（我认为当时还没有任何译本）。通过这些文本，我逐渐意识到德国传统中存在着另外一种思想体系，显然更具有辩证性，而法国的传统则明显带有政治性。另一方面，在德国传统中，在某种他们认为政治已经变得不可能的情况下，否定辩证法就明显带有政治性。这样，就有两种可行的方案：如果政治实践仍然可行，就采取萨特模式，如果受到阻碍或陷入僵局，那么在某种程度上就采用一种非常强大的反模式，而该反模式存在于具有否定和批判活力的德国思想中。事实证明，这两种模式都影响了60年代的美国，但鉴于马尔库塞的存在，我想德国的传统显然对美国的新左派和学生争取民主社会运动（SDS, Student for a Democratic Society）产生了更大的影响。

布：如今，我们将理论的存在视为理所当然的事。对于我这一代人而言，很难想象首次接触理论时所体会到的新奇感和迫切感。所以，我想请你描绘一下当时英美批评的状况，理论在那时似乎是一种激进的选择。

杰：从这一点上讲，尽管美国的批评做了一些修改和变动，但它才是真正的“新批评”。那时候，弗莱还不是非常有影响力，而我们已经有了神话批评和其它批评方式。不过，这些批评都是针对文学而言，而且我认为你只能在英语系了解这些东西——例如，在我的大学，哈沃福特学院（Haverford College）——文学如果真能学到勃朗宁就很不错了，勃朗宁确实是有点难，所以实际上他们也只能学到丁尼生。然而我是学法语的，在法语系人们向来都是阅读当代最前沿的文本，更重要的是，政治不受制于英美的审查制度，所以即使在20世纪50年代，法语系的人都知道左翼作家也是法国伟大的作家，特别是自巴尔扎克以来法国反资产阶级传统的作家。因此，这是一种令人匪夷所思的美国现象。在这方面，理论在美国的传播与其他国家完全不同：它真的发端于法语系，而且按照美国制度设置的院系结构使我们产生的影响力远远超出了直接的法文课程。据我的了解，在英国，法语老师被严格局限于法国文学这样的内容，相反，理论传播则需要借助公共领域，例如《新左派评论》这样的期刊。因此，这不是对作为基础的文学产生强烈抵制，而只是认为文学和文化比纯文学更重要。

当然，我的背景也有点不同：我的知识体系并非源于新批评，而是你很可能笼统地称之为语文学的东西，包括法国和德国；当时被称之为风格研究，例如像奥尔巴赫(Auerbach)这些人的工作，他是我在耶鲁大学的老师。与大多数英语系纯粹的审美鉴赏相比，那里的单个文本、风格、词汇等与运动和历史背景的联系更加密切，这也为我对理论的兴趣铺平了道路。但是，它也确实引出了关于语言、文本与社会之间的关系这样更大的问题，使得研究者能够在萨特的文本中借助列维·斯特劳斯与神话批评的结构人类学发掘更多的问题——我指的是列维·斯特劳斯的神话批评——和叙事功能的整个概念，即叙事如何在社会和意识形态世界中发挥其在文学中的作用；同样重要的是在巴尔特《神话学》中发展出来的意识形态概念。正是所有这些东西使我们认识到，文学领域中存在着一系列社会科学尚未察觉到的新的实验性状况，我想有人会说这是人文学科中一种新的理论的帝国主义形式，不仅涉及其他语言中的文学研究，而且也涉及社会科学。这是第一个真正的开创性使命，我们可能会在法国结构主义的语言学和人类学与马克思主义的结合中发现这样的使命。这的确是方法上的一次全新革命，发端于人文学科，经过很长一段时间，逐步地、并最终影响到其他学科。

布：我在你的作品中总能发现与众不同之处，这就是风格总是与政治联系在一起，对文本构成问题的密切关注成为了解其意识形态指涉的重要手段。我也想提到这样一个早期观点：你说在反动内部寻找进步元素是你想从事的工作之一。也许你可以将这两点联系起来，谈一下你阅读文本的方法。

杰：好，我就从风格问题谈起吧，因为它是至关重要的，而且能够解释你所感兴趣的转向问题，即后现代主义理论的出现。正如我所说，我的知识体系形成于斯皮策(Spitzer)和奥尔巴赫倡导的风格研究传统，也形成于一种现代方式，如萨特撰写的《情境》第一卷中一些关于福克纳的著名文学评论所体现的那样(我不知道它在英文是如何转换的)。但是，我在巴尔特的《写作的零度》对文学史解读方式的影响下开始有这样的想法，认为风格是一种特定的现代或现代主义现象。也就是说，我开始形成这样的看法：现代主义中个人风格的创造与个人主观的整体建构相联系，因而风格的变化不仅有整体的世界观作为先决条件，而且要为诸如温德姆·刘易斯(Wyndham Lewis)这样的作家含混的，甚至可疑的政治对立倾向提供具体线索。因此，贯穿这一切的后现代线索是认识到——我认为巴尔特在或许不太成熟的纯写作(white writing)概念中，就已觉察到这一点——风格本身就要终结，而且现代主义本身因耗尽产生全新风格的可能性而终结。其他的或新的东西可能已经开始，但却很难描述。没有人认为大卫·福斯特·华莱士(David Foster Wallace)那样的人是无风格的，而个体或个人风格的产生——也许你能在品钦(Pynchon)身上发现——再也不像现代主义风格那样。从这个意义上讲,产生风格的可能性会发生转变,而这种转变会与伟大的后结构理论问题——即所谓的"主体的死亡",中心主体性的终结——建立联系。所以在后来的哲学发展中,风格及其可能性问题变得至关重要。

所以,我早期偏于文学的著作确实是通过这种社会和体制突变的方式进入后现代性理论的。而现在,在进步或反动的问题上,我觉得我们被这些沿袭来的术语弄得有点尴尬,所以我想使用一个与众不同的术语,即乌托邦。因为对我而言,我逐渐意识到——正如人们看的那样,我说的不只是法西斯主义作家,而是在整个右翼文学和文化的"悲伤激情"(斯宾诺莎语)中——尽管意识形态利用了一整套的集体欲望,但它们在某种程度上也是集体的,因而在内心深处隐藏着一种乌托邦式的冲动。所以,慢慢地,这种观念和这个术语引出了这样的议题,那就是要对旧式马克思主义方法论中的议程进行重新修订。

例如,现在我们知道,福楼拜和波德莱尔对1848年的革命的确怀有同情之心,并且具有乌托邦式的思想认识。可问题不在于只是寻找那一类有趣的传记事实,分出哪些是进步的和哪些是反动的,而是要认识到甚至是在已达到反动目的的作品中,或者说,甚至是与政治无关的、自由主义的作品中,如果其作品足够有力,就应该能够找到有启示性的动机(informing drive),我认为这种动力最好称之为乌托邦冲动。这个信念确保文化研究具有一种完全不同的议程,也就是说,不仅在文化上,而且在社会和政治行动中确认了那种集体冲动,并对获得这种冲动的方式进行反思。这种方式与过去按照左右翼来分类的方法截然不同,为文学和文化研究定了某种政治承诺。

布:这就涉及到一个有关方法的问题。你的工作为多层次阅读文本提供了可能性。你能否进一步解释一下多层次阅读文本如何能够辩证地解读文本?

杰:文本是一种"利多比装置",可以被赋予许多力量和意义。当然,所有文本都对各种性别意识形态(gender ideologies)认同开放,同样地,它们也向一系列其他层次的欲望和人们可以称为意识形态性的取向(ideological orientation)开放,包括种族和阶级、国情本身和许多其他更具体的决定因素。尽管对文本中任何一个主题进行强有力的分析都会揭示出一些惊人的、重要的东西,但文本分析从来不受这些内容的限制。然而,文本始终是一种易于渗透、善于接受的客体,吸收各种复杂和共存的幻想或渴望。当然,人们从未达到理解一切的程度,也未达到全面认识文本的程度,因为每种新的关系都会带来一些新的问题。但是,作为一个方法论的准则,它对我而言是非常重要的,可以使这些多重决定性具有的开放概念保持活力。现在,我不太喜欢"开放"这个词,因为这个词反复向我们灌输有关"开放"与"封闭"社会、"开放"与"封闭"哲学体系的意识形态——一个真正具有倾向性和意识形态的冷战概念。作为意识形态的对应物,它认为如果这样的决定是不够的,那么我们应该更笼统地谈论文本的不确定性。我宁愿谈论文本的多重决定性,从而为更多的确定性留下可能性,而不是强加某种对立(开放对封闭)的意识形态视野,或者在不确定性或后现代的偶然性与这样或那样的老式封闭之间的视野。在我看来,问题不在这里,而在于文本是否具有多元投入(multiple investments)的可能性,这才是人们应该强调的地方。

布:现在,我想知道如何在后现代中展开分析?如果个人或个体的风格已经随着现代主义的终结而消失，如果没有留下任何可以聚焦的特殊性让人们可以以直接的方式链接意识形态的话，在我看来，文本分析将会面临一种全新的、显然非常困难的境遇。

杰：嗯，这是一个与我的工作转向有关的问题，即从具体的文本分析转换为对后现代主义形成问题的分析，而且也是一个非常难的问题。人们得通过一种间接或者调和的方式完成转换。首先要说的是，从这个角度上讲，旧的文本，旧的文本对象，无论是文学还是艺术，认知还是修辞，都已经在真正意义上消逝了。很多人都会谈到艺术品或艺术对象的消失，如架上绘画的伟大的个体性审美对象已经转变成类似于装置艺术一样的集群物(clusters)，或者被观念[艺术]所代替，甚至旧的文学作品或名著的观念也消散在大量的文化或大众文化运动中。就此而言，某种新的分析形式显然是必要的，而在我看来，这样的分析形式必然来自后现代性自身的模仿系统，其中所有这些对象不再作为个体主体性的表达发挥作用，而是参与到某种较大的晚期资本主义或后现代性的文化生产运动中。显然，这需要一种与旧式文本解读方法不同的分析方式。

人们认为，这里的危险在于将这些新的审美对象仅仅视为某个具有较大文化倾向的例子。另一方面，反对者的问题在于它们不再是真正的个体对象，它们在后现代文化的潮流中使用后结构主义语言和文本性的形式，因此必须以另一种方式理解它们。所以，像文学一样，它转变为文化本身或特定文化形式的角色问题；在这种情况下，正如我多次重申的那样，文化概念已被大大扩大了；在一定程度上，整个经济体系本身也变成文化的一部分，而且我们再也无法保证对个体对象研究能够指导我们的具体工作或具体的解读。但是，在这种新形势之下，当然也可以想象到某种严密的逻辑；它并不是简单地让事物接受某种模糊的、笼统的文化批评，至少我不希望是这样。在我的工作中，我一直关注这种模糊的社会学和大众文化意义上的“文化批判”(这是我的称谓)，尤其是关注“文化批判”的所有追求被抹黑这一问题。对我来说，有这样一些口号，如“以他者为导向”、“自恋主义文化”，甚至是法兰克福学派的“权威人格”概念、与法兰克福学派相关的埃里克·弗洛姆的作品以及福柯式的“微观权力论”，都是以通俗的心理学分析替代了对当前政治、社会和经济的真正分析。

布：据你说，我们今天在面对晚期资本主义时比以往任何时候都更需要马克思主义的问题意识，但我们必须找到新的解决方法。这就提出了两个问题：(1)今天的马克思主义问题意识是什么，它采取什么样的形式？(2)可以找到或者想象哪些新的解决方法？

杰：提到新的解决方法，我真的不知道；我的意思是，如果我们能想象到的话，我们就已经做到了，因此这可能是更难预见的。但是，即使没有“新的解决方法”，马克思主义的问题意识也具有两个方面的优势：一个是商品的概念，这是一个结构性概念，而不是一个道德或伦理的概念，因此，一方面它带领我们进入有关消费主义和商品化的政治，不涉及容易沦为清教主义和其他狂热主义的伦理冲动；另一方面是马克思主义的经济制度观念，具有强大的力量。作为一个局外人，我的印象是，如今正在实行的其它所有经济类型纯粹是实用性和经验性的，为生产或分配等这样那样的具体方面提供方法和补救措施，或为投资和资金重组提供具体的建议；而马克思主义经济学的优势在于，它真的是唯一将这个系统看作整体的方法。然而，马克思主义的这些优势，反映了它不再受早先马克思主义政治时刻和形式的约束。文化才是所谓西方马克思主义真理的时刻：坚持资本主义的文化维度[的分析]。而伴随着全球化和后现代性的到来，这些文化问题成为我们存在时刻的绝对核心。也就是说，正如列斐伏尔在他关于政治空间化问题的最后几本书中说的那样，列斐伏尔确实在呼唤一种新的空间辩证法。也许这就是一种马克思主义政治新概念所前进的方向，但我敢肯定，还有许多其他可能的方法，只不过我们还没有意识到这些方法的存在。

布：你曾在一些场合说过理论已经取代了哲学，这意味着哲学在某种程度上消失了。你能进一步解释一下你说的哲学正在消失是什么意思吗？

杰：人们可以看到，在20世纪70、80年代躁动期之后，哲学明显地回归到传统的分科及其各种分支中，如伦理，政治哲学和形而上学等等，我认为这是哲学思辨一种令人遗憾的衰退征兆。毕竟，自黑格尔以来的哲学历史中（如果你把尼采看做新的哲学起点）一直存在这样一种哲学批判，一种对哲学体系的批判。我不怀疑未来仍将继续产生和过去一样伟大的哲学家，但我想他们的思想力量将来自于对那些传统哲学分野的抵抗、对各种新事物的生产，而不是对哲学地位本身喋喋不休的辩护。人们当然可以看到，大多数哲学家的工作重点是将哲学重新理论化，并使他们所进行的实践合理化，甚至当他们成为德勒兹、德里达那样真正具有独创性和特质的思想家时也是如此。然而，在某种意义上，理论或我宁愿称之为“理论话语”或“理论写作”的东西至少是摆脱了那种自我辩护的必要性。它使得在哲学中对皮埃尔·布迪厄（Pierre Bourdieu）经典性的批判性攻击显得似是而非；在布迪厄看来，所有这些学科最终是为了重建和延续学科本身而进行自圆其说，并实施巧妙的利己诡计。因此，达到理论写作本身独特性的一个方法是从学科自我保护的本能中进行形式的解放，而在传统哲学中，这种本能仍在继续。我认为我之前提到的像德勒兹、德里达这样的人，就是把哲学推进到极限的哲学家。在这种哲学的极限地带，他们是从事理论工作的理论家，尽管他们不管这些而自我定义为哲学家。但我自己积极地学习哲学，而且哲学传统绝对是人们今天在理论方面所做一切的组成部分。所以，我希望这种对传统哲学的批评能够从结构方面加以认识，而不是从任何带有敌意的或意识形态的意义上来理解。

布：现在应该是提出神话批评这个问题的时候了，因为非常有趣的是，你暗示只有当确定我们今天的情况不同于原始社会的时候，人们才有可能正确使用神话批评（尽管你对此进行了批判）。你认为神话批评还占有一席之地吗，或者能否改造它以适应今天的情况呢？

杰：这是一个非常棘手的问题。本雅明在《拱廊街计划》中为自己提出了这个问题，并且非常关注法兰克福学派的批判。在对待这个问题上，法兰克福学派也许比他更加关注神话批评与荣格学派之间的亲密关系，甚至还关注神话批评中一种对法西斯主义和纳粹主义设法复活的古老冲动所给予的法西斯式的肯定。显然，采取这条路径的神话批评是不可接受的。我还想说的是，社会生物学就是这种尝试的一种实证主义版本，因为它试图把非常复杂的现代社会与最低级的生物冲动联系起来，并以一种神话的方式使社会现实简单化，虽然它肯定不太像是荣格主义。当然，从马克思主义视角来看，这些非常古老的社会也是没有权力和金钱的社会：人们是否将它们都称为原始共产主义形式是更为复杂的问题，因为有些社会当然存在种姓制度、贵族阶层和其他一些东西。但是，在我看来，列维·斯特劳斯的伟大之处就在于他重新打开了一条有效的路径，可以使我们回到那些古老社会的社会现实，回到我们在现代工业资本主义世界已经失去了的各种社会关系。与其说这是重新创造那些事物的问题,不如说是对适量的乌托邦能量的一种利用,那种乌托邦能量就存在于古老的社会中,人们也可以在原始的神话中找到。关键不是使现在重新神话化,而是将人类遥远的过去时刻(和过去的其他生产方式一样)作为了解我们历史上失去之物的方式,进而为我们可利用的乌托邦能量充电。因此,一方面,我当然感兴趣的是,从这种意义上被理解的神话能够提供给我们什么,另一方面,我非常担心的是,作为一种具有正面价值的神话概念可能产生各种误解,在我看来,这些误解大多具有意识形态倾向,应该抱着最大的质疑态度进行分析研究。

布:你曾在很多场合说过,今天的我们失去了想象未来的能力。现在你依然这样认为吗?如果是的话,你找到任何可能解决的办法了吗?

杰:我觉得,今天的人们很难把不把未来想象成现存之物的延伸——正如本雅明所言,灾难不是等待我们的东西,而恰恰是一切照旧、继续并不断继续,就像现在这样。显然,人类失去了未来感就不可能存在(如果你同意的话,这就是萨特存在主义的负担,或者关乎人类意识的任何雄心勃勃却艰涩难懂的现象学的负担)。然而,很多东西都会干扰人们有效利用这些面向未来的冲动,因而人们需要找到扫除障碍的方法。

如果回到十九世纪晚期工业化的初始阶段,即使是在技术领域,也存在着各种如同科幻小说似的、创造奇迹的未来愿景。在我看来,它们如今很少能发挥作用;我们真的认为会有小的修补——越来越小的电脑芯片等等——但本质上一切保持不变。保罗·维瑞利奥(Paul Virilio)和曼纽尔·德兰达(Manuel DeLanda)这样的人的优点是,他们也试图重新发明并开创一个未来技术变革的概念,至少在这个特定领域恢复一些未来发展和未来意识的形式,虽然我倾向于认为他们的努力和鲍德里亚(Baudrillard)的努力一样,本质上是一种幻想和诗的类型。我专注于使我们无法想象未来的方式,这似乎令很多人沮丧和悲观。对我而言,如果我们开始意识到自己是如何被牢牢关在一个没有未来的现在,开始觉察到阻碍未来想象的所有东西,那么,我们就会有所收获。我想,这是一个布莱希特的手法;从这个意义上讲,布莱希特总想让我们明白,那些我们认为是自然和永恒的事物仅仅是历史的、被建构的,因而是可以改变的。尽管自然观已经在后现代性中消失了,但我们仍然会以过去自然的方式把很多东西视为我们身处境遇的永恒特征:因此,正如我在《时间的种子》中所说,我们可以轻松地想象经历各种灾难的世界毁灭,但却很难想象资本主义的终结或被其它东西替代。在这方面和乌托邦领域,我的方法是消极的,即,剖析阻碍未来和乌托邦冲动的元素,而不是提出一种崭新的、积极的乌托邦愿景,比如在十九世纪从傅里叶到莫里斯这一重要的乌托邦时刻展现出的美好愿景。

布:在《马克思主义与形式》中,你说成功地应用辩证法会产生一种震撼,使人目睹真实,所以问一个略微愚蠢的问题,你将如何指导学生应用辩证法,你会如何开始你的讲解,告诉人们应该怎样去建构它,运用它,并最终产生那种震撼?因为最终,如你所说,作为一个知识分子,你的职责是传道授业解惑,所以,关于如何做的问题,你也许可以提出一些建议。

杰:好的,我想我可以通过重复萨特、海德格尔、甚至拉康的观点来回答这个问题,即我们永远无法掌握真理,我们总是处在错误、误认、各种意识形态和各种错觉中,真理不是我们能够处于其中的地方,虽然我们有时可以瞥见真理,并且试图抓住真实性的一刻,可它总是会溜走，受到各方的危害，而且备受谴责，最终消失在意识形态和物化中。人类总是不真实的，但偶尔能够有真实性的一刻。我想坚持这样的方式，一种真正的辩证思想以这种方式确实能够有使我们在真理或真实的短暂时刻重新定位自己的震撼，尽管那只是短暂的一瞬间。除了举例之外，我不确信辩证法是否可以教授——我指的并不是通过我个人的例子，而是通过有关时刻的例子，我们在那些时刻突然领悟到更大的辩证运动。例如，如果一个人思考当代历史，最近的过去对我们而言总是最模糊的，而对当前历史的最佳分析，就是使当前的形势和刚刚过去的各种事物之间的直接联系突然变得清晰和生动。因为，最近的过去我们已经忘记，或者说，我们之前从未真正理解最近的过去与现在的关系。人们获取辩证洞察力光芒的方式有很多，而教学的方法就在于抓住一些闪光点，并在实践中展示它们，使我们了解这一瞬间的启示是什么，然后对它保持更加警觉的态度，在未来对它保持开放的心态。但我真的认为，除了以最老套的方式教授之外，没有什么其它方法可以教授如何辩证地思考。如果有的话，其任务就是对前辈思想家进行解读。在黑格尔、马克思、以及很多其他看似非辩证的作家身上，我们可以体会到辩证法在发挥作用，我们也可以通过追溯的方式学习他们的一些经验。但是，这不是按照事先安排的方式加以运用的东西；这对所有的方法概念而言，都是一个问题。

杰：谢谢你。

出处：伊恩·布坎南著《充满生命力的杰姆逊理论》，Continuum 国际出版集团 2006 年版。译者，史岩林，北京工商大学英语系教师。

巴赫金的小说论(1935—1941):
巴赫金小说论的知识背景和独创性研究

G.提哈诺夫
余静远 译

在这篇文章中,我试图追溯巴赫金小说理论背后的俄国知识传统,然后从这点出发,以一种比以往更为确凿的方法去讨论他的独创性。令人惊讶的是,对19世纪晚期一直到20世纪30年代俄国知识界中巴赫金思想来源问题的研究,一直乏善可陈。尽管我们在研究巴赫金与康德主义及新康德主义的关系方面有很大进展,但对俄国的文化、宗教、哲学和文学的理论思想传统了解还不够。这方面有一些做得很好的研究,但在这篇文章中我将不去讨论这些思想家和学者们在他们研究中讨论过的问题。相反,我将集中围绕着文学理论和文学史,详细地讨论维谢洛夫斯基(Veselovsky),俄国形式主义者和弗雷登伯格(Olga Freidenberg),接着会谈到格里夫佐夫,以及1934年12月和1935年1月在莫斯科举行的关于小说的辩论。在这场辩论中,卢卡奇和佩列韦尔泽夫是最杰出的两位参与者之一。首先,在文章的第一部分,我将以对巴赫金论小说的作品有形成性的影响这点为参考,严格筛选维谢洛夫斯基、俄国形式主义者和弗雷登伯格的作品,然后再对它们进行列举和分析。在文章的第二部分,我将分析巴赫金对这个传承下来的理论传统的反应。

一、巴赫金小说论的知识背景

维克多·什克洛夫斯基在其1929年写的文章《概述与轶事》(Sketch and Anecdote)中,粗略地概述了俄国的小说理论,他最后得到一个令人沮丧的结论:

> 尽管希腊给我们留下了小说和小说的形式,其中有部分还一直保留到了今天,但它并没有留给我们一个有关小说的理论。小说已存在了几个世纪,但是并没有相关论述涉及小说本身,它处在理论之外。俄国文学中,情况也一样,小说和普维斯特(povest)[①]长期以来都是处在理论之外的文体。

什克洛夫斯基习惯于快速且具有学院偏见的概括,因此,他的评价只有部分正确。根据他的一位形式主义的朋友鲍里斯·艾亨鲍姆(Boris Eikhenbaum)1924年的记录,俄国早在1844年就出现了论小说的学术性论文,艾亨鲍姆进一步将这些论文解读为一种确凿的标志,标志着正在成长的俄国散文的自我意识。然而,直到19世纪90年代在亚历山大·维谢洛夫斯

① 译者注:俄罗斯古代的史诗文学体裁。

基的作品中,俄国才有了关于小说起源的正式记述。

维谢洛夫斯基的文章理论性并不强。用他自己的话来说,他觉得自己无法回答小说为什么逐渐成为了现代性的主要表达方式这个问题。于是,他选择考虑这个过程中"如何"的问题。尽管设定了这个限制性的框架,维谢洛夫斯基还是十分谨慎,不让随意的解释影响他的行文。如此一来,外界那些影射他的努力仅限在探索起源的言说就不攻自破了。在《从历史诗学的介绍说起》(Iz wedeniia v istoricheskuiu poetiku)中,他提供给读者的是一个"类比,这个类比也许不能清楚地说明小说的起源,但也许能告诉我们能够形成小说源起的社会环境的特点"。鉴于维谢洛夫斯基对小说源起方式的重构与巴赫金的观点有紧密关联,下面我将以一个更长的引用说明:

> 在希腊,戏剧仍然属于民族历史发展的范畴。亚历山大的征战打破了这种民族发展,自治的希腊变成一个融合了东西方的世界范围的君主国,在这样的背景下,小说的时代就出现了。政治自由的传统连同公民的理想一起黯淡了,在这个世界性的广袤空间里,孤独的个体因不再与社会性事物联系,逐渐退回自身,对内在的生活产生了兴趣,并建立起了乌托邦以代替传说。这些就是希腊小说的主要话题。它们缺乏传统元素,一切都与资产阶级格调接近,戏剧转移到了火炉旁,从戏台上跌入了日常生活的各种情境之中。

值得注意的是,维谢洛夫斯基狂热地相信小说的历史是连续的,从古典时期一直延续到他最喜爱的文艺复兴时期。鲍里斯·恩格尔哈特(Boris Engelhardt),这个少数研究俄国形式主义并卓有成效的学者,以他对薄伽丘和拉伯雷广博的研究,仔细研究了维谢洛夫斯基除纯粹个人偏好之外,钟爱文艺复兴的原因:"这里的'Renaissance'这个名称就表明了这位文学历史学家最关心的是传统的思想或艺术潮流,这些潮流在被其他的精神文化现象压制一段时间之后,在社会和个体意识中复苏"。维谢洛夫斯基与20世纪30年代的佩列韦尔泽夫(Pereverzev)一样,坚持主张资本主义前期和文艺复兴早期小说的重要性。他并不认为小说的历史中存在着一个关键的断裂,小说是在经过断裂之后,重新拥有了一个新的身份。对他而言,小说的崛起与矛盾的历史发展不可分割,这种历史发展允许对外在无尽的世界的探索和对内在个人火炉边的普通生活的挖掘同时存在。如此一来,小说就具有了多元的特质:它既能激发对外在世界的探索,同时又倡导一种孤独感;它既能拓宽人类存在的视界,又使得人们对于自身更为敏感。

形式主义者们继承了小说历史的连续观,并且在将之大幅度修改之后,保存了下来。他们的连续观缺乏发展之流中具体的历史界限。而当初正是这股发展之流的灵感给维谢洛夫斯基和佩列韦尔泽夫提供了方法。小说历史的连续观(后来)被洪堡式的一个观点取代了,此观点认为有一种永存的、塑形的"能量,它的本质是永恒的——它不会出现,也不会消失,因此它超越了时间"。这也许听起来很悖谬,艾亨鲍姆称这种能量是"历史性的",总结时又称这种特殊形式的历史性产生了大量能从时间中隐退的事实。

俄国形式主义者将连续性修改为持久性。他们认为许多文学体裁的命运是一连串可预测的变体形式。尽管充满了动力,这种升降交替(的能量/情景)却没有历史。文体被认为主要是一种内在的修辞系统,目的是“材料的变形”和疏远,因此它处于时间和社会变化之外。诚然,文体的位置在文学系统内部是不断地发生着变化的,因为它们不断地从中心退到边缘,又从边缘走向中心,承担起主导角色。然而,在这些争夺主导权的斗争中,最基本的要素一直都没变。人们的注意力转移到了它们的身份变化上,追寻文学体裁起源的问题失去了意义。文学形式不会产生也不会消失,它们仅仅是在文学版图上变换着音量和位置。因为缺少生死存亡那种真正的残酷,它们的战争是颇具戏剧性的。低级别的体裁永远不会消失,它们被流放到一个安全的地方,要么是版图的底部要么是版图的顶部。短期的被忽略之后,它们迎来的是被经典化的盛宴。迪尼亚诺夫(Tynianov)对这一过程的描述几乎呈现出一种童话的色彩:“在某一体裁解体的时代,它从中心退到了边缘,然后从文学的卑微琐碎之中,从它的‘后院’和‘低洼’里,一种新的现象出现在了中心。”

这种现象引起一个问题,即当一种文学体裁从“后院”到达文学阶梯的顶峰时,它有哪些表现。迪尼亚诺夫早期的一篇文章提供了答案,这一答案直接对巴赫金未来的理论产生了影响。以处于“高级别”阶段的体裁——颂歌——为例,迪尼亚诺夫强调“它不是一种结束的、封闭的存在,而是一种建设式的倾向”。迪尼亚诺夫的功劳在于,关于小说的起源特性,他提出了一种不同于前人的可能性:从他看来,体裁不再是一组被严格定义的、固定的符号,而是一组动感的词组,一个方向。这一点很关键,因为它提供了一种体裁间联系的可能。依靠一个方向开放的字群,高级别的文体吸引其他的文体,甚至直接带上它们,使它们变成自己的一部分,然后再依靠自己的身份使它们“活跃”起来。此外,之前被认为不合适的新的生命体,可以通过一个文体敞开的门进入文学领域。最终,在一个限制更加灵活的体裁里,安全的变形就有了更多的空间。“具有吸引力的体裁(颂歌)可以在依旧保持自己是颂歌的条件下不让人察觉地进行变形,只要那些发挥主要语篇功能的基本元素是固定的。”什克洛夫斯基(Shklovsky)引申了这个论述,将它运用到了小说这一体裁上:“作为体裁的小说经典比其它体裁的经典也许更能戏仿或修复它自身。”这样,在迪尼亚诺夫眼里,小说的界限更加灵活和松散,而体裁的经典也变得更有渗透力了。对他来说,小说的存在意味着自我模仿作为一种考察和肯定体裁身份的一种方式。《项狄传》(*Tristram Shandy*)是他用以说明小说不惧怕激活自嘲的过程的最极端和激烈的一个例子。

依照这种思路,体裁间的斗争就不再是为保持固定特质的斗争,而变成了一场对诗意语词方向或定位的争斗。这场在理解文体,特别是将文体等同于字组的趋势的革命性的转变,不可避免地造成了一场我们看到的对任何特定文体的命运史无前例的确证。从“高级别”体裁的位置上退下来以后,迪尼亚诺夫安慰地说道,颂歌并没有消失:“(它)注定了要荣誉扫地,过一种秘密的、地下的生活,然后在拟古主义者的反抗中,它重新崛起了。”

尽管文学体裁会遭遇各种变数,尽管文体的基本构成是不可改变的,俄国形式主义者们还是需要解释文体的兴起和扩张。评论俄国形式主义的学者一直在探究形式主义者们在面对防御森严的、封闭的文学领域时所体验到的无力感。形式主义者们对此在他们的理论中提出了解决方法,与此相关的研究也做的很好。这里我想谈到的是他们提出的这些解决方法与巴赫金后来思考的小说话语的关联。

早在1922年,迪尼亚诺夫的文章《颂歌作为演说》(The Ode as an Oratorical Genre)中,

就涉及了对文学"纯粹性"的质疑。这篇内涵丰富的论文毫不含糊地分析了文学系统与相邻系统的相关性,具体说来,是文学系统与"与之最接近的非文学的组织——口语,和与之相近的言语艺术和日常用语的关联"。文章中对非文学的口语组织的研究在形式主义者之间引起了不同的反响。艾亨鲍姆尽管原则上同意这一观点,但在短暂的对"神侃"(skaz)的兴趣之后,与迪尼亚诺夫分道扬镳,专注到距离更远的群组的重要性上去了,如文学制度和作者的社会地位等问题。科洛夫斯基曾指控他忽略了美学之外因素的意义,艾亨鲍姆的回应是将事情推到了另一个极端。1927 年他写的论文《文学字节》("Literaturnyi byt")推翻了迪尼亚诺夫的前提,使得人们对文学语言方面的关注大为减少。最近的研究还发现他 1924 年就计划要写一本书名为《文学劳动》(*Literary Labour*)的著作。

然而,迪尼亚诺夫的观点得到了形式主义内部最坚定的文学纯粹性的保卫者维克多·什克洛夫斯基的认可和支持。1928 年,什克洛夫斯基为了弥补错误,甘愿承认"非美学的因素能够也确实引起过艺术的改变,例如,因为一种语言对另一种特定语言的影响,又或者是因为一种新的社会秩序的出现"。如果这份声明在与"社会秩序"这一现实的和解的路上走的太远的话,什克洛夫斯基在其他一些声明中用更为委婉地方式表达他对迪尼亚诺夫观点的支持。在同一本书的后几页,他赞扬了迪尼亚诺夫的论文《文学事实》("The Literary Fact"),认为它奠定了文学这一概念的流动性。这一份褒奖之后,什克洛夫斯基又加上了他自己的一个生动的比喻性总结:"文学",他写道,"从边缘成长起来,吸收了非美学的材料,文学通过扩展到非文学领域生存下去。"这里尤其需要注意的是,在什克洛夫斯基对文学进化的理解中,非文学材料和文学边缘性地位是互以彼此为先决条件的,通过不断地将文学性的疆域向后推,文学加速前进。这个过程发生在边缘上,在"低洼"里。边缘地带是日常语言和生活中元素的主要入口。回到他在 1922 年那篇论文中提到的观点,以他及形式主义者同伴的作品为基础,迪尼亚诺夫论证了文学与日常生活的重要关联,这种关联最基本的模式是以言语为基础的:"日常生活主要通过言语与文学联系。"正是这个信念,激起了迪尼亚诺夫以及其他形式主义者对小说"将非文学的言语材料引进文学的不断变化的方法"的兴趣。

口语和日常生活与文学紧密联系的这一发现,不仅对巴赫金的理论构造有非凡的意义,对两次世界大战间隙俄国的文学和文化理论的整个图景都具有无比重要的意义。在文艺理论界,唯一能与这一发现相提并论的是形式主义"内在的文学性"这一具有开拓性的创新观念。从自主的文学性到文学与日常生活和言语互动,形式主义运动经历了一个危险的通过仪式。然后,通过接受随着这一转变而来的自我毁灭性的后果,它保持了自身知识的正直性。

文学形式的连续观主导了 20 世纪 20 年代到 30 年代的俄国小说理论。这一观点在弗雷登伯格的作品中也可以看到,巴赫金曾在《拉伯雷研究》(*Rabelais*)中引用了她在《情节和体裁的诗学》(*The Poetics of Plot and Genre*)一书中的观点,该书于 1935 年完成、1936 年出版。弗雷登伯格在彼得堡是被作为一名古典主义者来培养的,她接受的是一批在希腊古典文学方面最著名的学者的指导,这些著名学者后来也教授过巴赫金。弗雷登伯格在希腊小说中找到了她毕生的兴趣点。在她未出版的回忆录《生命之芽》(*The Shoots of Life*)中,她谈到了自己是是如何进入这个领域的:"我对希腊小说几乎一无所知,对它研究的并不是一件已经完成了的事。罗德(Rohde)之后就没人去触碰它,而那些触碰过的人也并没有了解的更深入。"在彼得堡大学的时候,弗雷登伯格回忆,"文学课程当时局限在古典时期,希腊化时期被认为是倒退,他们甚至都没有提到小说。人们以它为耻就像它是一位失足的女儿一样。"在这样的环境下,弗雷登伯格立志为小说发声的勇气尤为震撼。她说她决定从事希腊小说研究的那一刻是她生命中最重要的时刻。

尼古拉·马尔通过"语义古生物学"的研究方法,证实了在历史发展的所有阶段都存在单一的、原始的神话遗产的痕迹(通常被马尔和他的学派认为与马克思主义意义上的社会—经济形式说吻合)。借助这一方法,弗雷登伯格提出了"差异是同一性的一种形式,而同一性存在于异质性当中"的核心观点。然而,实际上这个公式微妙的平衡在她的作品中却被打破了,因为弗雷登伯格明显的倾向于"同一"这一边。她又直接地将这个观点放到《情节和体裁的诗学》中去,根据"同一"这一原则,小说也不过是史诗的另一种形式。它们都是从一个共同的神话遗产那里发展而来的,而这共同的神话遗产保证了它们文体的相似:"希腊小说与史诗一样,都使用了相同的民间故事传统,从它情节的基本要素就可以得出它是小说的一个变体的结论。"(P. p269)。然而这并没有消除马尔主义者们想要发现的差异类型,而就算真是无法发现,马尔主义者也会将其设想出来。弗雷登伯格明显受了马尔的影响,她认为共同遗产处在不同的历史阶段,被不同社会阶级的人掌握,形式都会不一样:"就像在早期的奴隶制度时代产生了史诗,而在希腊化时代那些富裕阶级的奴隶主却欣赏小说一样。"(P. p268)

弗雷登伯格坚持认为史诗和小说的内在本质是同一的,她同意维谢洛夫斯基的观点,认为小说其实是史诗穿着日常的衣服。"希腊小说",她写道,"是非常人性化且非常真实的,英勇的功绩,随着社会结构和思想的变化,在这里成为了冒险。"(P. p273)小说中,命运已经表现为低一格的"好运"。(P. p 276)

弗雷登伯格观点的问题在于,因为有共同的神话起源,所有的文学体裁最终都会融和。小说不仅与史诗融和,与抒情诗,与耶稣受难剧等都会融和。这个列表可以很长,因为每一种文学体裁最终都会变成另一种体裁的另一面。吊诡的是,尽管弗雷登伯格承认古代文学为后来的欧洲一直到工业资本主义时代的艺术提供了模式,她却不愿意承认希腊小说为后世创造了很多重复的叙述模式(P. p332) 她认为,那些不是产生于小说自身体裁内的特性,而是产生于"原始思维"。因此,弗雷登伯格辩述道,"希腊小说并不像据说的那样,所有欧洲冒险小说都是从其稳定的体裁复制而来的"。(P. p277)小说在这位倾向于相信"原始思维"是所有人类文化的共同起源和基本特性的学者的严肃注视下,时时都能感到丧失身份和消解在永恒的神话之域的危险。

最后,我们简单地来看一本有明显折中主义的书,这本书题为《小说的一种理论》(*A Theory of the Novel*),作者鲍里斯·格里夫佐夫似乎是从卢卡奇那里借用了这个书名,书中好几次他都赞许地提到了卢卡奇的名字,卢卡奇的《小说理论》(1920 年第一版)也出现在格里夫佐夫的参考书目里。格里夫佐夫的书缺少一个清晰明确的原则,它只是一本粗略的文学体裁的历史介绍夹杂着一些一般性的评论。与他的同辈人一样,格里夫佐夫也承认罗德的(T. p147)权威性,并指认希腊为小说的发源地。(T. p17)我们需要注意的是,格里夫佐夫将小说的历史描绘成一个"与其它更人为化的文体逐渐分离"的过程,最后变得"更为清楚地意识到自身的自然性和拥有自然性的独特权利”。小说逼着其他的文体退出、灭亡(T. pp9—10),它把他们逼到一个“凄惨的境地,并占领了言语文化的全部领域”。(T. p19)当然,这并不就意味着格里夫佐夫赞同小说的连续观:“小说有一个断裂的历史,它曾几次繁荣过,但总是断断续续的,区域性的。”(T. p18) 他认为小说“无所不能”的这个想法“是虚幻且危险的”。(T. p19)在开列这一文学体裁的历史的时候,格里夫佐夫强调,散文体裁地位的上升和下降是交替的,而当它下降的时候,就是诗歌兴盛的时候。格里夫佐夫的这个观点很大部分上受了俄国形式主义的影响。格里夫佐夫认为小说不应当是无所不能的’,尽管他的原因表述的并不完全清楚,但是他暗示过小说内容是可以道德败坏的。他举了福楼拜的《包法利夫人》的例子,以证明对小说创造和营设的幻象的信任会给个人带来毁灭的后果。格里夫佐夫的结论很有启示意义,他似乎完全赞成卢卡奇的观点,即史诗比小说更具有道德优越性:“小说确实可以描绘一切,但是小说的描绘不是总是歪曲的吗?……过去有没有小说的世纪,未来可能还会有。”回归史诗,就像卢卡奇说的那样,被认为是人类解放的标志:“意识到史诗的力量,它自我实现的权利,人类能够回归史诗,而不必去羡慕可怜的爱玛的命运。”(T. p148)

说到这里,有必要简短地做一个总结。我已经表明,巴赫金开始写他第一篇关于小说的文章的时候(1934—1935),俄国就已经奠定了小说理论化的传统。抛开所有的繁缛和细节不论,这个传统的核心是由三种主要的观点组成的:这一文学体裁的连续性;这一文学体裁多变、灵活、不稳定的特性;最后是小说与日常话语及生活现象有紧密关系。形式主义是唯一一场强调日常生活言语的文学运动,它在这一方面的功劳很大,不仅将活生生的语言引入了小说的研究,而且提出了小说是披着日常的外衣的史诗的观点,这一观点在其他主要的理论学派中也被反复的提到(维谢洛夫斯基和弗雷登伯格)。如果由此再想到1934至1935初的讨论,再想到卢卡奇有力论证了的小说是史诗暂时的中断的观点,那么巴赫金文章的背景便逐渐显出了更清晰的轮廓。

二、巴赫金的创新:局限和实质

巴赫金的论文是严格按照时间顺序进行的,中间有一些规律的短期中断:1934—35年(《小说中的话语》);1937—38年(由S.G.波查罗夫 和V.V.科斯罗夫发表,标题为《小说中时间和时空的形式》,其“结语”和结语前的一段为1973年所写);1940年(《从小说话语的前历史说起》);1941年(《史诗与小说》)。我选择对这四篇文章进行解释和评论,将重点特别集中在巴赫金创新性的局限和性质上。俄国的理论传统和1934—35年关于小说的辩论留下了很多问题,其中有两个尤其重要:小说与日常词(世界)的关系问题和小说体裁的起源问题。巴赫金的独创性与他回答这两个问题的方法有关。

似乎有充分的理由将这四篇文章认为是巴赫金与不同时期的对手的辩论。巴赫金很早就参与了这些辩论,而他对小说的言说所走的道路表明了他致力于辩论的决心。所以在他第一篇文章里(虽然这篇文章写作于1934—35年那场辩论期间及之后),他首先就回到了形式主义的遗产。这对20世纪20年代的巴赫金社(Bakhtin Circle)的自我定义非常关键,他现在要对其进行清算。卢卡奇作品的回音从一开始就在场,但在这篇文章里稍弱。

巴赫金将他自己的方法论定义为"言语艺术的研究中,对抽象的'形式主义'和同样抽象的'意识形态主义'间分离状态的克服。"(DN. p259)。这种克服被写在了日程表上,因为"一旦我们理解了话语是一种社会现象,话语中的形式和内容就是合一的"。(DN. p259)话语的社会本质这个观点,直接回应了巴赫金和沃罗辛诺夫20世纪20年代的观点,现在又得到了另一个观点的支持:话语"伟大的历史使命"与文学体裁使命的交错。(DN. p259)在这篇和下篇文章中,巴赫金都采用了社会学方法。这两篇文章讨论的是艺术话语"伟大"或"无名"的命运由文学体裁的命运决定的论点。这一论点给了文学体裁一个重要的社会维度:由于它有决定话语命运的权利,因此,文学体裁是超个人的,是无法缩减为个人的才华的。

巴赫金最初从分析小说的文体特征着手,决心弥补传统文体学区分风格和体裁的弱点。然而,他并未断言这一点自己的独创性。他间接提到了形式主义者,将自己对小说体散文的最初兴趣点放在20世纪20年代。这似乎是他向形式主义唯一的致敬,在接下来的文章中他竭力地想要把自己与形式主义者拉开距离,尽管有时候这种努力显得徒劳。

1. 小说与日常的、非正式的词(世界)

顺着形式主义者们的道路,巴赫金认为最重要的一步就是把注意力放在小说的话语特征上。与形式主义者一样,他视小说为"有结构的艺术系统"(DN. p262,PND. p47)。然而,与形式主义者不一样的是,巴赫金的系统是由言语和语言组成的,而不是由修辞组成的。巴赫金的中心论点是,小说是一个艺术地组织成的"社会言语类型的多样体和个体言语的多样体"。(DN. p262) 巴赫金从来没有想过要详细区分言语多样性和语言多样性(杂语性),他迅速地转到了另一个观点上,即小说总是(不仅仅是"有时")"语言间社会对话"的场所(DN. p263)。这个定义表达了一种强烈的信念,那就是小说不应该简单地被视为是仅仅有关社会的故事,它也是社会本身的一种言语模式,它典型地体现了社会性的而非个体性的不同态度之间的冲突与矛盾。

无疑,如果没有形式主义对"神侃"(skaz)和对其他日常生活中的言语表现予以特别注意的传统,巴赫金也不可能对小说的话语跨度如此关注。然而在他追问这些问题的时候,巴赫金却明显地采取了一种与形式主义者们不同的方法,他在语言和世界观之间建立了一种紧密的关联。语言,巴赫金明确写道,不应该被视作抽象的语法类别的系统,而应被视作"渗透着意识形态的,作为一种世界观,甚至作为一种具体的观点"。(DN. p27)因此,小说中一种语言的"形象"就是"社会所持有的(或流行)的那些观点的形象,就是一种社会意识形态元素(ideologeme)的形象"。(DN. p357)小说表达了语言形式的混杂,从其背后可以辨认出"不同世界观间的相撞和冲突"。(DN. p360)在新的一轮对形式主义的方法的攻击中,巴赫金总结道,语言不是一种形式主义的东西,艺术地进行语言游戏也不可能是一种形式主义的游戏。(DN. p357)

巴赫金将小说中语言间的互动称为"对话",这也许会令人误解,因为他描述的并不是一种和睦的、平静的、开放的交流。相反,对话的主要面目是斗争,是一种几乎有形的"社会—语言观点间的斗争"。(DN. p273)诚然,巴赫金援引了一种解释学的对话观点,这种观点的基础是被他称为“字词的内在对话性”的一种机制，但是，这种耐心关注对方的理想情况很大程度上局限于读者/听者的空间，而在“物内部与异己的词直接相遇”(DN. p282)的场域里则很少发生。这种语言和世界观之间竞争性的互动标明了巴赫金接近于现代性的认识论模式，以及这种认识论模式的流动观、变化观，以及各种看法同样神圣但最终却短暂的观点。更具有启示意义的是，在《小说中的话语》(Discourse in the Novel)中，文学想象和社会分析之间的鸿沟被证明是不存在的，因为，杂语性作为物体内在矛盾性的表达含而不露地展现出来。对话明确地类比为辩证：

> 除了物体自身内部的矛盾，文章的作者也目睹了围绕着这个物体的社会杂语性慢慢展开，任何物体周围都有各种语言混合的巴别塔，物体的辩证与围绕着这个物体的社会对话交织在一起。
>
> (DN. p278)

在巴赫金1970—71年的笔记中，他不承认对话和辩证之间的亲密关系。他颠倒了这两者的初始立足点，将辩证法作为认知的产物而不是过程。在这些前提下，他警告道，对话会消失在辩证法里。然而，20世纪30年代的时候，他还是很乐观的，他相信在物体本性及从中得到的知识和小说中这种知识的丰富展现之间有一种必然又清晰的纽带。小说再次被视为一种反映社会现实的模式，尽管这个模式是虚构性、调解性的。

如果说小说是唯一可以为不同的语言和世界观提供互相竞争的场所的体裁，那这肯定只是一个结果而不是起点。巴赫金重建了小说包含世界上不同的、甚至是敌意的图景的方法，在此过程中，他不断地表明这是出于一种显而易见的形而上的需要。在人类历史的每个阶段，总有两股对立的力量在起作用：一股是不停制造言语—意识形态世界的集中统一和尊奉意识形态系统的向心力(DN. p271)，一股是试图破坏这一过程的离心力。巴赫金从未将任何一个定义明确的社会团体或阶级归为这两股力量中的任何一个，也从未说明这种对立的具体的历史动态，这也就是为什么他的表述有形而上色彩的原因。相反，他将两组文学体裁分为离心/向心两极：小说，以及“向小说靠拢的那些艺术—散文式的体裁”；另一极则包括诗歌、戏剧和史诗。巴赫金认为小说式的散文，“出生在地方集市和斗牛场上”(DN. p273)，因而是低俗的、流行的、日常的，而诗歌则是处于“更高的更正式的社会—意识形态水平”。(DN. p173, PND. p67)这种分类不仅令人想起沃罗辛诺夫1929年将未成形的和非正式的(“生活—意识形态”)神圣化的举动，也让人想起后期形式主义者们对字节(byt)的关注。日常生活的世界在小说中寻找自己的词汇并通过小说表达自己，而“正式的”文体只对业已形成的、成功的意识形态的需求有所回应。巴赫金认为，杂语性是一种前定的必要特征，就算是在被推翻的情况下，它的痕迹在一切言语艺术作品中还是可以发现的。并不奇怪的是，从诗歌中发现这种“痕迹”的唯一方法是细心考察讽刺诗和喜剧诗等“低等”体裁。(DN. p287)所有那些“不正式的”体裁都不在从亚里士多德到现在的诗学的“观念视界”之列(DN. p269)，巴赫金狂热地想要将它们从——用什克洛夫斯基有关小说的话来说——“外于理论的体裁”的地位重新解救回来。

我来总结一下。巴赫金在证明小说复调杂语本质的时候，仍然继续着他和形式主义者们的辩论。他应该感谢形式主义者们,正是因为他们的刺激,他才转向对字词、日常生活的世界和对非正式言语的关注。他也与形式主义者们共享同样的一个理论模型。两者都认为艺术是一个系统,也都认为文学体裁的命运是被对立的形而上的原则之间的斗争所决定的:要么是修辞的非自动化/自动化,要么是语言和世界观的分散/集中。在形式主义者和巴赫金共享的文学形式非经典化/经典化观念中,上述两组力量也可以被认为是重叠的。除此之外,对巴赫金和形式主义者来说,之前的理论都把小说忽略了,这非常不合理。然而,巴赫金明显与形式主义者们不同的地方在于,他往这个理论模型里填充了不一样的内容:他没有去分析文体修辞,而是专注在语言的斗争上。与形式主义的"修辞"不同,巴赫金所说的语言是与世界观和态度联系在一起的。

因此,社会语言和艺术修辞分别是巴赫金和形式主义者们理论中艺术的主导因素。作为主导因素,它们决定了系统中其它要素的功能。两者在这方面的惊人相似,从情节的角色就可以看出。对什克洛夫斯基和艾亨鲍姆来说,情节主要是为修辞的进化服务的,或,用什克洛夫斯基的话来说,情节是被修辞"推动的"。相反,在巴赫金的理论里,我们读到:"情节是受语言间联系和接触这一任务支配的。"(DN. p365) 然而,他们理论内在机制的等同不应该让我们无视这样一个事实:形式主义者对小说作为一种"低等的"、日常的文学体裁的兴趣只是一种不成熟的倾向,而巴赫金果断地转换了视角,将小说看做是一种重写文学理论及其对社会思想含义的主要手段。

2. 小说的起源:小说和史诗

在巴赫金讨论到小说的起源及小说与史诗的关系时,可以很明显地看到巴赫金深受俄国理论框架的影响和启发,这个理论框架主要是由前期俄国的传统和1934—35年关于小说的辩论组成的,巴赫金的独创性与之有很大的关联。对小说与史诗关系的探究其实是他对小说起源问题探究的继续。从这点来看,他的论文《史诗与小说》("Epic and Novel") 最初的标题为《作为一种文学体裁的小说》("The Novel as a Literary Genre") 是很有道理的。

因为研究方法带有过深的形而上学色彩,巴赫金对小说起源的研究极大地受阻。早在1934—35年他就提出了小说起源的问题,且以极其矛盾的方式给出了答案。他明确指出,"在历史性存在的任一时刻,每一种语言的内部分层是小说作为一种文学体裁的不可或缺的前提。"(DN. p263)如果语言一直是内部分层的,而且这个过程一直贯穿它整个"历史性的存在",包括"任一时刻",那么小说的起源这个问题还有什么意义?既然小说存在的前提似乎永恒地存在着,这要么消解了对小说起源的追问,要么自动地排除了语言作为有历史重要性的因素。

那么,到底什么重要呢?巴赫金在一段容易使人联想起卢卡奇《小说理论》的章节里,改述了卢卡奇的话,强调了他称之为"文学意识的一种特定的语言失落感,它不复再拥有一种神圣单一的语言媒介去保存意识形态的思想"的重要性。(DN. p367)接着,他试着为这种抽象的情况提供一个社会学的解读:

> 言语—意识形态的世界的分离在小说中得到表达。它的前提是存在一个与其它社会团体密切互动的根本分化了的社会团体。处于内部核心统一不变的等级、阶层或阶级,不能为小说的发展提供具有生产力的社会土壤,除非他们腐朽不堪,改变了内部平

衡和自足的状态。

(DN. p368)

这就是巴赫金最具体的讲述了。他似乎陷入到当时苏联文艺批评流行的语言惯性中去了,认为小说应该是一个特定阶层的境况与兴趣的表达。但他仍语焉不详,也拒绝在具体的历史阶级群的问题上进行详细阐述,人们也许会推测他是反对而不是赞成官方的理论。然而,可以肯定的是,他并不认为这是小说兴起的一个充分条件:"但即使这样还不够,即使是一个被社会斗争打破了的社会整体,如果作为国族整体来说仍然处于隔绝封闭的状态,还是不足以为小说提供社会土壤。"(DN. p368)

在解释小说起源的时候,人们一定会注意到巴赫金对维谢洛夫斯基坚决拥护的世界主义原则的忠诚,虽然他未明确承认这一点。尽管维谢洛夫斯基对社会差异可能是小说兴起的一个决定因素这个观点缺乏兴趣,但他仍然明确地提到过,地理位置的置换和多元文化主义是小说的摇篮。如此一来,我们便了解了,巴赫金所列的三个因素早已经是俄国文艺批评理论界的观点了:小说的社会决定论(阶级决定论)的观点被社会学的方法所坚持;小说产生于一个国家超越它狭隘的限制的过程中,这一观点是从维谢洛夫斯基继承而来的;最后一点,一种语言对其它语言的影响是进化和变化的要素,这首先是由形式主义者们提出来的。巴赫金的独创性与其说在于他修正和重新整理了这些因素,不如说他看到了这些因素间的联系,这是之前被忽略了的。但这并不是说每一因素的自主行为的结果与其它因素有联系,而是说每一个因素都有复杂的双重本性:社会的是话语的,话语的也是社会的。社会团体的分层也是语言的分层,反之亦然。同样,世界主义既有社会维度也有语言维度。巴赫金认为这些因素间是互相联系,同等重要的,因此他无法排列它们的重要性。某些时候他强调,就像前面的例子表明的那样,世界主义是小说兴起的决定性条件,在其他情况下,他又纠正这个平衡,再一次偏向了社会因素。他对骑士散文小说的讨论就是一个例子。他写道,"当然不仅仅是对外国文字的自由翻译这个明显的事实,也不是原作者的文化国际主义",决定了骑士散文小说的特性,而"主要是这样的一个事实,即这种散文小说缺乏一个统一牢固的社会基础,缺乏与固定的社会阶层相联系的安全可靠的自足性"。

1940年,巴赫金写了《从小说话语的前历史谈起》("From the Prehistory of Novelistic Discourse"),看来他终于试图在历史的具体化和指称性上更进一步了。与他的前辈罗德和维谢洛夫斯基一样,在这篇文章中,巴赫金也认为小说最初兴起的过程发生在希腊化时期。(PND. pp63—4) 然而,小说体的定位是巴赫金小说起源模型中唯一一个具体的历史指称点。当他接着分析决定小说兴起的因素时,他再一次求助于宏伟的形而上学假设。这证实了人们的印象,即他喜欢复杂的直觉胜过可检验的事实。毫不奇怪,这些因素中的第一个是复调。在巴赫金的表述中,它完全剥去了外在历史或社会的决定因素。第一次被严肃又鲜明地引进的另一个因素是笑。正是在这个阶段巴赫金对历史理性的漠视显得尤为突出。巴赫金断言,笑"组成了代表语言的最古老的形式"。(PND. p50)笑和语言紧密联系,它们似乎是人类文化内在的人类学恒量。通过赋予笑原始形式的杰出地位,借其表达特定的普遍态度,巴赫金突出了笑作为一直伴随人们生活的一种形而上的典范力量的角色。巴赫金对古罗马的笑的描述都几乎没能改变这个专断的结论。他勾勒的罗马的笑的是本质主义的、无历史的,人们从他的前提中都能看到这一点。他将笑缩减为一种在世界的矛盾性中获得关于这个世界丰富的、足够的、永恒的知识的认识工具:"严肃直白的形式只是一个片段,只是整体的一半;整体的完整只能依靠给这个形式增加喜剧的对应物来恢复。"(PND. p58)无怪乎巴赫金这里用了"恢复"这个词:它意味着一种对知识被动性更强烈的感觉,知识的命运被认为是揭开业已存在的真相而不是去寻找新的真相。

在笑的所有类型中,巴赫金尤感兴趣的是戏仿。在描述它展开的过程时,巴赫金尽管从未承认,但他确实受惠于迪尼亚诺夫。在成为或融入一种文学类型之前,戏仿只是一种话语倾向,或用迪尼亚诺夫的说法,一种"方向"。在令人想起卢卡奇和迪尼亚诺夫的一个段落中,巴赫金写道:"古代戏仿作品的词是无根的,所有不同戏仿的形式似乎组成了一种特殊的超体裁或体裁间的世界。"(PND. p59)依照迪尼亚诺夫的模型,巴赫金的戏仿字词很快就不再无根地漂浮在各种体裁之间了,因为这种体裁间的世界是由一个共同的目的组成的,那就是"给所有直接存在的体裁、语言、风格、声音提供笑的纠正和批评",它"内部统一,看起来就像同类组成的整体"。(PND. p59)然而,巴赫金从这里出发的下一步则不免牵强。对巴赫金来说,这个统一的世界的轮廓逐渐变成了小说中的那些:"但是我总把这一切想象成一部巨大的小说,属性丰富、风格多样、评论独到、讽刺辛辣,其中充分地展示了一个特定文化、民族、时代的多声性和多层次的声音。"(PND. p60)这里,让人困扰的根源不在于巴赫金认为戏仿最终呈现出了文学体裁的样子的这个结论,而在于他武断地相信这种体裁必然是小说。在这个紧要关头,巴赫金使用了循环论证的方法(petitio principii),这是一种在论证中用于隐藏缺失的一环联系的修辞手法。从巴赫金最初的前提,他需要用令人信服的逻辑去证明小说作为文学体裁的存在,现在这一论题已经成为一个正当的、无条件的事实:小说不是产生于戏仿或笑,它仅仅是对一个已经存在的"超体裁或体裁间世界"的命名。(PND. p59)

除了这一处的前后矛盾之外,巴赫金的论证从另一个不同方面来说极其重要。他证明了迪尼亚诺夫研究文学体裁方法的可行性,他将小说视为不同话语交织形成的动态力量的中心。他以追踪戏仿的命运开始,以小说是不同话语的产物,是"多体裁的体裁"这个观点的形成结束。巴赫金声称小说是一种通过不停地摆脱自身的身份以保持自身身份的文学体裁。我们现在知道了他之所以这么说的深层原因。作为被戏仿和戏仿、直接与曲折的交汇点,小说本质上就是自相矛盾的,它注定处于永远的躁动与自我批评中。

巴赫金进一步揭示了小说自身内部容纳的它的"他者",他也努力分析了史诗和小说的区别,在小说的界限之外,进一步确定小说的"他者"。如果说,在形式主义者们所确立的理论的压力下,巴赫金要定义小说文体就必定要区分小说与诗歌,那么,将小说和史诗并置的观点肯定是来自卢卡奇。然而,巴赫金在两个重要方面与卢卡奇不同。首先,与俄国理论传统和罗德的观点相同,他力证小说的历史是连续的。他确实突出了作为小说的成熟与完善期的文艺复兴时期,(DN. p415)但从来没有隔断它与古典主义时期、与中世纪的联系。第二,他摒弃了传统贬低小说的看法。传统观点认为小说不过是对史诗的糟糕模仿,是史诗的有机性和整体性的暂时替代。巴赫金参考了布兰肯堡(Blankenburg)和黑格尔的观点,但他仅仅是部分地同意他们的看法(后来这些观点无条件地被卢卡奇认可了),即认为小说之于现代世界，应当如史诗之于古代世界。这个想法有某些创造性，是将小说从文学“低洼”上升为杰出的、受人尊敬的文学体裁的必要一步。(EN. p10)但是这仍然不够，巴赫金并不想说明小说与史诗的价值是可比的；他旨在说明，虽然两个体裁在审美价值方面具有可比性，小说和史诗作为世界的图景依旧是不可替换的。另外，他还决心奠定小说在现代社会作为唯一一种能胜任于表现现实的体裁的地位。这项任务要求他在沉闷的博物馆灯光下研究史诗，同时也要求策略，某种程度上，这种策略类似什克洛夫斯基对待旧的艺术形式的不屑态度：“对形式的斗争就是对新形式的斗争。我们要像研究青蛙一样研究旧的形式，生物学家研究青蛙并不是为了学习如何呱呱叫。”

在《史诗与小说》这篇文章中，巴赫金第一次试图简洁地列出那些使得小说成为一种不可取代的艺术形式和表现现代性的文学体裁的突出特征。除了他在前面文章里证明过的那些特点之外，在这里他特别强调他称为“当代区域”的地方，作为小说文体真正的领土，这个新领地被巴赫金定义为“与现代接触最多的地方”(无限接触着当代现实)。(EN. p11)巴赫金同意歌德的观点，认为史诗记载的是“绝对的过去”，而小说则是关于无限的现在的文体。巴赫金特别注明，小说的“现在”并不是一个准备好了、仅仅需要被反映的世界；它是小说创造的一个现代世界。只有从这个意义上讲它才是一个无限的世界，因为当代与过去一样，(在小说中)可以在场，也可以向个体观察的无限的可能性开放。小说，巴赫金最终承认，正因它的认识论差别，才具有属性差别。与史诗依赖“民族传说”不同，小说是依靠不断改变的自我的体验而存活的。小说文体根植于瞬间的、短暂的不稳定中，植根于将迅速“消失在空气里”之物，它甚至能重塑过去。早在1934—35年，巴赫金在《小说中的话语》(Discourse in the Novel)这篇文章中，为了揭示小说融和古今的能力，尝试着重新书写历史小说的本质：“历史小说的特点是一种积极进取的现代化，它消除了时空范围的限制，它是一种在过去中对永恒的现在的发现。”(DNP. pp365—66)从“永恒的现在”一词我们可以窥见巴赫金的小说哲学。但这并不意味着现在的长存性，而是指它向两个方向的延伸性。小说中，如果从个人的“经验，知识和实践”(EN. p15)间断的、常新的、具体的视角去看，过去和未来都呈现出具有现在特点的存在模式。“绝对的过去”，巴赫金坚持认为，“并不是像我们对这个词精确而又有限的理解一样，是和时间结合的”，它是“按等级划分的时间—价值表”。(EN. p18)然而，巴赫金却忽略了一个事实，在他的理论直觉里，“绝对的过去”和“永恒的现在”变成了永恒的(不受时间影响的)“时间”，还承载着对现实的价值态度。

无需说，巴赫金坚持认为小说与现代性“永恒的现在”之间存在着牢不可破的联系，这让我们想起关于低等的、日常的、非正式的熟悉主题。他提醒读者记住，“与史诗的过去相比，当代是‘更低等’的现实”(EN. p19)，小说起源于通过笑声熟悉化的民间文化(EN. p20)，小说文体的最终目的是强调时代全面的“今日性”。(EN. p26)

应该认识到，巴赫金与卢卡奇一样，使用了黑格尔的概念框架去区分史诗与小说。在他看来，小说的兴起实际上是由于对男女私人生活关注的上升。(PND. p108)如果对卢卡奇而言，这是与有机性的衰弱相应的腐朽、顺从的标志，那么对巴赫金来说则是一个需要仔细辩证分析的自然过程，而不是一种对于回不去的过去的哀叹。

黑格尔《权利哲学》中私人与公共的辩证关系与马克思关于资本主义时代生产的公共性

与私人形式的占有与消费之间的内在矛盾的表述,无疑影响了巴赫金关于古代小说起源的因素,他讲道:

> (在希腊化时代)文学形式的公共性与其内容的私密性构成了矛盾,私人文学体裁的发展过程开始了……对于长一点的史诗(大型史诗)的形式来说,这一点尤为关键。在解决这个问题的过程中,古代的小说出现了。
>
> (PND. p123)

这也许听起来难以置信,巴赫金比卢卡奇更像是一名辩证主义者。但与卢卡奇不同的是,他仅仅接受了黑格尔方法中有关这个现象发生的假设,并没有接受这个现象发展方向的假设。如果说卢卡奇期望资本主义的灭亡和史诗的重生,巴赫金则更愿意看到小说一直成长直至达到文学完全小说化的理想阶段。毕竟,对巴赫金和卢卡奇而言,史诗与小说是两种不相容的文体,两者间不可能"相处融洽"。从他们定义中就能看到这种不相容:对巴赫金来说,史诗是"绝对过去"的文体;对卢卡奇而言,小说是"绝对罪恶"的文体。两人分歧的焦点实际上围绕一个问题,那就是这两种文体,哪种决定了文艺和社会进化的进程。

巴赫金采用的黑格尔主义理论框架还有另一个更重要的维度。巴赫金声称认识论特征决定了小说的文体特性,这样,他黑格尔式地将各种文化形式严格辨认为(自我)意识的进展的阶段。小说标志着这种意识发展的新阶段:"当小说变成了主要的文学体裁,认识论就变成了主要的哲学原则。"(EN. p15)小说与认知的这种统一性,在他对苏格拉底对话的分析中也被强调过,他认为,从这些对话中我们看到了"科学观念与新的艺术—散文小说体形象的同时产生"。(EN. p24)

无论是否合理,巴赫金欲为小说话语赋予形式多样的意识,这种意识随着小说取得主导地位而渐臻完善。这反映了现代性的典型信念,即科学和认知意识是人类智性能力解放的标志。在巴赫金的叙述中,小说不断探索的精神和人类理智不断的努力呈现为一对彼此匹配的组合。

在论文的总结部分,我再一次强调,巴赫金作为一名文化和文学理论家的日程表很大程度上已经预先被决定了,他一方面受益于俄国强大的理论传统,另一方面被复兴黑格尔文艺方法的知识气氛所影响,尽管这种黑格尔主义被伪装成有阶级基础(或偏见)的马克思历史主义。巴赫金对小说起源及其与非正式的、日常的、非经典的之间密切关系等问题的回答,既得益于也修正了由维谢洛夫斯基和形式主义者们提出的理论框架,以及黑格尔范式的理论框架。巴赫金的独创性在于,他坚定又执著地相信,小说仅仅是对形成人类文化的几种基本和永恒原理的运作的表达,它具有强烈的历史感和美好的艺术感,因此从这个视角出发,巴赫金合成了已有的假设(多元文化主义、世界主义、社会分化论与社会决定论、语言对话语和和对文体的依附)。对巴赫金来说,小说起源的问题变成了庆祝人类永恒的一种状态(意识)的托辞,这种状态在其完善自身不可改变的本质时,经历了很多不同的阶段。而对小说文体的描述则意味着一个不受历史变化影响的文化和社会运作的模型。

“儿童的发现”与文学诸问题

——试论中日现代文学中的“童心”观念

高华鑫

【内容提要】 “儿童的发现”是近年来引起学术界种种讨论的一个命题。本文围绕这一命题对中国和日本现代文学中的某些现象进行了考察，试图通过对两国作家的儿童观、儿童文学观的比较分析，特别是对浪漫化的“童心”观念的梳理，揭示出其中映射的某些关于文学现代性的问题。

【关键词】 童心　儿童的发现　中日现代文学

Discovery of the Children and Literary Modernity

—A Comparative Study on the Ideas of “Childlike Heart” in Modern Chinese and Japanese Literature

【Abstract】 “Discovery of the children” is a proposition that has caused many academic discussions in recent years. Focusing on this proposition, this paper examines some phenomena in Chinese and Japanese modern literature, and tries to uncover the literary modernity in the ideas of “children” and “children's literature,” especially in the romanticized idea of the “childlike heart.”

【Key Words】 the Childlike heart　discovery of the children　Chinese and Japanese modern literature

引　言

“儿童的发现”这一命题被提出已经有一段时间，无论是在西方还是在中国、日本，都产生了相当的影响。按照柄谷行人的说法，最早对心理学领域的“孩子”这一不证自明的观念提出质疑的是梵·丹·伯杰(Van den Berg)和米歇尔·福柯；不过之后他发现，更早的其实是法国年鉴学派菲利普·阿里埃斯(Phillipe Ariès)的《童年的世纪》(1960)。另一些历史学家，如美国的塔奇曼(Barbara Tuchman)、塔克尔(M. J. Tucker)也较早地关注了历史上儿童地位的变化。近年来又有学者在此基础上进一步探讨电子媒体时代“童年”的危机。在中国，也出现了《儿童的发现——现代中国文学及文化中的儿童问题》这样的论文集。在对中国儿童文学和儿童观的反思中，柄谷行人的《日本现代文学的起源》经常被引用，不过很少见到有进一步拿日本文学史上的相关内容来作比较和参照的。这便是本文试图做的工作。尽管“儿童的发现”广泛触及了文学、历史、社会学、心理学、教育学等领域，但本文只能聚焦于文学家对儿童和儿童文学的观念，特别是审美上的“童心”观念。

一、“儿童”的所指：隐喻与实存

虽然我们讨论的是现代的文学问题，但首先需要指出，儿童这一形象自古就具有隐喻性。比如《周易》“蒙”卦卦辞中的“童蒙”，孩童的无知这一具体的“象”背后是抽象之理。《道德经》第十章所谓“专气致柔，能婴儿乎”，也是以婴儿来体现“任自然之气，致至柔之和”（王弼语）的境界。值得注意的是，这两个例子本身已经预示了儿童观念中的两种向度。前者包涵着教化与启蒙的萌芽，后者则指向对纯洁本真之物的保持与恢复。前一种向度内在于中国古代社会的教育中，反映在《童蒙止观》、《童蒙须知》、《童蒙养正诗选》等种种读物中，直到清末，新兴的儿童读物往往仍以“蒙学”为名。[①] 而后一种向度在社会实践中也许不那么重要，但作为譬喻在文艺批评中占有一席之地。李贽的《童心说》大概是最有名的例子。李贽以“绝假纯真，最初一念之本心”，来抨击道学家的保守文学观念，为市井文学作辩护。这样的童心，与《读律肤说》中的“自然”一致，都是对礼义纲纪的超越。

中国如此，日本又如何呢？我们可以拿江户时代的国学家本居宣长在《紫文要领》中的一段话作为例子：

> 或问：以源氏为代表的书中的好人们，其性情都像女童一般脆弱幼稚，缺乏男性的坚强。为什么要如此描写？
>
> 答曰：一般而论，真实的人情就是像女童那样幼稚和愚懦，坚强自信不是人情的本质，常常是表面上有意假装出来的，如果深入其内心世界，就会发现无论怎样的强人，内心深处都与女童无异。对此引以为耻，极力隐瞒，是不正确的做法。中国人写的书就是这样，极力装潢门面，而忽略了对真实人情的描写。[②]

本居宣长在这部著作中提出了著名的“物哀”论，指出《源氏物语》的意义就在于深刻细腻地描写人情，而学者们用儒家和佛典的说教来作解释是完全错误的——后者便是宣长所谓“汉意”。考虑到当时江户幕府的官方学术正是日本化的儒学（特别是理学），宣长对“汉意”的敌视就不是那么难于理解了。

李贽和本居宣长在使用“儿童”这一譬喻时，都试图以一种自然本真的范畴来对抗压抑性的文化规范，但显而易见，这与现实中的孩子们毫不相干。对现实儿童教育的关怀与对理想儿童的崇拜结合在一起，是现代的“儿童”被发现之后的事。

关于这一发现，周作人在1927年的《〈蒙氏教育法〉序》中有精炼的表述：

> 儿童这样东西原是古已有之的，但历来似乎都不知道，虽然他们终日在大人们的眼

---

① 如1897年上海时务日报馆创办的《蒙学报》。

② 本居宣长：《紫文要领》，见王向远编译：《日本物哀》，长春：吉林出版集团责任有限公司，2010年，第106—107页。由于篇幅有限，引文有删减。

前……直至很近的近世，还在夷地，这才被人家发现，原来世上有一种所谓儿童的物事，与人及女人的发见并称为三大发见之一……少数的明智的教育家与学者承认儿童是灵长类的一种小动物，并不是缩小了的成人，把它另眼看待，其结果是发生了幼稚园的制度与儿童学的研究。①

这一现代性的发现要追溯到西欧。法国学者阿里埃斯的研究表明，中世纪时孩子只是被当作“小大人”，与成人一同出没于各种日常生活场合，到17、18世纪才逐渐被当作天真无知的存在而被隔离出来。荷兰精神病理学家梵·丹·伯杰则着重研究了把“大人”与“孩子”进行分割的认知图式的形成，他发现蒙田、洛克都没提过“成人”这件事，唯独卢梭的《爱弥尔》主张把孩子当作孩子，从此童年才成为一个单独的阶段，而成年一事也成为了问题。② 不过单从卢梭出发也有些不足。尼尔·波兹曼(Neil Postman)在《童年的消逝》中总结得更为全面，他指出现代的儿童观分为“洛克派”(新教的)和“卢梭派”(浪漫主义)两支。前者认为儿童是未成形的人，要靠识字、教育、理性、自我控制和羞耻感来改造成文明的成人；而后者认为未成形的儿童不是问题，问题出在畸形的成人，儿童与生俱来的能力被后天的教育和控制淹没了。③ 这种二分法与我们前面提到的两个向度有些相似。

当然，要说古代完全没有“儿童”的观念恐怕也是成问题的。一些学者批评阿里埃斯的《童年的世纪》与史实不符，指出古代人(比如古罗马人)就已经把人生划分为数个阶段，认识到儿童与成人的不同。在古代中国，成年与未成年之间也有明显的界线，在男子是“加冠”，在女子则是“及笄”。④ 不过与古代相比，近代的“儿童的发现”仍然具有根本不同的意义。这不仅仅是因为人们更加强调儿童的特殊性，更是因为社会状况的变化：儿童确已被分离出来。

柄谷行人认为，人们对明治时代教育思想的种种批判，以及与此相关的童心主义的兴起，正是在现代学制基本稳定，儿童被从传统家庭中剥离到学校中之后才成为可能的。阿里埃斯认为“儿童”的诞生有三个条件：印刷文化、中产阶级和新教伦理的形成。波兹曼则尤其强调印刷术的作用：

> 儿童被从其他人群中分离出来，并非因为他们据信有“不同的本质和不同的需求”。他们据信有不同的本质和不同的需求，是因为他们已经被从其他人群中分离出来。他们被分离，是因为在他们的文化中他们要学习如何读书写字，如何成为印刷文化所要求的那种人。⑤

儿童被分离出来之后，对他们的观察和分析也就越来越成为专门的学问。蒙台梭利、赫尔巴特等人的研究，把卢梭对儿童问题的抽象思考推进到更加具体的实践层面。19世纪末，在美国心理学家霍尔(G. S. Hall)和克里斯曼(O. Chrismann)等人的推动下，儿童学

---

① 周作人：《〈蒙氏教育法〉序》，见刘绪源辑笺：《周作人论儿童文学》，北京：海豚出版社，2012年，第255页。

② 参见[日]柄谷行人：《日本现代文学的起源》，赵京华译，北京：三联书店，2003年。

③ [美]尼尔·波兹曼：《童年的消逝》，吴燕莛译，桂林：广西师范大学出版社，2004年。

④ 参见吴其南：《20世纪中国儿童文学的文化阐释》，北京：中国社会科学出版社，2012年，第11、12页。

⑤ [美]尼尔·波兹曼：《童年的消逝》，吴燕莛译，桂林：广西师范大学出版社，2004年，第68页。

(Paidology)正式出现,不仅在欧美扩展开来,也传到了日本。1902年高岛平三郎等人设立日本儿童研究会,发行月刊《儿童研究》,日本的儿童学从此起步。周作人也是留学期间接触到高岛平三郎等人的研究之后才开始关注儿童学的①。不过中国知识分子普遍开始关注儿童教育则是在1919年杜威来华讲学以后。至1935、1936年,国内对儿童问题的讨论更为广泛,于是有了所谓"儿童年"。

与西方不同的是,中国的"儿童的发现"从一开始就与民族救亡和社会启蒙观念密不可分。启蒙二字,最早见于汉代应劭《风俗通·黄霸·六国》"每辄挫衄,亦足以祛蔽启蒙矣",意思是开导蒙昧,使明白事理,②后来有了向初学者教授入门知识的意思。而今人用"启蒙"一词描述五四新文化运动时,既引入了西语中"enlightenment"或"Aufklärung"的内涵,又保留了汉字原来的意义,可谓触到了这场运动的要旨:中国知识分子正是要以西方的新思想、新知识来教育民众,使整个社会摆脱蒙昧状态。儿童的发现,只是巨大进程中的一环,与人的发现、妇女的发现勾连在一起。举例来说,鲁迅在《我们今天怎样做父亲》中提出的"幼者本位"观念,同《狂人日记》中"救救孩子"的呼喊相一致,并非以儿童为言说对象,而是对成人的提醒和警告,是颠覆旧的伦常纲纪的一种努力。

前面已经提到,儿童观念有两种不同的向度。在风雨飘摇的现代中国,"教化"、"启蒙"这一向度无疑占据主流。但另一方面,理想化、浪漫化的"童心"观念也在悄悄形成,作为隐喻,它具有更多的文学和美学内涵,也是本文重点要讨论的。儿童文学史则是印证这些观念的重要材料。

二、童话的意义与文学的功用

1904年"癸卯学制"颁布后,各地新式小学堂纷纷建立。伴随着教育制度的更新,晚清已出现一些冠以"少年"、"蒙学"之名的儿童读物。1909年,商务印书馆的孙毓修开始编撰《童话》,这套丛书的内容基本是西方和中国古代故事的改写。日本现代儿童文学的起始则以1891年出版的《少年文学》丛书为标志。其名称,据岩谷小波说是对德语Jugendshrift的翻译;其内容包括一些创作,但主要也是历史小说、民间故事、伟人传记的改写。③ 由于较早关注儿童的阅读需求,专门为儿童编写读物,孙毓修和岩谷小波在两国各自的儿童文学史上都占据了里程碑式的位置。(岩谷小波由于自己创作《黄金丸》而影响更大。)不过他们的观念与后来的"童心主义"有很大的不同,并未深入审美的层面。孙毓修编书的目的是帮助儿童"周知世故,练达人事"。岩谷小波也只是强调寓教于乐,并且保证随着年龄增长孩子自然会分清幻想和现实;为了培养积极进取的气质,他还主张让儿童少看"人情物",多看军事谭、冒险谭。④ 这使我们想起卢梭让爱弥尔在很长一段时期里只读一本书:《鲁滨逊漂流记》。

---

① 参见周作人:《儿童文学》,见刘绪源辑笺:《周作人论儿童文学》,北京:海豚出版社,2012年,第367页。

② 罗竹风主编:《汉语大词典》缩印本,上卷,北京:汉语大词典出版社,1997年,第1611页。

③ 菅忠道:《近代日本児童文学史論》,见《日本児童文学大系》(卷一),京都:三一書房,1955年,第3页。

④ 岩谷小波:《家庭と児童》,见《日本児童文学大系》(卷一),京都:三一書房,1955年,第354页。

从审美层面上"发现"儿童，在中国以周作人为先驱，在日本则以铃木三重吉创办《赤鸟》(『赤い鳥』)为标志性事件。

1913年，周作人发表《童话研究》，这篇文章首先从民俗学上分析了童话(Märchen)的起源，它由神话和世说(即民间传说)演变而来，本质上是"原人之文学"。然后他进一步讲到用童话进行教育的问题。

> 盖凡欲以童话为教育者，当勿忘童话为物亦艺术之一，其作用之范围，当比论他艺术而断之，其与教本，区以别矣。故童话者，其能在表现，所希在享受，撄激心灵，令起追求以上遂也。其余效益，皆属副支，本末失正，斯昧其义。[①]

周作人从艺术审美而非教化的角度来把握童话的本质，这就与孙毓修大为不同。对周作人来说，儿童文学的功用从根本上不会超出文学的功用，而文学具有独立的审美价值，不是实用的工具，"是人类的，也是个人的，却不是种族的，国家的，乡土的及家族的"[②]。因此，他反对唤起少年儿童"不适当的英雄崇拜和爱国心"，主张采用各国的材料，"使儿童知道人性里共通的地方"。[③] 后来他在介绍《阿丽丝漫游奇境记》时，抨击拟古主义和军国主义的教育，指出儿童对空想作品的需要，大人无论凭了怎样的神圣之名，都没有剥夺的权力。这种儿童文学观念与周作人更大的"文学"观是同构的。

另一个值得注意的问题是，周作人在文中提到"个体发生与系统发生同序"，所以幼儿与原始人思想感情相近，而童话是"幼稚时代之文学，故原人所好，幼儿亦好之"。这正是他后来反复提到的"复演说"。"复演说"可以追溯到维柯，他在《新科学》中开创性地描述了人类的原始思维。德国生物学家海克尔则进一步把个体童年看作人类童年之复演。真正在童话和原人之间建立起本质联系的则是19世纪的文化人类学，特别是英国的民俗学家安德鲁·朗(Andrew Lang)的工作。他不仅把大量民间故事作为原始文化遗留物加以整理，而且建立了整套的理论。[④] 文化人类学在19世纪末传入日本，推动了以柳田国男为代表的日本近代民俗学的诞生，进而影响到大正时代的儿童文学。菅忠道《近代日本儿童文学史论》指出，大正童话研究与明治时的重大差异，正在于引入民俗学、人类学，主张儿童和自然民族的相似，进一步发现了童话的超历史的本质。[⑤] 周作人对文化人类学的兴趣也正是在日本形成的。他靠这种来自人类学的"复演说"认识了儿童心理，从学理上证明了：儿童是完全的个人，有他自己内外两面的生活。

既然文化人类学表明，童话故事本非为儿童而作，那么"童心"自然也不再是儿童的专利。周作人一面研究古有的童话，一面介绍以安徒生为代表的"人为童话"，这已是艺术创作，"非熟通儿童心理者不能试，非自具儿童心理者不能善"[⑥]。后来他进一步说，"近代文艺

---

① 周作人：《童话研究》，见刘绪源辑笺：《周作人论儿童文学》，北京：海豚出版社，2012年，第14页。

② 周作人：《新文学的要求》，同上书，第117页。

③ 周作人：《儿童的文学》，同上书，第122页。

④ 吴其南：《20世纪中国儿童文学的文化阐释》，北京：中国社会科学出版社，2012，第43到45页。

⑤ 菅忠道：《近代日本児童文学史論》，见《日本児童文学大系》(卷一)，京都：三一書房，1955年，第7页。

⑥ 周作人：《丹麦诗人安兑尔然传》，见刘绪源辑笺：《周作人论儿童文学》，北京：海豚出版社，2012年，第34页。

上童话只是文学的一种形式"。比如王尔德的童话就是诗人的、而不是儿童的文学。而安徒生的无与伦比之处在于"他是诗人,又是一个'永久的孩子'"。[①] 1920年,周作人翻译柳泽健原的《儿童的世界》,指出儿童文学作家的任务并不是完全变成儿童,而是生出儿童与大人的世界之外的"第三世界";安徒生便是这"第三世界"的典范。[②]

周作人的儿童文学观有时被同日本大正时代的"童心主义"联系起来。"童心主义"主要表现为以《赤鸟》为中心的童谣和童话运动,这一运动对周作人有哪些具体的影响,尚需实证的考察[③],不过这场运动的领军人物的意见,常常与周作人不谋而合。同周作人的《人的文学》一样,秋田雨雀在《作为艺术表现的童话》中也提到,"女子和儿童"是最近才受到关注的对象。然后他进一步提出了儿童本位的主张:

> 儿童的世界,是儿童自身的世界。既非大人的世界,亦非父母或教育者的世界……儿童不是为了某个国家、某个社会或某个人而出生的,而是为了做人而出生的。
>
> 作为艺术的童话,实是由于人类对下一时代的人的爱,而生出的一种艺术样式。[④]

小川未明的《孩子默从于虐待》[⑤]一文则把大人对孩子的压迫与男人对女人,资本家对劳动者的压迫并置起来。他不仅批判家庭对儿童的禁锢,更把矛头指向学校生活,明言资本主义已经腐蚀了教化精神,学校生活等同于牢狱。这篇文章发表于1926年,是大正的最后一年,也是昭和元年,从中可以感到新的时代气息,但它还远不是日后的"无产阶级儿童文学",其艺术功用观仍然与童心主义一脉相承。小川未明创作童话,并不是要宣传政治理念,只是要做孩子的"代辩者",并用艺术抚慰孩子的心灵。另一方面,童话又并不全是为了孩子:

> 我的童话,并非只要使孩子感到有趣便好,也不是单做成一篇寓言便够。在更广阔的世界中、在万物中求索美,以及这样的美应该怎样调和才是正确的存在——这些才是我想要作成诗的。[⑥]

在另一篇文章中,小川未明说"真正美丽之物,真正正确之事,真正悲哀的事实"本是大人和孩子都能理解的,但某些大人因为失去了纯真的感情反而不能理解,因而他的童话也是为这些大人而作的。这种思想与周作人所感慨的"童心的丧失",以及他赞扬的"第三世界"是一致的。秋田雨雀也说:

> 童话中表现的思想和世界,也可以看作大人的理想的世界。在这一世界中孩子与大人可以合而为一。此时大人和儿童的灵魂并无差别……童话不应当是大人为儿童创作的,而应当是为人类心中"永远的孩子"创作的。[⑦]

---

① 周作人:《王尔德童话》,同上书,第146页。

② 周作人:《童话的讨论》,同上书,第164页。

③ 刘军的《周作人儿童文学论探源——以绍兴时期日本儿童文学的接受为中心》列出了1913—1916年周作人从日本订购的相关书籍的清单。比起文学作品,周作人更感兴趣的似乎是日本和西方的儿童研究。

④ 秋田雨雀:《芸術表現としての童話》,《日本児童文学大系》(卷二),京都:三一書房,1955年,第328页。

⑤ 小川未明:《子供は虐待に黙従す》,同上书,第378页。

⑥ 小川未明:《今後を童話作家に》:同上书,第383页。

⑦ 秋田雨雀:《芸術表現としての童話》,同上书,第329页。

“永远的孩子”可以说是浪漫化的“童心”最精炼的表述形式。“儿童”一词自古以来所具有的“纯真无邪”的隐喻意味经过同现实的儿童的结合，重又升华到普遍人性中去，变成一种诗化的理想，同时也是一种文学功用观的表达。由此可见，“儿童本位”与“童心”还是有区别的。如果说“儿童本位”只是要求把儿童当作儿童来看待，那么“童心”则是把大人乃至人类也当作儿童来看待。

三、浪漫派、童心与宗教

周作人进入儿童问题的视角是比较独特、比较个人化的。我们还需要更广泛地观察现代文学中的童心观念，更多地揭示其中的文化因素。

五四诗坛上有一种“童心崇拜”的现象。最常被提及的诗是冰心的《繁星》，如第十四章，“我们都是自然的婴儿，卧在宇宙的摇篮里”；第三十五章，“万千的天使，要起来歌颂小孩子/小孩子！他细小的身躯里，含着伟大的灵魂”。[①] 具有代表性的作品还有朱自清《睡吧，小小的人》等等。这些诗作有一个共同点：它们的用词和意象似乎与西方文化特别是基督教有着某种联系。在日本，视儿童为纯洁无垢的存在这一视点的形成，也同基督教有关。若松贱子在著名译作《小公子》的序文中把儿童称为“浊世的莲花，家庭的天使”，可谓预示了后来的浪漫主义儿童观，而登载《小公子》的《女学杂志》便是一份基于基督教理念的启蒙杂志。事实上，这一杂志又是《文学界》的前身，而后者正是北村透谷等浪漫派作家的根据地。

《圣经》中确有赞美小孩子的段落，比如《马太福音》说像孩子这般在人间最小的，在天国里反是最大的。(Matthew 18:4)不过这主要是教导人在主面前要像孩子一般谦卑。作为审美对象，散发着圣洁光辉的“孩子”毋宁说主要来自美术中的圣子形象。而在“儿童的发现”这一历史进程中，基督教更重要的作用大概在于保护儿童、反对婴儿屠杀等社会实践。但基督教本身并不会提供“童心崇拜”的观念，只有在经历了浪漫主义文学的洗礼之后，这种观念才成为可能。浪漫主义假设了一个与“人为”相对立的自然，正是在对这个自然的讴歌中，儿童崇拜诞生了。雨果曾兴冲冲地宣布自己“发现”了儿童，这其实是欧洲各国浪漫派的共通之处。英国文学中这方面的先驱大概是布莱克和华兹华斯，后者写出了“儿童是成人之父”这样的名句；德国的蒂克与霍夫曼等人则留下了浪漫主义童话的实绩。而中国现代诗坛上最早的童心崇拜者，如冰心、郭沫若等，也具有鲜明的浪漫主义的倾向：尽情地讴歌自然，直白地抒发自我，并且带有某种泛神论的影子，如此等等。不过，他们的童心崇拜并非直接承自西欧，更多的倒是受到泰戈尔的影响。比如郭沫若作于1920年的《岸上》一诗，在描写儿童在海边嬉戏的场景时，直接嵌入了《吉檀迦利》的诗句，接下来又写道：

> 我也念着泰戈尔的一首诗，
> 我也去和着他们游戏。

---

① 冰心：《冰心全集》，卓如编，福州：海峡文艺出版社，1994年，卷一，第235、243页。

> 唉！我怎能成就个纯洁的孩儿？[①]

借助“儿童”的意象，同时也借助泰戈尔式的诗句，中国诗人唱出了对自然的礼赞，并且（或许是更重要的）唱出了新文学中大写的“我”。与西方诗人相比，中国诗人之“童心”的宗教因素更加难以指认，而它作为一种自我解放的文学装置的功能则更为凸显。

在日本，最早从“永远的孩子”中看见自我解放的希望的，可能是国木田独步。[②]（值得注意的是，在柄谷行人看来他同时也是“风景”的发现者。）他在1897年写了一篇题为《春之鸟》的小说：一个智力不发达的孩子想像鸟儿一样飞翔，结果从石墙上坠地而死，而作为叙事者的教师则想起了华兹华斯的一首诗（“There was a boy”）中的类似情节，并认为这个孩子的事比诗更深刻地揭示了一种永远的生命。这样一种脱离尘世，投身于精神的、审美的世界的决绝姿态，带有西方现代文艺的痕迹。不过一些日本学者在考察独步的文艺观时，特别强调在西方文化之外，老庄思想和俳谐中自然无为的观念也对他有所影响。[③] 这提示我们，考察中日的浪漫主义童心观，也要注意两国原有的文化传统。

中日两国均有悠久的佛教传统。丰子恺的“儿童崇拜”就与佛教观念密不可分。1927年他在《剪网》一文中写道，世间仿佛有一张大网，一切事物都牢结其中，难以看清，所以自己想找一把快剪刀，剪破这网，来认识世界的真相；又说艺术和宗教也许就是这剪刀。而他在同年所作的《从孩子得到的启示》中则说：

> 唉！我今晚受了这孩子（华瞻）的启示了：他能撤去世间事物的因果关系的网，看见事物的本身的真相。他是创造者，能赋给生命于一切的事物。他们是“艺术”的国土的主人。唉！我要从他学习。[④]

在丰子恺的眼里，艺术的精神正是宗教的，其根本之义在于认识世界，安置生命。而现在“孩子”也获得了与艺术和宗教同样的高度。如果说冰心礼赞儿童时，主要是通过他们去体会充溢宇宙的“爱”，那么丰子恺在儿童身上看到的则是一种智慧，是勘破因果之网，通往“万法从心”、“诸相非相”境界的启示。无怪乎他在《儿女》中写道：“近来我的心为四事所占据了：天上的神明与星辰，人间的艺术与儿童。”[⑤]

在中国作家的“童心崇拜”中，基督教和佛教的因素比较容易区别，而在日本文学中要作这样的分辨就困难一些。北原白秋的《童谣私观》是一个很好的例子。白秋认为童谣源自乡愁，而他所说的乡愁并非简单的故园之思，而具有某种神秘感和宗教性。

> 啊，乡愁！乡愁正是人类最本真的灵魂的眷恋。怀念故乡风土山川之心，进而升华为渴慕寂光常乐之彼岸的信与行，依恋生母的眼泪也终于化为对神的憧憬。这乡愁的

① 郭沫若：《女神》，北京：人民文学出版社，2000年，第142页。

② 这里采用的是河原和枝的观点，参见河原和枝：《子ども観の近代「赤い鳥」と『童心』の理想》，東京：中央公論社，1998年，第62页。

③ 同上书，第64页。

④ 丰子恺：《丰子恺散文全编》，丰陈宝、丰一吟编，杭州：浙江文艺出版社，1992年，第122页。

⑤ 同上书，第116页。

起因存在于出生之前。这乡愁永是存在，并成为更高的存在，成为我的救赎。[①]

这种乡愁是具有时代普遍性的。借用日本学者的话说，当时存在一种"怀旧观念的扩大再生产"[②]。但白秋没有像谷崎润一郎那样把乡愁寄托于江户风情，而是描述了一个更为抽象的精神上的故乡。他认为日本的人情和童谣的故乡存在于遥远的往昔中，是那悠久的自然风土，那常年与自然相交接的祖辈，那"常住的闲与寂"。这"故乡"与其说是他生于斯长于斯的土地，不如说更多的是一种想象。要说这玄虚的想象物为什么具有感染力，那也许应当归功于作者那带有宗教式热情的修辞。像日本的很多浪漫主义作家一样，白秋也有基督教的背景，但如果考察一下这篇文章使用的特殊词汇，就会发现它们并非来自一种宗教，而是杂糅着多种文化传统的色彩。比如"思無邪"来自儒家，"万有流通"、"寂光常乐の彼岸"、"常住"和"法悦"都是佛教用语，而"救い"和"信と行"则具有基督教色彩，更不必说那个既可指耶和华，又可指八百万神灵的"神"。总而言之，各种宗教的教义对白秋来说并不重要，重要的是宗教式的情感和运思，他依靠它们建构了一个超历史的童谣的故乡。

值得注意的是，这个故乡不仅指向浪漫化的"自然"和"生命"等，它的另一端还连接着"民族"。白秋强调"日本的童谣是日本的童谣，日本的孩子是日本的孩子"，这种民族性是万世不易的。现实的国族与遥远的想象中的时空连接在一起，而具体的历史变迁和历史距离却消失了。

早在白秋之前，浪漫主义理论家高山樗牛也强调过，在社会一味追随西方的时代，儿童故事具有保存民族传统的重要作用。在这里我们隐约可以窥见童话、浪漫主义与民族认同之间的联系。这种联系并非日本独有，1812 年格林兄弟出版《儿童与家庭的故事》时，或者 1899 年叶芝与道格拉斯·海德、格里高利夫人出版《爱尔兰民间故事集》时，都有发扬民族精神的意图。[③] 中国的情况有些不同，儿童文学中从来不缺救亡图存的民族使命感，但缺少浪漫主义的一环，浪漫化的童心停留在成人的诗歌和散文里，未对童话创作的实践产生重大影响。

四、重审童话与文学

关于理想化的童心的例子，已经举得很多；而对此的批评，不妨以梁实秋的《现代中国文学之浪漫的趋势》(1926)为例：

> 新文学运动里有所谓"儿童文学"者。安徒生的童话，王尔德的童话，都很受读者的欢迎，而这些读者大概什分之九分半是成年的人，并非是儿童……浪漫主义者就是儿童，至少在心理上是如此。他们所最尊贵的便是"赤子之心'……浪漫的天才即是儿童的天真烂漫，同为不负责任的自然发生……由现实生活逃避到幻想生活，由成年时代逃

① 北原白秋：《童謡私観》，见《日本児童文学大系》(卷二)，京都：三一書房，1955 年，第 335 页。

② 原子朗：《大正期の童話》，见《日本文学研究資料叢書 児童文学》，東京：有精堂，1977 年，第 35 页。

③ 周舟：《从蒙学到童话——作为文化策略的儿童文学观念之诞生》，北京大学硕士学位论文，2006 年。

> 避到儿童时代，由文明社会逃避到原始社会。简单说，浪漫主义者把文学当做生活的逋逃薮。①

做出这样一针见血的批判之后，梁实秋重新提出“儿童毕竟是不完全的人”。他认为通过教育发展人的身心，这是自然的历程，并非天真的损失。他又引证孔子和西塞罗，说明思想成熟的老年才是人生最幸福的时候。梁实秋对古典的援引使人联想起柄谷行人关于成熟的论述：

> “如幼儿一般”这种认识乃是过剩的自我意识所生出的颠倒，可以说这是经由浪漫主义而普遍化了的认识。相反，若质疑“成熟”这一问题必追究到宗教性的问题上去。尼采和海德格尔要走向遥远的希腊艺术，就是因为要避免这种“浪漫的形式”之不证自明性，仅仅追溯到中世纪乃是不可能的。②

追溯到古代并非简单的复古。梁实秋所说的“成年”也包含了现代性的意识。培根在《新工具》里曾把古/今二元结构做过一个颠倒，从知识积累、理性成熟的角度看，他认为古代社会才是幼年，现代社会则是老年。梁实秋所说的成年，也正是通过教育，把人培养为有理性、负责任的现代公民。然而梁实秋所提倡的理性和道德，与浪漫化的童心同样植根于先在的“普遍人性”。也许我们还需要引入一种非本质的思考。这里以坂口安吾《文学的故乡》为例。

17世纪法国作家夏尔·佩罗(Charles Perrault)的童话集中有《小红帽》这样一篇故事。小红帽去森林里看望外婆，被化装成外婆的大灰狼吃掉了，这个情节是我们所熟悉的。但是佩罗的故事到这里就结束了——就只是这样一个故事。对于我们来说它是如此突兀，令人不知所措。但这只是因为我们对这一故事后来的大团圆版本过于熟悉。事实上这一民间故事原本比佩罗所写的还要残酷，佩罗为了照顾上层女性读者，已经删掉了不少东西。对此坂口安吾写道：

> 我们仿佛突然被推了一把，感觉这和约定好的不一样，因而不知所措。但是，在眼睛毫无防备地遭了一击之后，在那“铮”的一下断开的虚无的空白之中，是不是能看见一个非常安静的，而且透明的，悲伤的故乡呢。③

坂口安吾并不是在说“民间故事本不是为儿童而作，儿童是后来发现的”这一类的事情。他说的是在文学中(或者世界上)本无道德。但是他也并不是主张返回到这无善无恶的原始混沌状态中去，因为“成人应做的，决不是回到故乡”。他只是强调，文学的道德和社会性必须建立在这样的“故乡”之上。康德的“实践理性”似乎也正是这样区别于古典的“理性”：世界本没有目的，但为了人类生活应当假设其目的。苏联解体后，柄谷行人从康德出发，在《跨越性批判》中呼吁重建社会主义理想，他屡次引用坂口安吾这篇文章，大概与此也不无关系。

现在我们再回到梁实秋的批评上来。其实童心的倡导者们并不总是反对“成年”。比如

---

① 梁实秋：《梁实秋文集》，厦门：鹭江出版社，2002年，第一卷，第51页。

② [日]柄谷行人：《日本现代文学的起源》，赵京华译，北京：三联书店，2003年，第122页。

③ 坂口安吾：「文学のふるさと」，『堕落論・日本文化私観』，東京：岩波書店，2008年，第92页。

丰子恺在《送阿宝出黄金时代》中，对于女儿的成年是"悲喜交集"，悲的是她失去了黄金时代，喜的则是她"开始在尝人类之爱的辛味了"。另一方面，我们要把主张和实际的作品区别开来。以叶圣陶和张天翼为代表的中国现代儿童文学从一开始就不是安徒生式、或者王尔德式的。看一下《稻草人》就会明白，中国社会的"灰色云雾"是怎样无可避免地弥漫于童话的世界中。本文开头提到的儿童观念的两种向度，其中"发蒙""教化"一脉在现代中国仍然是主流。新的思想，新的社会运动总是试图通过教育儿童来获得更广阔的影响。30年代以后，反映政治运动、阶级斗争的儿童文学作品越来越多。在这样激烈的历史进程中，"童心"是一种具有自我抚慰、自我解放功能的想象，但它只停留在少数文人抒发性情的诗与散文中，并未对儿童文学实践产生重大影响。也就是说，我们并没有能够和大正童心主义文学相对应的作品。

这样说来，似乎是中国的"童心"发展得不充分。目前在学界对中国现代儿童文学的反思中确实有这样的声音，同时日本的大正文学也被举做例子反证中国的"童心"之不足。但事实上日本的"童心主义"在昭和时代也同样受到批判，并为"无产阶级儿童文学"所替代（与中国不同的是，日本的"无产阶级儿童文学"又败给了压倒性的军国主义教育和与之配套的通俗作品）。由此可见，拿"童心"来衡量儿童文学的水平，仍是基于对"儿童"的简单想象。"儿童文学"这个概念包含了两个词，其中哪一个都不是不证自明的。说到底，这一概念只能从功能上（而非本质上）去理解。我们无法证明安徒生童话就是儿童文学，《水浒传》就不是，除非我们对儿童的定义就是"他们只读安徒生"。

结　语

关于中国现代儿童观与儿童文学中的"启蒙"之维度，已经有不少研究文章甚至专著。因此本文选择将重心放在"童心"这一维度上，比起文学启蒙，更关注作家个体生命的安置，自我解放的想象，总之是那些似乎"艺术本位"色彩更浓的侧面。"为人生而艺术"与"为艺术而艺术"的分分合合，在现代文学研究中已经被论述过无数遍，在此本文并无新的论点，只是尝试着把日本文学作为参照系引入，使中国现代文学中某些问题的世界普遍性更清晰地浮现出来。这一工作也许有进一步展开、深化的价值。

作者简介：高华鑫，北京大学中文系比较文学与比较文化研究所在读硕士研究生。

崇高风格呼唤崇高心灵
——马修·阿诺德翻译思想探析

黄　弋

【内容提要】 19世纪60年代，马修·阿诺德与弗朗西斯·纽曼就《荷马史诗》的翻译以及翻译标准与译作风格等问题进行激烈论争。在其撰写的两篇相关论文中，阿诺德批判了当时英国译者过于拘泥"信"，而忽略"达"的普遍作法，并特别强调译者个人的文化修为与道德素养。

【关键词】 马修·阿诺德　翻译思想与理论　《荷马史诗》的翻译

The Sublimity Is the Echo of a Noble Mind: An Analysis of Matthew Arnold's *Thought on Translation*

【Abstract】 In 1860s, there was a controversy between the poet and thinker Matthew Arnold and Francis Newman over a series of questions, such as the Homeric translation, translation criteria, translation style, etc. In his two related essays, Matthew Arnold criticized the translation trend then prevailing in Britain, which overemphasized the Truthfulness to the original works at the cost of the Truthfulness of the translation works; besides, he considered it vitally important for a translator to be noble-minded so as to form a grand style.

【Key Words】 Matthew Arnold　Homeric translation　translation theory

马修·阿诺德(Matthew Arnold, 1822—1888)是英国维多利亚时期重要的诗人和评论家。终其一生，他在诗歌和散文方面都取得了非凡的成就。他的散文著作涉及文学、政治、社会、宗教、教育等各个相关领域，社会的各种问题无不成为他持久关注的对象，可以说他的整个思想生涯都与他所处的时代息息相关。他不但为当时英国社会把脉，更要开出良方。有英国评论家指出，阿诺德"在其诗歌和批评散文中引入了对西方社会和文化的核心问题的一种新的、微妙的、比较的态度，帮助形成了现代意识。这一点实在令人吃惊。对我们来说，理解他要对理解上个世纪任何一个英国人更加有用。"[1](P1)

阿诺德的很多著作都是在与他人的激烈思想论争中写就的。例如，在与斯宾塞(Herbert Spencer)等人就教育中自然科学和人文科学孰轻孰重之争中，阿诺德坚定地站在人文主义者的立场上，认为人文教育相比于自然科学教育更为重要。他在伊顿公学的讲演中曾说过："人类通过教育了解自己，了解世界；为了达此目标，他必须首先了解人类最好的思想和言论；而古希腊、罗马的经典著作则构成了这些最好的思想和言论的最主要的部分，也是最让人满意的部分。意识到这一点,人们必然会坚定地支持人文教育。”[2](P243)在其主要的批评著作中,阿诺德特别强调“最好的思想和议论”的启智与开化作用,他认为批评应该是“以公正无私的努力,来研究与宣传世界上最好的思想和言论”。这实际上是提倡一种新批评,主张批评不应局限于文学,也应用于神学、历史、艺术、科学、社会与政治等各个领域。

阿诺德最重要的作品无疑是《文化与无政府状态》(*Culture and Anarchy*, 1869),在书中他对英国维多利亚时代的偏狭、崇尚实际、反理想主义等时代缺点进行了无情地抨击。他认为英国社会由三个阶层组成:一是野蛮的贵族,他们精神充沛,态度沉静,举止正经,却闭目塞听,不接受任何新道理;二是市侩的中产阶层,他们信仰自由,颇有事业心,但顽固愚昧,唯利是图;三是平民,他们只是粗野而盲目的群氓。在阿诺德看来,这三种人都是“没有文化”的人。[3](P65—95)由于受沿袭而来的“希伯来主义”的约束,尤其是清教主义的偏狭的约束,他们中没有一个阶层真正同情或赞成一种真正典雅的、能够抵御政治和宗教秩序中深层腐败的文化。在这种情况下,英国更需要用古希腊的更柔美、更温馨的艺术来平衡,以便创造一种更加宽容、更加舒畅的文化。文化,在阿诺德看来,是用来确定新的社会和道德的聚合力,这种聚合力有助于将不同阶层联结起来,也提供了一个能够取代宗教宗派的精神回音。[4](p257—258)普遍的启蒙和个人正直的精神能够大规模地改变民主,促进社会的和谐与进步,这正是阿诺德一生孜孜追求的最终落脚点。

阿诺德在翻译领域虽涉猎不深,但绝非浅尝辄止。他的翻译思想也是在他与时人论争时阐发的。就翻译而言,他强调译者的文化修为和社会责任,这与他在所有著作中一以贯之的“文化”、“诉诸人的心灵”等思想内核可谓一脉相承。

在 19 世纪的英国,翻译作品渐多。许多翻译名家提出了衡量译作风格和准确性的新标准。就准确性而言,这一时期普遍采纳的原则是,必须再现“原文,整个原文,唯独原文。”[5](p169)由此也产生了一个严重的问题,即因为过于强调表达的准确性,译作很难为当代读者看懂。卡莱尔译的哥德,形式上是英语,但结构上是德语;伯顿(Richard F. Burton)译的《一千零一夜》充满阿拉伯语的表达法。这些问题引起了当时学者的关注,从而引发了一场著名的论争。这场论争主要涉及荷马史诗的翻译,同时也澄清了许多翻译的一般性理论和原则问题,对 20 世纪的翻译研究产生了一定的影响。

论争一方为阿诺德,另一方为伦敦大学拉丁语教授弗朗西斯·纽曼①(Francis W. Newman)。19 世纪 50 年代,纽曼翻译出版了《伊利亚特》。1861 年,阿诺德写了一篇《论荷马史诗的翻译》,评价纽曼的译作,兼及其他译者,如蒲柏、查普曼等人。纽曼不服,写了一篇长文予以回敬,题为《荷马史诗翻译的理论与实践:答马修·阿诺德》(“Homeric Translation in Theory and Practice: A Reply to Matthew Arnold”)。阿诺德也不让步,于 1862 年再发表一篇论文,题为《再论荷马史诗的翻译:答弗朗西斯· 纽曼》(“Last Words on Translating Homer: A Reply to Francis W. Newman”),进一步批评纽曼。

在这两篇颇有分量的论文中,阿诺德提出了许多有价值的见解,不仅限于荷马史诗的翻

① F. W. Newman (1805—1897),英国学者、作家。红衣主教亨利·纽曼(John Henry Newman, 1801—1890)的兄弟。亨利·纽曼的《大学的理念》为人熟知。

译，还兼及整个诗歌翻译艺术。

在论文的开篇，阿诺德即以纽曼为靶子提出了什么是信实的问题。关于信实标准，纽曼认为，译者的首要责任，是历史的，是对原文的信实；译者应该“保存原文的一切特点，使译文越像外国口气越好。这样就使读者不会忘掉译者只是在摹拟，在摹拟别人的作品。”[6](p2)阿诺德对此提出了针锋相对的批驳：“我还要忠告译者们不要专为翻译创造一种特殊的文字；不要专为荷马风格的某些特点，而定出理论以排斥某些英国字，并专用某种英国字。”[6](P4)阿诺德认为纽曼的理论本身是错误的，对译者是危险的。这一理论不但很难遵守（阿诺德在文中列举说明纽曼本人也“不能很好地尊重这一理论”），而且更为严重的是，它“表现出一种惊人的迂阔；而迂阔则却是世界上最不合于荷马的一种风格”。[6](P5)要翻译好荷马，必须正确认识荷马。“不能正确地认识他，怎能正确的翻译他呢？”[6](P5)那么究竟什么才是荷马风格呢？他对此进行了详加说明：

> 他[荷马]是非常轻快的；在思想发展和表现上，也就是说，在句法与文字上，他是非常朴素与直接的；在思想实质上，也就是说，在内容和观念上，他也是非常朴素与直接的；最后，他是非常崇高的。[6](P6)

阿诺德指出，只有全面把握荷马风格的这四个特点，方能翻译出好的荷马史诗。正是由于忽略了第一个特点，即荷马的轻快，库柏①的翻译失败了；由于忽略了第二个特点，即文辞的朴素与直接，蒲柏②的翻译失败了；由于忽略了第三个特点，即观念的朴素与直接，查普曼③的翻译失败了；由于忽略了第四个特点，即荷马的崇高，“那位把前人的一些短处看得清楚的纽曼先生，便使自己的翻译失败得比前人更显著”。[6](P7)

阿诺德对库柏、蒲柏、查普曼等人的译文进行一一剖解，指出“库柏译文的缺点，在于声调迂缓，句法拖累；蒲柏的缺点，在于造句遣辞，唯尚雕饰；查普曼的缺点，在于观念离奇”[6](P49)，这显然与荷马的声调轻快、字句朴素、观念简洁的风格背道而驰，所以他们的翻译失败也就不足为奇了。

如上文所述，阿诺德论战的对象是纽曼，因此他对纽曼的译文和有关翻译理论进行了详细分析和有力批判。纽曼说，他是抱着为普通读者之阅读目的而翻译了荷马，应以普通读者的阅读感受作为评判译作好坏的依据；阿诺德则认为只有学者（scholar）才是最终的“裁判人”（judge），且必须是“不迂腐的学者”（the scholar who is not pedantic），因为学者通晓原语文字且能鉴赏诗文，只有他们能说出译作是否和原作基本一样，能否给他们带来与阅读原作一样的感受。由此可见，阿诺德认为，译作正确与否、成功与否，只有“高水平的读者”即“不迂腐的学者”才是合格的评判员。

---

① William Cowper (1730—1800)，所译荷马于1791年出版。译文的音律为无韵体。无韵体和十音步的双韵体一样，有五个音步的轻重格，但行末不押韵。

② Alexander Pope (1688—1744)，1720年译《伊利亚特》，1726年与他人合译《奥德赛》。

③ George Chapman (1559? — 1634?)，所译《伊利亚特》于1611年出版，所译《奥德赛》于1616年出版。译文的音律是七个音步的轻重格，行末有韵。济慈为此写过后来广为传诵的十四行诗《初读查普曼的荷马史诗》（“On First Looking into Chapman's Homer”）。

阿诺德认为，对于一个译者而言，他的明确目标应该是："给那些通达的学者，尽可能地译出荷马的整体印象来。"[6](P24)在翻译过程中，重要的是译出"整体印象"(general effect)，而不是过于关注个别文字(single words)。纽曼的谬误之处在于他一方面对荷马的"整体印象"把握完全不当，另一方面在于他过于注意细枝末节。纽曼以为，"荷马的文体是直截了当的，通俗的，有力的，怪僻的，流畅的，饶舌的；""荷马是常随主题起伏的，主题平淡时他便庸俗些；主题卑贱时，他便粗鄙些。"[6](P25)阿诺德认为，纽曼对荷马风格的看法除了部分是正确的，大多都是荒谬之极。再没有任何词语比"怪僻、饶舌、庸俗、粗鄙"更不适合用来形容荷马了。无论主题是什么，荷马的风格永远都是崇高的，而绝不会堕入"庸俗、粗鄙"的境地。"谁要用它们来形容荷马风格，我可以说他永远不会把荷马翻译出来的。"[6](P25)纽曼为了表现他所说的荷马的"怪僻、饶舌"，不遗余力地使用古僻的词语、怪诞的用法，如将"骄傲的帝王"("the proud princes")译成"the princes orgulous"，这的确很古僻、怪诞，但这却不再是荷马了。荷马永远是简单的、朴素的。

纽曼翻译荷马使用的是歌谣体(the style of ballad-poetry)。阿诺德认为这种诗体虽然有利于表现荷马的简单、自然、朴素，但却不能展现荷马风格的实质。因为纽曼的歌谣体一点也不崇高。相反，"他用以表现思想的句法，有点超越了无拘束的范围——那简直是太随便了；有点超过了平易的界限——那简直是放任而平易了……他的声调节奏尽管还有优点，也不够崇高；即使他避免了迂缓拖累的错误，但他又失之于另一极端——他有点油腔滑调。"[6](P31)阿诺德认为，采用歌谣体翻译荷马，是纽曼最大的错误。"歌谣体和歌谣律显然是不适宜用来翻译荷马的。荷马的风格与声调一定是崇高而有力的；歌谣体的风格与声调，不是飘浮轻佻，因而不够崇高；便是懒散庸俗，因而柔弱无力。"[6](P35)因此，正因为歌谣体与荷马风格之间，本质上存在着这么深的一道鸿沟，就是"能力最大、精力最强、才力极高的人，也不能用这样的文体造出荷马的境界来"。[6](P35)那么，什么诗体最适合翻译荷马呢？阿诺德的答案是六步律(hexameter)。他认为，六步律最能帮助译者获得荷马的轻快、朴素、直接；另一方面，"六步律具有那种天生的庄严，也会排斥歌谣体自然带来的那种得意忘形的或懒洋洋的文体。"[6](P43)

针对什么是"崇高风格"(the grand style)的问题，阿诺德在《再论荷马史诗的翻译：答弗朗西斯·纽曼》作了详细说明。他认为荷马的"崇高风格"在很大程度上是很难定义的，往往只可意会不可言传。"只有用心感知，方能真正了解"。[7](P398)阿诺德认为，在诗歌史上，除了荷马外，也只有但丁和弥尔顿能称得上是具有"崇高风格"。但是如果一定要定义的话，也只能通过例举来定义。阿诺德认为，"当某一心灵高贵、诗才横溢之人，以或简洁或苍劲的笔法处理某一严肃主题时，崇高风格就出现了。"[7](P399)这让我们想起朗吉努斯在《论崇高》中给"崇高"下的定义：崇高是高贵心灵的回声(The sublimity is the echo of an noble mind.)[8](P109)。两者都强调作为主体的诗人、译者的道德素养、自身修为在文艺创作中具有决定性的作用。阿诺德认为，诗应该是诗人对于"生活的批判"，诗人之所以伟大，"在于他把个人的道德观念有力地应用到生活上，解决一个根本性的问题：教人们如何生活。"[9](P147)试想，一个道德低劣、心灵龌龊的诗人如何能有力地批判生活、教人们如何生活呢？阿诺德劝告想译荷马的人"必须培养一种希腊人的美德，一种一般现代人，尤其英国人所稀有的温和性格。因为荷马不只具有英国人的活力,还具有希腊人的优雅。”[6](P81)论文最后,阿诺德不无戏谑地说,那些以嘈杂叫嚣的方式谈论、赞扬荷马的英国人与荷马是没有丝毫共通之处的;“我时常在幻想,如果荷马听到了他们,一定会这样说,‘朋友们,承蒙你们夸奖,我觉得很荣幸;但你们说话有点儿像野人似的。’”[6](P81)他认为,荷马的崇高是一种完美无瑕、优雅可爱的崇高(a lovely, a perfect grandeur)。他的诗不但包含英语诗歌里所表现的那种矫健雄浑(energy and power),“此外它还有伊俄尼亚地平线上的那种纯净和它的天空里的那种清明。”[6](P81)后者是一般的诗人很难展现的,即使最伟大的英国诗人如查普曼、蒲柏或者如纽曼这样的知名学者也不例外。这正暗合了阿诺德在《文化与无政府主义》对英国人的“劣根性”所进行的有针对性的批判。阿诺德希望他的国人能摆脱偏狭的“岛国心态”,学习希腊人的优雅、温和与宽容,而作为知识分子的翻译家理应成为这方面的典范。

阿诺德在评价别人的译本的同时,也按照自己的理论翻译了荷马史诗的个别诗句。由于译笔有好有劣,有高有低,这自然也给纽曼攻击他留下了口实。两人的争论很激烈,各不相让。我们可以看出,两人作为语言文学和翻译领域的佼佼者,各自观点和理论在今天看来实无绝对高下之分,只是截然不同而已。例如,纽曼认为,应该尽力保留原作的所有特征才是忠实于原文;而阿诺德则强调,译作应该保留的是原作的整体印象,不必过于拘泥细节。这本质上是“直译”和“意译”之别,我们并不能妄加断定二者孰优孰劣。

不难看出,阿诺德的翻译思想与其倡导的“文化”理念一脉相承。阿诺德尤其强调译者的重要性。他认为,译者要译诗,必须具有诗人的洞察力;更重要的是,译者作为传播“文化”的媒介,不仅需要高超的语言技巧,更需要心灵高尚、道德完美。在论及翻译技巧时,他认为,在翻译过程中,要对原作进行整体把握,理解原作的整体风格,在译作中传达出原作的“整体印象”,而不是过于忠实于原作的细枝末节,更不是肆意曲解原作的基本风格。在译荷马时,译者应同时传达出荷马的明快、朴素、直接和崇高等四个特点,缺一不可。只有这样,才能达到信实,才能使译作具有与原作相同的感染力。至于谁是译作优劣的最终裁判者,阿诺德认为在这方面学者最有发言权而非普通读者,因为只有前者方能说出译作是否与原作基本一致,能否给他们带来与原作一样的感受。阿诺德的这些翻译思想为后人所重视,并对翻译理论的发展产生了一定的影响。

参考文献:

[1] 刘锋.《圣经》的文学性诠释与希伯来精神的探求——马修·阿诺德宗教思想研究[M]. 北京:北京大学出版社,2007.

[2] Arnold, Matthew. *Thoughts on Education: Chosen from Matthew Arnold*, Ed. Leonard Huxley. London: John Murray, 1912.

[3] 马修·阿诺德. 文化与无政府主义[M],韩敏中译. 北京:北大出版社,2007.

[4] 安德鲁·桑德斯. 牛津简明英国文学史[M],谷启楠、韩加明、高万隆译. 北京:人民文学出版社,2006.

[5] 谭载喜. 西方翻译简史[M]. 北京:商务印书馆,1991.

[6] 马修·阿诺德. 安诺德文学评论选集[M],殷葆瑹译. 北京:人民文学出版社,1958.

[7] Arnold, Matthew. *Essays by Matthew Arnold*. Oxford: Oxford UP. 1914.

[8] Longinus. "On the Sublime." *On the Art of Poetry*. Beijing: China Social Science Publishing House, 1999.
[9] Sherman, Stuart P. *Matthew Arnold: How to Know Him*. Indianapolis: The Bibbs-Merrill Company Publishers, 1917.

作者简介:黄弋,北京大学外国语学院在读博士研究生,主要研究方向为英国浪漫主义文学。

比较视野下的国别文学史写作

——以现代中国的文学史写作为例

张　珂

【内容提要】 比较视野在现代中国的国别文学史写作中不仅表现为一种世界的意识，世界文学的观念，也体现在从自发到自觉的批评视野中，更体现在对中国文学发展方向和范围构成的探索与理解上。它代表了一种更广阔、更宏观、更高远的观念和方法的出现，有力地促进了文学研究的现代化进程，生动地诠释了“比较”作为一种“沟通之道”的价值与意义。这对今天反思比较文学与外国文学的关系以及国别文学研究的思路与方法有着重要的启示意义。

【关键词】 比较视野　国别文学史　世界文学 比较文学 现代中国

A Study on the Comparative Perspective in the Writings of National Literary History in Modern China

【Abstract】 Comparative perspective in the writings of National Literary History in Modern China is not only about world consciousness and the idea of world literature, but also a critical vision from spontaneousness to consciousness. It is deeply rooted in the exploring and understanding of Chinese literature's future and composition. It represents a kind of new idea and approach which is more profound, macroscopic and broadness that promotes the modernization of literary study. As a result, comparative study proves itself an effective communication way. It can give us some important implications when we rethink about the relations between comparative literature and foreign literature, and also the methods of studying national literature.

【Key Words】 Comparative Perspective　National Literary History　World Literature　Comparative Literature　Modern China

对于中国学术的发展而言，文学史的出现无疑是一件具有现代转型意义的事件。随着现代民族国家意识的觉醒和确立，国别文学史的写作成为中国文学研究现代化进程的一个必然选择。在中国人开眼看世界的大背景下，不但中国文学被纳入西方文学史的发展模式加以理解，外国文学史对于渴望了解异域文化知识的中国人来说也有着巨大的吸引力，现代中国的国别文学史的写作可谓蔚为大观。随着西学东渐的深入，特别是比较文学在中国的萌生，比较视野的运用成为这一时期国别文学史写作的一个显著特色，反映了人们更为世界化的学术视野。本文通过考察现代中国具有代表性的国别文学史写作，分析比较视野的引入对于国别文学史写作所具有的意义，总结其特色和价值，反思比较文学与外国文学的关系，以及今天我们进行国别文学研究时的思路与方法。

一

对于早期的国别文学史写作者而言，比较的视野首先是一种世界的意识、世界文学的观念在文学史中的运用和呈现。许多传统的中国文人士大夫在晚清的大变局中仍然充满了对中国文学的盲目自信，对于域外文学的价值和地位不屑一顾。1895 年甲午中日战争失败以后，中国的民族意识和世界意识被空前地激发出来。一时间，走近世界，了解世界成为人们最迫切的知识诉求。伴随着大量世界历史、世界地理等出版物的普及，文学史作为传播世界文明的方式也逐渐被有识之士重视起来。因此，晚清民初的世界意识在文学学科和知识体系中的呈现最具发生学上的价值和意义。

在这方面，写出第一部《中国文学史》(1907)的黄人做出了不可忽视的历史贡献，世界意识和世界文学观念在这部文学史中明确出现："盖我国国史，守四千年闭关锁港之见，每有己而无人；承廿四朝朝秦暮楚之风，多美此而剧彼，初无世界之观念，大同之思想。历史如是，而文学性质亦禀之，无足怪也。"[①]在作者看来，缺乏世界意识，世界观念，以文学为"载道垂训"的工具，正是中国文学的弊病所在。

> 创世之记，默示之录、天方夜谭，希腊神话，未尝非一丘之貉，不当独为我国诟病，惟彼之贤乎我者，华与实不相掩，真与赝不相杂，而除一上帝外，无赞美指纹，除几种诗歌小说外，无神怪直说。即间有之，而语有分寸，尚殊奴隶之卑污，事有依据，不等野蛮之迷信。故其国民皆以诚为至善，以诳为极恶，外交内政，昭如划一，以固其国础，文学未始无功焉。[②]

可见，黄人以为必须正视域外文学的优点与价值，才能发挥文学对国家和国民的精神功效。黄人在写作中国文学史时，并没有局限于中国文学自身，而是自觉地观察世界文学史的发展历程和规律，拥有以世界文学史的发展审视中国自身文学症结的比较意识。在他看来，从"服从之文学变为自由之文学"，从"一国之文学变为世界之文学"的关键在于言语思想的自由平等，不能仅仅"以国界为交易"。这些结论，正是黄人比较地观察了世界文学史的通例之后才得出的。黄人还参照世界各国学者的学说，获得了关于"文学"现代意义的崭新理解，确认审美是文学的最终目的，传递了西方自浪漫主义以来对文学的理解。[③] 可以说，黄人在文学史的写作中自觉地引入了比较的视野、世界的意识，使这部中国文学史在眼光和见识上明显高出同代人的著述。

世界的意识及比较的视野也出现在此后的各种外国国别文学史中。在英国文学史方面，中国学者王靖写作于 1917 年夏，出版于 1920 年 6 月的《英国文学史(上编)》是我国第一

---

① 汤哲声，涂小马：《黄人 评传 作品选》，北京：中国文史出版社，1998 年，第 39 页。

② 同上书，第 44 页。

③ 同上书，第 65 页，第 67—72 页。

部系统的英国文学史，分六章叙述了从古代至十九世纪英国文学发展的主要历程。作者还有向国人介绍“世界文学史”的宏伟愿望[①]。尽管该书采用了文言写作，对文学家及文学现象的叙述沿用了中国传统的纪传体模式，但在具体的文学批评上却有着不少的突破。例如，许多传统的《文苑传》常常涉及人物及作品风格的比较，但基本局限在一国文学范围内。而王靖却创造性地以中国文学的典故比附英国文学，从而将比较的视野扩大到了国别文学之间。例如，谈到十八世纪英国文学家爱狄生“生性嗜酒，奋髯箕踞，雅有刘伶风范”；称柯勒律治与华兹华斯的交往“雅有管鲍分金之谊”；湖边诗人“可与吾邦虎溪三友相颉颃也”。[②] 除了人物之间的品评比较，还有文体风格的类比。如认为史诗 *Beowulf*“格调似弹词”；华兹华斯的诗“神韵淡远，用字亦浅现，如白香山之诗，老妪都解”；德·昆西的笔记作品“雄丽隽永，似中国六朝小品文字”。[③] 有时著者还以“歌、行、吟”这种传统的中国古诗样式指称英国的诗歌。不难看出，作者深受中国传统文化浸染，又对英国文学有着较深入的了解，因此旧学新知的相互激发，使其看到了中外文学之间的互通性。

这样的以中释西，实际上是一种自发的比较文学批评视野，这在晚清民初的许多文史论著中乃是一种普遍的思维方式。或许是因为在东西文化激烈碰撞的时代，知识分子更强烈和更深刻地感受到了异文化的冲击，但同时又试图以自身的主体意识去消解异文化的陌生感。早在 1914 年，留德学生应时在专述德国诗歌发展史的文章《德诗源流》中就曾以中国古代文论中特有的文质概念来分析阐述德国诗歌的不同风格：“德人有诗以来，文质二家，家法各承一系。”“质家之诗直笔朴辞，止于事理；文家则灵思隽语，穷究事理者也。”[④]他将歌德和席勒归纳为“质”和“文”两种风格的代表，认为诗人“阅历世道”的深浅导致了他们风格的差异。这里的解读颇有中国传统的知人论世的味道。在另外一些受过比较文学训练的现代学者那里，比较视野的运用则有着自觉的意识和明确的目的。1920 年代，吴宓在编译理查生和欧文合著的《世界文学史》之希腊文学史部分时，曾以按语或注释的方式借题发挥，阐述对当时各种文学问题（如印度梵语诗歌的价值、中国的白话诗泛滥等）的看法。他虽然也以文言翻译文学史著作，但其意义却已经大有不同。他的文学史实践是其自觉的比较视野和问题意识的一种呈现，有着明确的现实指向性。由此可见，现代中国学者的比较批评视野经历了一个从自发到自觉的渐进过程。

二

正如有学者指出的那样：“国别文学史的写作与研究不一定是比较文学的研究，但最好是具备世界文学的视野和比较文学的观念。”[⑤]这一点在现代中国的国别文学史中有着丰富的实践，无论是中国文学史，还是以民族国家为主体的各国文学史，都有不少值得今天借鉴

① 王靖：《英国文学史》，上海：泰东书局，1920 年，序二。

② 同上书，第 39、64、62 页。

③ 同上书，第 1、65、79 页。

④ 应时：《德诗汉译》，上海：世界书局，1939 年，第 4—5 页。

⑤ 王向远：《比较文学学科论》，银川：宁夏人民出版社，2007 年，第 238 页。

的东西。国别文学史写作如果不在一个更为宏观的角度进行考察分析，就无法把握一个国家文学的特质，也无法评判其文学作品在历时和共时层面的价值。由于具备了比较的视野和宏观的角度，早期的许多国别文学史在勾勒国家文学整体轮廓，把握一国文学特性方面都显示出了自己的主体立场和学术特色。

例如，曾虚白将英国文学史的写作范围延伸至20世纪的现代时期，注意了英国文学所受到的外国文学的影响，在对比分析中考察英国文学的特色：

> 英国人的文学，可以说，大半含着教训的意味。文学家自认为高出群众的特殊阶级，他们作品的目的是其实人群真理的正轨。所以他们永久是超出群众的，不是混入群众的；他们是高坐堂皇的教师，不是代表多数人的呐喊者。他们作品最伟大的力量，能令读者们欣赏、佩服、和领悟，却不能拨动他们共鸣的心弦，觉得作者所说的话，句句都是自己心坎里发掘出来的。十九世纪写实派的作家，像莎克莱，依廖德，即使像最近逝世的花带，我们看了他们的作品，的确十分感动；可是这种感动，好像只在心灵平静的水面上打起了一层微皱的波纹，一会儿淡了、隐了。他们不能像法国作家的掀起你情感的大浪，又不能像俄国作家的深入你心灵的微奥。这是什么缘故呢？恐怕就因为英国作家始终没有走下他们尊严的讲台来吧？①

这里点出的是一种特殊的文学接受现象，作者敏感地发现中国人对英国文学产生共鸣的困难与隔膜，并在与法国、俄国文学的对比中深入分析了背后的原因。作者认为英国作家"道学家先生的态度"使其文学"充满了严重的色彩"。站在中国学者的角度，作者还专门列出"英国最要作家中国纪元的生卒表"，意在表明"一部伟大的英国文学史的时间，实在只能比上我们清朝一朝的历史而已"。既肯定了英国文学史在相对较短时间内所取得的成绩，也始终将中国乃文学大国的自豪感藏于胸间。这些结论虽然只是作者的一家之言，却富有个人的特色及见解。作者表现出的中国立场与世界意识，微观分析与宏观把握相结合的思路也清晰可见。

国别文学史中的比较视野不仅体现在对各国文学之间的关联分析上，也体现在一国文学范围内的各种对比和类比。作为一种国别文学的研究方法，内部比较有它不可忽视的价值和意义，有助于读者加深对于文学史传承流变的认识和对作家作品的理解。徐名骥的《英吉利文学》(1933)就十分善于在比较中指出作家的风格异同。例如，对比华兹华斯和柯勒律治："华兹华士要使平凡变为新奇，辜勒律已却要使神奇的化为平凡。"②简单的两句话，却一针见血，切中要害。又如，对比华兹华斯和哈代："哈代是英吉利文学中最愁苦的诗人。他和华兹华士一样，是对于自然的绵密的观察者和爱好者，然而他没有像华兹华士这样的从自然获得稳静和安慰。"作者还指出哈代诗歌的艰深"并不是由于他的音律，乃由于他的思想。"③这种特色在金东雷的更为详尽的《英国文学史纲》(1937)中发挥到了极致，后者特别重视英国文学史上不同作家之间的比较，善于从对比分析中显现各家特色。书中进行比较的作家

---

① 曾虚白：《英国文学》，上海：世界书局，1935年，第161页。

② 徐名骥：《英吉利文学》，上海：商务印书馆，1933年，第19页。

③ 同上书，第40页。

包括乔叟与斯宾塞，理查生与菲尔丁，拜伦、雪莱、济慈三家，丁尼生与勃朗宁，卡莱尔与麦考莱，狄更斯与萨克雷等。这些比较分析体现了著者对英国文学深刻的理解和认知，在今天仍有借鉴意义。

三

国别文学史有着自身的价值评判体系，但是国别文学史并不能止于在一国范围内评价作家和作品。比较视野的运用有助于研究者在世界文学的范围内确定一国文学的特色和地位，从而使国别文学史研究上升到世界文学的高度。对于国别文学在世界文学中地位和特色的认识是早期国别文学史写作的普遍诉求，这种诉求有时甚至发展成对民族国家文学的热情追逐。欧阳兰编写的《英国文学史》(1927)评价道："英国文学，在世界文学园里，差不多要算最灿烂最鲜丽的一朵花儿了！"①刘大杰的《德国文学概论》(1928)对德国文学在世界文学中的地位极力推崇："综观各国的文学，最伟大最有特殊个性的，要算德国与俄国的作品。在他两国的文学里面，能深深地看出他们的民族性，体验当时的时代精神。""德国的文学，与俄国的作品有同样的伟大，兼有比俄国悠远的历史与富有理想的民族精神为背景，我敢说德国文学，在世界文学中，为最优美的一部分"。② 另一位我国较早的德国文学研究者杨丙辰也曾评价道："我们简直可以直接断定德国古典文艺是世界各国文艺之冠，放射着奇异伟大，掩遮了一切的光明"。③ 这些论断试图在世界文学范围突显对象国文学的特色和地位，虽然带有绝对化倾向和过激成分，但它们表现出来的研究思路却是值得肯定的。

这方面的实践比较成功的要数夏炎德的《法兰西文学史》(1936)，该著不单单研究法国文学，更重要的是能由法国文学推及文学研究的整体，看到法国文学对于中国新文学的可资借鉴之处，并在比较分析中获得对世界文学发展趋向及潮流的认识：

> 文化是有传播性的，研究并理解先进国文学是创造中国新文学必要的步骤。称为"欧洲之花"的法兰西文学，是世界文学府库中一部分非常的宝藏。
>
> 我们在西欧文学的发展中可以看到，每个思潮或运动的兴起，法国不是占着领袖的地位，便是占着次重要的地位，没有一次是落后的。一部法兰西文学史处处充满着光与热，从来很少衰落的时间。而且以历史言，比利时与西班牙文学差不多是法兰西的附庸，德国与俄国是后进，在西欧诸国的文学中，除英吉利足以与之并驾齐驱外，也没有一个国家比他更悠久的。④

这段话纵论法国文学在世界文学中的地位和特色，且用词谨慎，可以说是对国别文学与世界文学之间关系的一个综合性阐述。在作者眼中，法国文学属于世界先进国的文学，有着广泛的世界影响，其特殊的民族性格也影响了文学艺术的表现。作者虽是谈论一国文学，但

---

① 欧阳兰：《英国文学史》序，北京：京师大学文科出版部，1927年。

② 刘大杰：《德国文学概论》，上海：北新书局，1928年，第1页。

③ 杨丙辰：《魏兰之介绍》，上海：商务印书馆，1934年，第25页。

④ 夏炎德：《法兰西文学史》自序，上海：商务印书馆，1936年，第1页。

却能自觉地联系更为广阔的世界文学背景，其议论就十分具有说服力。作者还明确谈到了文学的世界化倾向，认为现代的法国青年作家没有固步自封，而是“一方面跟时代学习创造新的，一方面也尽力吸收各国的文学”，“这是文学世界化的趋向”。① 正是有了世界的眼光，有了对国际经济、文化交往趋势的了解，才会做出这样的归纳和总结。法国文学的世界化发展趋向，也正代表了国别文学走向世界文学的潮流。作者还提出了自己的文学史观：“文学不是作家个人孤立的产物，文学是反映时代精神社会生活的镜子。文学史不能单是作家作品的汇集，文学史须要是文学演进有机的叙述。”②因此，必须从经济生活、政治制度、思想潮流与社会风尚等多个层面入手，才能了解文学的特质。这也是进行国别文学研究时的方法和依据，充分考虑到了历史发展与普遍联系的双重因素。他所举出的“文学演进有机的叙述”、“时代生产关系的说明”、“作家个别的研究”、“征引权威的论断”、“重要作家的主要作品一一举出”等多种角度，实际上是一种综合性的文学史写作方法，也是比较视野下国别文学史写作的必然呈现方式。可见，比较视野的引入能够使研究者不局限于文学自身，而是能在更为综合和复杂的社会历史语境中考察文学的发展。

四

理解一国文学的特质，必须通过与其他国家文学的比较研究才能获得。而这种比较研究又不单单局限于文学，有时还会涉及整个民族特性，国情历史的比较研究，从而将文学研究引向深入。早期中国文学史学者在阐述一国文学的发展时，大都秉持着自觉的世界意识及历史精神，其比较的基点却是对中国文学自身立场和发展方向的宏观思考。这一点不仅表现在文学史著作对于国民性与文学关系的理解上，也表现在对借鉴什么样的外国文学改造中国文学的择取上。在特殊的历史语境中，中国学者对于外国文学的认识始终立足于中国文学与文化发展的现实。

国民性及其与文学的关系可以说是近代以来知识分子关注的焦点问题。早在1902年，梁启超在《新民说》中就诠释了崭新的民族人格，认为凡一国之能立于世界，必有其国民独具之特质。③ 早期的文学史家也经常在著作中讨论国民性与一国文学之关联，并且赋予文学改造国民性这一重大的历史使命，这是那个时代问题意识集中呈现的必然结果。而关于一国国民性及文学特色的认识必须建立在世界眼光与比较视野的基础之上。这样的探讨有助于人们更深地理解不同国家文学的差异。

例如，王靖《英国文学史》序言明确宣称：“一国文学，多为一国国民性之表征。”“所谓‘沉潜刚克’舍英人殆末与归。”这一点正与中国文学的好高骛远，“期伪相尚”、“花而无实”等缺陷形成对比，因此英国文学史的写作被赋予了改造中国国民性的使命。④ 这种看法具有一定

① 夏炎德：《法兰西文学史》自序，上海：商务印书馆，1936年，第673页。

② 同上书，自序，第3页。

③ 梁启超：《梁启超全集》第3卷，北京：北京出版社，1997年，第657页。

④ 王靖：《英国文学史》，上海：泰东书局，1920年，序一。

的片面性，但其间反映出来的比较意识和引入外国文学改造中国文学的观念却具有时代特色和进步性。欧阳兰也断言：英国文学在世界文学上的特色在于既拥有“热烈的情绪”而又“不失其严正的态度”，“既有沉痛的调子”，“又不脱其滑稽讽刺的风味”，保持了“中和的气质”。① 这是其特殊民族性格的表现。胡愈之则通过对德国国民性的分析，指出了德国文学的特色：“德国国民性雄壮刚强而且智慧。所以德国诗人，大都豪放壮烈，具有超脱的见解；在小说剧本里更多闳大的结构和瑰奇的辞藻。德国人是抽象的国民，哲学的国民，富于思索和归纳的才能。”②在论者看来，德国的国民性不但造就了他们独特的文学，而且使其产生了伟大的艺术。

对于法国的民族性格与文学特色，夏炎德指出法兰西人是“神经质的民族，天性流动，情智兼富，精于修辞，长于社交，有爱美的心理，特别适于文学艺术的表现。”③吴达元也认为法兰西民族理性特别发达，同时富于感情。尽管他们也明白人生有很多痛苦，但却不像日耳曼人似的思考宇宙之谜。法兰西民族的最大特点是爱美的观念，这是使法国文学史光明灿烂的最主要原因。④ 这些论述可谓纵横比较和层层推进，虽然在今天看来并不新鲜，但它们背后透露出论者世界文学的眼光和综合宏观的提炼能力。吴宓曾指出，“各国各族之中，以法兰西人为最明于辨理，工于运思。故近世各种新学术、新思想、新潮流，靡不发轫于法国，由此导源，而后传于他邦，法兰西人诚智慧之先驱者也。惟然，故欲究近世学术思想变迁之迹者，首当于法国文学史中求之。”⑤可见，吴宓不但在比较的视野下指出了法国民族与思想的特色，而且把研究法国文学史的目的提到观察“近世学术思想变迁之迹”的高度，集中体现了不拘泥于一点一面的整体研究意识。这正是今天我们学习国别文学史最应该注意的问题，不能只看到一个文本而忽视整体风貌，只见树木不见森林，必须从个体到整体，从局部到全局，从具体到抽象，这样才能对一国文学的审美风貌和历史沿革有更深入的理解。

五

比较的视野还使中国学者看到了建设中国新的民族国家文学的希望。例如，美国文学因为历史的短暂及英国文学的辐射，在当时很不受研究者的重视。曾虚白就认为美国文学是英国文学的一个分支，但他也承认不能“轻视了美国文学”，因为美国文学有“最多数努力的作家，这是英国文学的旧家里分出来最繁昌的一个大族”。⑥ 到了1930年代，中国学者看到：“现在的美国，是在供给着到二十世纪还可能发展出一个独立的民族文学来的例子了。这例子，对于我们的这个割断了一切过去的传统，而在独立创造中的新文学，应该是怎样有

① 欧阳兰：《英国文学史》序，北京：京师大学文科出版部，1927年。
② 胡愈之：《近代德国文学概观》，《东方杂志》1921年第7期，第55页。
③ 夏炎德：《法兰西文学史》自序，上海：商务印书馆，1936年，第1页。
④ 吴达元：《法国文学史》，上海：商务印书馆，1946，第1—6页。
⑤ 吴宓：《福禄特尔评传》，《出版周刊》1935年第128号，第8页。
⑥ 曾虚白：《英国文学》，上海：世界书局，1935年，第6页。

力的一个鼓励啊!"[1]美国文学洋溢着创造的自由的精神,成为一切新的东西的摇篮,甚至反过来影响到了其他国家。美国文学成为中国新文学学习的榜样,因此当时的美国文学研究取得了不低于同时代其他西方国家的水平。

由于将中国文学自身的发展使命时刻铭记在心,中国学者能够自觉地在文学史研究中为中国文学的发展树立榜样,寻找对策,不断地为中国新文学的建设呼吁呐喊。这种迫切的建设心态决定了研究者们的开放意识,使其能够自觉地在比较研究中为中国文学的发展把脉助阵。进行国别文学研究的目的也是为了比较参照,给本国文学的发展提供养料。这也决定了国别文学研究离不开比较视野的运用。再如,中国现代知识分子在引进外国文学时,发现俄国国情与中国国情的相似,于是主张引入俄国文学以建设中国新文学。郑振铎的《俄国文学史略》(1924)就谈到,俄国文学与英国、德国、法国及其他各国的文学相比,虽然是一个"很年轻的后进",但近代俄国文学的辉煌不但照耀了欧洲各国,而且在日本和中国也引发了持续不断的热潮。[2] 俄国文学可以成为中国建设新文学的榜样。这种思考背后蕴含着自觉的比较意识。它不仅促进了我国对俄国文学研究的精进,而且为中国新文学的建设提供了有益的参照。日本学者升曙梦认为,俄国与中国在国民性及思想特质等方面有着很多共通点,"俄国文化,比之世界任何一国"[3],在中国最能得到正当的理解。可见,当时的中外学者在研究国别文学时,普遍地将比较的视野自觉地纳入思考的范围,从而发现了国别文学之间的差异性及共通性,正是这一点使国别文学之间的相互学习和借鉴成为可能。

早期国别文学史写作中的比较视野还体现在世界文学史的参照下,对于翻译文学及文学传播与交流的重视上。就翻译文学来说,由于晚清以来大量翻译文学在中国的出现,对翻译文学的重视在民国时期的中国文学史中不乏其例,胡适的《白话文学史》、陈子展的《中国近代文学之变迁》、王哲甫的《中国新文学运动史》等都专章讲中国的翻译文学。在外国文学研究领域,金东雷的《英国文学史纲》在国别文学史写作中对于翻译文学的认识颇具代表性。该著明确地提出了"翻译文学"这个问题,为莎士比亚时代的"翻译文学"列出了专章,除举出当时主要翻译文学作品,还探讨了"翻译文学发达的原因":

> 文艺复兴以后,一般读者已扩大眼光,注意到世界文学。乔叟时代遗下的作品既陈腐不堪,难以研习;而当时的教育又十分发达,人民求知心切,颇有供不应求的情形,因之,英国文坛上一时添了不少由外国文翻译过来的英文读物。这些读物在形式上是英国的,但在精神上仍是富于外国的口味。加以那时英国自己的新文学正在将成熟与未成熟的时候,热心的文学研究者比较平时增加了数倍,创作者则正在酝酿,尚未尽量发露,故外来的读物,备受欢迎,这都是翻译作品所以发达的原因。[4]

这段文字从时代发展、读者需求及文学变迁的角度论述了文艺复兴以后英国翻译文学兴盛的原因,深入浅出,可做一家之言,显示出著者自己的思考。最后,著者不无幽默地说

① 施蛰存:《现代美国文学专号导言》,《现代》1934 年第 6 期,第 835、836 页。

② 郑振铎:《郑振铎全集》第 15 卷,石家庄:花山文艺出版社,1998 年,第 417 页。

③ [日]升曙梦:《俄国现代思潮与文学》,许亦非译,上海:现代书局,1933 年,第 2 页。

④ 金东雷:《英国文学史纲》,上海:商务印书馆,1937 年,第 117、118 页。

道："翻译文学发达的结果，拉丁文和希腊文的伟大著作，一时都穿上了英文的衣服，移居到英国，内容是拉丁文和希腊文，而外貌都像英国的。"①这里的论述似乎也映衬了翻译文学在中国的近代化历程，对于我们重新认识翻译文学和国别文学之间的关系提供了参照。任何国家的文学都需要外来文学的刺激和更新。翻译文学对于一国文学的发展而言具有重要的补充和更新的作用，理应成为国别文学史的书写和研究对象。因此，比较的视野还丰富了人们对中国文学构成的理解，这种理解直到今天仍具有先锋意义。

六

从以上对比较视野在现代中国的国别文学史写作中运用的分析，我们可以发现，比较视野在早期国别文学史中不仅表现为一种世界的意识，世界文学的观念，也体现在从自发到自觉的批评视野中，更体现在对中国文学发展方向和范围构成的探索与理解上。这种视野的出现既缘于研究者个人深厚的中外文学修养，又是特殊历史时期时代召唤的必然文化表达。还需要指出的是，比较的视野体现在、但并不止于本文所描述的几个方面。

就比较的含义而言，正如学界所认识到的，比较文学不等同于文学比较。从比较文学的学科历史来看，比较文学的起源离不开文学史研究的发展。法国学派认为比较文学是文学史研究的分支。正是为了克服国别文学史研究中狭隘与孤立的倾向，法国学派从学理和实践上注重挖掘了法国文学与其他国家文学之间的事实联系。对于法国学派而言，比较的视野意味着法国与欧洲其他国家之间文学交流事实联系的求证、挖掘与处理。因此，从起源上来看，国别文学史研究与比较文学研究有着不解之缘，后者拓宽了国别文学史研究的视野和思路。对于美国学派而言，比较的视野意味着建立在共同审美基础之上的平行比较研究，它既发生在有事实联系的文学现象之间，同时又可以发生在没有事实联系的文学现象之间。更为全面的对比较视野的理解则是艾金伯勒所提倡的比较诗学式的综合，"将历史方法与批评精神结合起来，将案卷研究与文本阐释结合起来，将社会学家的审慎与美学家的大胆结合起来。"②比较视野既是历史的，又是审美的。它既可以是历时的寻踪，也可以是共时的观察。比较视野既可运用于同一种文明价值体系当中，也可以在迥然相异的文明价值体系中找到用武之地。它是一种综合性的研究方法和思维，包含了对比、类比、分析、归纳、演绎、解释、描绘等多种内涵。

韦勒克曾指出，比较文学并不含有忽视研究各种国别文学的意思，事实上正是"国家性"（或译"民族性"）以及各个国家对这个总的文学进程作出独特贡献应当被理解为问题的中心。全球文学与国别文学相互影响，必须讨论国别文学是如何成为更大文学传统的一部分的，这样才能写出不单单是地理或语言分类上的国别文学史。③ 因此，比较的视野不仅需要而且必须运用在研究国别文学自身以及国别文学对世界文学进程的贡献中。虽然早期国别

---

① 金东雷：《英国文学史纲》，上海：商务印书馆，1937年，第118页。

② 干永昌、廖鸿钧等：《比较文学译文集》，上海：上海译文出版社，1985年，第102页。

③ 同上书，第182—183页。

文学史写作中的比较视野并非都是严格的比较文学学科意义上的，但却从不同的层面接近着比较文学的真谛，其历史价值和意义不能忽视。这些尝试代表了一种更广阔、更宏观、更高远的观念和方法的出现，有力地促进了文学研究的现代化进程，生动地诠释了“比较”作为一种“沟通之道”的价值与意义。它们的得失在某种程度上对于今天的重写文学史、宏观比较文学研究等命题也有一定的启示意义。回顾这些历史资源，不仅有助于我们反思比较文学与外国文学的关系，对于我们今天的国别文学史研究和写作同样意义重大。

作者简介：张珂，中央民族大学外国语学院博士后。

关于召开中国比较文学学会第11届年会暨国际学术研讨会的通报

经中国比较文学学会10届2次常务理事会(天津)研究决定,中国比较文学学会第11届年会暨国际学术研讨会定于2014年9月18—21日在吉林省延边市延边大学举行。会议主题为"百年中国比较文学:回顾与展望"。主办单位:中国比较文学学会、延边大学、吉林省比较文学学会。承办单位:延边大学暨延边大学跨文化研究中心、延边大学朝鲜—韩国学学院 、延边大学外国语学院、延边大学汉语言文化学院、延边大学人文学院中文系、延边大学《东疆学刊》编辑部。协办单位:吉林大学、东北师范大学等。

会议将设立以下分论题和圆桌(暂定):

(1) 中国比较文学的历史、现状与未来(曹顺庆 王向远)

(2) 普遍性与差异性:比较文学的学科方法与文化分野(陈跃红 周小仪)

(3) 中国作家、批评家与世界文学(钱林森 高旭东)

(4) 汉学与国际中国人文研究(严绍璗 王晓平)

(5) 多民族国家的比较文学疆界与研究范式(叶舒宪 徐新建)

(6) 诗学的世界性与民族性(张辉 刘耘华)

(7) 比较文学、国别文学与世界文学(王宁 李庆本)

(8) 比较文学与世界文学的教学与师资培养(孟昭毅 杨乃乔)

(9) 翻译与比较文学 (谢天振 宋炳辉)

(10) 中韩文学及东北亚文学关系研究(金柄珉 徐东日)

(11)【圆桌】比较文学与宗教学(杨慧林)

(12)【圆桌】海外华文文学研究(程爱民)

(13)【圆桌】文学符号学(赵毅衡)

其他(待定)

自即日起向学会理事、会员及国内外比较文学同仁征集论文,论文提纲提交截止日期为2014年3月31日,4月底筹委会通知入选论文作者,5月底提交完整论文,6月30日前发出正式会议邀请。

论文请提交至相关论题负责人,邮箱地址如下:

严绍璗	ysddyf@pku.edu.cn
曹顺庆	shunqingcao@163.com
谢天振	swgfxtz@163.com
王　宁	wangning@mail.tsinghua.edu.cn
叶舒宪	ye6208@163.com
钱林森	linsenqian@hotmail.com

高旭东	gaoxudong116@aliyun. com
陈跃红	ychen@pku. edu. cn
张　辉	zhui@pku. edu. cn
程爱民	amcheng@nju. edu. cn
徐新建	scxxjian@sina. com
刘耘华	liuyh1964@aliyun. com
孟昭毅	wxy@mail. tjnu. edu. cn
宋炳辉	songbinghui2000@126. com. cn
周小仪	xiaoyizhou@hotmail. com
赵毅衡	zhaoyiheng@gmail. com
杨乃乔	yangnaiqiao@126. com
徐东日	Drx2005@sina. com

中国比较文学学会秘书处

2013 年 11 月 25 日

关于参加2013年度国际比协理事会暨第20届国际比协年会的报告

周小仪

2013年6月16、17日，国际比较文学学会在巴黎索邦大学召开了理事会。国际比协秘书长John Forster教授总结了上一年的工作，并介绍了学会期刊《文学研究》的编辑情况。三位司库分别汇报了本年度各大洲的会费收支情况。其中亚洲司库上垣外宪一的报告列出了亚洲各国的缴费情况(每人每年10美元)，即：日本约8340美元，中国1130美元，韩国850美元，印度800美元。我国已连续多年在亚洲地区名列第二。

理事会在讨论了学会的一些组织结构和学术奖项等问题后，又听取了学会下属的各研究分会负责人所作的本年度研究和出版情况的报告。这些研究会包括翻译研究会、文学理论研究会、世界文学研究会、数码时代研究会、印度次大陆研究会等。中国比较文学学会双会长之一、人民大学杨慧林教授，作为“经典释读研究会”负责人向理事会做工作报告并提交了本年度出版的《基督教文化研究》刊物3期和研究著作2本，颇获好评。此外理事会还讨论了关于2016年度选举的网络投票议案并表决通过。届时我国会员也可以电子邮件的方式直接选举理事会成员，并投票决定下一届年会的开会地点。这将使我国国际比协会员拥有更多参与决策的机会。

2013年7月18至24日国际比协在巴黎索邦大学召开了第20届年会暨学术研讨会。会议主题为“作为批评方法的比较文学”。大会期间，主办方共组织了九场学术报告，其中著名学者斯皮瓦克的报告以“自由的实践”(The Practice of Freedom is not impractical)为主题做了大会发言。来自世界各地约900余名比较学者分别参加了11个专题的分组讨论及数十个圆桌、工作坊的讨论。

与会的中国学者共组织了两个圆桌讨论会。上海外国语大学谢天振教授与北京大学孟华教授共同主持了题为“西方文学概念在东方的历史境遇”的圆桌讨论。共有来自美、法、德、中国香港、中国内地的14位学者发言(详见张丽华博士报告)，鉴于两天共五场的讨论具有较高学术水平，圆桌组织者已决定会后将论文结集出版。人大杨慧林教授主持了“经典释读”圆桌会议，有来自英、美、日、中国香港、中国内地的13位学者发言，其间各国学者讨论热烈，彼此都觉得很有收获(详见张辉教授报告)。此外，浙江大学的沈弘教授参加了“中国与英语文学”的小组会并作了有关弥尔顿作品汉译的发言。

此次大会各分组会议讨论的问题非常丰富，除了我们比较熟悉的如现代性、翻译学、诗学、美学、艺术理论、文学研究对象、比较文学观念、全球化、民族国家、多语种文学、东方主义等的专题讨论之外，还有一些我们过去关注不多的问题，如文学与医学、文学与神经科学、意识与脑研究、文学与公共卫生叙事、文学与恐怖主义、人类学情感问题、后殖民主义文学记忆、文学中的机场空间、文学与其他社会科学的关系等等。这些引人入胜的讨论对于我们开阔视野、启发思路、拓展比较文学研究领域不无帮助。

会议期间，各国国际比较文学学会会员还进行了无记名投票选举，选出了新一届理事会。由于中国学者有备而来，每位参会者都携带了另两位会员的投票委托书，新一届理事会共有三位中国学者当选：周小仪连任副会长，杨慧林当选为新一届理事会理事，香港城市大学张隆溪连任理事。这是历届理事会中中国学者当选人数最多的一次。

在大会闭幕式上，前国际比协会长、杨百翰大学教授 Steve Sondrup 作了离职演讲，题为“作为礼物的文学”。论文总结了从马歇尔·莫斯到德里达以来的社会学礼物交换理论，并把文学看作是生活存在的一部分和思想交流的载体。新任国际比协会长、后现代文学理论专家、荷兰乌特勒支大学（University of Utrecht）教授 Hans Bertens 也作了幽默而简短的就职演讲。在对大会进行总结时，杨慧林教授应邀做大会发言，介绍了经典释读研究领域在中国和其它欧美国家的研究状况和成就、经典释读理论和实践的比较研究性质和方法，以及与传统比较文学研究的关系。此外各国国际比协会员还投票决定了下一届年会的主题和开会地点：下一届年会将于 2016 年 7 月中旬在维也纳大学召开，主题为“比较研究与世界文学的多种语言”（Comparaticism and the Many Languages of World Literature）。由于主办单位经费紧张，下一届年会的会务费较为昂贵，可能达到 300 欧元，但维也纳市的旅馆较为便宜。会议分组议题目前尚未发布，感兴趣者可关注国际比协网站http://www.ailc-icla.org。

闭幕式后随即召开了新一届理事会的第一次全体会议，会议决定 2014 年国际比协理事会将由中国比较文学学会承办。目前中国比较文学学会秘书处在乐黛云、杨慧林两位会长的领导下正在积极协商、筹备这次理事会。它将与中国比较文学学会的下一届年会同时于延边大学举行，而国际比协全体理事也将应邀参加中国比协下一届年会暨国际学术研讨会。

“比较文学与世界文学学术文库”总序

张　辉　宋炳辉

“比较文学与世界文学学术文库”第一辑即将与读者见面。从动议编辑这套文库到今天，转眼已3年。“风雨如晦，鸡鸣不已”，这是“中生代”比较文学学人一次小小的集结；“虽不能至，然心向往之”，这是我们献给自己师长们的一份迟交的作业；“嘤其鸣矣，求其友声”，这又是我们向各位同仁、乃至更年轻同行们发出的对话与批评的邀请。

3年的酝酿筹划，3年的协同努力，使我们逐步将自己的工作与更深远而广大的时间和空间背景联系了起来，并开始慢慢融入其中。作为从1980年代开始接受系统学术训练的“新一代”比较文学学人，我们深深知道，自己的每一点成长与进步，都无不受惠于祖国的开放改革，受惠于师长们的谆谆教诲，受惠于同辈间的切磋琢磨。我们是这15年、30年乃至更长时段文化积淀的受益者，也是一批如饥似渴的学习者和无比幸运的历史见证者。我们也许注定是行色匆匆的“过客”，但我们却也应是承先启后的“桥梁”，必须发出属于我们自己的“声音”。而这里记录的正是我们探索行进的脚印，也是我们对自己所从事的学科一点微末的贡献。

百年中国文学“走向（进）世界”的历程，给了我们思考过去、筹划未来的“底气”；新时期中国比较文学的复兴与发展，为我们准备了难能可贵的学术资源和不可或缺的学科建制。我们将这套丛书命名为“比较文学与世界文学学术文库”，以之与我们所属的学科名称相呼应，因为我们有一个共同的默契：打破界限、超越语言与文化的限制，乃是我们比较文学学人的使命乃至宿命。是的，我们无疑拥有不同的学术爱好、志趣和观点，但至少有一个基本的共识把我们联系在了一起——那就是，我们必须在世界的语境中，以比较的眼光，从多学科的视域，面对并尝试回答我们所浸润其中的文学与文化问题。

“德不孤，必有邻。”非常幸运的是，我们身处富于活力和学术追求的知识与精神共同体之中。我们的工作得到了中国比较文学学会许多老师和朋友的无私帮助；也得到了具有远见卓识的上海文化发展基金会以及复旦大学出版社的大力支持。在这里，我们要送上我们衷心的谢意。

同样值得高兴的是，与这套“文库”相呼应，《比较文学与世界文学》辑刊、“比较文学与世界文学讲座系列”等姊妹项目也已陆续启动。

在“文库”第一辑即将面世的这个特殊时刻，先贤们的声音似乎又一次在我们的耳畔响起。鲁迅先生说，中国文化的发展应“内之弗失既有之血脉，外之仍不后于世界之思潮，取今复古，别立新宗”；而陈寅恪先生则说，华夏文化的崛起须“取塞外野蛮精悍之血，注入中原文化颓废之躯，旧染既出，新机重启，扩大恢张，遂能别创空前之世局”。响应先贤的号召，集结这8本著作，仅是我们的第一次尝试。希望有更多的朋友加入到这“取今复古”、“扩大恢张”的行列中，贡献他们的智慧与力量；希望我们会有继续编辑以后各辑的荣幸。

是所望也，谨为序。

（“比较文学与世界文学学术文库”顾问：乐黛云，杨慧林，谢天振，陈思和，陈跃红；主编：张辉，宋炳辉。第一辑（2013年9月，复旦大学出版社）：王宏图：《东西跨界与都市书写》；严锋：《跨媒体的诗学》；宋炳辉：

《视界与方法：中外文学关系研究》；张华：《跨学科研究与跨文化诠释》；张旭春：《浪漫主义、文学理论与比较文学研究论稿；张沛：《比较文学：人文之道》；张辉：《文学与思想史论稿》；周阅：《比较文学视野中的中日文化关系研究》。第二辑（预计 2014 年 8 月，复旦大学出版社）：陈戎女：《女性与爱欲：希腊与世界》；陈晓兰：《性别·城市·异邦——文学经典的跨文化阐释》；刘洪涛：《从国别文学走向世界文学》；刘耘华：《中西文学与诗学关系的实证与诠释》；叶隽：《文学·比较·侨易》；周宁：《跨文化形象学》；程巍：《幻象的见证人》；季进：《彼此的视界》。）

中国高等教育学会外国文学专业委员会 2013 年年会纪要

董 晓

2013 年 7 月 20 日—23 日，中国高等教育学会外国文学专业委员会 2013 年年会在美丽的塞上明珠银川市北方民族大学举行。21 日上午，开幕式由此次年会的承办方北方民族大学外国语学院院长闫丽君教授主持。北方民族大学副校长赵杰教授致了热情洋溢的欢迎辞。学会副会长刘建军教授代表学会致了开幕辞。刘建军教授宣读了学会会长杨正润教授致大会的公开信，并对会议承办单位北方民族大学外国语学院表示诚挚的感谢。刘建军教授在致辞中针对目前外国文学教学与研究的现状，强调了改革和深化外国文学教学与研究的重要性。

大会发言分别由刘树森教授、黄铁池教授、郑体武教授、张冰教授、周明燕教授、闫丽君教授、梁坤教授、曾艳兵教授和曾思艺教授主持。在大会发言中，北京大学李明滨教授介绍了俄罗斯扩充托尔斯泰全集的进展情况；复旦大学英语系孙建教授从一尊佛像这一细节出发，讨论了品特剧作《看门人》的艺术特色；河南大学文学院李伟昉教授讨论了《悲惨世界》中对滑铁卢战役的叙述，阐述了雨果对战争、民族等问题的思考以及对拿破仑的看法；江西师范大学傅修延教授讨论了对“穿越”这一概念的看法；北京师范大学刘洪涛教授从《朗曼世界文学作品选》出发，探讨了对世界文学教学的看法；北京大学林丰民教授谈了阿拉伯现当代文学与社会文化变迁之间的关系；天津师范大学孟昭毅教授讲解了《我的名字叫红》的艺术内涵，分析了土耳其作家奥尔罕·帕默克的创作与绘画的关系；南京师范大学文学院杨莉馨教授论述了贝尔的绘画艺术对弗吉尼亚·伍尔芙小说创作的影响；北京大学东语系魏丽明教授介绍了北京大学东方文学的教学状况；四川大学刘亚丁教授分析了孔子形象在俄罗斯文学中的流变；广州大学冉东平教授论述了瑞典剧作家斯特林堡的戏剧对于 19 世纪戏剧的创新性和对 20 世纪现代戏剧的影响；中国人民大学陈世丹教授讨论了在大学讲授后现代主义小说课程时应当注意的后现代主义小说的知识结构；南开大学王旭锋老师谈论了苏联作家布尔加科夫的作品《大师与玛格丽特》中的“疯狂”叙事特征；北方民族大学外国语学院车凤成老师讨论了《伯罗奔尼撒战争史》中的正义叙事与伦理意义；河南教育学院苏永旭教授谈了教学阐释学与 21 世纪中国世界文学史教学之关系的问题；华东师范大学王亚明教授介绍了当代俄罗斯电影的现状；复旦大学李征教授以具体实例生动地说明了外国文学教学中文本细读的方法与意义；河北工业大学石梅芳老师介绍了当代苏格兰小说家詹姆斯·凯尔曼小说中的工人阶级书写；北京大学张冰教授谈了俄罗斯著名汉学家李福清院士对“东干故事”的比较研究；东北师范大学柳东林老师对劳伦斯的小说《虹》做了个性化的阐释。

在分组讨论中，来自全国各个高校的代表进行了为时 3 个小时的自由讨论，就外国文学的研究与教学中的诸种问题广泛而富有成效地交换了意见。

7 月 20 日晚召开了学会第六届常务理事会，讨论并通过了新一届理事名单。21 日晚举行了第七届理事会，选举产生了新一届常务理事会，随后，在新一届常务理事会上，选举产生了新一届副会长、秘书长和会长。东北师范大学刘建军教授当选为会长，上海外国语大学郑体武教授、南开大学王立新教授、北京大学刘树森教授、中国人民大学杨慧林教授、厦门大学王诺教授、北京大学张冰教授、南京大学董晓教授当选为副会长。并在 7 月 22 日的大会上，由学会秘书长张冰教授宣布了学会换届选举的结果。

大会闭幕式由刘树森副会长主持。他宣读了3个新入会的单位名单，学会名誉理事李明滨教授在闭幕辞中回顾了学会的发展史。学会新一届会长刘建军教授对本次年会做了总结。他指出，这是一次成功的年会，是一次各种学术观点相互碰撞、相互交流的学术盛宴，中国高等教育学会外国文学专业委员会将继承和发扬学会好的学术传统，进一步提高中国高校外国文学教学与研究的整体水平。尤其是一些青年学者在大会上的发言，给学会带来了新的学术气息。他还代表理事会宣布了理事会的决议：在2015年年会上举行本会建会30周年的庆祝活动。

中国翻译学学科建设高层论坛暨中国比较文学学会翻译研究会第十届年会在重庆召开

谢天振

2013年10月19—21日，中国比较文学学会翻译研究会、中国翻译协会翻译理论与翻译教学委员会、教育部全国MTI教育指导委员会和四川外国语大学，联合在四川外国语大学举办“中国翻译学学科建设高层论坛暨中国比较文学学会翻译研究会第十届年会”。来自中国内地、香港、台湾两岸三地的两百多位译界同仁，包括中国译协、教育部全国MTI教指委领导、在翻译理论与教学研究领域卓有成就的专家学者，以及关注中国翻译学学科建设的广大师生和研究者，共同交流和探讨翻译学学科建设尚存在的许多疑惑和问题。

四川外国语大学校长李克勇教授在开幕式上代表承办单位向与会学者表示热烈欢迎。中比翻译研究会会长谢天振教授回顾了研究会成立以来每届年会的发展历程。中国译协常务副会长许钧教授指出当今翻译研究在整个社科研究中的地位、作用和发展机遇。研讨会主要围绕翻译教学、翻译史研究、翻译理论研究三大议题展开深入全面的讨论，共安排了6场大会发言和12场分组发言。

与会代表多对翻译史感兴趣，共有40多名学者分别就特定历史时期、特定地区的翻译史问题、翻译史观以及其他译史问题做了发言。香港中文大学王宏志介绍了香港殖民时期翻译史上三个极具研究价值却未及深入探究过的课题。复旦大学邹振环指出当前翻译研究在文献学、校勘学、版本学等史学方法运用中存在的问题。台湾辅仁大学杨承淑描述了日据时期台湾《语苑》中的译者群像。台湾师大张思婷阐述了“戒严时期”中国流亡青年在台湾的文学翻译活动。

另一个引起大家关注并热烈讨论的话题是中译外及相关问题。清华大学王宁从跨文化阐释角度对翻译的定义进行了新的理论辨析，并以葛浩文对莫言作品的翻译为例说明跨文化阐释式翻译达到的效果。南京大学许钧认为译学研究需积极参与中国文学对外的构建，研究重点应从外译中转向中译外，客观地分析外译作品的传播与接受效果，为国家决策提供依据。上外高翻学院谢天振从译者的隐身与现身角度剖析了译学理论从传统到当代的发展线索，指出译学研究视角的变化，以译入为主的理论不可能有效指导文化走出去战略中的译出行为，译学研究需探索出新的契合时代发展的理论。

翻译教学研究也是研讨会上的讨论焦点之一。上外高翻学院柴明颎指出在专业翻译教学探索国际化途径中，需要明确本科生和研究生不同的培养目标，认识翻译及相关岗位工作的任务要求，并以理论研究推动实用人才的培养。北京语言大学刘和平对翻译专业教育的理念和方法发表了意见，认为不同类型翻译人才培养目标上的差异要求我们探索不同的教育教学方法和课程体系。广外高翻学院穆雷基于国内700篇博士论文的文献计量分析，对中国翻译学博士培养的历史进行回顾与思考，指出翻译学高层次人才培养取得的成绩和存在的不足。

大会期间，翻译研究会举行了第十届第一次全体理事会，选举产生了新一届理事会成员。经过充分的酝酿和讨论，在力挽无效的情况下，理事会最终接受谢天振教授主动辞去研究会会长职务一事，并一致同意聘请他担任研究会名誉会长，由南京大学许钧教授接任会长。理事会还重新调整并任命了新的副会长：柴明颎任常务副会长兼秘书长，廖七一、穆雷、王东风、赵稀方任副会长。同时，增补高彬等14位新任理事，加上原有28位理事，理事会现共有42位成员。新老会长都发表了讲话，他们表示对研究会的支持一如既往，希望研究会继续大力开展学术活动，为多元思想的碰撞创造平台，为青年学者的成长创造机会。

中国比较文学与翻译研究高峰论坛综述

刘贵珍

中国比较文学与翻译研究高峰论坛于2013年10月15日在清华大学举行。论坛由清华大学外文系和比较文学与文化研究中心主办,清华大学外文系长江学者特聘教授、比较文学与文化研究中心主任王宁等主持了论坛。清华大学副校长谢维和代表主办方对论坛的举行表示衷心的祝贺,并希望清华大学的人文学者为中国文化和文学走向世界作出独特的贡献。在开幕式上致辞的还有中国比较文学学会副会长、四川大学长江学者特聘教授曹顺庆,国际比较文学学会理事、国际权威刊物《比较文学与世界文学评论》(*Neohelicon*)主编彼得·海居(Peter Hajdu),清华大学外文系主任刘世生,上海外国语大学高级翻译学院教授谢天振。简短的开幕式之后,王宁教授和美国著名文学翻译家、莫言作品的主要译者葛浩文(Howard Goldblatt)以及谢天振教授做了主题发言。

葛浩文在发言中探讨了译者的主体性作用。他认为,翻译尽管不是一种走近异域作品的完美方式,但也的确是一种方式,而且几乎总是一种能够让作者获得国际声誉的方式。他高度评价了诺贝尔文学奖得主莫言的几部主要作品,认为无论何时,莫言的写作都足以将他本人推入中国顶级作家之列。关于作者与译者的关系,葛浩文提到,正是由于有了像他这样的国外译者的参与,才使莫言的作品得以与国外读者见面,莫言的国际知名度已经达到了新的高度。而译者主要是为读者而翻译,没有必要尽力去忠实原作的词句。译者的责任在于忠实地再现作者的意思和风格。翻译可以延长一部作品的生命,并可以揭示原文本中所隐藏的东西。因此我们不应该把翻译看成全球化或跨文化的工具,而应该把它看成一种对个人的拯救。

王宁的发言题目为《世界主义、世界文学与中国文学的世界性》。他首先以世界主义在中国的实践作为参照,追溯其在中国和世界其他地方的源头,并提出他本人主要从文化和文学的视角对这一概念所做出的新的建构。然后他以世界主义作为参照,着重讨论了中国现代文学的国际化进程。他认为,随着全球化时代的到来,中国经济的飞速发展,以及莫言荣获诺贝尔文学奖,中国文学的国际化应该提到议事日程上来,因此翻译的重点应该从外译中转向中译外,通过中外合作的方式加速中国文学和文化的国际化进程。他认为莫言的成功,很大程度上在于,他恰到好处地把中国人所面临的一些基本问题放到了一个广阔的世界语境下来探讨,而这也正是世人共同关心的问题。

谢天振发言的题目是《中国文学走出去:理论与实践》。他认为,在中国文化如何"走出去"这个问题上,存在一个严重的认识误区,以为只要把中国文化典籍和文学作品翻译成外文,中国文化和文学就自然而然地"走出去"了。他运用译介学理论,对制约中国文化走出去的诸多因素进行了考察与分析,同时结合中国文化"走出去"的两个具体译介个案,即中国古典名著《红楼梦》的百年英译史和上世纪80年代以来国内推出的外文版"熊猫丛书"在国外的传播与接受实际,对中国文化如何才能真正有效地"走出去"这一问题进行了全面深入的探讨。

关于中国文化与文学"走出去"这一主题,另有学者从其他角度进行了探讨。例如,孙艺风(香港岭南大学)从翻译与跨文化交际的关系入手,认为在中译英研究方面,文化差异造成的跨文化交际上的障碍并未引起学界足够重视。为保证跨文化交际的顺利进行,有必要进行跨文化重写,同时有必要挖掘国与国之间的审美共性,超越狭隘的文化民族主义。彼得·海居则介绍了匈牙利对中国古典小说,如《金瓶梅》、《水浒传》、《西游记》和《三国演义》等的译介状况,在他看来,中国文学在匈牙利的译介总体而言不容乐观。张平功(广东外语外贸大学)认为,伴随着全球化的进程,作为跨学科的英国文学研究的内涵和外延都发生了深刻变化,呈现出教学、研究和批评的多元化,同时也给中国文学和文化走出国门带来了有益启示。陆薇(北京语言大学)则以《青衣》英译本的叙事方式为个案,探讨了译者的主体性问题。

关于翻译在历史上曾发挥的重要作用,亦有两位学者对此进行了专门研究。罗选民(清华大学)以早期清华大学为例,探讨了翻译行为的多重角色,如从宏观角度而言,翻译行为促进了政治、文学和教育改革,而个人翻译行为则可以修身养性;同时,他以《清华周刊》为例,详细探讨了清华的翻译对教育的影响等核心问题。卢明玉(北京交通大学)则介绍了 1894—1911 年在华美国新教传教士及其西学译介,指出这一译介行为使得我们得以窥见文化和知识体系如何与民族身份的探索、译介策略的选择以及文化间的交流相联系。最后,马军红和李程(北京第二外国语学院)分别在发言中探讨了生态批评在中国的译介状况。马军红介绍了美国生态批评与生态文学在中国的译介,指出上述译介积极参与了国内生态文学的形成。李程则做了《跨文化对话语境中的中国生态批评研究》的综述,着重指出中美生态批评界存在的差距,认为有必要开展跨国别的对话以及发展中国自己的跨学科研究。

众所周知,清华大学外文系在翻译方面有着辉煌的历史传统,老清华的一大批学人通过翻译将大量外国文化理论思潮和文学作品引入中国,从而推动了中国的现代性进程。而在当今的全球化时代,新一代清华学人继承了这一优良传统,为中国文化和文学走向世界做出了独特贡献,得到国际学界的高度重视。此次高峰论坛的召开,为中外学者探讨这一历久弥新的话题提供了契机,具有重要学术价值。

博雅大学堂—2013 年全国高校比较文学与世界文学高级研修班成功举办

初艳红

为提高我国高校比较文学与世界文学的教学研究水平，增进各高校教师间的交流与合作，由北京大学比较文学与比较文化研究所、四川外国语大学英语学院、《国外文学》杂志、《中国比较文学》杂志、《比较文学与世界文学》编辑部、北京大学出版社联合举办的“博雅大学堂—全国高校比较文学与世界文学高级研修班”于 2013 年 10 月 11—13 日在重庆成功举办。四川外国语大学副校长董洪川和北京大学出版社外文部主任张冰分别在开幕式、闭幕式上致辞。

本次研修班培训对象主要针对国内高校从事比较文学与世界文学教学的骨干教师。为本次研修班授课的专家有北京大学教授、北京大学比较文学与比较文化研究所所长、中国比较文学学会副会长兼学术委员会主任严绍璗(“北京大学比较文学学术文库”主编、“21 世纪比较文学系列教材”主编)，北京大学教授、中文系主任、中国比较文学学会副会长兼秘书长陈跃红(主要著有《比较诗学导论》、《比较文学原理新编》(合著)等)，《中国比较文学》主编、上海外国语大学教授、上海外国语大学高级翻译学院翻译研究所所长、中国比较文学学会副会长谢天振(主要著有《译介学导论》，“翻译专业必读书系”主编)，北京大学教授、北京大学比较文学与比较文化研究所副所长、中国比较文学学会副秘书长张辉(主要著有《比较文学原理新编》(合著)、《审美现代性批判》等)，《国外文学》主编、北京大学教授刘锋(主要著有《〈圣经〉的文学性诠释与希伯来精神的探求》等)，四川外国语大学教授、四川外国语大学英语学院院长张旭春(主要著有《政治的审美化与审美的政治化》、《世界语境中的中国文学理论》(合著)，《国外英语语言文学研究前沿》主编)，以及厦门大学外文学院英语系副系主任、副教授林斌(主要著有《美国文学选读》(合著)等)。

严绍璗教授的报告是《文本中“文化元素”的测定与比较文学》，阐释了什么是比较文学研究；张辉教授则以对《哈姆雷特》等三部名著的开头部门的细读为例，阐述了从“小”事实发现“大”问题；谢天振教授告诉我们如何做学术研究，从而达到学术创新，并谈及学术论文的写作与发表；张旭春教授的报告《浪漫主义与政治—历史:兼论国内“英国文学”本科教材诸种问题》解释了为什么北大版罗经国的《新编英国文学选读》更适合本科的教学，其优势表现在哪些方面；陈跃红教授以对钱锺书比较诗学方法论的研究为例，告诉我们怎样做到从“游于艺”到“求打通”；林斌教授以北大版《美国文学选读》为例，阐述了英美文学本科教学的理论视角嵌入的问题；刘锋教授则结合其自身的文学研究，告诉大家怎样写出好文章，《国外文学》会采用什么样的论文予以发表。

两天的研修班课程，专家们为学员准备了丰富的精神食粮，介绍国内外比较文学与世界文学研究的最新理论和成果，讲授先进的教学研究方法，交流与沟通近年来我国比较文学与世界文学课程教学方面的教学经验与心得。这次培训切实提高了教师的教学能力，达到了推动课程的建设与发展，从而提高教学质量的目的。研修班结束后，统一颁发了结业证书。参加培训的教师们纷纷表示希望以后能继续举办这样的研修班。

“比较文学与世界文学学术讲座系列”陆续在北京大学举行

缴　蕊

2012年10月，由北京大学中文系、北京大学比较文学与比较文化研究所主办，北京大学出版社和《比较文学与世界文学》杂志协办的“比较文学与世界文学学术讲座系列”正式拉开帷幕。活动开始以来，陆续邀请海内外知名学者前来演讲，到2013年10月底为止已举行过十一讲。前六讲的纪要刊载于《比较文学与世界文学》杂志第二和第三期，以下为第七至十一讲的简要内容。

2013年5月17日，系列讲座的第七、第八讲于北京大学中文系连续举行。第七讲由来自弗吉尼亚理工大学的贾内尔·华生(Janell Watson)教授主讲，北京大学张辉教授主持，题为“文化作为存在之域：21世纪的生态智慧家园——以瓜塔里的文化思想为中心”；第八讲杜克大学肯尼斯·苏林(Kenneth Surin)教授主讲，北京大学蒋洪生老师主持，题为“美国大学对批评理论的接受谱系”。

上午的讲座中，华生教授从21世纪初的大规模群众性异见运动出发，展开了对菲力克斯·瓜塔里(Félix Guattari)的文化思想的探讨。瓜塔里将伊朗革命(1979年)和波兰团结工会运动视为对主体性特异化(subjective singularisation)的追求。华生教授认为，当下出现的种种抗议运动，也都可以解读为集体性、主体性和存在性嬗变(collective, subjective, existential mutation)的表达。瓜塔里相信一体化的资本主义(integrated world capitalism)使传统的生活方式不再可能，必须创造新的生活方式，而这就要靠社会嬗变来实现。但这种嬗变既可以带来好的结果，也可能走向坏的结局，那么我们应该如何分析，如何推动这种嬗变？为此，华生教授在瓜塔里思想的基础上总结出几种模式：1、传统的人民革命；2、从混乱中产生秩序(Order out of chaos)；3、辖域化(Territorialisation)；4、原模式(Meta-modeling，或译原形塑)，亦即瓜塔里所说的生态智慧(Ecosophy)。

当下的各种群体性抗议运动，具有自发性、无组织性和诉求的不确定性，与其说是为有意识的话语性(discursivity)所激发，不如说是由“感受性强度”(affective intensity)激发的。华生教授认为，这些运动可以理解为瓜塔里晚年所观察到的存在性变化(existential transformations)的延续。他以嬗变中的装配(mutating assemblages)来描述历史变化，装配是自创生性的(autopoietic)，能够不断地自我组织、自我再生产，从无法预测的方向发动，形成新的装配。在无定形的集体运动的“民主混沌”中，战斗性分析的任务就在于寻找“社会创造的吸引子”(attractors of social creativity)，从而推动主体性的特异化。

装配唯有与某种界域(territory)相联系才能存在，而界域正如生物学家于克斯屈尔(Jakob von Uexküll)所说，是一个环境的问题，表征了一种完全的主体性产物。人类和动物都能根据其相互关系及其与环境的关系来调适其行为，在此意义上它们具有主体性。这种主体性不是话语性的，而是运作于消极的(pathic)、感受性的和强度性的维度之中。当下的集体运动和骚乱作为社会装配，其感受能力(capacity for affect)显示出了一种元主体性(proto-subjectivity)，也许在这种元主体性的基础上自治将得以达成。

作为社会性的动物，人的生存需要各种装配。瓜塔里认为，80年代以来历史进入解域化(deterritorialisation)的阶段，人从原初的界域中被剥离，因此人类需要新的装配以取代那些已崩溃的装配，而生态智慧为此提供了有意义的框架。生态智慧是对贯穿于各种装配和嬗变中的伦理美学的制图，是对互相缠绕的精神和社会场域、机器界、生物界和宇宙的制图学的探索。它将容贯性平面(plane of consistency)绘制在四个象限上：存在之域(existential Territories)，价值世界/宇宙(或参照世界/宇宙，Universes of value,or of reference),机器系(machinic Phyla),流(Fluxes,or flows)。许多关于全球资本主义的描述集中于后二者,而瓜塔里更关注前两个象限,这些虚拟的领域恰恰是主体性得以出现的地方。华生教授认为,今日的全球精英的行动导致了极度的超解域化(hyperdeterritorialisation),而在这一时代中寻找某种特异性的家园,需要的正是生态智慧。

瓜塔里注意到,1990 年代早期以来,通过大众传媒而得到全球传布的集体表达,将主体性真正推向了世界事件的前台。今天,数字媒体、信息技术被进一步整合进人类生活,但进步和反动势力都可以以这些技术为依托,因此它们有着双刃剑的效应。我们是否已经进入了瓜塔里所期待的异见性(dissensual)、进程性(processual)的后媒体时代(post-media era)?解放性、保守性和毁灭性冲动的奇怪混合表明,后媒体时代只能零星地到来。它更依赖于主体特异化的程度而不是技术。

总而言之,存在之域对任何装配都是必要的。它需要容贯性的平面、主体性的维度和辖域化的模式。它是一种"行动的界域,物质总体化(physical totalisation)的界域,感受地带和元历史的界域"。没有界域,就没有主体性的形成,而主体的特异化可以激活装配,从而创造新的世界。21 世纪的家园不一定对应于原有的国家、种族和宗教,各种旧装配的残留物和符号学的替代物都可以作为材料和催化剂去参与新装配的生成,创造新的界域,不同的元素将在存在性算子(existential operators)的作用下结合起来。

在详细阐释了生态智慧的理论之后,华生教授又结合伊斯兰妇女头巾问题等具体事例,说明了残留性文化物作为组分(component)、作为存在之域和价值世界的中继站(算子)的复杂作用。对于不同的个人,有不同的算子、不同的主体化的核心;而在生态智慧的帮助下,文化可以成为提供这些元素的水库。最后,华生教授总结道:她之所以与大家分享瓜塔里的文化观念,是因为它对文化的重组,对我们如何在解域化的时代过一种有意义的生活,具有启示作用;其中也许有理想主义的成分,但瓜塔里思想中的乌托邦维度正是她所欣赏的。

演讲结束后,华生教授与在座的老师和同学就"一体化"的概念、占领华尔街运动等许多话题进行了进一步交流。

5 月 17 日下午的讲座由肯尼斯·苏林教授主讲。苏林教授首先回顾了 20 世纪 70 年代之前美国的文学研究,然后分段介绍了自 70 年代至当下的状况。

70 年代前,美国文学研究中已出现批评和文化理论的制度化,占主导地位的是新批评。新批评将文学文本看作自足的整体,拒绝以"外部"学科研究文本的起源、背景和影响等,只关心文本的"技术效果",将"细读"作为首选方法。同时代比较文学的主导范式则是比较两个或两个以上的西欧民族文学的文本,以来自语文学的解释方法为基础,最重要的代表是埃里希·奥尔巴赫的《摹仿论》。在 70 年代的新形势下,新批评和传统的比较文学失去了影响力——历时语言学谱系的概念和自足的文学文本受到了质疑,而且不可逾越的问题是它们局限于印欧语言而排斥其他的语言和文学传统。

取代新批评与传统比较文学的是"理论"。60 年代末和 70 年代初,批评理论在美国出现,主要表现为对几种思潮的接受:结构主义和后结构主义、解释学、精神分析批评、女性主义理论、马克思主义理论、黑人研究、文化研究和欧洲大陆哲学(法兰克福学派、现象学等)。这些理论范式在 20 世纪 70 年代发生了显著的变化,如黑人研究变为非裔美国人研究,女性主义理论辅之以性别研究等。这些理论范式推动美国文学研究产生了先前所没有的元理论:预设(presuppositions)、立场(standpoints)等问题开始受到讨论。

70 年代发生的一些变化一直持续到 80 年代。黑人研究继续向非裔美国人研究转变,文化研究在北美越发得到认可。与此同时,其他学术领域内也发生了新的变化:与罗蒂和普特南联系在一起的美国实用主义的复兴,显示了哲学与文学研究相关的一个特点;同时由于斯皮瓦克,文化和文学研究开始涉及历史学家们关于印度贱民的著作。范式之间的互相融合,形成了新的子域,后殖民理论和酷儿理论最为明显。此外,新的理论对象成为某些研究子域关注的焦点:控制论和信息技术的发展使"超文本"成为文化研究的一个新领域;全球化的现象(包括国家属性,民族主义,集体记忆,移民社群等)也变得非常重要。

20 世纪 90 年代,又出现了新的变化。此时很多评论和阐释性研究已经建立了二十年或更久,对于这些范式的接受本身成为了研究的对象，如齐泽克与克里斯特瓦对拉康的解读，迈克尔·陶西格和阿甘本对瓦尔特·本雅明的诠释，霍米·巴巴对法农的解释等等。

接下来，苏林教授重点介绍了文学和批评理论的当下，与未来的可能性。当今的文学研究和批评理论中，并不存在标准的课程设置。此前这一领域有着“关键范式”，有一系列被普遍承认的“主要思想家”；根据一位学者的研究和教学所侧重的范式和“主要思想家”，可以清晰地确认他或她在该领域的地位。而现在情况发生了变化。范式及其相关的主要思想家已经越出了“文学”，进入其他学科领域；而许多来自其他领域的思想家充当了“文学”教学的生力军。这种困境并非美国的文学研究所独有，几乎所有人文学科和社会科学都是如此。

与此同时，新的范式已经开始出现。90年代的“超文本”现象现在已发展成一种成熟的“数码文化”，昭示了一个“后文本”文化的方向，与此相关的知识领域越来越多。传统的文学研究与新媒体研究之间的关系有待解决。同样重要的是，性别研究中的一些新发展已经开始影响到性别的概念和男性女性的身份问题。女性主义、精神分析，文化研究和媒体研究（尤其是对日本动漫的研究）显然受到了新的性别观念的影响。另一个值得注意的现象是，以英语授课的世界文学课程，在过去十年中迅速发展，与之相伴而出现的是一种新型的英语学习，像“全球英语”和“无国界英语”这样的课程不断增殖。这些课程兼顾了被称为“英联邦文学”或“英国以外的英语文学”的特征，并侧重于英语中的混合语形态。

最后苏林教授还提到，未来几年财政拮据的状况对文学研究的影响不可忽视。由经济衰退引起的经费削减已导致一些部门的合并，而且跨学科中心（如人文学院）正在升级以将几个院系的工作合并到一起。很难确定这些事态将来会发展成什么样子。

演讲结束后，苏林教授同在座的老师和同学们就自己的著作、中国的思想家和批评理论等话题展开讨论，气氛热烈。

5月29日下午，系列讲座的第九讲在中文系举行。此次讲座由来自山东大学的盛宁教授主讲，北京大学严绍璗教授主持，题为“文学与文学批评的审美回归”。

盛宁教授说，“文学与文学批评的审美回归”这一题目的产生，动因有两个。第一个就是去年莫言获得诺贝尔文学奖的事件。盛宁教授认为，就当下英美文学状况而言，就近年来诺贝尔奖评定过程中非文学因素的日益凸显来说，莫言得奖不仅当之无愧，而且是一件好事。但在这个问题上也有很大的争议。一些人主张莫言不应得奖，因为他同政府意识形态关系密切。从国内许多普通读者对莫言作品的反应来看，也能发现他们多将文学作品当做新闻报道、当做现实或意识形态的简单再现。而盛宁教授认为，“文学的本质是什么”这个问题需要进行再讨论。

促使盛宁教授思考上述问题的第二个动因，是去年10月底召开的全国美国文学年会。这次年会的主题是“回归审美”，对美国近几十年来后结构主义统领下的意识形态批评进行了反思。盛宁教授强调，需要做的不是简单的否定或纠偏，而是放宽视野，作进一步的思考。他指出，美国自90年代（特别是1999年）以后也在这一问题上出现了激烈的讨论，保守和激进两派分别把审美（aesthetic）和政治正确（ political correctness）作为各自的大旗。盛宁教授认为，文学具有跨越时空的特征，仅仅强调族裔、性别等方面并不能解决文学交流的问题。90年代以前，在解构主义的大趋势下，美国多数理论家都倾向于反本质主义，但现在情况已经有所不同。比如 Terry Eagleton 从2000年后写了 *How To Read a Poem* 等多部讲授审美分析方法的著作，在2012年的 *The Event of Literature* 中他更是明言，自己过去虽然主张反本质主义，但现在却要证明文学具有自己的本质。由此可见，不能把理论家一时一地的言论视为绝对的结论，审美问题现今仍然需要考虑。

那么，我们应该如何进行进一步的思考？盛宁教授认为文学可以用“三个 W”来概括。第一，是“word”，这就是说不能把语言轻易地与现实画上等号。语言是不透明的、无法穿透的，可以无限阐释，创造出艺术形象。正如黑格尔所说，艺术就是让人冥思和欣赏由人的精神的自由驰骋所创造出的形象（image）。

而如果没有审美的关照，就会把语言的意义简化为字面义，理解得很浅薄。第二个“W”是“work”，这就是说要像新批评一样把作品看做一个有机体，意义建立在整体结构、建立在作品所有要素的支撑之上，不能断章取义。第三个“W”是“world”，就是说文学相对于现实世界，应该具有“另一个世界”的地位。文学作品并不是对外部世界的直接反映。文学内部虽有引起行动的冲力，但并不能直接产生行动。不仅18世纪以来的美学家一直关注审美问题，就连马克思本人也认为文学作品并非政治的传声筒。一些人（比如Perry Link）声称莫言是政治的喉舌，不应该拿诺贝尔文学奖，这种看法是很肤浅的。

最后，盛宁教授以库切的《耻》为例，说明了对作品进行审美分析的方法。《耻》描写了南非种族隔离制度取消后白人面临的困境，一些人批评这是种族歧视的延续。而盛宁教授认为，不从文学形式入手，这部小说无法得到充分的阐释。小说的前后两部分似乎有某种“分裂”，为了把作品作为有机整体来解读，需要注意两部分之间的联系。主人公在小说的前一部分中同一些具有黑人血统的女性发生的违背意志的性关系，事实上为后来他女儿的遭遇埋下了伏笔，种下了历史重演的种子。这样来读，就会发现《耻》中包含着对“耻”的认罪，不能简单理解为对黑人掌权后的社会的诽谤。库切曾宣称自己不是任何共同体的代言人，他借用柏拉图的洞穴隐喻，说自己并不是要揭示洞穴外的自由世界，只是要描写人挣脱锁链而转身的过程。这其实正是文学的使命。

演讲结束后，盛教授与在座师生就意识形态与审美经验的关系等问题作了进一步交流。

10月16日下午，系列讲座的第十讲（秋季学期的第一次）于中文系举行。此次讲座由中国社会科学院高建平研究员主讲，北京大学张辉教授主持，题为“从‘他’到‘你’：他者性的消解——读弗朗索瓦·于连《间距与之间：如何在当代全球化之下思考中欧之间的文化他者性》”。

高建平研究员指出，在对中国与欧洲文化的比较研究中，“互看”是学者们早就提出的话题，但这一视角有其盲点。说是“互看”，其实在很长时间里西方只是把东方视作“田野”，作为自己的思想和研究的例证。而东方“看”西方的方式，大致有三种：其一是借用西方的目光来看东方，前辈学人正是这样构建起现代中国的学术的，但其局限性也很明显；另一些人出于民族自尊心，发掘材料证明西方有的东西中国也有，结果常常把例子抽离原本的语境，错过了东西文化互相启发的机会；第三种方式则是证明东西文化本来就不同，东方文化优于西方，把文化保守主义与后殖民、后现代主义结合起来。“互看”发现的是差异，而正如弗朗索瓦·于连所说，与差异相伴的只有认同。如果每个非西方文化都以自我—西方的二元逻辑来言说，那么世界仍然是一个以西方为中心的扇形结构。

于连提出“间距”的概念，正是对二元对立的“差异”的纠正。差异是寻找、分析的结果，而间距先于寻找，是原本就在那里的。外在性先于他者性：各种文化未相遇时，并没有“他者”，它们相遇之后才开始发现彼此的差异，于是“他者”出现了。“他”（或者“她”、“它”）是一种缺席的在场，由于是被言说的对象，所以需要对其保持客观，持科学的、分析的、非价值评价的态度。但知道“他”的存在，言说“他”，不等于对“他”的认识就是正确的，人们往往又在他者身上寄托某种幻想。使“他文化”成为“他者”，曾被视为一个进步，然而这个进步又使我们陷入到文化的皱褶之中，这是我们今天需要打开的。打开的办法，是使“他”变成“你”。

与“我”和“他”的关系不同，“我”和“你”是面对面的，可以互相观看，可以交谈，可以一道从事某种活动。这种具有生长性的交流，对双方都有启发。当代的中国和欧洲文化，就处于从“他”到“你”的过程中。高先生认为，“我”和“你”的对话，不仅是为了解“你”，更重要的是了解“我”自己。从当下的文化进程上看，文化多样性并不会被交往所抹杀，不同文化总是共存并且互相启发。我们能够预见的，不是一种同质的未来，而是共同的发展，各自的进步；是多元共生的“你”，而不是一体化的“我们”。

演讲结束后，高建平研究员与在座师生就新技术与传统文化等问题展开了进一步讨论。

10月21日下午，系列讲座的第十一讲在中文系举行。此次讲座由四川大学、北京师范大学教授曹顺庆先生主讲，北京大学陈跃红教授主持，题为“比较文学前沿问题研究”。

曹顺庆教授指出,长期以来,西方原有的比较文学学科理论认为比较文学的可比性在于求同,即寻求"同源性"或"类同性",从这种角度出发,东西方之间的文学比较是没有合法性的。而实际上,在当今的全球化语境下,全世界学者都不得不面对不同文明的交流、碰撞、对话与比较;东西方文学的比较研究也早已成绩卓著。因此,比较文学学者有责任从学科理论上阐明东西方文学比较的合法性问题。

许多学者,比如韦勒克和钱钟书,都认为东西方不同文明的文学可以比较,不过他们的立足点大多还是放在相同性之上。正如弗朗索瓦·于连批评钱钟书时所说,只看到同,忽略差异,是一个失误。不同文化之有着不可通约性,仅仅求同,并不能根本解决东西方文学比较的合法性问题,而只有在这个学科理论问题上做出推进,比较文学才能摆脱"危机论"、"死亡论"而获得"重生"。

曹教授认为,比较文学变异学的提出,正是解决上述难题的一个重要突破。变异学肯定了差异也是具有可比性的,比较的合法性就在于异质性和变异性。在国外,影响研究中的形象学,韦斯坦因所谓影响过程中的"创造性转变",以及赛义德的"理论旅行",都可视为变异学的萌芽;在中国,严绍璗先生、王向远教授等学者的研究更为变异学开辟了道路。曹教授对"变异学"(Variation Studies)作出了定义:变异学是指对不同国家、不同文明的文学在影响交流和相互阐发中出现的变异状态的研究。变异学重点在求"异"的可比性,以开启一个注重异质性和变异性的比较文学学科理论的新阶段。

异质性为何会成为比较文学可比性的基础?曹教授对此进行了解释。异质性的第一层意义是文学交流和影响中的变异。变异学强调变异性和同一性实际上是影响过程的一体两面,从而弥补了过去重"同"轻"异"的影响研究之不足。异质性的第二层意义则是东西方文学的可通约性与不可通约性。只有充分认识到不同文明间的异质性,平行研究才能在一种"对话"的视野下展开,实现不同文明间的互证、互释、互补。突出异质性,有利于实现不同文明的沟通和融合,建构一个"和而不同"的世界。曹教授认为,中国比较文学学者提出的比较文学变异学,将开创比较文学学科理论的新阶段,推动全世界比较文学的发展。

演讲结束后,曹教授和在座的同学就"比较文学与比较文化的边界"等问题进行了进一步交流。中文系严绍璗教授作总结发言,再次肯定曹教授的研究对比较文学学科理论建构所具有的意义。

据悉,"比较文学与世界文学学术讲座系列"将继续邀请国内外优秀学者参加,依托北京大学、中国比较文学学会以及《比较文学与世界文学》杂志,营造海内外学人特别是比较文学学者的高端学术平台,促进学界的深入交流。讲座内容将继续在《比较文学与世界文学》杂志上报道。

“人文学科关键词研究”丛书出版学术研讨会在京举行

刘　爽

由中国人民大学文学院主办的“西方文论在中国学术语境的空间和张力”学术研讨会于2013年9月21—22日在北京召开。会议主要就“人文学科关键词研究”丛书,进行研讨,与会专家一致肯定了丛书的重大理论意义、学术价值和出版品质。

国家出版基金项目“人文学科关键词研究”丛书于2013年5月由北京大学出版社出版。该丛书选取了当代西方思想中的十个重要概念进行讨论研究,以跨学科的原典梳理为分析线索和立论依据,从诸人文学科交叉概念入手,深入探讨当代西方神学与人文学的内在关联、相互借鉴及深层对话,同时又从中国自身的学术处境和问题意识出发,试图把握当代西方思想的关键概念、核心命题和基本逻辑,其问题意识、研究方法、学术文献等涉及当代中西方人文学科各个领域,具有重要的理论价值和实践意义,对我国人文领域学术研究具有重大推进作用。

参加这次会议研讨的有中国人民大学副校长杨慧林教授、中国人民大学文学院院长孙郁教授、北京大学中文系主任陈跃红教授、中国社科院文学所所长陆建德教授、清华大学哲学系王晓朝教授、北京师范大学文学院方维规教授、北京大学出版社外语编辑部张冰主任、《文艺研究》陈建澜副主编等专家和学者。中国人民大学文学院副院长耿幼壮教授主持会议。

会议首先由“人文学科关键词”丛书主编杨慧林教授致辞,杨慧林向与会嘉宾介绍了这套丛书的研究背景、主旨思想、问题意识、理论意义,以及项目团队从项目启动到出版历时五年的学术钻研。与会专家研讨热烈,指出本套丛书:第一,视角新。孙郁教授谈到,本套丛书基于不同的视角,对于不同的文学意境和学术视角给予了不同层次的解读,提出了许多问题,也解决了许多问题;陆建德教授强调说,从更高的人文精神层次上进行概念的梳理,把有价值的问题提出来,这对于中国的语境是一种丰富,是一种提升,也是一种大胆的、有价值的尝试。第二,学术规范性强。方维规教授认为这套丛书从基本的概念入手,进行复杂的学理分析,这对作者的知识面、学术功底和研究时间要求都非常严格,本套丛书得到了学术界的极大认可,充分说明作者们扎实的学术功底和认真态度;王晓朝教授也非常赞同这一观点,他认为这套丛书把如此复杂的题目做得深入浅出,为相关领域的学术研究提供了样板,这对我国人文学科的发展将起到非常积极的作用。第三,学科的交叉性。陈跃红教授指出,中国传统的学术视角往往缺少他者,缺少反思,此套丛书从交叉学科的角度入手,对其关键词进行了解析和补充,极大地丰富了中国人文学科学术研究的视角。陈建澜副主编从中西思想互相激发的角度对本套丛书的主导思想等诸方面进行了阐发。耿幼壮教授还宣读了因故未能到会的张旭教授的书面发言。张冰主任向丛书作者对北京大学出版社的信任和支持表达了由衷的谢意,对丛书作者以深厚的学养,扎实的学术功力,将西方文论置于更广义的人文学背景,探寻西方文论在中国学术语境的空间和张力,表示了由衷的敬意,她表示,北京大学出版社是一家具有悠久学术出版传统的大学出版机构,出版“人文学科关键词研究”丛书,是对人类文明和思想的发展有所担当的努力追求。

“人文学科关键词研究”共 10 本，包括：《意义——当代神学的公共性问题》（杨慧林）、《倾听——后形而上学时代的感知范式》（耿幼壮）、《行动——从身体的实践到文学的无为》（汪海）、《礼物——当代法国思想史的一段谱系》（张旭）、《身体——从感发性、生命技术到元素性》（夏可君）、《书写——碎片化语境下他者的痕迹》（王涛）、《焦虑——西方哲学与心理学视域中的焦虑话语》（杨钧）、《道说——从逻各斯到倾空》（芮欣）、《法则——现代危机和克服之途》（葛体标）、《动物（性）——传统与现代之间的人性根由》（赵倞）等。

“探寻中国梦的缘起 重现失落的远古文明”

——中国“玉石之路”与玉兵文化研讨会综述

夏陆然

2013年6月15—16日，陕北古城榆林市，暑气初临，群贤毕至。上海交通大学与中国收藏家协会联合主办的“中国‘玉石之路’与玉兵文化研讨会”在这里盛大召开。来自上海交通大学、中国收藏家协会等国内外数十个单位、高校的80余位专家学者齐聚一堂，见证了此次会议的盛况。

这次会议是我国考古界与玉器收藏界的一次重大交流与合作，具有突出的学术意义。结合石峁古城遗址的最新发掘成果，以及早年流失于民间的石峁古玉，与会专家学者针对如下问题展开讨论：1.西部玉料是如何沿着黄河及其支流的水道东输至中原地域，从而成为夏、商、周三代建构政权所依赖的玉礼器的生产原料，并由此形成中华玉文化大传统的？2.玉钺、玉戈、牙璋等玉质兵器在我国玉文化体系中占据着怎样的位置？与会专家学者希望通过广泛的学术交流，摸索出代表着中华玉文化辉煌历史的“玉石之路”。

在本次会议中，19位专家学者的发言围绕“‘玉石之路’的证明与反思”和“中国玉兵文化研究”等两大主题展开。

一、“玉石之路”的论证与反思

此次会议召开的重要契机是陕西省神木县石峁遗址最新成果的发掘。石峁遗址考古队领队孙周勇首先作题为《陕西神木石峁遗址考古新发现》的主题发言。他对该遗址的研究现状等进行了详细的汇报。他指出，城址年代始于龙山中期或晚期，延续至龙山晚期到夏代早期，“其规模为目前所见中国最大史前遗址”。该遗址的发现“为进一步研究中国文明起源多源性发展提供了全新的研究资料，对进一步理解古文化、古城、古国框架下的中国早期文明的格局具有重要意义。”

上海交通大学讲席教授、中国社会科学院研究员叶舒宪作题为《玉文化先统一中国说》的主题演讲。他认为，通过石峁古城及玉器的新发现，说明玉石神话信仰作为精神文化要素，率先开启统一中国的历程。石峁玉制建筑的新发现，一方面验证了古书上关于夏代帝王修筑玉门瑶台之类神话建筑记载的相对可信性，另一方面也验证了中国人信仰玉石避邪驱魔功能的史前渊源之深厚。玉兵器的功能在于从精神上防御和化解实际的武力攻击，由此看出“化干戈为玉帛”的中国式和平理想的由来。石峁古城建筑用玉的发现，还提示了华夏文明特有的资源依赖之“西玉东输”现象，以及“玉石之路黄河段”的存在，比所谓“丝绸之路”更早也更值得关注。

陕西师范大学教授朱鸿推断，石峁城建立在上古洪水的史前背景，可能就是史书中的“幽都”，也就是尧世的北方政令重镇、祭祀中心、陪都。他还结合中华玉文化的大传统，对石峁玉器的功能、制作、传播、玉料来源，以及黄河作为玉石运输水道等问题做出推论。

甘肃省文物考古文物所所长王辉对甘肃北部马鬃山古代玉矿的最新挖掘状况进行了介绍。马鬃山发现古矿坑百余处，遗迹单位65处，出土遗物千余件，初步断代为战国至汉代。出土遗物中除中原陶器外，还发现有河西走廊西部的骟马文化遗物等，为“玉石之路”提供了一些晚近的证据。

中国收藏家协会学术研究部主任古方将近期对甘肃马衔山玉矿的调查情况进行了一次报告。通过考察，他认为马衔山的玉料是齐家文化玉器原料来源之一。同时，在甘肃东部地区也发现类似马衔山玉料的齐家文化玉器。又进而说明，在距今4000年的玉石之路上输送的不仅是和田玉，还包括了甘肃地区出产的玉料。

《丝绸之路》杂志总编冯玉雷以亲身经验和图像资料，生动地介绍了他和叶舒宪先生以齐家玉为线索，寻访“玉石之路”的过程。

中国社科院人类学与民族学研究所易华研究员在发言中指出，上古时代的西域与中原之间，存在玉文化的交流与互动之路，玉器的材料与器形便是证明。除玉器之外，还有许多其他证据可以对“玉石之路”进行补充论证。他还论述了羌夏之间的关系：二头里文化与齐家文化不仅时空接近，性质也大同小异，在龙山文化基础上发展起来的二头里文化中的新因素大都来自齐家文化。

台湾“中央研究院”历史语言研究所王明珂研究员从华夏认同的角度去看待石峁遗址所处的历史时期。他认为：4000年前左右的气候变化是中原地区以外的石峁、良渚、齐家、石家河等文化衰落的重要原因。气候变化带来的资源缺乏导致了战争侵略的增加，加速了防卫性建筑的产生，也促使了中原地区夏商等早期国家形态的出现。虽然华夏文明形成的过程是一个中原文明“月渐明”，周边族群“星渐稀”的过程，但这些周边族群依然延存至后世，与中原文明有所互动。

中国文学人类学研究会副会长徐新建对“史前表述”一词进行了深刻的反思。他指出，受到西方“进化主义”的时间分割的影响，当代中国对于自身文明的表述与年代划分也限制在西方科学时间与科学主义的藩篱之下。博物馆是国民认知与国民教育的重要方式之一，而中国各地的博物馆大多被这种西方的“史前表述”所占据，这就对中华文明的发展与延续带来了很大的现实问题。

四川大学杨骊博士以三星堆金沙玉源为个案，论述了考古学实证与文学人类学阐释之间的互动与对话。她运用文学人类学的多重证据法，结合了三星堆、龙溪玉料的考古学证据、羌族释比经文的口传证据、羌绣金星树的实物证据，对三星堆金沙玉源的问题经行了考究。她还列举出了多条“玉石之路”的文学人类学研究路径。

石峁文化收藏研究会胡文高会长与参会者一起分享自己多年来收藏石峁玉器的经验与心得，他总结了石峁传世玉器的玉料、形制、出土分布等问题，为“玉石之路”提供许多实物证据，并对石峁玉器与良渚、齐家等玉器的关系进行了推断。

二、中国玉兵文化研究

中国社科院考古研究所王仁湘研究员从新石器晚期的红山、凌家滩文化等出土的戉出发，结合古文字学分析，梳理了“戉”与“王”的关系，分析了各种颜色戉的区别与功能。他指出，以钺为代表的兵器通过玉化的途径完成了王权的符号化。可以说，以玉戉为代表的玉兵器指示了一个时代的变换过程，可看作早期文明时代的重要标志。

成都金沙遗址博物馆王方研究员对古蜀国出土的各种玉兵器尤其是玉璋，进行了逐一的介绍。她认为，三星堆、金沙遗址的玉器形制精美，是通神、娱神的礼器、祭器。

中国社科院考古研究所研究员许宏指出：在中原二里头时代，青铜礼兵器渗入并局部替代既有的玉礼器，形成“金玉共振”的局面。以戈为代表的二里头文化青铜兵器，奠定了中国古代兵器的基本格局。进入二里岗时代，集实用征伐与仪仗象征意义与一身的钺、戈等形成了以戈为中心的兵器组合。

中国社科院考古研究所研究员曹楠对已出土的夏商周三代玉质兵器进行了统计学的分析。她指出，三代的玉质斧钺是新石器时代的玉质斧钺的延续，数量与前代相比呈锐减趋势；玉戚是对玉斧钺的改造，商代最多，西周时锐减；而玉戈是三代的新器形，西周时达到鼎盛，东周衰退。总之，至东周时期，玉质兵器诸多功能已经衰微，并最终为铜兵器所取代。

中国社科院考古研究所李健民研究员指出，殷商仪仗玉器多见于大中型墓葬与祭祀坑中，且与玉、铜礼器共出，表明玉石仪仗用具是象征权力的专用道具。青铜兵器用于征伐，即“戎”；玉石兵器用于仪仗，即“祀”。同时，殷商仪仗玉器多表现出中原文化的地区特色，也反映出殷商王朝与周边的文化交流。他还认为，考古学者不能回避古史传说，人文学者也应当与收藏界、考古界紧密结合。

纽约大都会博物馆孙志新研究员结合良渚文化的实物，梳理了玉钺形成发展的历史脉络，指出，玉钺源于史前的实用石斧，其定型以良渚文化为始，发展逐趋精细繁缛，且通常在大墓中出现，象征王权。到商周之后，玉钺逐渐被青铜器取代，但造型上仍有延续。

山西省考古研究所吉琨璋对玉戈的形制特点、历史演变等进行了讲解。玉戈约出现于仰韶晚期，成型于龙山晚期，流行于夏商周，消失于春秋时期。它脱胎于玉刀，最初是兵器，很快就进入玉礼器、玉仪仗器系统。西周时期，在其他玉兵器衰退之时，玉戈依然是重要的礼器，还是重要的陪葬品，甚至还具有祭祀的功用。

陕西省文物局副局长刘云辉追溯了东周至汉代玉兵器的历史演变轨迹。他认为，玉兵对青铜武器的形状有所仿效。但受玉材本身的局限，只能象征军权。他选取了考古发现的和海内外公私收藏的25件东周至汉代的玉兵资料，分析了这一段时期内玉质兵器衍变、式微的历史过程。

此次会议的顺利举行，是国人弘扬、传承中华玉文化的又一次成功。在这次会议中，与会学者带来了他们最新的研究成果，为中华文明起源、“玉石之路黄河段”论证、玉兵文化研究等相关学术问题提供了新的证据和新的阐释方法。

崛起中国的“新汉学”①

A. B. 罗曼诺夫
张冰 译

2012年11月3—4日，主题为“汉学与当今世界”的第三届世界汉学大会在北京中国人民大学举行，大会主办者为国家汉办(国家汉语国际推广领导小组办公室)与中国人民大学。汉学的振兴，汉学对世界上中国角色飞速变化的适应，扩大与深化中国在国际汉学发展中的参与成为大会的核心问题。

主题为“文明对话与和谐世界”的首届世界汉学大会2007年春天在中国人民大学举行。当时关注的中心是各种文明间和谐关系形成中汉学的作用。这一主题延续到2009年秋天举行的第二届世界汉学大会的主题——“汉学与跨文化交流”，基调是探寻中国与西方文化传统的共同性。

第三届大会讨论中国研究中的过去和当今的联系，寻求汉学的未来发展之路。大会主办者试图强调传统汉学与当今“中国学”研究的承续，并推进中国学术界与海外中国学界间的沟通。会议认为，世界正在发生巨大的变化，产生了新的重要的议题“中国道路”——汉学也应该顺应这些趋势。

大会提出了建立“新汉学”和“大汉学”的构想。认为“新汉学”将更能顺应时变，更具对话能力和更有责任意识。“大汉学”需要的是走出研究的传统界限，探讨新的议题。中国教育部副部长郝平在大会开幕式上发言时，强调汉学要为“当代中国”和“当今世界”的理解做出更多贡献。他还指出，汉学是加深中国和世界文化相互沟通和相互理解的重要渠道。

依据大会惯例，本次学术会议的大会议厅装饰着两幅中国和古希腊的古典箴言字幅，象征着人类共同的精神求索。与中国古籍《周易》中“与时偕行”，互为补充的词句是柏拉图的话——“因势而道”。中国人民大学校长陈雨露的发言充满了对这两句箴言的重视，他指出，把握“时”“势”，是自古以来，也是当今意义重大的论题。汉学需要融通古今，“察古”而立于今，“视往”以知来者。这些箴言出自古籍《管子·形势》：“疑今者察之古，不知来者视之往”。

大会第一天的主旨报告人为第十届全国人大常委会副委员长许嘉璐。他强调指出，应该在面临人类“觉醒”的重大问题的全球反思的视野中认识汉学的发展。报告者认为，人们开始意识到金钱和技术至上的思想已经使人类迷失自己，需要的是新的对人类、社会和自然关系的阐释，为此必须重视传统文化。中国传统基于三家：这是儒家以“仁”为核心的伦理观、道家以“道”为中心的宇宙观、佛教“缘起性空”的本体观。这三家都在唤起人们以敬畏、感恩的心态遵从自然和社会规律。类似的理念也存在于其他传统中，只是人们已经忘却了它们，应该以敬畏、感恩的心态，因此重新认识先代哲人圣贤的时代已经到来。

在“回归源头”的旨归背景下，许嘉璐提出，汉学应该面向当下、面向世界、面向未来。关于中国的现世，他谈到当下诸多问题的解决和对人们担负的职责，特别是对青年人，对于中国传统知识的职责。世界需要汉学，因为汉学稳固的古代中国丰富的经验研究，能够运用于构建人类新的伦理。与此同时，为了攀上下一个高峰，为中国和全世界贡献丰富的智慧，汉学同样需要世界。

报告人呼吁扩大与世界汉学界的交流，拟定政策“走出去”，“请进来”，以期中国学者，特别是年轻学者，能够长时间地在外面工作；外国的学者则在中国住下来。这些交换，有助于在把握异质文化和理解其思维

---

① Ломанов, А. «Новое китаеведение» для растущего Китая. —Проблемы Дальнего Востока № 1 за 2013г. С. 171—176.

特点的体验基础上发展文明对话。与此同时，应该深化中外合作为中国和全世界培养汉学人才的工作，合作开展问题研究和合作举办教学研究机构。需要更多地向外国民众介绍中国文化，除去由于误解对其产生的“神秘”光环。

类似的关于当今世界汉学天职的阐述回响在中国人民大学前校长纪宝成的发言中。他指出，唯科学主义思想、对市场和消费的崇拜对人类的历史命运形成了挑战，因此，崇尚技术，蔑视道德，在最近二三十年的中国同样存在。在这种情况下，我们要讨论的就不仅仅是不同文明的开放互动、相互借鉴、共存共荣的问题，而是还要讨论所有这些问题是为了什么的问题。汉学问题的研讨应该成为解决全人类共同难题的人文社会科学界努力的一部分。

北京大学高等人文研究院长杜维明谈到1974年发表于《外交事务》杂志美籍日本学者埃德温·雷绍尔的颇具开创意义的论文。这篇论文对日本“经济奇迹”的解释——国家西方化的结果，进行了质疑。文章指出，日本的成就可归功于传统的文化实践——团队精神，努力工作，节俭，精英意识，互助和选贤举能。然而这些价值理念不仅仅属于日本，而是属于整个“汉文化世界”。因此，雷绍尔得以预言未来韩国、中国台湾、中国香港和新加坡的经济增长。并且，他还有先见之明地提到，中国如果能够摆脱计划经济的桎梏，她也会繁荣富强。

杜维明以中国“龙”的形象为例来说明儒家文明的特点。他强调说，他永远不会将“龙”这个词译为дракон(“龙”)。这位学者指出，“龙”是儒家整体学说的象征，因为它将人们所熟悉的诸多动物原型的种种特征融为一体。儒家学说以此类形象突显出和谐的特性，这一学说具有包容性，尊重多样性，并可以做到兼容并蓄。龙象征着中国传统中对人文主义的全面的整体理解，而这种理解是以核心概念“仁”为基础的。

著名的老一辈专家汤一介在对杜维明的报告进行点评时肯定了中国文化中包容性论题的重要性。就此，他呼吁重视中国应该如何将自身历史形成文化与人类文化交融研究的问题。他以宋代儒学和由于与印度文化交流产生的新儒家学说为例，强调指出中国文化中创造性问题的重要。他认为，目前的中国正在吸收西方文化，因此或将出现一个创造性潜力实现的新的时代。

中国人民大学美国中心主任时殷弘的报告题为“普遍主义、特殊主义和民族主义：在当代世界的当代中国涵义”。他描述了普遍主义和特殊主义作为相对立的世界观和思想方式的特征，指出，为了达到特殊主义需要战胜对“普遍最高存在”的迷信。在报告人看来，现当代中国思想史的巨大成就是特殊主义最好形态的创新，它由于毛泽东和邓小平得以出现。中国充满了自信地向全世界昭示，西方的现代化模式不是唯一的现代化形态。每个民族人民的未来取决于其自身的历史和实践，谁也不能从外部为其做出选择。因此，普遍主义有可能转变为自身文化传统的反面，报告人指出：毛泽东不仅仅坚决抵制了共产国际的革命普遍主义，他也同样拒绝了中国传统的儒家世界观及其礼教普遍主义。

时殷弘发言的最后部分涉及了当代中国的爱国主义和民族主义。就其政府主持的形态而言，它的特征是：前瞻、镇定、耐心和更尊重中国特性。然而，它的非政府的形态表现出的特征是：对外部世界简单粗鲁的态度，还有对本国政府“软弱政策”的常有指责。报告者强调指出，如何合理地引导公众及其舆论，是一个复杂的问题。但是，在中国的条件下不可忽视。

英国政论家、伦敦经济政治学院教授马丁·雅克呼吁“理解中国，理解世界”。从前，西方思维是理解世界的前提，中国曾经只能接受这一切，实用主义地专注于学习西方和顺应西方世界。现在，中国对其独一无二的自然的自信日益增长，全世界都向着“中国中心时代”行进，即使那些受到西方普适经验培养的人很难接受她的前行。西方难以想像其不再是世界的中心，它尚未准备好去迎接这个新的时代，它的时代还是试图以自己的思维理解中国。然而，21世纪的任务正是以中国的观念理解中国。范式的深刻更替在于，几个世纪前被边缘化的多种文明重新取得了全球话语。

报告人指出，美国汉学家卢西恩·派伊(白鲁恂)将中国描述为“伪装成民族国家的一种文明”。在马丁·雅克看来，民族国家是解放了的国家被迫穿在自己身上的后殖民主义的“拘束衣”(病号服)。目前，中国这个文明国家变为全球强国深刻地改变了世界秩序，因此，中国为其他国家做出了榜样，将会引起对自身同一性过程进行重新思考的过程更加广泛。尽管中国和美国一样，固有其普遍主义性，具有着另外的特征，但是，她没有将自身力量向全世界扩散的传教愿望。中国的全球化霸权有别于西方强国，其不是根基于政治，而是经济和文化。中国这个国家与维护文明发展的天命紧密相关，因此，对中国的角色的理解将有别于西方思维。

张隆溪教授(香港城市大学)发言的主题关系到外国汉学与中国学术知识。他批评了西方研究者漠视进行中国古典文化研究的中国学者的著述，在报告人看来，这与传教士们宣称的中国学者不能接受基督教义的负面论述有关。另一原因在于20世纪下半叶的诸多事件：西方研究者因此认为，中国的所有学术研究都受到政府的管制，都不过是种政治宣传。但是，当今的中国学术界充满了各种各样的观点表达，进行中国文化和历史研究的海外学者不能够忽视。

用报告人的话说，心理和认识论方面的成见(而这种成见被描述为西方“社会科学的自负”)有碍于两种学术传统的交流。根据这种观点，只有西方的理论才是正宗的，而东方的学术传统只不过是一种异域情调，仅此而已。这种观点是西方长期统治的结果，西方思想和观念普遍地渗透于其他各国。从西方社会科学理论的角度而言，被理解为研究中国的汉学，无论如何与中国本土学者的工作毫不相干。张隆溪指出，为从内部体验历史西方研究者提出了“变成中国人”的方法，这一方法无助于问题的解决，因为个体的有限经验无论如何也涵盖不了整个历史进程。(看问题的)视角并不能保证获得更富成效的探知结果，因此，认为中国人由于可以从内部获取经验便能更好地理解问题，而外国人依据批评性的反省和更为完善的研究方法便能够更好地从外部理解问题——这种想法并不正确。报告人呼吁将中国和外国的学术力量联合起来，将探知中国的“内部”和“外部”知识整合起来。

大会举行了分组会议：“‘新汉学’的趋势与展望”，“中国道路与世界经济秩序”，“文化差异与国际政治走向”，“传统伦理与人类未来”，“中国典籍的翻译及其当代意义”。与此同时，进行了专题论坛“孔子学院与世界多元文化交流”，以及“中外文学获奖者论坛”。

在一系列的报告中有些论及俄罗斯汉学。李明滨(北京大学)谈到1960年代Б.Л.李福清发现的两种中国抄本：在列宁格勒发现的《石头记》和在莫斯科列宁图书馆发现的《姑妄言》。张冰(北京大学出版社)的发言阐述了Б.Л.李福清在20世纪下半叶俄罗斯汉学传统发展中的作用特点。方维规(北京师范大学)报告了欧洲汉学中创作的首批中国文学史纲的历史，他注意到В.П.瓦西里耶夫的书(《中国文学史纲要》)(1880)的结构与之相访，以及德国研究者肖特的著作(1854)更早面世。

阎国栋(南开大学)注重的是18世纪俄国作家笔下的中国形象问题。赞扬中国的时尚从西方传向俄国，然而有别于西方作者，俄罗斯作家们的溢美之词没有指向清朝。俄罗斯的中国形象特征是对邻国文化传统的理想化与对乾隆皇帝的国策充满了戒备评价的融合。俄罗斯的理想化的中国形象源自西方，当时现实的中国观则来自东方，是在与中国直接的政治和经济交往过程中产生的。

А.В.卢金(俄罗斯外交部外交学院)概述了17世纪至今的俄罗斯汉学研究历史。А.Д.吉安德(俄罗斯科学院东方研究所)阐述了对俄罗斯举行的“中国社会与现状”学术会议论文材料(1970—2012)进行的定量分析结果。А.В.罗曼诺夫(俄罗斯科学院远东所)强调指出，增强中国潜在的“软实力”和建设“文化强国”的新的口号，表明了研究当今中国了解传统文化重要性的加深。

“‘孔子新汉学计划’与汉学的未来”专题组成了大会的一个亮点。专题组宣布了一系列支持国外汉学研究的规模宏大的具体计划。国家汉办主任许琳女士在主旨发言中介绍了“孔子新汉学计划”，她说，2007年以来，世界各地的孔子学院已经有398所，孔子课堂526个，注册学员(学习超过3个月)逾50万人。目前，在孔子学院的工作中，融入国外的当地大学，提高学生的素养(这种素养已超出标准化的汉语语言与文化基础知识)被确定为具有发展前景的工作方向。许琳希望，在孔子学院的学生中将来能有1%的人获得汉学专业方面的知识素养。

中方宣布，希望通过来华学习，中外合作培养各国青年汉学家等方式，为提高国际汉学水平，培养新一代研究者做出贡献。“孔子新汉学计划”应该成为实现这一目标的工具。许琳说：目前的这一“计划”呼吁

“凝聚各国汉学家的力量”,“为各国汉学研究提供服务与支持”,壮大汉学家队伍,扩大汉学的影响力,也促使文化间的真正的相互影响。

“孔子新汉学计划”包括六个活动项目:第一和第二个计划与在华培养外国博士有关,关于来华学习1至2年,完成其最后答辩,由外国大学授予学位,亦或外国学生完成全部中国博士课程,同时授予中国博士学位。这两个项目的申请者都要通过汉语知识水平考试,申请者年龄一般在40岁以下。下面的两个项目旨在使外国人了解中国。子项目“理解中国”规定了组织外国教师、研究人员和博士后人员为期2周至10个月的来华访学。子项目“青年领袖”旨在吸引外国大学高年级本科生和硕士生,以及外国政界、商界、学界等各界优秀青年来华考察访学,时间为2周至6个月,使他们能够获得更好的了解中国文化和现代中国社会的体验。

还有两个呼吁促进国外汉学学术活动的项目。第一,中方保证资助举办中国学国际会议。这些学术活动不仅可以在中国,也可以在外国举行,主要的是,它们进行的是中国的人文和社会科学研究。第二,是关于国外汉学家的出版资助项目,资助他们出版学术著作和专业学术期刊。

许琳指出,“计划”的制定工作持续了两年左右,所采用的模式是西方结构,如:富布莱特计划、艾森豪威尔项目、英国使馆项目。为了像这样“便于记忆”,此项新“计划”便以“孔子”命名。中方进行了大量的准备工作,为了保证子计划——博士培养工作的实施,已经组建了14所重点高校的联盟。他们提出了100个人文和社科课题。一份列有800位指导外国来华留学博士生的中国教授名单也已拟定。

“计划”引起了参加会议讨论的海外人士的兴趣和反响。英国伦敦国王学院的姚新中教授希望“计划”有助于扩大具有文学和哲学造诣的汉学家队伍,他们的人数在英国明显减少,其中有一部分原因是人才流入了实用型的研究领域。他强调,不了解中国的历史、哲学,便不可能取得中国经济和对内、对外政治方面的重要研究成果。参加讨论的其他人士指出,在“计划”的实施过程中,最应该在乎的是研究成果的质量,避免急功近利,对学术研究这一部分造成损害。

聚焦意大利汉学研究:新动态与新提议

狄霞娜

AISC,意大利汉学协会,是一个汇集了所有对汉学感兴趣的意大利学者和研究者的协会。它自1979年创建以来,就一直致力于汉学这个领域。每半年举行一次会议是该协会的主要活动之一。在当前的会议上,协会所有成员将对意大利关于中国及其多层面社会的研究现状进行讨论和反思。协会的其他活动包括:发表会议文集,继续致力于搭建公民社会与汉学之间的桥梁,为那些有志于中国问题研究的人搭建网络平台。

美丽的普罗斯达位于那不勒斯湾一个迷人的小岛上,意大利汉学协会第十四届代表大会于今年9月19至21日在此召开。许多协会成员都参与了此次会议,经过三天的讨论与辩论,会议取得丰硕的成果。

十二个主题专家组分别对意大利汉学研究的不同方面进行了讨论和分析,其中包括如下方面:古典文学和哲学、古典语文学、古典艺术、考古学与宗教、人类学研究、现代文学与翻译、中国当代互联网与影院、20世纪中国—意大利关系、西方传统视野下的中国文学理论、蒙古历史、文化研究、汉语语言学和汉语教学、当代中国诗歌和中国1949年社会与政治背景研究。

来自23所不同高校的67名学者均认为,当今汉学研究具有前所未有的重要性。这一方面是因为中国在全球化语境下变得越发重要,另一方面是因为意大利社会迫切需要了解中国知识和中国文化的竞争力。汉学家们必须对这一需求做出回应,必须对中国的方方面面具有真知灼见。

会议以"当代中国和互联网"的专题组讨论开始。来自瑞士意大利语大学的Gianluigi Negro首先对诸如新浪微博和微信那样的社会媒体进行了经济政治学分析。而来自萨兰托大学的路易莎Luisa Prudentino则讨论了汉字与意象的关系,这种关系表现出一种美感,至今仍然影响着中国电影的进程。

意大利的威尼斯大学是研究古代中国的中心(重镇),在毛里齐奥·斯卡尔帕里(Maurizio Scarpari)教授的指导下,威尼斯大学组织了一个专题讨论组,从一个新视角去研究古代和传统中国。Attilio Andreini、Luca Vantaggiato和Amina Crisma在最近发现的中国古代手稿的帮助下,明确指出,在进行哲学研究时,从语文学研究入手是不可避免的;此外,如果哲学研究脱离对文本的语文学研究,那么对中国传统文化的研究成果将非常有限,其价值也会大打折扣,从而难以揭示前帝国时期的中国是如何使用及查阅文本的。

某些人类学视角下的研究引发了热烈的讨论。来自伊苏布利亚大学的Daniele Cologna研究了最近随家人迁移到意大利的中国移民子女的融入问题;来自佩鲁贾大学的Daniele Parbuono在普拉托(意大利西北部城市)的佛教寺庙里开展了关于移民的人种学的研究。普拉托是中国移民最密集的城市,而在该城市的一所寺庙中,这些华人似乎找回了一种因山隔水阻而逐渐消失和遥不可及的中国性。另外,威尼斯大学的Martina Bristot和Daniele Brombal,那不勒斯大学的Alessandra Cappelletti也对一些中国热点问题进行了探讨。

文学和翻译专题讨论组以宋春芳(Song Chunfang)和她1921年在《东方杂志》上改编的四部意大利戏剧为开场议题(Alessandra Brezzi,罗马大学)。意大利的先锋戏剧因此被认为促成了中国本土话剧的形成。戏剧和当代中国社会的关系也是Barbara Leonesi(都灵大学)论文的主题。她集中讨论了郭世鑫的两个"三部曲",即《闲人三部曲》和《尊严三部曲》。罗马大学的Monica Romano和Gabriele Tola更深入地探讨了翻译方面的问题。Monica Romano发表了一篇关于圣经的中文翻译的论文,Gabriele Tola则在论文中分析了约翰·弗莱和徐寿翻译的《化学材料中西名目表》(1885)中外来词的运用,以及其中对一些具体名目的语音拼写。

第二天上午的第一个议题——20世纪中国与意大利的关系——引发了激烈的讨论,集中讨论了天津租界和上世纪初意大利传递给中国的形象(Maurizio Marinelli,萨塞克斯大学)。接下来的议题涉及1949年中华人民共和国成立后中国与意大利的关系(Enrico Fardella,北京大学)以及最近十年中国与意大利的关系(Giovanni Andornino,都灵大学)。来自都灵世界事务研究所的Simone Dossi分析了自2009年至今中国与意大利在非洲索马里反海盗行动上的合作问题。

另一专题讨论组探讨了文学理论和中国历史进程中理论范畴的定义,并讨论了其与西方模式和理论的关系。Barbara Bisetto(米兰比可卡大学)是该专题讨论组的推动者之一,她让人们认识到需要从社会学角度考察文学的范畴和体裁。讨论组中,有两篇论文研究传统文学,另两篇研究现当代文学。Bisetto的论文研究的是16世纪到20世纪的演义这一文体,试图探寻演义作者的创作意图。她关注的焦点落在类文本成分和序言上。演义这个术语第一次出现是3世纪潘岳(Pan Yue)的《西征赋》。这次演讲的目的在于以历时性的方式来探讨,在文本实践和前现代批评话语中,演义这一术语的用法和意义,以便突出其在不同的社会文学语境中的流变与永恒。这一文体的意图就是为了让文本适应社会。来自威尼斯大学的Giulia Baccini致力于从历时性的角度来考察幽默文体的角色塑造和它自汉代以降的传统。Baccini认为不同时代的作者能将他们的幽默小说置于整个幽默文学的传统中。这通过许多作家将他们的作品集取名为《笑林》得以证明。这一文类被用来与西罗马和古希腊的滑稽文章乃至文艺复兴的文学传统做比较,因为这一文体的用法、类型和口口相传的成果似乎与西方的这些传统有许多共同的方面。来自威尼斯大学的Nicoletta Pesaro深入到现代文学领域,分析了"五四"时期的"类型翻译"。正是从这个时期起,中国学者开始从西方视角反思文类这一概念,即使他们的反思是以中国传统为基础,而且对文类定义的反思并不系统。鲁迅、胡适、郑振铎和俞平伯被认为是这个时代试图定义文类的主要学者。根据陈平原的看法,鲁迅仍然是中国文学的主要权威,这些学者给中国文学归类的需要同时也是为中国传统文类正名的需要。必须从此类学者捍卫中国文学和对中国文学的理解出发,来重新认识和看待他们"破除旧习"的做法。鲁迅和郑振铎似乎在攻击传统文学上表现得过于偏激,但不可否认的是,他们试图重新定义传统并使其系统化。与其说这是一种毁坏的需要,不如说这是一种系统化学习的需要。Federica Passi(威尼斯大学)谈论了台湾现代主义者和本土文化保护主义者间的辩论,并反思了西方的同化作用和本土传统的延续。

"20世纪诗歌"讨论组继续展开对文学的讨论。其中有些主题是关于中法互动交流过程中陈敬容(Chen Jinrong)和波德莱尔的诗歌的关系(Giusi Tamburello,巴勒莫大学),这是诗歌翻译领域中的问题;或者是关于冰心诗歌中涉及到基督教的意涵(Silvia Canuti,萨兰托大学)。在这里,作家被看做是一个对现代新中国进行界定的成熟的主人公,他不是把西方视为一个仿效的对象,而是一个可以进行对话的革命的和民主的伙伴。在中国现代诗歌讨论的最后环节,Patrizia Dadò(罗马智慧大学)和Anna Simona Margarito(萨兰托大学)分别对梁秉钧(Leung Ping Kwan)与顾城(Gu Cheng)展开了讨论。

一个专门的讨论组对作为二外的汉语和汉语教学展开了饶有兴趣的讨论。来自佩鲁贾大学的Chen Hsueh Li,关注动词的"体",他讨论了"体"这一概念与中文动词的联系,及其在汉语教学中的使用。有三本可以参考的教材:《新使用汉语课本》(2002),《意大利人学汉语 》(2006),《中文天地》(2006)。来自罗马第三大学的Chiara Romagnoli让人们关注趋向补语在中文和意大利文中的用法。这两种语言似乎都习惯于通过动词定位来指示动词的方向。Romagnoli准确的分析奠定了一个初步的基础,通过对中文—意大利语翻译的研究,我们可以厘清汉语中动词表达的结构。

来自罗马大学的Luisa Paternico阐述了EBCL(欧洲汉语基准)研究项目,这一项目由四所大学用时两年发展而成,力图根据《2001年欧洲语言共同参考框架》建立起在中文教学上的欧洲共同框架。来自米兰天主教大学的Victoria Bogushevskaya,深入分析了中文色彩词汇的语义,她阐述了中文中"褪色"这一概念在历史上的演变,并分析了像"青"这样的词。根据她的解释,"青"是介于蓝和绿之间的概念,同时拥有这两种颜色,在语义上还有很多其他内涵。

其他会议主题包括:东巴文,《全唐诗》中诗歌的真实性,甘肃地区少数民族以及中央一边陲关系研究,晋朝的制陶技术,20世纪的绘画身份,龙门石窟的奉先寺和佛教艺术,近现代佛教在中国的发展趋势,从成吉思汗时期至明朝的蒙古历史,萨法维王朝(伊朗)和奥斯曼王朝(土耳其)。还有讨论组致力于研究中国和非洲的关系,意大利的中国旅行者,中国书法及其文化内涵。

意大利的汉学研究是一个蓬勃发展的学科,需要鼓励和培育,以便继续为西方视角下的中国研究提供新的见解。这一研究领域涉及文化和社会的许多方面,值得我们给予关注和研究。下次会议将在两年后举行,在此期间,意大利的学者们将继续探索新的兴趣点,从而促进中意学术关系的发展。

北京第二外国语学院
古典学视野下的哲学与文学夏季青年论坛综述

周晓丽

以古观今，鉴察今日之利弊；以今观古，烛照古人之得失。历览前贤，博古融今，正是我们作为跨文化研究者及学人、学子之重任及使命。北京第二外国语学院跨文化研究院自诞生之初，就以古典学为基，贯通古今，广容并包，秉承尽心做事、虚心治学之院训，在美学、哲学、文学等相关领域的交叉互动及平等对话中独树一帜，在与众多学界同仁的交流、互助中不断成长。

6月18日，北京第二外国语学院跨文化研究院又组织了一场精彩的学术演讲。这次青年论坛于下午2时在求是厅举行，由跨文化研究院黄薇薇博士主持，主讲人分别为中国人民大学文学院讲师娄林博士和北京第二外国语学院跨文化研究院杨平副教授，由北京大学中文系比较文学与世界文学博士生导师张辉教授和北京师范大学哲学与社会发展学院刘成纪教授作点评，我院的胡继华教授、刘燕教授、曲茹教授出席了本次活动。与会人员还包括跨文化研究院的全体研究生及我校其他院系的学生。

议题一：克塞诺芬尼——诗化的整全智慧

第一位主讲人是娄林博士，他的论题是《克塞诺芬尼的哲学与诗歌》。

克塞诺芬尼(Xenophanes，约公元前565—470)，在希腊哲学史上享有盛名，是爱利亚学派第一位哲人，亦是巴门尼德之师。西方思想中念念在兹的"理念"之说，其发端就是这位哲人；所谓一神教的最早说法，他也可谓开其端绪。以此两点，对其做何赞誉似乎都不为过。

娄博士从哲学与诗歌的迥异的品性入手，引出自古以来就存在的"诗与哲学之争"的问题。他认为文体本身与政制相关，除了文明早期的传统礼法(甚至包括传统礼法本身)，后世的任何一种文体或者政制的确立，背后都有一种哲学的权力意志之手在起作用。而现在我们所面对的论文(散文)和诗歌的严格分野，肇始于现代启蒙哲学确立的学科范式。借用柏拉图的句式来说，便是"诗歌与散文之争早就出现"。为表明这一点，娄博士从古希腊先哲泰勒斯谈起，引出三位"逆流而动"的哲人：克塞诺芬尼、巴门尼德和恩培多克勒，他们不同于新派哲人，不用其惯用的散文(或论文)形式，而依旧采取传统的韵文诗歌写作。为解释这一问题，娄林博士以克塞诺芬尼为例，层层深入地展开了论述。从克塞诺芬尼的身份认知上讲，他是一位真正的哲人，即进行哲学思考的人。西方哲学诞生于泰勒斯对世界本源的思考。从"水是万物的本原"中归纳出"万有为一"，一种形而上学的普遍化的信条出现了，这便是"凝视存在之为存在的存在"。柏拉图借苏格拉底之口为哲人和哲学下定义，亚里士多德也将学问的终极目的归于事物本身的"善"。由此得出结论：哲学之为哲学，其根本不是爱智慧，而是对智慧之爱必须要达到对整全的智慧之爱，对世界作为一个整体的存在之爱。而克塞诺芬尼正是非常明白地以"一"来解释万物的哲人，其残篇27、29、30传达了与泰勒斯自然哲学非常类似的学问，以尼采的观点，这些自然哲学可称之为科学。中国人称之为经世致用之学，是有益于人生的。接着，娄博士讲到了克塞诺芬尼对毕达哥拉斯等先哲的批评，借此说明克塞诺芬尼的传统的政治伦理观：一个真正高贵的人，应该言说对美德的追求，而不是智性的炫耀。苏格拉底和柏拉图等哲人，都从自然哲学转向政治哲学，克塞诺芬尼也有这种政治哲学的自觉，他采取诗歌这种文学样式，根本原因在于：哲学是少数极富才智的人的事情，但诗歌却关乎所有人的共同存在。以会饮为例，这种场合看似闲适放松，但最宜凸显人的性情，既是一个展现的场合，也是一个受教育的场合。这样的场合歌唱的歌曲反而更要故事庄严，言辞纯洁，也更恪守传统。谈到克塞诺芬尼对荷马和赫西俄德的批评，娄博士说，这恰恰是因为他秉承传统教化的原则，故而反对二者虚妄神话的态度。克塞诺芬尼的第二首残篇嘲讽了希腊传统的竞技体育，针对的是沉迷体育而不追求美德者。竞技比赛应该呈现个人美德，令胜利者可为城邦的"法度"尽自己的卓越之能。娄博士最后总结说，在梭伦变法、品达凯歌、荷马史诗及赫西俄德的《神谱》中，都有对良好法度的歌颂。对一个城邦来说，最深处的不是哲学，而是良好的礼法秩序。克塞诺芬尼正是看到了这一点，才会对自己哲人的身份稍加隐匿，而敞开自己的诗人身份。

张辉教授对娄林博士的论文给予了充分的肯定，认为他打开了我们的思路，是一种用全新的角度去审视"诗与哲学之争"这一古老的问题的尝试。克塞诺芬尼只写过诗歌（城邦诗歌），诗是最早的文体形式，我们应更深入地去探讨诗对良好法度的内在吁求。还有，在思想史上，也应对保守的思想的位置加以重新认识。张教授还特别提出了个别关键词的翻译问题，例如关于 Poetry 一词，张教授建议翻译为"诗"，而不是"诗歌"。刘成纪教授也对论文进行了精彩的点评。从东西方文明史的进程中看，诗的形式占主导，而散文写作只是一个阶段而已。他从西方古希腊、古罗马、德国古典时期，谈到中国先秦的《尚书》、《舜典》，孔子的春秋笔法，认为从诗到史，再到哲学，是一个歌者的时代到辩者的时代。这一进程中，散文并不是主流。

娄林博士对各位点评人的问题和意见分别作出了详尽的答复，认为古今之争，是"心性"上的产物，而并非只是时间上的概念。胡继华教授和刘燕教授也对娄博士的论文提出了自己的学术见解，胡继华教授认为"启蒙乃个人之事，绝非众人一哄而上，散漫无边"，他从神话诗学的角度，结合对普罗米修斯的"盗火之行"及"成人之罪"的分析提出了对启蒙的独到之见解。学生们也针对娄博士对亚里士多德"次等学问"的评价提出了疑问并得到了满意的答复。

议题二：翻译的美学——康德的《判断力批判》重点句段中译论辩

第二位主讲人是杨平副教授，论题是《〈判断力批判〉的汉译及其问题》。

众所周知，康德美学是德国古典美学乃至西方现代美学公认的起源，美学作为在近代产生的独立学科，其学科规范、问题意识、理论形态、价值取向都根植于康德美学及其后继的德国古典美学的发展脉络之中。对康德著作的汉译本研究是中国美学史上的重要一环。在美学领域，《判断力批判》是重要的一部著作，如何翻译康德术语的概念和范畴，如何理解翻译过程中的得失，这需要对不同译本进行横向对比与纵向对话。

杨平老师以第一节第一段汉译的对勘为例来探讨四个汉译本的翻译所导致的问题。他首先按时间顺序，介绍了《判断力批判》的四种汉译本：宗白华与韦卓民的"分工"翻译、牟宗三单挑康德三大批判的翻译、杨祖陶与邓晓芒的"双打"拍档及李秋零翻译康德全集的单打独斗。接着，以第一节第一段的对勘为例，论述四个汉译本的得与失。选取的段落涉及康德美学中的核心问题和核心概念，涵盖了德文原文、三种英译与四种汉译。杨老师从"信"等方面看各种译本的差异，分辨翻译的理论效果。如对"Geschmacksurteil"这一关键术语的翻译，宗氏、邓氏与李氏将其译为鉴赏判断，而牟氏则标新立异地将其译为审美品位之判断。这些译法都是差强人意的，因为在西方美学史中，从概念史的角度看，Geschmack 有诸多含义，比如"趣味"、"鉴赏"等等，的确没有审美品位之义，牟译将翻译复杂化了，改变了这一重要术语的含义，造成译文"信"的缺失。杨老师还对"Verstand"，"Einbildungskrafe"等术语的翻译得失作出了阐释，认为学术译名对我们正确理解哲学文本尤为关键，确定译名为翻译的首要任务。译者必须有坚实的语文学、哲学史的基础，并且不能盲目照搬原有的译名。接着，就选段译文的"达雅"问题，杨老师结合康德要旨及行文方式、语气等，分别探讨了四种汉译本的疏漏得失，指出邓、李译本较好地遵照原著，术语译名尽量趋近原文的含义，译文平实顺畅，可读性与可理解性较强。最后，结合翻译美学及译者任务，杨老师整体关照20世纪中国学术史，从晚清严复“信达雅”的翻译标准谈到哲人陈康“直译”的标准，认为虽标准不一，但都可作为参考，去评价汉译的西学著作。然而真正把握“新语”的最佳途径还是要精通西文、读原著。关于译者的任务，依照本雅明的观点，“真正的翻译是透明的”，“如果句子是挡在原文语言前面的那堵墙，那么，直译就是拱廊”。

刘成纪教授首先作出点评，认为杨老师的论文很有必要，这是将价值问题转化为学术问题；其选取的段落也很有必要，因为都涉及了康德美学的核心问题。杨老师谈到的如何走进真理、美学，翻译技法及准确性等问题，很有启发性。然而翻译是不可能完全符合愿义的，而只能无限接近本义。如“青山”一词的翻译就很难找到绝对完全对等的英译。刘教授还以中国历史上佛经的翻译为例，谈论了语词的非对称性及意义的错位、游移性。针对汉译文字本身的曲解所导致的误译，是否有意义的添加等问题，刘教授也提出了自己的疑问。张辉教授亦高屋建瓴地作出精辟的论评，他以交叉对话关系来总结两位青年学者的演讲论题，从诗哲之分到诗哲相合，从康德的理论中剥离出审美关系。并结合莱辛《拉奥孔》中对鲍姆加登的“美学”的批判与否定，来对比康德《判断力批判》中对“美学”一词的态度。他指出莱辛从事物本源出发来研究具体问题，而不是像鲍姆加登一样从抽象的概念出发，探讨感性的问题。张教授建议将探讨的问题置于康德的整个三大批判体系之中，通读全篇，回到事物本身。

杨老师对两位专家的点评一一做出回应，指出由于语言、理解等方面的问题，翻译具有不彻底性。误读不等于误解，20世纪中国的美学问题与翻译相关，翻译的重要性毋庸置疑。

最后，师生们还进行了精彩的对话，对学生的“怎样看待生活与哲学的关系”之问题，娄林博士作出了自己的阐释和理解，认为诗歌具有本源性，我们的生活本身，是被哲学规范了的世界，过于理论化、制度化，将会限制哲学、败坏哲学。所以建议我们学习中国古典哲学，做“可上可下”的君子。针对刘燕老师关于共同体的提问，娄博士说，全球化时代，虽然不断遭到碰撞与改变，但共同体不会消解，其核心仍在。

本次论坛在热烈而祥和的氛围中圆满结束，各位专家、学者以诚恳的态度、朴质的学风、严谨求是的治学精神感染着在场的每位学子，其豁达的胸襟、谦和的为人，为学子们树立了榜样。这次青年论坛给全体师生带来了一次难得的学习和交流机会，使各位学子们如浴春风、受益匪浅。

观之古今，人文以化成，在相隔千年的对话中，彰显了诗与哲学的冲突和交融。古典学以不断丰富的形式重新焕发青春和热情，人文精神也在超越政制的禁闭和物欲的诱惑而继续着对真与美的探寻。学界待有才人出，再领风骚数百年！

《文贝:比较文学与比较文化学刊》投稿须知

一、《文贝:比较文学与比较文化学刊》为国家重点学科——上海师范大学比较文学与世界文学研究中心——主编的刊物,每年两期,定于6月15日和12月15日分别出版,发表的内容为比较文学、比较诗学和比较文化等领域之原创性学术论文及书评文章。

二、原创性学术论文之字数不限,书评文章以2500字以内为妥。中英文皆可。

三、学术论文之撰写格式、顺序及注意事项:

1. 首页:题名、作者简介及联系方式;

2. 中英文摘要(各以500字为限)、关键词(以5个为限);

3. 注释的格式,请遵循本刊"注释范例"。

四、来稿请向本须知之第十条提供的通讯地址及电子邮箱分别邮寄纸质稿件及电子稿件各1份(后者为必须提供);本刊收悉来稿即登录收稿时间,并回复投稿人。三个月内未收到处理意见,作者可自行处理稿件。

五、本刊严格实行双向匿名评审制度。来稿由程序审查决定是否刊登:首先由编辑推荐至编委会初审,初审通过后送交两名相关领域学者匿名评审,最后由编辑委员会集体终审。终审通过,即可进入刊登程序。匿名评审结果,由匿名评审专家返回之后,本刊将尽快告知作者。若审稿人要求修改,则已完成之修改稿须经匿名再审(不同意修改之申辩,亦一并转送审稿人)。通过终审的稿件,须遵从本刊注释格式,仔细审校正文并核对引文,编委会收到合格定稿之后再通知作者预定刊登的时间与期数。

六、投稿本刊的著作人,其稿件一旦通过终审且同意由本刊发表,须填写授权书,同意本刊拥有此稿件之版权,即,本刊具有再授权其他刊物或数据库进行转载、复印或网络下载、打印等行为之权利。授权书等相关表格,可由编辑寄送,亦可从网络下载(www.cclaa.cn)。

七、著作人若将本刊发表之论文收入自撰著述,请事先通知本刊,并在该著述中注明发表出处。

八、本刊刊登的稿件,作者文责自负,一概不代表本刊观点。

九、稿件刊登之后,本刊将按每千字100—200元人民币之标准发放稿酬,并赠送当期刊物2本。

十、来稿请寄:上海市桂林路100号,上海师范大学人文与传播学院《文贝:比较文学与比较文化学刊》编辑部收,邮编:200234。电子稿件请寄:cowrie2012@163.com。

《文贝》编辑部

新书快递

不可消解的他者为意义的源头

——《意义》书评

林鸿信

杨慧林教授所著《意义——当代神学的公共性问题》实在是令人耳目一新，自由出入于文学、哲学与神学的精彩著作，从齐泽克到经文辨读、从诗性到灵性、从文论到神学、从传统传承到后现代解构以致重构，生动地见证那不可消解的他者为意义的源头。

这是一本洋溢智慧而有关文化与意义的著作，从开篇论及“名词的动词性”与“动词的交互性”起，指出“文化”即“传播”，而“传播”即“相互传播”，呈现一个文化传播相互激荡而衍生意义的世界，既是“沒有任何文化可以一成不变、可以保持其本原的状态，卻只能是在交往中不断生成和繁衍”，又是“文化间从来沒有什麼单向的传播，而必然是‘施动’与‘受动’的相互影响和相辅相成”。

“意义”往往来自相异之间比较，这意味著自我须要他者对照才能深入理解意义，因此不只有主张包容异己的必要，而且唯有在异己激发下才能迈向对意义的深层理解，进而在与自我极限之外者的对照下才能经历启发与光照。然而，开创现代性的笛卡儿之“我思故我在”却把意义收纳在自我里面，孤立的自我成了意义源头，有如拿著指挥棒不断地挥出意义音符的大师，只是这样的音乐其同质性太高了，不论指挥棒如何飞舞，所呈现的音乐都是单一调性，这正是现代性的悲剧。

不过，现代性挟其科技高度发展带来的千军万马之势，有如洪水猛兽泛滥，从满街四处可见自我中心的低头族看来，似乎“我玩手机故我在”更加契合笛卡儿式自我的精神，面对这种大势所趋的潮流卻有意中流砥柱者是万分不易的，《意义》一书卻另辟蹊径，精彩地批判意义的自我內在化。

当挑战现代性的源头笛卡儿式自我时，若是过于正经的话，恐将落入另外一种自我中心的窘境—反笛卡儿式自我的自我中心，举凡以正面作战强攻方式挑战自我中心者往往陷入凝聚出更强之自我中心的噩梦。于是，德里达选择调皮文字游戏展现延異，呈现千变万化不可穷尽——惊喜之必要；齐泽克则采用嘻笑人间出语惊人地揭露基督教的颠覆性，呈现千山万水我独行——反向之必要，《意义》一书深深地领略“另类思想家”策略性地迴避在反对自我中心时不陷人另一自我中心的智慧，书中在行文流畅无碍中尽量避免了自我中心的风格特质与思考方式。

“故说诗者，不以文害辞，不以辞害志；以意逆志，是为得之。”(孟子万章上)“以意逆志”原本用意是反对以文害辞而以辞害志，主张作者意向优先于文辞，读者应当越过文字障而让己意迎向作者本意，然而如杨教授指出卻转而成为后来“诗无达诂”之滥觞而展开了丰富意义世界之追寻。(11)“以意逆志”毕竟带有一模糊性，究竟是他意明白彰显于己意中，抑或己意主道宰制了他意。当孟子选择由“己意”出发时，毕竟难以掙脫“以己观他”的色彩，而不是“以他观他”。《意义》一书呈现了让众多文本互相对话的深厚诠释学功力，始终避免介入过多“己意”而干扰“他志”，又能适度投人“己意”于“他志”中而呈现投入性理解。

本书反映作者博览多闻的为学精华，收集了四类文章以切入意义问题，其一观察当代人文学术的演变而主要借由齐泽克的反向思维追问意义问题，其二从理雅各翻译中国经典以及圣经和合本的译文观察他者(西方)究竟如何诠释自我(中国)而展现经文辨读所追寻的丰富意义，其三从诗性智慧角度诠释文学、文化研究如何与神学研究会遇而呈现有限与无限、自我与他者对照所开创的视域，其四从汉语语境中的基督教诠释如何维持天上与地上、信仰伦理与世俗伦理之间必要的张力以呈现意义的丰富面貌。

第四编论及基督教与中国文化会遇所面对的意义问题十分精彩，如作者所观察，宗教"'本地化'既可能'转变、再造原有的文化'，也可能被原有的文化所消解"(165)。这个具有洞察力的观察既可应用于摩尼教，亦可应用于汉语语境中的基督教。文化与文化的会遇有如他者与自我的会遇，既可能转变、再造自我，也可能是他者被自我消解，前者是意义丰富的泉源，而后者则是意义单调的标志。当穿戴西方文化肉身的基督教传到中国时，不只面对西方文化与中国文化的他己之争，而且还要面对宗教与人文之间的张力；不只是信仰之道如何更换文化肉身的问题，而且是信仰理想中的无限视域如何与现实世界中的有限视域维持必要的张力之问题。

从基督教与中国文化会遇的历史来看，如果"适应化"的结果是"信仰伦理"转化成"世俗伦理"而不再有二者之间的张力的话，究竟是道成肉身抑或是随波逐流呢？其实连基督教本身都有从陷溺尘世而在世上一帆风顺的"宗教"里释放出来的呼吁，如书中引述朋霍非尔之"非宗教的基督教诠释"，(181－182)追问如何让信仰又出世又入世，而非以宗教之名陷溺于世呢？如何能够让信仰在地上不断地发出良心声音而丰富地繁衍意义于世上呢？

于是本书期盼，以"知"的探究发现"神学诠释学"展现的空间，以"意"的界说追寻"神学伦理学"揭露的意义，而以"情"的价值指向拓展"神学美学"描绘的期待。(182)基督教信仰的真正价值不在于其"适应性"，而在于其"不可适应性"。基督教信仰始终坚称无限者对于有限者的颠覆性，一直确信上帝国价值对于尘世价值的提升。

本书主张当神学议题还原成为人文学的议题时，以未知之视域扩充已知之视域，可望提供更加成熟的人文学视野，作者说："如果人文学是非常地自以为是，就无从谈人文学。人文学的所有批判的前提都是自我批判，自我批判就是自我敞开、自我倾空，这在学术语境和信仰语境中都非常值得强调。说实话，我认为中国人从这个角度去理解基督教信仰的还不是太多。"(218)

这是一本具有宽广神学视域与深刻人文学反思的著作，作者对基督教信仰特质——道与肉身之间的张力的必要性的深入理解，对理当带有颠覆特质与生命热情的基督教信仰竟陷溺社会建制、意识型态、伦理化诠释的提醒，在在指向其副题：当代神学的公共性问题。

全书读来行云流水，赏心悦目，令人目不暇给地惊喜于作者多年来神游于东西方学术领域的心得，书中处处可见诗性智慧与灵性智慧的会通，人文学与神学的相辅相成，辛勤耕耘已逐渐地成长为灿烂园地。诸如对于理雅各翻译中国经典的洞察细微，对于圣经和合本翻译基督教经典的细腻辨析，不只具有深刻洞察力，而且是难得一见深入文本之际的诠释典范。

如同作者心仪的当代法国哲学家巴丢所主张，从事件到决定、而后到忠实、而后建构主体、最终形成普遍形式，"事件"是一个走向真理的思想过程，《意义》的出版"事件"正参与文化传播而衍生丰富意义。

作者简介：林鸿信，台湾神学院教授，台湾大学哲学系兼任教授；图宾根大学神学博士，诺丁汉大学哲学博士。

“一字见乾坤”:还原坛君神话的原始形态
——读张哲俊教授《韩国坛君神话研究》

毛建雷

1936年,陈寅恪先生读完沈兼士的《“鬼”字原始意义之试探》,复函赞道:“大著读讫,欢喜敬佩之至,依照今日训诂学之标准,凡解释一字即是作一部文化史。中国近日著作能适合此义者以寅恪所见,惟公此文足以当之无愧也。”[1:202]沈兼士的文章能否当得起此语,姑且不论。但是,“解释一字即是作一部文化史”却鲜明地揭示出陈寅恪先生的心仪的治学门径,给后生学术研究提供了可资借鉴的方法启示。一字往往就蕴含着丰富的信息,今人治学当从一字一字细读开始,揭示每一字背后的牵连,将其落实到实处,借由一字探得历史的源流脉络。

张哲俊教授近著《韩国坛君神话研究》是足以配得上此评语的学术著作之一。坛君神话是韩国民族的建国神话之一,是关系到韩国国家起源的重大课题,尤其是上世纪90年代朝鲜挖掘了平壤的坛君陵之后,更是成为学术界的热点问题。然而,坛君神话正文353字,故事部分286字,核心部分只有100多字,且13世纪之前的文献极度缺乏,如何研究这篇短短的神话,历来是困扰学术界的一大难题。而作者此书的篇幅却多达45万字,平均每一个字写了数千字。张哲俊教授有着清晰的方法论和方向性定位,如其在《后记》中所言,“一个字一个字地研究,而不是大而化之地主观分析,随意宏论”[2:416]。从二三百字到45万字,不仅仅是字数翻了多少倍,更重要的是从一字一字的研究中发现了新天地,解决了困扰东亚世界七百余年的诸多难题。正是通过这样的研究,论著在蛛丝马迹中寻找事实,竭力还原坛君神话的原始形态和生成过程,不仅将韩国学研究提高到一个新的高度,而且为中国的东亚比较文学研究提供了新的文化视野和方法论启示。

这种一字一字研究的理路,从章节的安排上就可以窥见一斑。第一章“坛君神话的原始形态不是建国神话”,首先研究了坛君神话中“桓雄”“桓因”“太伯山”“妙香山”“三危山”“阿斯达”人名地名等要素,得出结论,佛孙降临建立坛君神话是僧侣的翻案,改换了其中人名地名。同时坛君神话的国家因素是箕子朝鲜之后添加的,而不是坛君神话的原始形态。第二章“从坛君神话到檀君神话”,重点研究一个“坛”字,由一字的“考掘”,纠正了一个困扰东亚已700多年的标记错误。第三章“坛君神话的文化因素”,研究了坛君神话中的“天符印”“三师”(风伯、雨师和云师)和“五主”(主谷、主命、主病、主刑与主善恶)的来源和进入坛君神话的时间。第四章“坛君神话中的灵艾、蒜与中医”,重点研究了坛君神话中的“蒜”“艾草”“不见日光百日”“忌三七日”,论著认定这些因素都是在中韩物质交流和医学交流的基础之上进入坛君神话的,同样属于坛君神话的衍生因素。第五章“熊神崇拜与祖先神话”,主要研究了最富于神话色彩的部分——熊变女人的故事,讨论了熊神信仰的源流与族源神话、始祖神话的关系。

从章节安排上,就可以清晰地看出,论著将坛君神话分解成诸多要素,每一章均是探讨相关词要素为主,也就是从解释一个词开始,探索这个词在坛君神话文本的生成和演变过程所起的地位和作用。通过这种以小见大的方法,还原坛君神话的生成与发展过程。在这个过程中,笔者认为,以下几点尤为值得注意。

其一,突破有机文本假说,认为坛君神话经历了从简到繁的过程。

之所以要从“解释一字”开始重新研究坛君神话,不仅是作者严谨不尚空谈的学术态度决定的,同时也是由坛君神话本身的性质使然。论著认为坛君神话经历了从简而繁的过程,各种因素形成的时间不同,最后形成了完整故事形态的神话。正因如此,要还原坛君神话的原始形态和生成过程,就要首先分别研究各要素进入坛君神话的时间和来源系统,区分哪些是原始因素,哪些是衍生因素。这也正是论著的一大创新点,即对以往认为坛君神话是有机文本观点的突破。先行研究关于坛君神话形成的时间众说纷纭,有的学者认为其生成于5000年前,有的学者认为生成于12到13世纪,还有学者认为生成于期间的某个阶段。时间跨度之大令人咋舌。原因在于,这些研究研究之前,已经预设了这样一个假说,即坛君神话生成于一个特定的时间。因而在研究过程中,往往抓住其中一个因素,就判断坛君神话生成的时间,就如同盲人摸象,难免失之偏颇。在坛君神话一百多年的研究史上,众多知名的学者,包括东京大学教授白鸟库吉、京都大学教授今西龙认为坛君神话是13世纪僧侣伪造的,错误原因正在于此。坛君神话固然有佛教化因素,但以此断定其全部都是伪造的,就有以偏概全的危险。"根据的部分性与判断的完全性构成了坛君神话形成的基本问题,也是一百多年来难以突破、视而不见的障碍。"[2:16—17]论著一针见血地指出了先行研究存在的核心问题。

与此同时,论著的行文充分证明了坛君神话由简到繁的论点是可靠的。比如坛君神话的原始因素(天神、熊女、神坛和坛树等)可能在新石器时代已构成神话的原始形态;而国家因素中的王权、都城、法律等,最早也要在箕子朝鲜建立的公元前1100年之后;"桓因""桓雄"等构成的佛教因素进入坛君神话的上限时间只可能在佛家传入朝鲜的5世纪之后;平壤地名最早载于5世纪,其进入坛君神话只能在此之后。这些观点都掷地有声,修正了国内外流行的看法。由诸因素进入神话的上限时间综合考虑,才能绘制出一副坛君神话生成发展的图谱。事实也充分证明,只有全面细致地分别对待各要素,具体研究各要素的形成,才能最大限度地还原坛君神话形成的事实。可以说,每一个词都潜藏着解开坛君神话生成的密码。

其二,考辨得出檀君神话是标记错误,应为坛君神话。

"坛"字的解释尤为关键,也是全书解决问题的一个典范,更是此书价值的一大表现。第二章"从坛君神话到檀君神话",作者用了5万字,来解释一个"坛"字,由此可见其重大意义。是坛树,还是檀树?有没有王沈的《魏书》,又有无记载坛君神话?这些问题都是由这一字派生的。《三国遗事》记载为坛君,而几乎同时的《帝王韵记》记为檀君,《帝王韵纪》之后檀君成为了700多年来的标准写法。如果据此判断,就会认为坛君神话是佛僧所编,产生于5世纪之后。一字之异会影响最初生成时间的判断,一字之误会掩盖坛君神话的原本状态,必然会引起一系列的错误结论。论著通过确凿证据,认为应为"坛君神话",檀君神话是后世标注错误。

作者首先考察了各种版本的坛字,认为一然《三国遗事》引用王沈的《魏书》是可靠的。作者多方搜罗文献,详加考辨得出结论早在3世纪中期王沈的《魏书》就有记载坛君朝鲜,这就比13世纪第一次记载的说法提前了1000年。中间的一千年正是坛君神话生成、变异并逐渐定型的关键时期。作者认为坛君神话的"坛"指神坛,"坛树"是神坛的树。坛的历史极为悠久,可以追溯到红山文化。有关坛与坛树的功能见于各种文献,江华岛堑星坛是与坛君神话有关的建筑,这是对坛与坛树的解释。而檀树蕴含的是神树崇拜,一般认为檀树是檀香树,或者弓矢材料的檀树,17世纪后又有朴达树之说。从坛树到檀树是李承休的有意改动,也是坛君神话佛教化的结果。王沈的《魏书》记载的是坛树,而不是檀树,表明坛树是原始因素,檀树与朴达树是衍生因素。坛君神话的坛与坛树是在山顶上,这与东亚神坛坛树的体制相合,也与红山文化的神坛特征相合。因此檀君神话应是坛君神话。"坛"字的确定无疑是坛君神话研究的一大突破。

其三,坛君神话熊神崇拜与红山文化的关系,及历史实证方法。

坛君神话与红山文化的关系是学术界比较关注的新问题,也是论著做出开拓的一点。第五章第二节"熊神崇拜的另一起源"详细论述了红山文化与坛君神话熊神崇拜的关系。论著从考古遗物中找到了在西辽河流域与朝鲜半岛的中间地带找到了熊神崇拜的相关物证。与此同时,作者搜集材料,分析材料的能力着实令人佩服,张哲俊教授在文字文献中找到证据证明红山玉龙是熊龙,而不是猪龙,无疑印证了考古遗物的确实性。红山文化的熊龙与后世的熊神崇拜在形象和意义上都有渊源关系,红山文化是东亚熊神崇拜的源头之一,从而纠正了先行研究过分夸大通古斯文化要素的错误认识。

同时，我们还应注意到作者解决这一问题的方法，充分利用考古遗物与文字文献，很容易使人想起王国维所谓“纸上之材料”与“地下之新材料”相互印证的双重证据法，陈寅恪先生也曾说“取地下之实物与纸上之遗文互相释证”[3:247]。张哲俊教授将考古与考据结合起来的实证方法运用到研究之中，相互验证，将坛君神话研究提高到科学的高度，远离了先行研究随意猜想的弊病。作者的研究思路其实是用历史实证的方法解决文学的问题，从看似荒诞的神话传说之中析离出历史的因素，还原坛君神话的生成过程。同时，通过研究神话中诸事物在历史层面的生成过程探索神话的形成，也能够突破没有文献的困境。

其四，历史减法的模拟研究方法及方法建构的启发。

作者的研究方法的制定和发现，总是能够给人眼前一亮、豁然开朗的感觉。张哲俊教授在《杨柳的形象：物质的交流与中日古代文学》中曾提出“第三种比较文学”和“文学考古学”的方法，而这本著作，作者又创造性地建构出“历史减法的模拟研究方法”。“这一方法要求研究文学作品中出现的各种事物，研究事物形成的空间与时间。要追溯和确认神话中出现的历史事物的上限时间，然后根据历史事物的上限时间顺序，逐一删除后来添加的衍生因素，保留最初形成的原始因素，由此可以还原坛君神话形成的模拟过程与模拟原始形态。”[2:20]这一方法的提出，一定程度上是为了弥补十三世纪之前文献匮乏的不利条件，但最终却给广大学人在研究此类问题时，提供了新的研究思维和以资借鉴的机会。

事实上，值得反思的不仅仅是历史减法的方法本身，还有作者提出这种新方法的发生过程。张哲俊教授专注于实证研究，其研究范式的选择，要由研究对象的实际情况决定，而不是照搬照抄西方前人的固定模式。文论“失语症”的出现，不是由于我们东亚文学比西方文学差什么，文学本身并无高低之分，每个民族都有自己深深眷恋的文学土壤，而文学研究也应立足于自身文学语言的实际情况。一旦放弃对自身文学实际涵咏回味的自觉，不知不觉间就会落入了西方话语中心主义普适性的陷阱，文学理论研究方法的生产也就只能亦步亦趋，创新更是奢谈。当然，我们不能否定世界文学有相通之处，但是，完全的普适性却要打上大大的问号。以该书为例，日本学者大林太良用法国杜梅斯的三机能体系理论研究坛君神话中虎的象征意义，然而却与实际存在诸多违合之处。张哲俊教授的著作在此给东亚比较文学研究提供了反思的机会。作者专注于一字一字地研究坛君神话，从小而精的个案研究入手，从具体的文学研究实践中提炼适合文本发生实际的研究方法，扎扎实实地研究具体问题。无疑值得肯定。

可以肯定，《韩国坛君神话研究》将是东亚比较文学研究的一部典范之作。张哲俊教授精通中日韩三国语言，从事比较文学研究已数十年，这部著作又是历数年之功锤炼而成。从二三百字到45万字，不仅是字数的翻倍，更是对坛君神话每一字背后所蕴涵世界的再发现，及对其理解的提升。一字一字地细读，一字一字地“考掘”，分别研究神话的诸要素，最终还原了坛君神话生成发展的源流脉络；论著运用原典文本实证的方法，发现并解决了许多困扰中日韩三国学术界多年的难题，将坛君神话研究提高到新的高度；同时也为我国乃至中日韩三国学者的东亚文学研究提供了新的思路和方法论启示。

参考文献：

[1] 沈兼士．葛信益、启功整理．沈兼士学术论文集[M]．北京：中华书局，1986.
[2] 张哲俊．韩国坛君神话研究[M]．北京：北京大学出版社，2013.
[3] 陈寅恪．金明馆丛稿二编[M]．北京：三联书店，2001.

作者简介：北京师范大学文学院硕士研究生，研究方向比较文学与世界文学。

稿约

《比较文学与世界文学(中国比较文学学会学术集刊)》稿件体例

《比较文学与世界文学(中国比较文学学会学术集刊)》是中国比较文学学会主办的以比较文学与世界文学研究为核心的人文社会科学综合性学术集刊。为方便作者写作和读者阅读,现将投稿注意事项规定如下:

1. 来稿以15,000字以内为宜。欢迎简明扼要而又论证充分的万字以内文章。所论重大理论问题、重要学术问题的论文允许篇幅稍长一些。稿件正文之前请附论文中文摘要(300—400字左右)、英文摘要(允许与中文摘要有所不同,不必对应翻译,约200个英文单词)、关键词(3—5个)、作者简介(包括姓名、工作单位、学位、职称)。如果所投稿件是作者承担的科研基金项目,请注明项目名称和项目编号。
2. 对于人文学科的论文不再区分注释(对文章中某一内容的进一步解释或补充说明,或作者对自己观点的阐发)与参考文献,二者均放在当页,以脚注形式出现。对于社会科学的论文,仍然可以将注释和参考文献分开,放于文末的参考文献采用"作者—出版年"制。
3. 注释与参考文献著录项目要齐全(不需要加文献标识码)。

   专著:

   主要责任者,文献名,出版地,出版单位,出版年,起止页码。

   译著:

   原著者国名,原著者,文献名,译者名,出版社.出版单位,出版年.起止页码。

   期刊文章:

   主要责任者,文献题名,刊名,年,卷(期):起止页码。

   报纸文章:

   主要责任者,文献题名,报纸名,出版日期(版次)。

   专著中的析出文献:

   析出文献主要责任者,析出文献题名,专著主要责任者,专著名.出版地:出版者,出版年,析出文献起止页码。
4. 外文参考文献要用外文原文,作者、书名、杂志名字体一致,采用正体;不得用中文叙述外文,如"牛津大学出版社,某某书,某一年版"等。
5. 来稿请寄送电子本与纸本各一份,电子本请寄:clwlcontribution@163.com;纸本请寄:【100871】北京大学比较文学与比较文化研究所内中国比较文学学会秘书处收。请注明详细通讯地址(含街道路名)、邮政编码、联系电话。
6. 来稿一般不退,请作者自留底稿;也不奉告评审意见,敬请海涵。

《比较文学与世界文学(中国比较文学学会学术集刊)》编辑部

Call for Papers

Comparative Literature and World Literature, sponsored by The Chinese Comparative Literature Association, is an academic journal focused on Comparative Literature and World Literature. Submissions are welcome based on the following guidelines:

1. Papers should not exceed the length limit of 15,000 words. The papers proper should be preceded by, in the following order, an abstract in Chinese, an abstract in English, 3—5 keywords, and a short biography of the author.

2. Papers written in English should follow the MLA format in their documentation.

3. Submissions should be both in electronic forms and in hard copies. The electronic version is to be emailed to clwlcontribution@163.com. The hard-copy version is to be mailed to this address:

Institute of Comparative Literature and Culture
Office of The Chinese Comparative Literature Association
Peking University
Beijing 100871, P. R. China

Please specify your mailing address and telephone number. Inquiries are to be directed to clwlcontribution@163.com.